FAR FROM THE A-LIST

FAR FROM THE A-LIST

STEPHANIE BURNS

MIRA

MIRA™

Recycling programs for this product may not exist in your area.

ISBN-13: 978-0-7783-8751-0

Far from the A-List

MIRA
22 Adelaide St. West, 41st Floor
Toronto, Ontario M5H 4E3,
Canada
MIRABooks.com

HarperCollins Publishers
Macken House, 39/40 Mayor
Street Upper,
Dublin 1, D01 C9W8, Ireland
www.HarperCollins.com

Printed in U.S.A.

To my mother, Cheryl, who was everything good in the world.
Best of all, she was mine.

FAR FROM THE A-LIST

CHAPTER ONE

2007, New York City

If you've read my mother's tell-all in the tabloids, you might be under the impression that I was born destined for remarkable things. I'm certain she meant the Honorary Emmy I earned at eight for Outstanding Performance by a Child Actor, the four Macy's Thanksgiving Day Parades I appeared in before I was twelve, or the dolls made in my likeness that flew off the shelves the Christmas I was ten. Now that I was twenty-six, buying shoes on a Wednesday afternoon with no job to speak of might fit her narrative that I was squandering my potential, but judging by the pink-faced sales associate standing across from me, my shopping trip was as noteworthy as any award or brand deal.

"You're Daisy Breyer." The woman blinked, like she was waiting for me to turn back into the girl on TV, the girl I was before I grew six inches and needed a bra and the world stopped knowing what to do with me.

I slid my credit card across the counter, knowing she was about to go from thrilled to disappointed in thirty seconds. "It's Michaela—"

"Turner. I know. I watched you every Wednesday growing up!"

Her and everyone else. I glanced around for the shopping companion I'd brought as a buffer for this exact situation, but she'd escaped to take a phone call twenty minutes earlier and had yet to resurface.

"When I was little, everyone said I looked like you."

Of course they did. She was roughly my age with brownish hair. I forged as polite a smile as I could and gave her the response I'd mastered by the time I turned sixteen. "Really?" Anything more, I'd end up with a stalker. Anything less, the headlines would call me a bitch.

She nodded as if this was her proudest achievement and not something I heard once a week. "What are you doing now?"

I tried to pry the shopping bag out of her moistened grip, but my casual dabbling in elementary Pilates was no match for her adrenaline. "Buying shoes," I said.

Again with the red-cheeked laughter. "You're still funny."

At least someone thought so. If she only knew that buying shoes felt like all I could do some days. I didn't act anymore. My attempt at college had been a disaster. I'd once tried to get a job just like hers and it caused such a scene that they let me go before my first lunch break. Buying something to make myself feel good was often all I could manage, and I couldn't even do that without being interrogated about what I was doing with my life.

She rolled my receipt back and forth, clearly trying to think of something witty to say. She came up with, "So, what's he like?"

She could have been talking about anyone, from my TV dad to the countless guest stars I'd met over the years, but I knew who she meant before she said it.

"Burke Sanders. You're seeing him, right?"

Burke—or the Colonel as he was known on the pitcher's mound—had been my boyfriend for four months, though whether or not I was seeing him was another question entirely. We hadn't been in the same city in over two weeks, when I'd been his date at some ESPN charity event, and I hadn't actually spoken to him in days, but ever since our picture had landed on *Page Six*, he was all anyone could ask about. I was sure that was exactly what his publicist had in mind when she set us up the week queenofthesocialscene.com ranked me number one on their list of New York's Hottest Party Girls.

I knew not to answer the salesgirl's question. Whatever I said would end up in a tabloid. Whatever I didn't say might end up there, too. "If I could just have my shoes?"

And there it was: the look. She was thinking that Daisy never would have brushed her off like that. Daisy would have beamed and told her everything she wanted to hear. Daisy loved chitchat.

She handed over the bag, her last sliver of hope hanging on the question everyone asked eventually: "Will you say it?"

It wouldn't kill me to give her what she wanted: a story. She wanted to be able to tell her friends that she met Daisy Breyer and got her to say the catchphrase "holy cannoli," but grown women didn't go around talking like fictional children, and I didn't owe this person anything.

"Have a nice day," I said instead, making my escape and rounding the corner in search of CeCe. Not quite a friend, not quite an employee, CeCe Johanssen came from a family wealthy enough that she didn't have to work, but not well-known enough to get her on anyone's guest list. She needed a social stepping stone. I needed someone to manage my social calendar. Somehow, the relationship worked.

CeCe hung up the phone when she saw me and said, "There you are," as if I were the one who'd wandered away. She peeked at my bag. "Oooh, what did you get?"

I tucked it under my arm, knowing she would run over and buy an identical pair if I showed her. "A gift."

Her eyes glowed, certain that said gift was for her. Freebies and never-worn hand-me-downs were an unspoken perk of our arrangement. "Well, I have a gift for *you*. I scored us the most epic plans ever tonight."

"Oh, yeah?" I tried to muster up the enthusiasm to go out for what had to be the eighth night in a row. It was getting harder, compared to when I was twenty and could go out for a week straight without ever coming home.

"Is Burke in town?"

"No," I said. "He's in . . . Kansas City." It wasn't like CeCe was keeping tabs on the American League. Plus, he could have been in Kansas City for all I knew.

"Too bad. That club Intuition opens tonight and one of their VIPs backed out. I got us a top spot on the guest list." Translation: I got you a top spot and I'm your plus-one. She eyed my shopping bag again. "You can thank me later."

I could have pointed out that she should have been thanking me—especially because she'd get a cut of my appearance fee—but I supposed I could use a night of drinking, dancing, and debauchery. Again.

I know what you're thinking. For someone who'd been such a remarkable child, I should have been doing a lot more as an adult than getting paid to have my picture taken at clubs, but you have to understand that I got my first job at age four, a starring role in a cereal commercial, and my life went into high-speed reverse from that point on. I had a thriving career and a record-breaking paycheck from ages seven to twelve. By my mid-teens, I was stuck with middle-of-the-road jobs, like Monday night TV movies. (Anyone remember '95's *Jennifer's Secret*? Didn't think so.) That was followed by the failed attempt at college and ever-plaguing "who am I?" questions most kids ask themselves during puberty. If I kept this up, I'd be using finger paints by the time I turned thirty-five.

"Intuition," I repeated. "Why not."

As we made our way to the exit of the store, my long-lost twin of a salesgirl reemerged, clasping my shoulder. The pit of my stomach tingled as I turned to face her, and I could still feel the outline of where her warm fingers had been. It took all my strength to not scream when she asked her final question.

"Are the rumors true? Is there any chance of a *Breyer's Town* reunion?"

BREYER'S TOWN. I'M SURE YOU WATCHED IT BACK IN THE day. Everyone did. That cheerful yet sentimental show about a young widowed doctor, Robert Breyer, who solved everyone's emotional and physical ailments while raising his two adorable daughters at home. There was brainy and quiet Veronica, the older of the two, played by Katrina Wilder. Then there was Daisy, the smart-alecky, precocious little girl America fell in love with in the pilot and stayed infatuated with until the series ended five seasons later. Fifteen years after its cancellation, the show continued to run in syndication, which meant that everyone still had an impossible time separating Michaela Turner from Daisy Breyer, despite the fact that I didn't live in a pink-and-green bedroom in the suburbs of Illinois, didn't have a wise-cracking neighbor named Heidi Firestadt, and was not, last I checked, seven years old.

Phil the Doorman greeted me with his usual distaste when I got back from my midweek shopping spree. Phil had never liked me. Maybe it was because for the first two years I lived there, I thought his name was Carl.

"Good afternoon, Miss Turner." His judgmental expression traveled south to my bags from Bergdorf's, Barneys, and Bloomingdale's. It was the same look he gave me every time I brought a new guy home. At least he seemed mildly impressed when I brought Burke around.

I nodded, gave my usual, "Phil," so he knew I remembered his name, and headed past him to the elevators.

I'd lived in the building for eight years—a record compared to almost everyone I knew in New York—but it still didn't quite feel like home. It felt homier than it had when I was eighteen, so I often tried to convince myself that in a few more years I'd finally be comfortable there. It really was beautiful, with all-white carpeting and vibrant walls lined with black-and-white art prints of Paris, London, and Venice. The pièce de résistance was the baby grand piano in the center of the living room. I once dated this photographer named Lewis (still unclear if that was his first or last name) who wanted to take pictures of the entire place for some magazine, because he loved the way the white leather furniture offset the fuchsia and turquoise walls. I turned him down. I didn't want a magazine crew snooping around where they didn't belong, and I didn't need everyone who read the thing to say, "Daisy wouldn't have decorated like that."

I threw open my closet to find an outfit for the night. I hated to admit it, but since becoming Burke Sanders's girlfriend, my already long getting-ready routine had nearly doubled. It was one thing to go out as Michaela Turner, Club Darling. It was something entirely different to go out as Michaela Turner, Arm Candy of the Colonel. It didn't matter that he was never around. One errant eyelash, one slightly undone zipper, and everyone would wonder why the hell he was with me. There was a reason why my paid-to-party rate had gone up and why paparazzi photos of me had skyrocketed in the past four months. For every person who wanted to admire me, there were a dozen more waiting for me to fall.

When I finished getting ready that night, my phone buzzed like clockwork. If there was one thing that could be said for CeCe, it was that she was always on time. She texted, I'm downstairs!!! at exactly 9:30. She put three exclamation points after everything.

I got down to the lobby just as Josh was coming in. If you were a teenager, had a teenager, or even knew any teenagers in the '90s, you'd know Josh McKenzie as Joshie Mac, the cutest boy-bander from Boyz of the Nation. Josh and I dated when we were sixteen—when his career was on the rise and mine was on the decline—and ten years later, we were essentially in the same place: far from the A-list. Any romance between us ended before Y2K, but he was the one person in my life I could never bear to lose touch with. His living two floors below me didn't hurt.

"Hey," he said, but his expression when he took in my minidress said so much more. "Forget your pants?"

"Very funny. And don't make that face. You'll get premature wrinkles." I gave the bottom of my dress a tug. Maybe it was a little short, but I didn't know how many years these legs had left.

He shifted his gym bag under his arm. Of course he was coming from the gym. When you were expected to have the world's finest six-pack in your teens, excessive workouts were a hard habit to break. "I take it you're not staying in tonight to watch your man pitch. What if he throws a no-hitter?"

Josh knew very well that I'd never actually watched one of Burke's games. He was also the only person who knew that while the picture on *Page Six* made us look like this incredible couple having this incredible night, the truth was I'd spent half the evening on the sidelines while Burke gave interviews and the other half coaxing him away from a mechanical bull that was calling his name so loudly he nearly forgot about his twenty-million-dollar arm.

"CeCe got us on the list at Intuition." Realizing that Josh had never paid attention to New York nightlife, I clarified, "It's a club."

"CeCe, huh?" He didn't like that I hung around with people who used me. And there was also the incident when CeCe went downstairs to his place and did a drunken striptease for him in the hall. I guess that left a bad taste in his mouth.

I ignored his comment and asked, "Do you want to come?" He may not have been on the list, but he had been in a boy band. He could have traded in that sweatshirt for a tight tee and thrown a little product in his shaggy blond hair, and he would have been in in a heartbeat. But I knew what his answer would be.

"Rather not." Josh never went out. His idea of a fun night was watching *The Godfather* trilogy while eating Cap'n Crunch.

He headed toward the stairs. "Have fun tonight. If the club turns out to be less amazing than CeCe promises, I'll be around if you want to hang out."

I almost considered taking him up on it, but miss one club opening and you're basically forgotten. I couldn't afford the risk. "I'm sure the club will be fine."

Looking back, I wonder if those words cursed me.

CECE MET ME OUTSIDE IN A RUNNING CAB. SHE'D CLEARLY gone spray-tanning—again—since the afternoon. I wanted to tell her that her naturally fair skin was turning tangerine, but that would only make her cry. After a few drinks, I'd offer her some powder.

I held my breath as I got into the cab, trying to ignore the ripped pleather seats and stale smell of whoever had been in there last. When I went out with Burke—which wasn't very often—we'd take a town car. CeCe and I didn't have twenty-million-dollar contracts, so we had to be more selective about where we spent our money. We preferred our couture and cocktails.

"You look amazing, MT." The first time CeCe called me by my initials, I thought she was saying *empty*. Even now, I couldn't hear it any other way. I'd almost asked her to stop a dozen times, but it seemed cruel when she was always coupling it with her favorite word: *amazing.* If nothing else, hanging out with CeCe was enough to boost my ego, even if it meant lowering my intelligence.

We pulled up to Intuition at a little past ten, and the city was just starting to come alive. Girls in heels they couldn't afford lined the block, offering their most practiced pouts in hopes that a bouncer would find them cute enough to be let in. Guys with a bit too much hair gel and far too much aftershave scoped out the scene, eyeing their potential bait. It was your typical Wednesday night crowd.

I was almost at the velvet rope, ready to flash my former celebrity status to the guy with the list, when I saw the poster on the door and realized this was anything but a typical Wednesday night. I looked at it again, hoping and praying that I was hallucinating and that it didn't actually read: **EXCLUSIVE CD RELEASE PERFORMANCE BY GRAMMY-WINNER DEACON KING.**

My lips buzzed in that way they do when something's not right, and my pulse was so rapid I could hear my skin vibrating, despite the music coming from within and the desperate pleas from the crowd outside. I wanted to melt into the sidewalk, to turn and run, to jump back into the cab. More than anything, I wished I'd taken Josh up on his offer, because somehow, I had landed in the one place I couldn't afford to be.

CHAPTER TWO

Deacon King was a mistake I made when I was nineteen. And twenty-four. Somehow, CeCe had neglected to mention that this club opening would be doubling as a mini-concert by the man who'd smashed my heart twice.

"Ohmigod," she whispered. "Didn't you two used to date?"

She made it sound so trivial. Like this wasn't the man I'd lived for and lived with for the better and worst part of my early adult years. The man I thought was the love of my life until he cheated and I cheated and I realized life wasn't a Julia Roberts movie.

"Michaela!" a paparazzo shouted, his flash going off before I even had a chance to react. I couldn't wait to see how that one would turn out. Not only did I appear to be hunting down my ex, I appeared to be hunting down my ex who was very publicly engaged to a rock journalist named Shaunn—with two *n*'s—who, according to recent reports, he was "head over heels in love with" and who had "changed him completely, making him a better man." Deacon always said phrases like that made him want to vomit. Apparently he'd grown a stronger stomach.

"Do you want to go home?" CeCe asked, knowing very

well what my answer would be. Leaving was the only thing that could make me look more foolish than showing up in the first place.

"We'll stay," I said, trying to sound casual, breathing from my diaphragm. As long as I stayed away from him, I'd be okay. If I could manage to stay away from him.

Assembling my face into a smile, I gave the crowd a wave and headed inside like I was about to have the greatest night of my life instead of the most uncomfortable. I was never going anywhere with CeCe again without doing my homework first.

I made my way through the club, nodding to acquaintances, posing for pictures, refusing to stop for a single conversation until I was safely ensconced in the VIP area with a vodka Red Bull. CeCe was saying something about Burke or the club or someone's botched lip job—I wasn't really sure. I could only nod and stir my drink and scan the premises for the nearest emergency exit. All I found was an eleven-by-fourteen poster of the man of the hour.

The man in the photo looked nothing like the man whose picture I kept buried in my underwear drawer. My Deacon was a mess, with a tiny chip in his eye tooth and wild black curly hair. There were times when he'd wear the same ratty Rolling Stones T-shirt for days and I'd have to physically force him out of it. In this picture—his new album cover, I assumed—all the things I loved about him had been replaced with a hideous maroon blazer and a pensive stare. His hair was short and groomed, and he was so clean-shaven you'd think he was waiting for his first trace of facial hair to sprout out. In that photo, there was nothing left of the one person who actually knew me.

CeCe must have spotted the poster, too, because she licked her lips and said, "Yum, am I right?" I knew she wasn't talking about her cocktail, and when I pretended not to hear her, she leaned closer. "Did you know he was thinking of going solo?"

I shook my head and said, "We don't exactly keep in

touch." Maybe I should have guessed he'd go out on his own one day, but I hadn't. He'd been with Reign since he was a broke kid sleeping on his friends' couches, and together they went gold, then platinum, then diamond. Watching it unfold was beautiful. Then things sort of blew up. Everyone's heard the story. Hot lead singer gets all the attention. Hot lead singer makes the cover of *Rolling Stone*, sans band. Hot lead singer goes solo. It was like an episode of *Behind the Music*, but I never would have believed it could happen to Deacon. If he'd kept me around, I wouldn't have let it happen. Yet, here we were, celebrating said former lead singer's first solo venture. Celebrating that he ditched the band he'd played with for over a decade for a group of studio musicians-for-hire.

"Whatever," CeCe said in a tone that was anything but *whatever.* "You have Burke now."

Oh, yes. I had Burke. Burke who was in—Sacramento? Or San Diego?—probably hooking up with one of his teammates' wives. I hadn't spoken to him in days, which was fine because he wasn't much of a conversationalist. The last thing he said to me was, "First pitch is for you, babe!" Josh had informed me that Burke lost that game.

I felt a tap on my bare shoulder, and I turned, expecting one of those "Do I know you from somewhere?" conversations, but unfortunately, I did know this person.

"Michaela." Jay, Deacon's bodyguard, was one of those too-muscular-for-his-own-good types who mistakenly thought wearing skintight T-shirts made him look hot. "Deacon know you're here?"

Jay absolutely hated me.

"Since I didn't know he'd be here, I highly doubt it." For added effect, I shrugged one shoulder. "Though you never know. Does he have a tracking device on me?"

My humor was clearly missed on him. "You didn't think he'd be at his own show?"

"Last I checked, it was a club opening."

He replied with another unsmiling nod. "I'll let D know you're here."

"Please don't." I hoped it would come off as indifferent, but I could hear my desperation oozing out. "I wouldn't want to distract him from his performance."

Jay took in the green minidress that turned more than a few heads when I walked in the door. "I'm sure you'd do just that." With that, he walked away, flashing his VIP pass as he made his way through the crowd. He was such an ass.

"Who was that?" CeCe asked—her usual routine.

"Deacon's bodyguard." *Glorified personal assistant* was more like it. When Deacon hired Jay for his own private security, I'd actually thought he was kidding—I couldn't imagine why he'd need something like that. As it turned out, Jay became quite handy when Deacon needed to lie about where he'd been.

The lights dimmed, and I had this flicker of fear that my vision was fading, the first sign of a panic attack. The crowd erupted into a deafening, suffocating sound, and I could smell Deacon in the air. I took a deep breath, wishing I'd stayed in with Josh, wishing I'd told CeCe at the door that I was leaving. The blinding stage lights came up and his backup band—not his true band—appeared. I hated them instantly. This wasn't Reign. These weren't the only people I could rely on to tell Deacon the truth when I wasn't around to do it. On stage right, there was a platform set up with three backup singers—two girls, one guy. He'd strayed even further than I'd thought.

I wanted to close my eyes and protect myself from what I was about to see, but the faux band started playing, the trio started oohing, and then, there was Deacon. The crowd was so loud, but I could still hear my blood rushing to my brain.

He looked just like that person on the poster—tailored jeans, a hideous blazer, and sunglasses, inside at night. Still, my heart, my pulse, every vein that coursed through my body signaled that this was the one man who harbored my every secret, like how when I was very young, I'd believe my mother when she'd tell me my father was a photographer from Paris or a journalist from Brazil or royalty from Monaco. This was the one man whose every desire I knew, like how his first love was his grandmother's piano, and how all he wanted in life was to write a song as magnificent as "Good Old-Fashioned Lover Boy."

"Holy hotness." I'd almost forgotten CeCe was there. "Why did you let him go?"

I hadn't let him go, and now that I was facing him—or this formulated image of someone who used to be him—I couldn't quite forget that. All I could think of was that moment on a Tuesday, at 12:37 a.m., when we were lying in bed and he said those six dreaded words: "Mickie, this is never gonna work."

I couldn't look at CeCe. "It's a long story."

"This song is amazing. Don't you think it's amazing?"

I did not think it was amazing, and if Deacon's dream was still to pen the greatest rock ballad of all time, this wasn't the way to do it. It didn't sound like him at all. The lyrics were probably brilliant—his always were—but they were drowned out by the techno-electropop hybrid passing for a melody. If he wanted to ruin his life by pretending to be someone he wasn't and by marrying someone he surely didn't love, that was one thing, but it pissed me off that he could waste the most gifted, talented mind I'd ever known. I couldn't tell CeCe that—she'd think I was a bitter ex-girlfriend—so I shrugged and ordered another drink.

After the second song, which sounded exactly like the first, I started to believe there were no traces of my Deacon left. It almost made me feel better, because it meant there was no one to miss. Then he spoke into the microphone.

"How are my beautiful people tonight?"

I guzzled half my drink. The first time he said that at a

show, I told him he'd sounded like a complete asshole. He responded by wrapping his arms around me so I couldn't move, kissing me, and saying, "Just for that, I'm going to say it every night." And he did. Not just onstage, but when he came home from the recording studio, or when he cooked me an evening omelet, or when I climbed into bed. This was my Deacon. And he was marrying someone else.

From up onstage, he had to have known he was getting to me, because he took off that ridiculous jacket, got rid of the sunglasses, and sat down at the piano. "This one's from a long time ago, but it will always mean the most to me."

After only one chord, I knew it was "The Queen," the first in the lengthy catalog he had written for me. Despite what the title suggested, it wasn't the most flattering song in the world. He wrote it after one of our many fights, after he said I thought of myself as some high and mighty queen. But after he wrote it, the instant he sat down at his piano and said, "Mickie, you gotta hear this," all was forgiven.

CeCe indicated my drink. "How many of those have you had? You're all pink."

"I'm fine." I couldn't breathe, but I was fine. "This is boring. Let's get out of here. Beat the crowd."

She looked at me like I was insane, because beating the crowd had never been a concern for Michaela Turner. "Oh." She laughed. "You're totally kidding. I love you, MT."

Nice to know someone still did. I swirled the straw around in my drink, wondering if I should order another but deciding that if I did, I'd probably throw up. Even without the cocktail, there was a good chance of my getting sick. Just watching him play that piano, watching his shoulder blades pulsate under his T-shirt, I was reminded of the night we met. I was reminded of how I'd felt about him, and I was reminded how, even after everything, that feeling never seemed to go away.

WHEN I MET DEACON, I WAS NINETEEN AND HE WAS twenty-three. I'd dropped out of college and was so sick of being called Daisy Breyer everywhere I went. (My roommate, it turned out, was a huge fan of the show.) After one semester as a theater major, I was certain I didn't want to be an actor anymore. I didn't know who I wanted to be, but I figured dancing until dawn every night would help me figure it out. I'd started hanging out with this aspiring model named Fiona, who, after a night of clubbing, told me that I had to come check out this guy she'd been trying to hook up with. He was the talent at a piano bar on Friday nights. So I went, and I saw him. And twenty seconds into "Try a Little Tenderness," I was hooked.

He was possessed by the piano, consumed by the words he was singing. At the end of his shift, he joined our table and greeted me with the most intense blue eyes I'd ever seen and the two words I most longed to hear: "Michaela Turner." Something in Deacon's manner, in the way he said my name, made me think that maybe this one person had the potential to see me for who I was, whoever that may have been.

I clung to every word that came out of his mouth, and before long, Fiona and all the other hangers-on were gone. It was just me and him. He didn't ask me about the show, about the episode where Dr. Breyer dated Daisy's teacher or what the deal was with all the green wardrobe. He talked about his band and how writing music sustained him more than food or oxygen. His passion made me wish some of it would rub off on me. We went outside so he could have a cigarette, and even though I hated smoke, I stood as close to him as possible, desperate to soak in every bit of this stunning creature's presence. It was out of character for me to be that taken in by someone, but that was what Deacon did to me. He made me lose all my senses. He slid his hand up the back of my shirt and kissed me right there, on the sidewalk. Three weeks later, he moved in.

I WATCHED THE REST OF THE SHOW, DOING ALL I COULD to distance myself from the person onstage. Trying to forget about touching him, craving him, loving him. Trying to remember the fighting, the cheating, the lying. But I didn't want to think about that, either. And I certainly didn't want to think about the "I've never been so in love" interviews he was giving about Shaunn. I wanted to get away. I wondered what Burke was doing.

During the last song, I felt another tap on my arm. Jay. "Upstairs," was all he said, as if I were at his beck and call. He glanced over at CeCe. "This one can come, too, I guess."

If I were CeCe, I would have been offended. Clearly, I was not CeCe, who jumped up like she'd been waiting for this all night. "Come on, Michaela, let's g-o."

I couldn't pry myself off the seat. If Shaunn was backstage, I didn't know what I'd do. I didn't have it in me to face her.

I closed my eyes and took one more sip of my drink. I didn't know how I could go back there and talk civilly to Deacon. I also couldn't seem to say no. I only hoped that we'd get up there and he'd have press to do, or he'd be too busy doing shots with his band to notice me.

A staff security guard stepped aside to let Jay through. He stared at me for a long moment before asking, "Do I know you from somewhere?"

Jay didn't look at him but answered, "*Breyer's Town*."

I flashed the guy an embarrassed smile and wondered how Daisy, if she had grown to twenty-six, would have handled a situation like this. Then again, Daisy wouldn't have dated someone like Deacon in the first place, and she certainly wouldn't have gotten herself into the mess that I was walking into. Daisy might have been married with children by now. She probably would have been a doctor, like her dad.

A group of women somebody had found attractive enough to give passes to started whispering as soon as they spotted me.

I didn't know if they recognized me as Daisy or as the girl who was once Deacon King's muse, but I ignored them and tried to pass myself off as comfortable on one of the couches. CeCe scooted down next to me.

"Shaunn's not here."

"What do you mean?" I asked. "Why isn't she here?"

"I don't know. I heard it on the way in. She's on assignment in LA or something. I guess she's out of town a *lot*."

The crowd erupted before I could react. It had to be the shortest show Deacon had ever done—a teaser of six new songs, plus, of course, "The Queen." I told myself that at least there'd be an encore, that I'd still have another fifteen minutes to figure out what I was going to say to him—if I was going to say anything to him—but then the faker backup band started filtering into the lounge.

"Shit," I said, mustering up my long-dormant acting skills. "I think I lost a bracelet downstairs. I'll be back."

CeCe looked at my wrists. "Are you sure?"

"Yeah. Definitely sure. I'll be back. Don't worry."

She wasn't worried. She probably figured that with me gone, she'd have a better shot at Deacon. I considered telling her that she should set her sights on the male backup singer—that was just the order of the chain—but I'd let her figure that out on her own.

I headed down one floor but was faced with the throngs of people making their way to the bar, the bathroom, or the exit. I'd been living in clubs for nearly a decade, but I'd never felt so claustrophobic. I turned and went back upstairs, but instead of going into the lounge, I slipped out onto the fire escape. I just needed air.

When we were together, Deacon would laugh at how, no matter where we were, I always managed to find some private area to clear my head—a fire escape or a balcony or, on more than one occasion, a maintenance closet. Half the time, I was trying to hide from someone who'd called me Daisy, but the other half of the time, I was trying to get away from him, because he'd said or done something to infuriate me. He'd come out and find me, and we'd fight some more, and I'd think it was all over between us, but then he would take me in his arms and tell me that he wasn't like my mother, and that I wasn't going to get rid of him that easily. Again, one of his many lies.

I sat outside for a while, not caring that I was wrecking my dress on the rusted stairs. I practiced the breathing exercises my mother taught me on set, and as I inhaled the cluttered air of the city, I wondered what it would be like to live somewhere with fresh air, somewhere I wouldn't have to wash grime off my face every time I went outside. I listened to the horns and taxis below, feeling that even with the collective noise of the city, it was more peaceful out there than it was inside, with the phony smiles and snide remarks and haunting memories of the past.

I heard the shuffling of footsteps and just for a moment, I thought CeCe had come out looking for me. Then I smelled his cigarette.

"Some things never change."

I didn't turn to look at him. I didn't trust myself to, even when he sat next to me on the step. "How you doin', Mickie Mine?"

Deacon was the only person I ever let call me Mickie. Normally, it made me think of the mouse or the dancing cheerleaders from that '80s video. But from the day I met him, he could murmur in my ear that I was so fine I blew his mind and I'd let him get away with it. I'd let him get away with anything.

"I don't think you're supposed to be smoking out here," I said. "I'm pretty sure it's still technically part of the club."

He blew a cloud of smoke away from me. "You're probably

right. But I don't know if either of us should be out here at all, should we?"

It was just the kind of statement I would have analyzed over and over when I was younger. I wouldn't do that now. I told myself the smart thing would be to get up, go inside, collect CeCe, and get the hell out of there. But I couldn't move. His elbow was a mere inch from mine, and if I moved, I might have touched his skin, and if I touched his skin, I'd be right back to where I was two years before.

"I'm glad you could make it," he said.

"Someone put me on the list for the club opening. I didn't know you were going to be here."

He nodded, stubbing his cigarette out, moving his arm a little closer. "Well, I'm glad you came."

The stench of smoke lingered in the air, but I could also smell that clean-soap, coconut-shampoo, cologne-less aroma that was Deacon. I had to remind myself he wasn't the same person anymore, and he wasn't mine.

"I hear congratulations are in order," I said.

He scratched the back of his neck. His nervous habits were the same. "Yeah, well, it comes out next week, so hold off the congratulations until then."

I turned and looked at him. Some things never changed. "I wasn't talking about your album." For the briefest instant, I held on to hope that the engagement was nothing more than a rumor.

"Oh. Right. Thanks." Another beat. "How about you? Is it true you're with some ballplayer?"

I should have told him that I wasn't with some ballplayer, I was with *the* ballplayer, but my mind was so muddled that all I could manage was, "I am." I wanted to say that Burke was incredible, that he was thoughtful and he meant something to me and he was a much better lover than Deacon ever had been, but Deacon always knew when I was lying.

He twisted the cap off his bottle, and for the first time, I noticed that Deacon King, whose two best friends were Jack Daniel's and Jose Cuervo, was drinking mineral water.

He glanced down at it. "I've taken up clean living?"

"Right." I nodded toward the stubbed-out cigarette. "How's that working out?"

He flicked the cigarette butt off the fire escape. "Let's just say I'm a work in progress." He was quiet for a second, probably debating whether his next statement would work for or against him. "I don't suppose you'd believe I'm a vegan now."

I nearly choked on my gum. "You're a vegan."

"Yep."

"And that was your idea?"

"Who else's would it be?" He was waiting for me to say her name. He could wait all night.

"Just seems like it would take a lot of commitment." We both knew commitment had never been his strongest suit.

"Ah, you know, health benefits. Sustainability. Plus, we don't believe in cruelty to animals."

We. And I knew he didn't mean it in the royal way. Something in the way he said it fueled me enough to say, "Clearly. Nice shoes."

He looked down at his leather loafers and smiled. I missed that smile. I hated that I missed that smile.

"So. What did you think of it?"

"Think of what?" I knew very well what he meant.

"The show, Mickie."

"Oh." I shrugged. "The crowd seemed to love it."

He stopped scratching his neck. "I didn't ask what the crowd thought. I asked what you thought."

I wasn't going to lie, and I wasn't going to coddle him, but he had hurt me—more than once—and he had chosen to give a ring to somebody else, so it really wasn't my job to give constructive feedback anymore. All I said was, "I think you'll sell a million records."

I could tell by his expression that he knew there was more to my answer, and that it wasn't good. "I couldn't do all new stuff. Had to throw in an old favorite."

I knew he was picturing himself in our living room, on that Sunday afternoon when he sat down and played me "The Queen" for the first time. Like so many of his songs, it was completely personal, yet completely universal. That day, I told him it was a guaranteed hit. Now I said, "Mm-hmm."

"Come on, Mickie, you don't have anything else to say? Seems to me you used to have quite a bit to say."

I looked at him square on—the one man I'd told my every secret to, my every fear, my every everything. I'd trusted him with my untrusting heart, and he had only made it weaker. I wasn't going to be reeled in again.

"I told you what I think." I repeated, "You'll sell a million records."

He knew what I meant. He could read me better than anyone, and I could read him, so I should have known not to answer when he said, "Where's the Colonel tonight? I'd love to meet him. I'm sure he's a stellar guy."

I didn't blink. "He's in Kansas City."

"Kansas City."

I nodded.

"That's interesting."

I looked away. "It's not that interesting."

"No, it is. Because Jay and I were flipping channels earlier, and I'm pretty sure we saw him give up a home run in Baltimore." He took a swig of his clean-living water. "Sounds like you two really have something special."

My entire body turned hot. I didn't know why he had to follow me onto the fire escape. I didn't know why I'd agreed to stay at the club at all. I didn't know why I was sitting there talking to the asshole who for years had haunted my every moment.

"You want to know what I thought of your show?" I asked. "I thought that music in there was not you. This image, this hair, this veganism? Absolutely not you. That's what I think."

He stood up and brushed the dirt off his hideous jeans, trying to pretend he was so much more mature and above me. "You know what? I came out here because I thought we could have an adult conversation. Clearly, I was wrong."

A conversation. He thought we could have a conversation. That was why he brought up my glowing relationship with Burke. Conversation.

"You asked my opinion and I gave it to you. I can't help it if you don't like what I have to say. And based on what I heard in there, and based on whatever this is?" I gestured to the blazer, the shoes, the clean-shaven face. "I think you know the truth yourself."

He looked like he was about to argue but thought better of it and turned to go inside. Maybe he had grown up.

"Hey, Mickie."

Or maybe he hadn't.

"I'm really glad you have it all figured out. I'm glad Blake and all of your adoring friends in there are giving you exactly what you need. Really."

I knew not to reply, but I still heard myself say, "It's Burke."

He nodded. "Right. Well, I'm sure there will be a Blake soon enough."

I tried not to let it sting. I tried to think of a remark to snap back, but he'd already done what he did best.

He'd disappeared.

CHAPTER THREE

People loved pointing out that my apartment was seriously lacking in framed photographs, as if framed photographs were the key to happiness. The thing was, I'd never been into pictures. Even if they didn't feature someone who'd been cut out of your life completely, there was a good chance they'd remind you of some other time you'd rather forget. This was why I only hung pictures of cities, all places I'd never been to. No people, no questions, no memories. Unfortunately, I did have a music collection that was filled with history. You know what I'm talking about: songs that remind you of a relationship, songs that remind you of a breakup. But in my case, half of those songs were written about me.

There were my Boyz of the Nation CDs from my puppylike romance with Josh, the only ones in the stack that still made me smile. To the public eye, Josh wasn't allowed to have a girlfriend, so we claimed we were "the very best of buddies"—and aside from a few awkward make-out sessions and a handful of innocent gropes, that was basically the truth. The Boyz didn't pen their own songs, but there was one track off their sophomore album called "Alwayz Be Around" that Josh used to secretly dedicate to me in concert by giving his heart three little taps signaling, "For you, Turner." We were sixteen, and I'm sure he'd deny it to his death, but it meant something at the time.

Then there was Travis Howard and his hard rock band, Soul Infusion. Travis was my annual one-night stand, if you could call it that, since it happened regularly, once a year. You may be familiar with his 2002 hit "Michaela Rose."

And, of course, there was the extensive collection of work by the one and only Deacon King, which I had no excuse for holding on to, other than the fact that I was a complete masochist.

I'd like to say that after encountering Deacon at Intuition, I went on with my life as if it never happened. I'm not proud to admit that the next day, when I was waiting for Burke to arrive, I was standing in my bedroom, debating which would be the better option—listening to said albums or smashing them with a hammer.

There was the first recording Reign had ever made. It was a cheap demo, and mine was one of the only copies in existence. Prior to this, the guys had played in bars with the catalog of songs Deacon wrote as a teenager, along with a few covers. Their name back then was Slum Lords, which was completely unfitting, because they were definitely not a grunge band. Then Deacon met me, and I convinced him to change the name and inspired him to write so much more—starting with "The Queen," the song that got them signed.

Sometime after the release of their first album, also named *The Queen* (and yes, that is my back on the cover), our first breakup occurred. Anyone should have seen it coming. He thought I went out too much. I thought he smoked too much. He thought I acted like a spoiled brat. I thought he wasn't pushing himself enough. Still, he was my world, and when I discovered that he'd slept with someone else during his first tour, that world was ripped apart.

The second album, aptly named *Torn*, was filled with breakup songs. Cheating songs, mainly. Inspired by his heartache, Deacon's band skyrocketed. For some strange reason, he begged me to take him back. For some even stranger reason, I did. In my defense, it was three years later. I'd learned a lot during that time, like men are liars and cheaters and users, and why not use them back? I vowed not to get too close this time. So when Deacon told me that he had grown and he had changed and he was sorry, I never quite believed him. We lasted eight months, and during that time I slept with two other guys—maybe to prove to myself that I was detached, maybe to hurt Deacon like he'd hurt me. Deacon slept with three other women, just because he could.

So there I stood, CDs in hand, thinking about Deacon King, even though I had a guy on the way willing to spend his only twenty-four hours in the city with me. I didn't know who Deacon thought he was, judging my life and my behavior and my relationship, when he was the one acting like some clean-living vegan imposter.

When Phil called to tell me Burke had arrived, I told him to send him up, then tossed the CDs on a shelf. Getting rid of them would have been a useless gesture, since I still had his piano taking up a third of my living room. I was dressed in a white gauzy skirt and red top, because Burke mentioned one time that he liked me in red. I had three other outfits—sexy, casual, or sexy-casual—handy for a quick change once we decided where to go.

He dropped his bag at the door and picked me up in his perfectly sculpted arms, making me feel so petite against his six-foot-five frame. "Je-sus Christ," he said. "You are beautiful." It had been so long since we'd spoken, I'd almost forgotten he had a Southern twang.

"Hi, handsome." Every time I kissed him, I felt like we were posing for a magazine cover. With his sun-streaked hair and pale green eyes, he could have been a model or an actor simply playing the role of an athlete. It made sense that everyone was still talking about our picture. We did look great together.

He grinned at me. "Are you going to let me inside or are we going to stand in the hallway all day?"

"Come on in." I turned, led him into the apartment, and was in the middle of asking about his flight when he kicked the door shut, kissed me again, and started taking off his shirt. In a matter of seconds, he was lifting me in the air with one arm and unbuckling his jeans with the other. Normally, I couldn't wait to get Burke into bed, but we'd barely said hello, and I couldn't stop thinking about Deacon's sounds-like-you-two-really-have-something-special comment.

"Hey, wait," I said once we were halfway to the bedroom. "I thought maybe you'd want to go somewhere?"

He stopped and looked at me like I was crazy, like I'd asked him if he wanted to join the space program or something. Actually, scratch that. Burke would probably be all for that.

"I'm only in town for a day, babe. I haven't seen you in like a week."

Actually, it was going on three weeks, but it was nice that he was keeping track.

"You didn't really want to go somewhere, did you?" He said it like it was preposterous. Maybe it was. If I brought him out in public, if he talked to too many people, the illusion might fade.

"No," I said. "We can stay in."

By the time the words were fully out of my mouth, he'd already ripped my skirt off.

LYING IN BED WITH BURKE LATER THAT AFTERNOON, I TRIED TO think of something really interesting to say. Something that would engage him in a conversation. Something that would take his attention away from *SportsCenter.* So far, I had ruled out "Does that World Series ring hurt your hand?" and "How was your game last night?" He'd lost that game, and we didn't talk about losses. I had to think of something, because it was getting awkward—me, lying there, watching him eat Ho Hos. Our relationship had to be about more than sex and that one great picture in *The Post.* He shifted a little bit, his eyes still glued to the TV, but I could tell that finally, finally he was going to say something. I just didn't expect it to be, "Careful, babe. Don't lie on my arm. Gotta pitch on Monday."

He slid his arm out from underneath me and I sunk flat into the mattress. The sheets were covered in chocolate crumbs, and so was his face. This was so not the relationship those people on *Page Six* should have had.

I should have been relieved that he didn't want to talk. He never asked about my family, so I never had to tell him that the only family I had was my mother, Caroline, and that I'd only spoken to her twice in the past ten years—both times when she needed money, both times post-divorce. He never asked if I had any dreams, so I didn't have to tell him that my only dream was to one day wake up and be someone other than Daisy Breyer. He never asked about previous relationships, so I never had to tell him that the one man who knew all of this, who'd promised to love me forever, was now promising his life to someone else. The only thing he did ask me was, "Do you have any more Ho Hos?"

I shook my head. "I think that was the last of them."

"No big. Buy more before I come to town next?"

"Sure," I said. "You're coming next week for my birthday, right?"

I'd been afraid to broach the subject. The last time I brought it up, a few weeks earlier, he said he was sure he could make it. He'd said he had a day game in Boston and he didn't see why he couldn't shoot down for my party. He hadn't mentioned it since, but it was sort of assumed by everyone that he would be there. I mean, I was Burke Sanders's girlfriend. Obviously he would be at my party.

"What day is it?" He picked up his phone. I thought he was going to check his calendar, but he was only reading a text.

"Saturday. Next Saturday night. The eighth."

"I'll be there, babe." He drew in a breath. "Hot damn, you look good."

I was sure he was referring to the score of a game, a nude photo from a fan, or his own reflection, because his eyes never left his screen. Then he turned the phone toward me and I sat up.

I had yet to see a picture from my night at Intuition—partly because I'd been avoiding it, partly because I'd spent three hours that morning curating an outfit that Burke spent three seconds tearing off. There were two photos of me—one entering the club, one partying inside—and neither one betrayed what was going on under the surface. I scrolled through the article, relieved that it made no mention of my history with Deacon. It could have been shoddy journalism or that what we'd had didn't matter in light of his joyful engagement, but the truth was our relationship had never been all that public. It was sacred. At least I'd thought it was.

Burke took the phone back and zoomed in on my clingy green dress. "My girl is fine."

I leaned toward him. "Your girl is right here."

He finally peeled his eyes away from the screen. "Yeah, you are." He pulled me in for a kiss and slapped my ass like I'd just slid into home. "That'll get you back in the top spot."

There was no way he would blatantly acknowledge where I fell in his rotation of women. "What do you mean?"

"That website. Hottest party girls or some shit. You know you're down to number three, right? Can't have anyone outdoing my lady." He squeezed my thigh like I'd agree.

"I wasn't aware *Queen of the Social Scene* was part of your daily reading routine." I wasn't aware Burke read at all.

"It's not. But, you know, people talk." He said it so simply, like it was perfectly natural for his publicists, teammates, and the general public to not only care but actually weigh in on how hot his girlfriend was. "Hey, you hungry?"

"Sure," I said, though I didn't know how he was. He'd eaten literally an entire box of Ho Hos. "What do you want? Other than to be dating the hottest party girl in New York."

I waited for him to laugh or detect the edge in my voice, but he just turned his attention back to the 2D image of me on screen. "How about pizza? You know the kind I like."

"Green pepper?"

"Pepperoni. Extra pepperoni."

I didn't like pepperoni. I certainly didn't like extra pepperoni. But I had asked, so once again, I said, "Sure," hoping that if he had his mouth full of pizza, the weight of us having nothing to say to each other would be less palpable.

AFTER A STRING OF HOURS SPENT EATING PIZZA, HAVING sex, and watching *SportsCenter* (sometimes all at once—Burke Sanders was a talent), I awoke to him singing an out-of-tune version of "SexyBack" in the shower. It couldn't have been morning already. I sat up and saw that it was still dark outside.

Burke emerged from the bathroom, his hair and skin still damp, dressed in his jeans and pulling on a blue T-shirt. He kissed the top of my head, a drop of water from his hair falling onto my cheek. "Hey there, Sleeping Beauty."

"Nice song," I tried to joke. I thought we were past the sneaking-out-while-the-other-person-was-sleeping phase. "Going somewhere?"

He pulled on one of his Nikes. "Tampa."

Tampa. When he said he'd only be in town for a day, I

didn't think he literally meant the day. I started to say that I thought he'd be spending the night, but I was afraid of sounding pathetic. Of course he couldn't spend the night. The team probably had practice or weight training or whatever it was baseball players did. "Were you going to wake me up?"

I couldn't read what was behind his eyes. "You looked too cute to disturb."

I smiled, trying to act like I believed him, trying not to wonder if he already had the reigning hottest party girl (a toothpaste heiress—I'd checked) on speed dial. "Well, have a safe trip. Good luck on your game Monday."

"I'll talk to you before then." He wouldn't. "And I almost forgot—" He reached into his duffel bag. "I brought you something."

He yanked out a T-shirt, pitching it to me on the bed. I unfolded the back and read *Sanders 64.*

"Your very own Burke Sanders jersey." He looked so proud.

"I can see that." I didn't know what else to say. "Thanks."

"No sweat." He slung his bag over his massive shoulder. "You gonna fly out to one of my games before the season's over? I wanna show off my lady."

He said this every time I saw him, and every time I gave him the same answer. "Sure thing." He never pushed it any further and neither did I. The thought of having to be on as Burke Sanders's girlfriend, having my every reaction to a play scrutinized, was too much to bear.

I gave him one last kiss at the door before locking up, wondering how long it would be until I talked to him again. Three days? A week? Hopefully long enough for me to be happy to see him when he came back for my party.

I looked at the clock before heading back to bed. I wasn't tired anymore, and I knew that if I called CeCe and asked her if she wanted to go out, she would have been there in minutes. But I couldn't face going to another club, and after spending the day forcing conversation with Burke, I didn't want to force more with her. My new Burke Sanders tee was crumpled on the bed, and as annoying as all of his "babes" could be, a tiny part of me wished he was still there, not because we had some wonderful connection—or, as Deacon had said, something special—but because sometimes it was just nice to have someone else around. I wished things could have been different. I wished I had someone I could talk to without putting on a show, but I didn't. I had Burke.

I flicked on the TV to break up the silence. It was just after twelve thirty, and I knew what was on. For some reason—possibly comfort, possibly torture—I flipped to the channel.

Sometimes the *Breyer's Town* years blurred together, but this episode I recognized. Daisy kept wanting to change her name and personality and interests to suit different cliques at school—the typical family sitcom scenario. Deacon was the only person who knew that I'd watch these reruns whenever I was feeling down. Sometimes we'd watch together.

On-screen was one of the famous kitchen table scenes. At the end of almost every episode, Dr. Breyer would sit and have a chat with Daisy. He would make sure she learned her lesson, then they would hug and share an apple or a cake or whatever the prop master decided on that week. I watched the scene play out, feeling distant, as I always did, from the eight-year-old girl with the green eyes and dark pigtails, talking to her TV dad.

"Why would you want to be something that you're not, Daisy?" Dr. Breyer was asking.

"I wanted people to like me."

"Well, I like you," Dr. Breyer said.

"But you're old," Daisy replied. The studio audience erupted in laughter. Back then, I didn't get the joke, which only added to its delivery. Dr. Breyer was barely thirty-five.

"Well, then, Veronica likes you."

"But I don't like Veronica." Again with the laughs. Veronica was my TV sister. Nobody really liked Veronica.

"The point is, Daisy, you can't care what other people think. Don't pretend to be something you're not so people will like you. You're special just the way you are. Be true to *Daisy Breyer.* Do what makes *you* happy. Once you accept that, everything else will fall in line."

Just like that, Daisy smiled, apologized, and hugged Dr. Breyer, leading to a loud "aww" and applause from the audience. It was so sweet, so simple. But real life wasn't like that. Not everyone knew who they were or what made them happy. Not everyone had someone like Dr. Breyer giving them nice little speeches, and even if they did, they were hard to believe.

I guess that's why *Breyer's Town* was a TV show, and why it was canceled.

CHAPTER FOUR

The only birthday tradition I'd ever kept was having lunch with my TV dad, John Stevenson, and that was only because he refused to take no for an answer.

I was about thirty minutes late for our reservation, but Uncle John still beamed and hugged me as if I were his own child. "Happy birthday, darlin'. I was starting to think you wouldn't show."

"Was that an option?"

He laughed. Maybe I'd been watching too many *Breyer's Town* reruns, but he looked older than the last time I'd seen him. I wondered if I did, too. He looked less like America's favorite dad and more like America's favorite granddad, but that didn't stop him from sustaining a hearty string of work on sitcoms and procedural crime dramas. How different things would have been if he were a woman.

There was a third place setting next to mine with a half-drunk iced tea. I hoped Uncle John hadn't brought his wife or one of his kids along. That had never been part of the deal.

He winked. "Your surprise had to run to the restroom."

Before I could remind him that I detested surprises, Katrina Wilder, my goddamn TV sister, approached our table.

I almost didn't recognize her. When I thought of her, I always pictured her as Veronica Breyer. Whenever Uncle John talked about her accomplishments over the years, I'd envision her at twelve. Twelve-year-old Veronica going to college. Twelve-year-old Veronica teaching theater to inner-city kids. That made it easier to pretend that her many achievements were fictional, too. But there she was, grown-up Katrina, ready to witness how much less fulfilling my life was than hers.

She went in for a hug, but since I was too frozen to stand, it ended up as more of a shoulder squeeze.

"We were starting to think you wouldn't show." She said it with a smile, but unlike when Uncle John said it, I couldn't joke back. Of course she was on time. Of course they had discussed that I wasn't.

Uncle John raised his glass. "My two girls together." For years, he had tried to push us into being best friends. He always thought it was so nice how those girls from *The Hudson Family*, our competitor show, were in each other's weddings. He didn't realize that Katrina and I had nothing in common—and, quite frankly, never had—except for once sharing a dressing room.

"You look great, Katrina. I—can't even remember the last time I saw you." It seemed like the appropriate thing to say.

"It's been forever," she said. "Uncle John's fiftieth, I think."

Ah, yes. I vaguely remembered Katrina being there. I only vaguely remembered being there at all. That was because I got drunk and hooked up with a *General Hospital* star in the coatroom.

"Five years is far too long to go without seeing each other," Uncle John said. "You live in the same city. You should grab coffee."

Katrina squeezed my arm. "I'd love that." She sounded like she meant it. I hadn't realized she was that good of an actress.

By the time we got our food, I was completely caught up on her life. She'd just finished her master's degree, had two spoiled cats, and was marrying a dentist named Wes in November. Her ring was as annoyingly understated and tasteful as the rest of her.

"And what about you, kiddo?" Uncle John asked me. "What have you been up to?"

I knew he expected I was up to more than shopping, clubbing, and getting into fights with my ex on fire escapes, and I wished I could lie to him, think of something to make him proud. All I could manage was, "Not much to report."

"Things going well with the Colonel?"

"You know about me and Burke?" I didn't think Uncle John read *Page Six*.

"I think everyone knows about you and Burke. Is it not true?"

"Oh, no. It's true. We're dating. Four months. He's great." Apparently *great* had become my new favorite word.

"I hope he's good to you."

"He is." And aside from the not-calling, he was—comparatively. I mean, he wasn't blatant about his cheating on the road like some other asshole I knew.

"My mom will freak out if you bring Burke Sanders to my wedding," Katrina said. "Actually, everyone will freak out. Wes will probably want him at our head table."

Her *if* hung in the air. Her wedding was months away. The whole world knew my track record. I could have told Katrina not to hold her breath, but I said, "Tell your mom to save him a dance. My man's a ham."

It wasn't as if I expected them to fall over with relief that little Michaela had at least one aspect of her life together, but they could have done more than smile politely.

"And what about your mom?" Katrina asked. "How is she?"

Uncle John gave my knee a pat under the table. He knew I didn't talk about Caroline. Katrina must have been so busy with her education and her fiancé that she missed the memo.

"You know Caroline," I said. "Alive and thriving." As far as I knew.

"I still hear her voice anytime I wear something monochromatic. 'All it takes is one pop of color,'" Katrina said. "I always thought she was so glamorous. You're just like her."

I put down my fork. My salad wasn't appetizing anymore. "I wouldn't say that."

She gestured to her shirt. "It took me thirty seconds to dribble iced tea on myself. You show up looking like you're on the cover of *Vanity Fair*."

I reached for my water. "Always assume you're going to have your picture taken, right?" Another Caroline-ism.

She laughed. "No one is taking my picture. I maybe get recognized once every six months."

I wasn't surprised. She'd never been all that famous to begin with, and she looked nothing like she did as a child. I was, and I did.

She threw out a thousand apologies about having to duck out for work. Of course, if I'd been on time, that wouldn't have been an issue. When she exited the restaurant, not a single person turned to look at her.

"I really do hope you two will make time to see each other more often," Uncle John said. "She's always adored you."

"And Caroline, too, apparently."

"Katrina was a kid back then, too. She didn't see all the sides of Caroline."

"She didn't see the tell-all either, I guess."

I hated the way his eyes dripped with sympathy. "Have you spoken to your mother since then?"

"Let's talk about something else."

"Okay. Any thoughts on going back to school?"

We had the same conversation every year. I tried the college thing when I was eighteen, a year and a half after my mother took off to marry Tyler Richards, "a *gorge*ously successful investment banker." I went to theater school, thinking maybe it was my chance at normalcy, but within the first week, I realized I'd never be normal. I couldn't live in a twelve-by-twelve room with two other girls—one who spread rumors about me, one who was a fan. I lasted one semester before taking the rest of my tuition money and buying an apartment. It was the right decision. College lasts four years. I still had that apartment.

All I said to Uncle John was, "I'd rather not talk about that, either."

I thought he'd back off, and he did—but not before one last comment.

"You have so much potential, Michaela. And I'm not talking about getting back into acting, though you could if you wanted to. You're so smart, you always have been. You're so talented in so many ways. Just don't throw it all away, okay?"

It sounded like a speech straight out of *Breyer's Town*. Daisy would have told him he was right and given him a kiss on the cheek. I pushed my salad away and said, "Thank you, *Dr. Breyer.*"

I knew what I looked like to him. It was one thing when I showed up for my birthday lunch as a teenager, miserable and confused, but at twenty-seven, I was supposed to have it all together, like Katrina did.

When we hugged goodbye, he offered up the same invitation he did every year. "Come out to the house anytime. You know you're always welcome for the holidays."

"I'll think about it." I wouldn't. When I was seventeen, my first Thanksgiving alone, I actually took him up on it. I felt so out of place with Uncle John, his wife, Jasmine, and their kids that I ducked out before the apple pie was served.

This year, I would spend the holidays like I always did: staying in, watching TV, and eating Chinese with Josh. Everyone had their traditions.

THAT NIGHT I ARRIVED AT MY PARTY FASHIONABLY LATE, around eleven forty. I wondered how much of the crowd I knew and how much CeCe wanted to know. Decked out in a short white one-shouldered dress with fuchsia flowers and matching fuchsia Manolos, I definitely looked the part I was going for, that of the ballplayer's girlfriend. There was just one little exception—no ballplayer.

Burke hadn't called to wish me a happy birthday. I'd texted him a few times before his game that afternoon. No answer. I tried again once his game was over, even allowing a window for postgame interviews. It was becoming difficult to deny that he might not show, but I tried not to think about it.

With the exception of CeCe, everyone was too caught up in their drinking and dancing to notice that I'd arrived. I accepted the shot she offered me and clinked glasses with her. Maybe the night wouldn't be so bad, after all.

"Happy *birth*day, MT! You look *amazing*." She looked behind me and pouted. "Where's the Colonel?"

I shrugged, putting on my best unconcerned face, trying to ignore that on my birthday, at my party, the biggest topic of discussion was Burke.

"His flight was delayed. As far as I know, he's still going to try to come." That last part wasn't a lie, really. Before she could ask me any more questions, I indicated the so-so guy in the ugly green hat she'd been standing with when I came in. "Who's he?"

"Douglas!" she said, like I was supposed to know who *Douglas* was. "You know. Deacon's backup singer? We hooked up the night of the show. I basically haven't left his side since."

As if I needed any reminders of that god-awful show.

She handed me another shot of tequila and a sparkling tiara. "Since you're the woman of the hour, you need to wear this."

I found a nearby mirror and adjusted the crown. It actually looked pretty good, and it was my party, so I'd wear a tiara if I wanted to. Uncle John's speech had left me a little unsettled about the lack of direction in my life. But I was still young. And I was dating a professional baseball player, and we both looked pretty damn good—even if he didn't happen to be here. This was my night, so I promised myself that whenever anyone handed me a drink, I would take it, because I could.

I made my way through the inebriated crowd, and when I didn't see anyone I wanted to talk to, I hit up the bar.

"Appletini," I ordered from a shirtless bartender. Definitely CeCe's idea.

He turned and looked at me square on. "It *is* you!"

I prayed he thought I was someone else.

"Daisy!" he said with way too much enthusiasm. "My sister was you for Halloween one year."

The music was far too loud for me to logically explain that his sister wasn't really me for Halloween—she may have been Daisy Breyer, but she wasn't *me*.

I shrugged and smiled. "Appletini?" I said again.

He looked disappointed that I didn't want to go down memory lane with him, that I didn't want to ask what his favorite episode was or tell him some behind-the-scenes gossip from the set. He fixed my appletini like I asked—though I could have done without the wink—and slid it across the bar, but not before adding, "I really loved *Breyer's Town*."

An hour later, I was about four cocktails in and still minus one boyfriend, so I decided to separate myself from the sweaty bodies on the dance floor and find someplace halfway quiet where I could check my messages. Burke couldn't ditch me on my birthday. He was the whole reason we got a double-chocolate crumb cake. I found a nearby velvet couch where a passed-out girl was taking up residency. She didn't seem to notice when I shifted her legs over so I could sit down.

"Careful. I think she's a puker."

I turned to see Josh, drinking a bottle of beer, seated at the opposite end of Passed-Out Patty. I'd never been so happy to see anyone in my life.

"Happy birthday," he said. "Nice crown."

I touched my hair, hoping it still looked decent for when—and if—Burke showed up. "It's a tiara, Joshua." At that moment, those words seemed to rhyme like no others. So much so that I may have repeated myself a few times.

"I was starting to wonder if I'd actually see you tonight," he said.

"I'm shocked that you're here." Josh never made appearances this public. Normally, he could be found on his couch watching Pacino movie marathons.

"I haven't missed one of your birthdays yet, Turner. I don't know why I'd start now." He took a long drink from his beer. He was probably the only one at the party drinking beer. "Besides, you know how charming I find Miss CeCe to be. How could I turn her invitation down? It was pink, by the way. With glitter."

I looked around to make sure no one nearby could hear me. I wasn't too concerned with the girl lying between us, since she'd started snoring. "I don't think the Colonel is coming."

Josh was unfazed. "Was he supposed to come?"

He couldn't have been that oblivious. Everyone had noticed. Everyone was talking about it. I assumed.

"Just don't tell anyone, okay?" I knew I didn't need to say it, because he was Josh, and besides, he wasn't exactly making small talk with the other guests.

All he said was, "Course."

I fumbled with my phone, remembering that the reason I

sat down was to see if Burke had called. He hadn't. I turned to share this news with Josh, when I noticed him trying not to stare at a group of girls laughing in our direction. I knew they couldn't have heard me, but I figured they were talking about me just the same. By the way Josh put down his beer and said, "I think I'm gonna head out," I could see that he thought the giggles were at his expense.

"You're leaving?" Not that he was bringing much spice to the party, but he had changed out of his mesh shorts, and for him, that was something. "They're not even looking at you. They're looking at me."

Josh stood up and scratched his three-day scruff. "Nope, they're definitely talking about me. The tall one asked four times already if I'd show her my abs. Along with less-G-rated things I won't repeat."

I attempted to stand, but the combination of vodka and stilettos was working against me. "Do you want me to go beat her up?"

He cracked a smile. "Next time. Seriously, though, I'm just tired. Happy birthday."

Before leaving, he flicked my nose and said, "Don't get into too much trouble," causing me to call him a "party pisser," causing him to point out that that wasn't the expression.

After another round of shots and a mix of fruity martinis, I started to feel that Josh was right—this night could lead to trouble. I had the inkling that I'd had one too many when some girl in the bathroom called me a skinny bitch, to which I may or may not have replied with a ten-minute diatribe about the harmful effects of skinny shaming.

When I rejoined the party, I looked around for a familiar face, but came up with nothing. Sure, these people looked vaguely recognizable, and I knew some by name, but where were my real friends? I wanted Burke. I wanted Deacon. Hell, I would have taken Katrina Wilder, but she was at home with her dentist. Where was CeCe? She forced me to have this party in the first place, now she was nowhere to be found. She was probably off with Deacon's backup singer. They'd probably already left.

"Can I have your attention, please?"

I spoke too soon. CeCe's high-pitched voice over the microphone drew everyone's notice. She must have loved that.

"One of Michaela's *very* good friends was in town tonight, heard about her party, and not only agreed to stop by but also asked to sing a very special song for this very special girl."

Deacon. I couldn't believe it. I should have known he wouldn't forget my birthday.

The band took the stage, and in my blurred, hazy state, I couldn't place them. It wasn't Deacon's new band, and it certainly wasn't Reign. *Oh, shit,* I realized as soon as I saw the singer. Soul Infusion. There, onstage, was my standing once-a-year deal, Travis Howard, singing "Michaela Rose."

I probably should have left with Josh.

I have a boyfriend, I reminded myself. *I have a boyfriend.* Though, between the tequila and Travis, I could barely remember that boyfriend's name, or even why I was so angry with him.

I will be good, I will be good. I repeated it over and over, but watching Travis up there with his black spiked hair, tattoos blazing, I wondered how bad a little human contact could be. So when Travis beckoned me onstage, luring me in with his murky hazel eyes, I jumped right up. I could dance a little. Give him a peck on the cheek. Thank him for coming. He was singing my song. I owed it to him. We were friends, sort of. And I was twenty-seven now. I could restrain myself. So I went, and I danced. And the rest of the night was a blur.

CHAPTER FIVE

All Daisy Breyer wanted for her tenth birthday was a Merry Sunshine Bear. They were these stuffed animals that had names like Tickle Bear and Snuggle Bear and Princess Bear. Daisy wanted Giggle Bear. That was all she wanted. Due to the overwhelming popularity of the toy, all the stores were sold out, and Dr. Breyer couldn't get his hands on one. Consequently, Daisy's birthday was ruined, but she didn't let her disappointment show, because Daisy wasn't like that. But then, wouldn't you know it, Dr. Breyer found out that one of his patients was the creator of Merry Sunshine Bears, and on the day after her birthday, he surprised Daisy with not only Giggle Bear, but Tickle Bear, and Snuggle Bear, and Princess Bear. Daisy then proclaimed the day after her birthday to be the best day ever—not because of the Merry Sunshine Bears, but because she had someone who cared enough to go to that effort.

The day after my birthday wasn't like that.

On the day after my birthday, I woke up to the worst headache of my life, the inevitable nausea that comes from an evening with Jose Cuervo, and the distinct feeling that I had something to be embarrassed about. Rolling over and grazing a body next to mine only confirmed it.

I opened one eye and was not remotely surprised when I saw the rose-entwined cross tattoo on the arm of the man next to me. Wonderful. My favorite holiday of the year, Travis Howard Day, and I could barely remember it. Twenty-seven was going to be fantastic.

A muffled version of "This Is Why I'm Hot" echoed near my head, and I was almost relieved to discover that it was my phone and I hadn't permanently destroyed my brain with appletinis. I say *almost* because that ringtone was assigned to the last person I wanted to speak to.

Burke never called me. Especially at nine fifty on a Sunday morning. My mind was far too fogged up to think about how I should play this. I hadn't forgiven him for ditching me on my birthday, and I couldn't wait to hear his excuse, but I wasn't exactly in a state to be having any kind of intense discussion. Besides, Travis was in my bed, so I guessed, for now, we could call it even.

I fumbled the phone open, desperate for the music to stop. "Burke, I'm kind of in the middle of something. Can I call you back?" I hoped he couldn't tell that the dry heaves were about to kick in. I used to say hangovers were God's way of telling us not to drink so much. Deacon always countered that by saying if that were the case, He wouldn't have invented tequila. But I shouldn't have been thinking about Deacon, and I definitely shouldn't have been thinking about tequila.

"We need to talk, Michaela." He never called me anything but *babe*. I knew this was not the kind of conversation I wanted to be having next to Travis Howard—passed out or not.

"Hold on one second." I tiptoed out of bed and tripped over the black leather pants Travis had left crumpled on the floor next to an empty Trojan wrapper. At least one of us had been thinking responsibly—probably me. Even in a blackout I knew where I kept my stash.

I searched around for something to throw on, but the only thing I could find was that ridiculous Sanders jersey. I slipped it on and headed out to the living room, closing the door behind me.

"Sorry, Burke." I tried to sound as chipper as possible, hoping he'd forget whatever it was we needed to talk about. I didn't know how much longer I'd be able to suppress my nausea without vomiting. "I saw your big win yesterday. Congratulations."

"Thanks," he said. Then he said something that sounded like, "Michaela, we need to break up."

I couldn't have heard him correctly. I must have still been drunk. Nobody broke up with someone like that, so briefly, so matter-of-factly, at 9:52 a.m. on the day after her birthday.

"I'm sorry," I said. "I think my phone cut out."

He raised his voice. "We need to break up."

I really wished I'd started this conversation with the whole standing-me-up-at-my-party thing.

"Did something happen?" I thought he'd say he slept with a bartender or something, which I wouldn't be too thrilled about, but again, there was Travis, so we could work it out.

"Your picture is everywhere this morning. Some of the guys brought it to my attention." His statement was followed by a chorus of hoots and whistles. The queasiness in my chest expanded.

"Where are you right now?"

"In the locker room. We have a game in a few hours."

I couldn't believe he was breaking up with me in front of his entire team. I wanted to throw the phone at the wall, but I needed to hold on to some shred of dignity. Plus, I couldn't wake Travis. There was no way I was letting him witness this exchange.

"So my picture is everywhere," I said. "What else is new?"

Burke lowered his voice, as if he were trying to be a gentleman. "It was sort of—*incriminating.*"

I didn't even think Burke knew what incriminating meant. "How so?"

He was whispering now. "You're standing on a bar, with your skirt up in the air, kissing that tattooed dude from Soul Infusion."

The tequila was getting back at me. My head was pounding, and now I definitely had to throw up. Somehow, I managed to say, "You should believe none of what you hear and half of what you see, Burke."

"We had a fun time, but I have an image to protect."

An image. And I knew he didn't mean as a squeaky-clean baseball hero. The only image he was concerned about bruising was his stupid male ego. He was worried about his girlfriend kissing someone else because people would think he, Burke "the Colonel" Sanders, Major League stud, could not keep his woman satisfied.

"It was a birthday kiss," I said, leaving out the rest. "It was my birthday, remember? You were supposed to be there."

"I never said I'd be there."

Now I really wanted to throw the phone.

"You did." The pitch of my voice only made my headache worse. "You said it last week. Maybe you forgot because you were so consumed with me being demoted to third hottest party girl in New York."

For a second, he was silent. I almost thought he was going to apologize. What he said instead was, "You're actually number eight now."

Of course he was keeping track.

"This is the last thing I need right now," he said, and I didn't know if he meant Travis or my descending ranking. "I don't care if you're hooking up with other guys, but have you seen my picture anywhere with other girls? It's called discretion."

Another wave of nausea slapped me. I'd always suspected that he had a girl in every city, each armed with a Burke Sanders jersey of her own. I just never expected him to be so callous about it.

"So that's it, then." I wasn't going to embarrass myself any further by begging him to reconsider.

"There's nothing more we can do for each other," he said, so businesslike I wanted to scream. "I have the playoffs coming up, then once the season's over, I need to focus on my art."

Now I knew I couldn't have heard him correctly. "Your art?"

"Yeah. I want to get back into painting. Landscapes, maybe. Maybe ballparks across America."

"That has to be the dumbest thing I've ever heard."

He took another beat. I almost thought he'd hung up. Then he said, "You do realize I was an art major in college?" This was the moment he decided to share a piece of his life with me.

"Gotta go," he said. "We have stuff to do before batting practice." Then he hung up. No *goodbye*, no *we'll still be friends*. His last words to me were about batting practice.

The vomit that I'd been trying to suppress rose up into my throat, and I made it to the bathroom just in time, which is more than I could say about some of my other Travis Howard binges. As I lay sprawled on the bathroom floor, my head resting on the cool porcelain of the toilet, I caught a glimpse of the girl in the mirror, and there was only one word for it: *pathetic*.

There she was, the eighth hottest party girl in New York: twenty-seven and one day, throwing up from a hangover, wearing the stupid jersey of the stupid man who had just dumped her in front of his stupid team. Her makeup was still caked on from the night before, but was now smeared and running, and that hideous tiara was still tangled in her dark hair. To make matters worse, she had a thirty-nine-year-old rocker naked in her bed, luckily passed out because otherwise he would have heard her getting dumped. This was what had become of Daisy from *Breyer's Town*. That smart-alecky little girl America loved. I didn't know who would love her now.

AFTER I PEELED MYSELF OFF THE FLOOR AND SHOWED TRAVIS to the door—and believe me, I didn't have to twist his arm—I washed down two aspirin with ginger ale in hopes of quelling the worst hangover of my life. There were a few flashes from the night before—the tiara, the shirtless bartenders, Travis singing "Michaela Rose"—but other than that, it was a run of missing hours I would never get back, not that I wanted to. I'd seen the picture. About forty people sent it to me. I followed the link, and there I was—skirt up in the air, thong out for everyone to see, with my tongue down Travis's throat, just as Burke had described.

Once I had a visual, I could sort of understand where he was coming from. It still didn't excuse him for dumping me in front of his teammates, but maybe he was in shock. Maybe he'd get over it. Maybe we didn't have a perfect relationship and maybe it wouldn't have lasted much longer, but he wouldn't really toss me aside like that. He'd call a few hours after his game ended, and I'd give him a hard time, but I'd take him back.

For once, I watched one of his games all the way through, and he wasn't even pitching. I figured we should have something to talk about when he called. I could be more interested in sports. The camera kept cutting to Burke in the dugout while the commentators broke down his outstanding start the day before. I searched for any signs that he was a little sad, or embarrassed, or ashamed about the way he'd treated me. He looked totally unaffected, spitting on the ground, talking to his pitching coach, even laughing. He really thought nothing of dumping a girl over the phone on the day after her birthday. He really thought nothing of dumping me.

It wasn't like I was a stranger to rejection. I still had baby teeth when I learned the phrase "we're going in a different direction." Back then, when I'd get turned down for a job, I'd ask Caroline what was wrong with me, why they didn't want *me*. She'd tell me it wasn't personal—that I just didn't fit their needs. I had no idea that by sixteen, I'd stop fitting hers, too.

"She doesn't know what she lost," Deacon would say when I'd joke about being dumped by my own mother. "One day she'll realize that leaving you was the biggest mistake she's ever made." Of course, not long after, he made the same choice. The memory of it still burned. We had just made love, and I was lying in bed next to him, studying the dove-shaped freckle below his left nipple, and for the first time in a long time, I let myself be happy because I knew in my bones that the only time I didn't have to be the girl who played Daisy Breyer was when I was in his arms. And then he said those six words I'd never get out of my heart: "Mickie, this is never gonna work."

The three-hour window I had given Burke turned into five hours, then seven, then eight. I waited to feel something—some unbearable sadness, or devastation, or loss. I hated that it was so easy for him to get rid of me, but at the same time, I couldn't shake the feeling that it was happening to someone else. It felt like it was happening to that couple on *Page Six*. And for them, I felt sad. And for that girl with her tongue down Travis Howard's throat with her skirt up in the air, I felt embarrassed. But for myself, I didn't know how to feel.

After an entire day spent retching over the toilet and studying my face in the mirror for premature wrinkles, I caved. I called him. All I got was his voicemail.

"Burke, it's Michaela. I know this morning was a little . . . crazy . . . but I was hoping we could talk about it. Okay?"

He never called me back.

CHAPTER SIX

Ask anyone about the worst thing a woman can do. They won't say commit a horrific crime. They'll say cheat.

My phone hadn't rung for two days. CeCe hadn't even answered my texts. I forced myself to leave the apartment to get a coffee, and when I passed the newsstand, the goddamn shot of Travis, me, and my panties was on the front of *The Daily Sun & Star* under the headline:

Daisy Does the Colonel Dirty

As if Daisy would ever do something so horrifying.

I knew I shouldn't buy a copy, but tell me you wouldn't have done the same.

I got back to my building—completely forgetting the coffee—and stepped into the elevator behind some woman making a fuss about getting her stroller inside, like no one had ever had a baby before. She stared me down.

"Aren't you . . . ?"

"Yup." I didn't know if she was thinking of *Breyer's Town* or Burke, but I was in no mood for either.

"I didn't know you lived in this building." She said it as if I'd broken in or something. I'd probably lived there longer than she had.

We got to her floor before I could determine which Daisy she was talking to. While it took her another four minutes to wrangle her child out into the hallway, I noticed Josh walking a pretty blonde to the opposite elevator. That boy-band thing was clearly still working for him.

As the stroller-wielding mom finagled her way into the hall, she said, "My brother always liked you on that show." That sentence alone caused Josh to turn his head, and as the elevator doors were sliding shut, he shoved his arm in front of the sensor.

"Morning." His shaggy blond hair gave the impression he'd just rolled out of bed.

"I think it's afternoon."

"I think you're right."

I wanted to make some excuse to get away, a quip about him holding up the elevator, but there was no one else around. He leaned on the door like he had all the time in the world. Clearly, that high-pitched noise coming from the sensor wasn't bothering him.

"Have you eaten breakfast?"

"It's three o'clock." I held up my wrist, an ineffective gesture since I wasn't wearing a watch.

"That wasn't my question."

I hadn't had breakfast. I hadn't had lunch. I hadn't had anything but coffee and Skittles for the past three days. Josh could see it all over my face.

"Come on, let's go get something to eat," he said. "I'll grab my keys."

He walked toward his apartment, and though I had no intention of going anywhere with him, I folded up *The Sun & Star* and followed him into the hall.

I stopped inside his doorway. "I really don't feel like going out."

"You always feel like going out."

"Well, I don't feel like it today."

He ran both hands through the mess on his head. "You have a fever or something?"

He didn't know. Of course he didn't know. Gossip rags weren't exactly on his radar.

"Come on, Turner." He threw on a ratty blue baseball cap and locked his door. "Let me buy you a bagel. You haven't been taking care of yourself."

Translation: *You look horrible.*

I smoothed down my hair and stepped into the elevator. I should have told him that I was the last person he'd want to be seen with, but this was Josh. He hadn't listened to me a day in his life.

As we headed out of the building, I said, "I would have thought a guy like you would feed your dates before sending them on their way."

"Nah, I only feed the ones I really like." When he noticed I wasn't laughing, he said, "She had to go to class."

"Don't tell me she's in college."

"Med school."

"So she says."

"Hey," he said. "Be nice."

A group of frat bros headed toward us, and I kept my head low, waiting for them to holler about my thong or harass me for stabbing their hero in the back. One stopped in front of us, did an embarrassingly accurate impression of the Boyz' most famous dance move, then burst into laughter and high-fived his friends. He'd surely be solidified as king of the kegger once he told everyone how he'd mocked a former boy-bander. A former boy-bander who didn't appear fazed in the slightest.

"How does that not bother you?" I asked.

"Oh, come on, Turner. You can't let that stuff get to you. The fact that I was in some pop group doesn't define me any more than playing Daisy Breyer defines you. It's ancient history."

How he could say that so easily, I had no idea.

We turned into a café on the corner where Josh was evidently a regular, judging by the way the staff greeted him when he ordered "the usual." He turned to me. "Black coffee, six sugars?"

I nodded. I'd learned to drink it that way when I was sixteen and Caroline told me it would stunt my growth. It was my way of revolting, I suppose. Josh and I would sneak around, drink coffee (his manager told him it would stain his pearly whites), and make out. We were so rebellious.

"So, this is what you do with your days now?" I asked once we'd settled into a corner booth with our coffees and bagels. "Send the ladies on their way, come down here, and stuff your face?'

He bit into his bagel. "Yes, that's exactly what I do."

"Don't you worry what her motives are?"

"Whose?"

"Med student's."

"Morgan," he said. "And no, I'm not worried. You know as well as I do, you can tell when someone cares about you and when they're after something else."

The bagel turned sour in my stomach. I couldn't remember the last time someone fell into the former category.

"How long have you been seeing each other?"

He took a sip of his coffee. "I don't know. Few months?"

There was no way he'd been dating someone for a few months. I would have known if he had a girlfriend for a few months. "Does she work a lot?"

He shrugged. "I guess."

"Why haven't I met her?"

"I don't know. You've been busy."

I wasn't busy, but I did see his point. There was a time when Josh and I spent every minute of every day together. I didn't know what had changed.

"So, are you going to read that or are you auditioning for a remake of *Newsies*?"

He gestured to the paper under my arm. I'd almost forgotten about it. Almost.

"I need you not to judge me," I said.

"For buying *The Sun & Star* or for what I'm about to see?"

I laid the paper on the table and unfolded it. I'll give Josh credit. His wince was subtle.

"Why would you waste your money on this?"

"Because I need to see what they're saying about me."

"Why does it matter?"

"Because it does."

"Christ." He tapped his coffee cup on the table and stared at the headline. "Fine. We'll look at it together."

There were half a dozen pictures of me at different clubs with different men. None had been taken during my time with Burke—a few were at least two years old—but that wouldn't have fit the narrative. They'd even added censor marks to conceal nonexistent nip slips and crotch shots.

> "The Colonel knew what he was getting into," a source close to the couple reveals. "From day one, he imparted a 'three strikes' rule. With Travis Howard, Dirty Daisy struck out."

Josh folded up the paper and put it on the seat next to him. I didn't argue.

"Turner," he said. "This is garbage. You know that, right?"

"Sure."

He knew I didn't really know it. He also knew this wasn't new territory for me. At least this time it wasn't my own mother going to the tabloids.

"Needless to say, Burke and I have parted ways. He said there wasn't much more we could do for each other. Sound familiar?"

Josh was lucky enough to be dating me when Caroline cited that very reason for leaving me at sixteen. His jaw twitched at the mention of it.

"Let's hang out tonight," he said. "We'll order takeout. Watch a movie."

It would have been so easy to say yes, to stay inside until the news cycle moved on to some other girl's questionable behavior, but all I could think about were the words Caroline said to me the day *Breyer's Town* was canceled. She refused to look back as we walked out of the studio, her honey-colored hair bouncing with determination as she marched on. She didn't turn until I started choking back tears. The second she heard that first sniffle, she took hold of my shoulders and looked me square in the eye.

"Don't ever let them see you cry, Gorgeous. Tears mean you've lost something, and there's no such thing as loss in this life. There's only change. When something like this happens, your only thought should be what's next. As for all of that in there? Just tell yourself it never existed."

Caroline's words were always better in theory than they were in execution, but she was right about one thing. I needed to focus on what came next. If the world thought Dirty Daisy was going to hide out and cry, they had another thing coming to them.

MAGIC WAS A NEW CLUB GETTING A LOT OF BUZZ FOR ITS lack of indoor lighting. It was pitch-black inside, but everyone was handed a Day-Glo necklace with each drink, so as the night wore on, the entire place became illuminated. I gave it two weeks before everyone grew tired of the gimmick and moved on to someplace new, but for now, it was exactly where I needed to be seen.

After two days of silence, all it took to get CeCe to respond was one text asking her to get us on the list. She said we were *in* and she and Douglas would meet me there. I wasn't thrilled with the idea of her bringing that stoner, but as long as she made the calls to get us in, I didn't care what she did.

I walked past the long line when I arrived, trying not to wonder how many had seen *The Sun & Star* and how many were disappointed in what had become of little Daisy Breyer.

The bouncer didn't unlatch the rope. "You gotta wait a few."

I looked back at the line. He had to be joking.

"I'm on the list," I said. "Michaela Turner."

He gave me a greasy smile. "Oh, I know. But we have some big names here tonight. You gotta wait until someone leaves." His eyes scanned my violet dress and he leaned in like he was going to give me a kiss on the cheek. "Unless you want to give me a preview of what everyone's going to see in there."

I could have slapped him. I could have turned around and left. But the paparazzi were right there, cameras in hand, so I smiled and said, "I'll wait."

I started to text CeCe, Are you here???, then deleted the last two question marks so I didn't seem desperate. As soon as the photographers got enough pictures of me being denied entry for the first time in my life, the bouncer unhooked the rope and let me through.

Once my eyes adjusted to the dark, I found CeCe on a couch, two necklaces in. She stood up and hugged me. "What took you so long?"

I leaned close so no one else could hear. "I had to wait. How much are they paying me to be here? They made me wait?"

She bit her lip and tied on a third necklace. "So they're actually not paying us. Don't be mad, 'kay? We were lucky to get in at all."

It felt like a slap. "What's that supposed to mean?"

"I mean, look at this place. Everyone is here. And—I mean, you saw *The Sun & Star*, right?"

When Daisy Breyer was backed into a corner, she never really lied. She just made the truth work to her advantage by holding some of it back, like when she told Dr. Breyer that she didn't have any Girl Scout cookies left because she'd donated them all. She just left out that she'd donated them to her own stomach. It wasn't a lie, it was more like a half-truth, and the audience loved it.

"I have better things to do than read tabloids," I said.

"I bet you do," a voice said from the couch. Douglas—eyes red-rimmed, hat askew, leering. He clearly did not have better things to do.

I touched CeCe's arm. "I'm going to get a drink."

I made my way through the crowd, smiling, waving, proving to anyone who looked my way that I wasn't only fine, I was thriving. So I wasn't getting paid to be there. That would all change as soon as I reminded everyone what a good time I could be.

"Dirty Daisy."

I turned and saw Dyana Wynters, reality star turned TV correspondent and ex-girlfriend of Travis Howard. She had at least six neon bands around her neck, smudged eyeliner, and a drunken smile.

"Super cute picture of you on the front page." She stepped forward, like she was trying to intimidate me. Please. I wasn't the one wearing Day-Glo underwear to match my necklaces.

I'd learned over the years that with someone like Dyana, you couldn't engage, because then they'd think you cared.

"Thanks. I thought I looked pretty good." I could have

left it at that, but she had called me Dirty Daisy, so I threw in, "Travis has a new piercing, by the way. I'll let you guess where it is."

I pretended I didn't hear her utter "skank" as I walked away, and I pretended I didn't hear the crowd around her laugh. I pretended I didn't hear the catcalls as I made my way to the bar, or the shouts of "Where's the Colonel?" as I made my way to the dance floor. If they were waiting for me to break, they could wait all night. There was only one baseball-inspired headline anyone would write about me after tonight, and that was that Michaela Turner was playing the field.

I pulled CeCe onto a table with me to dance, and when she ditched me to go find Douglas, I danced on my own. I danced like everyone was watching, because they were, and my solitary Day-Glo necklace showed them I was in complete control. When the time was right, I would find the hottest guy there, an NFL player or a Calvin Klein model, and I'd show everyone just how little I cared about what the tabloids were saying about me. I would focus on what was next.

Or I would focus on the couple at the bar who immediately made me want to throw up my brunch.

They'd just arrived, judging by their lack of necklaces, although it could have been the clean living. I had never seen Shaunn with two *n*'s in person, and I hated to admit that she was striking, and the complete opposite of me. Deacon wore a velvet plum jacket with an *Abbey Road* T-shirt underneath, like a tiny piece of the real him was fighting to come out. I tried to avert my eyes, but all I could focus on was how she was talking, and he looked like he was listening—really listening—with his arm wrapped around her waist, gently caressing her left hip, a move he'd mastered on me.

I had to get away. Saving face for someone like CeCe or Dyana Wynters was one thing, but this I couldn't do. I scanned the club for the nearest exit, but all I saw was the sea of Day-Glo. I couldn't even get down from the table. Everyone was too damn close. As if he could smell my panic, Deacon turned his attention away from Shaunn and onto me. I didn't need to imagine what he'd say if I could hear him, what he'd say if he still cared. *When are you going to grow out of this? When are you going to stop pretending? Why can't you let the world see you like I see you?*

A lot of good that did me. It was one thing for Burke to toss me aside when he'd never known me. Here was the one man who got rid of me when he did.

Shaunn placed her hand on his stomach and said something in his ear. Just like that, his attention was back on her. Of course it was. She was the girl he was going to marry. I was the girl he left with a half-empty bed and a heart full of questions.

I managed to get down from the table and made my way through the illuminated, inebriated crowd. The least I could do was act like I was having a good time until I got out of there. I had an Emmy, for Christ's sake. When someone traced his hand down my arm, put his hand on my waist, and started moving our bodies to the music, I let him. I knew it wasn't Deacon—I'd recognize his touch anywhere—but I closed my eyes and let myself pretend that it was. I let myself pretend that I was in the arms of the man he was before, the man who sent my mother away when she came asking for money, the man who wove me into his songs and made me believe I could be someone other than who the world thought I was. I let myself pretend that that was all still true, and that the hands pushing my hair aside, the lips kissing my neck, the body grinding against mine belonged to the man who'd vowed to take my pain away.

"You *SLUT*!"

CeCe stood before me, her eyes bright with Day-Glo and tears, her trembling lips detached from Douglas for the first time that night. That's because his lips, his teeth, his tongue, were focused on my neck.

She pulled him behind her, as if he were a victim and not someone trying to acquaint himself with every inch of my bare skin. "You're pathetic. Is there anything or anyone you won't do to make yourself feel better?"

I could have defended myself, could have told her that I didn't even know it was him, but that wouldn't have mattered to her or the crowd surrounding us.

She raised her voice so everyone could hear her over the music. "Do you know she pays me to be her friend? *That's* how desperate she is."

"That's not true." Even as I said it, I couldn't deny that the dress she was wearing was one I'd given her. Her earrings were a gift from Burke that I passed on because they weren't my style. If Magic had paid me to show my face, she would have gotten a cut for making the arrangements. "I've been a good friend to you." I knew no one else could hear me. I wasn't even sure if she could.

"You are not capable of having friends." She came close so that only I could hear her, and that was what hurt—she wasn't saying it for show; she was saying it because she meant it. "No one has cared about you since you were eight years old. You know why? Because you're not Daisy Breyer."

It was the truth I'd wanted everyone to see for more than half of my life, and it offered no comfort.

"You're not Daisy," she said again. "You're nothing."

NOTHING COULD GET THE FEEL OF DOUGLAS'S LIPS OFF MY skin or CeCe's words out of my mind. Not the long cab ride home, not the steaming hot shower, certainly not the *Breyer's Town* rerun I put on in bed. At 3 a.m., I sat on the couch, cued up my white noise wave sounds, and stared at the art print of the Pacific Ocean hanging above Deacon's piano. He'd bought it for me shortly after he moved in, after I told him how when I was younger, I vowed to live in California, right on the beach where I could wake up every morning and have the ocean be the first thing I saw. He came home with that picture, hung it up, and said I could have the best of both worlds. Sometimes, staring at that image was the only thing that could calm me down. Not tonight.

A loud pounding shook me out of my attempt at reverie. At first I thought it was a neighbor's door, but the second bang undoubtedly came from my own. I hadn't buzzed anyone in, and I didn't know any of my neighbors except Josh, who was obviously not up at this unsightly hour. When the pounding got louder, I was convinced that this—3:58 a.m. on September 12—would be the fateful day a deranged fan of *Breyer's Town* hunted me down.

I grabbed my phone and tiptoed across the apartment so that the psycho/stalker/killer wouldn't know I was home. As I got closer, the knocking lessened, sounding less fierce and more pathetic. Hoping it was a drunken neighbor with the wrong door, I looked through the peephole.

Deacon.

This was too much for one night, even for me.

I stood completely still, hoping he'd give up and leave. I didn't trust myself to let him in, but I also couldn't bear to walk away, especially when he leaned his forehead on the door and whispered, "Mickie."

I unlocked the four bolts but left the chain up.

He'd lost the jacket and was now sporting his ripped *Abbey Road* T-shirt and more Day-Glo necklaces than I could count. The clean living hadn't lasted very long.

He stared at me for a long moment, looking lost now that I was standing in front of him, like he wasn't quite sure why he'd come. I wondered if he'd thought he still lived there.

"Hey, Mickie."

I closed the door a little bit. "How did you get in here?"

"You still got Phil."

That damn doorman. Deacon's and my drunken middle-of-the-night antics were his favorite form of entertainment. He'd probably been waiting for us to start back up again for the past two years.

"You really shouldn't be here."

He tried to open the door and didn't seem to notice when the chain blocked his way. "Can I come in?"

I stepped back. "No."

He leaned on the door and looked past me into the apartment. I couldn't let him see how much it still dripped with his presence. The bookcase he'd chipped with his foot one night when he had writer's block. The couch he had to have because it reminded him of the one at Graceland. The piano I bought for him, the one I wouldn't let him take when I kicked him out. I told him it wasn't his to keep, but I wished I'd let him have it. Every time I looked at it, all I could think of was him sitting there, singing Sam Cooke's "Bring It on Home to Me." It was all there, whispering, *Let him in. He's the balm that we need.*

He trained his bloodshot eyes on me. He always looked at me like that, like I was the only person in the world. "I heard what happened."

"What did you hear?"

"All of it, Mickie. Travis and the picture and Dougie and your girl—they're shits. I heard all of it. You okay?"

I couldn't let him do this to me. Burke was one thing. Burke could reject me and I could get over it. Deacon I couldn't handle, not again.

I should have sent him away right then. I shouldn't have asked, "Why are you really here?" I should have been thankful when he didn't answer.

I tried to close the door a little more, tried to shut him out. "Go home, Deacon."

He didn't turn away. He just stood there, fingering the

chain with one hand, tapping the door with the other. "I tried to find you after. I thought we could talk. Even checked the storage room for you."

I didn't respond. If I waited long enough, he would have to give up and leave, unless he wanted to piss himself.

"Hey, what'd you mean?" he asked.

I moved back another inch. "What did I mean by what?"

"At my show," he said. "You said I'd sell a million records. You said it wasn't me. You didn't say what you thought."

I stood up straighter but refused to look at him. It always came back to his music. "That is what I think."

He was silent for a moment. "What did you think, Mickie?"

He was drunk, he was vulnerable, and whatever his motives, he was the only person checking on me. I couldn't tell him he'd completely ruined the one thing he'd always been good at.

"I'll call Phil and have him get you a cab."

"Can't we talk?"

His finger was hooked over the top of the chain, and I wanted to remove it, but I couldn't touch him, because then I would let him in, and then we would go to bed, and then he would break my heart.

"I saw you dancing up there and all I wanted to do was talk to you. I miss talking to you. I miss hearing what you have to say." He didn't mean what he was saying. He probably wouldn't even remember coming here by the morning. I needed him to leave, now, before I caved and unlatched the chain from the door.

"Then why don't you come back when you're sober and not engaged?"

For a minute, neither of us moved. I could feel him looking at me, and I refused to look back. I started gently pushing the door shut, and he finally moved his hand.

"I'm gonna call you, okay? Just listen to my album and I'm gonna call you and you can tell me what you think."

Before he could say or do any more, I shut the door and bolted the four locks. Through the peephole, I could see he wasn't moving, and I was afraid that I'd have to go out there and help him to the elevator, but I knew if I opened that door again, neither one of us would be going downstairs. When he finally walked away, I called downstairs and told Phil to make sure he got in a cab okay, then I watched out the window and made sure he actually did.

There was no way I'd be able to sleep now. I went back to the couch, crawled under a blanket, and focused on that picture of the ocean. For the first time in hours, I wasn't thinking about CeCe, or Douglas, or the mess with Travis. I may have sent him away, but Deacon managed to get in anyway.

CHAPTER SEVEN

There had been exactly three instances in my life when I'd asked Josh if I could go for a run with him. Every time, he told me it was a bad idea, and every time, I convinced him it would be great. Every time, he ended up slowing to a mere jog, and every time, I nearly passed out from exhaustion.

It was nice to see some things never changed.

"Are you sure you don't want to find a bench somewhere and take a break?" He shifted to jogging backward like a show-off while I pumped my arms and tried to keep pace.

"I'm fine. I'm just out of practice."

"When were you in practice?"

He'd known something was up when I came downstairs in yoga pants and sneakers, and he asked if I wouldn't rather just talk about whatever was going on instead of forcing myself to wheeze through a fraction of a mile before deciding I wanted to tell him what was going on. There was no way I could tell him about Deacon—he'd told me under no uncertain terms that if I ever invited that asshole back into my life, he'd have me committed—so I handed him my phone and showed him CeCe's tell-all, and he threw on his shoes.

It had taken her mere days to go to the press with my story of betrayal. Scratch that. It had taken her mere days to go to a garbage D-list blog with my story of betrayal, which was fitting. She thought I was garbage. She thought I was nothing. She wasn't wrong.

I tried to focus on the running, or at least the burning sensation in my legs, but all I could think about was the headline:

Paid to Party, Paying for Friends: The Real Story of the Former Queen of the Social Scene

That's right. *Former.* A couple bad nights and I was persona non grata in the very circuit I had made famous.

> "Clubs would pay her just to show up and look like she was having a good time," Johanssen reveals. "She'd pay me to go with her, to cover up that she doesn't have anyone else. Did she pay guys like Burke Sanders and Travis Howard to keep her in the public eye? I wouldn't put it past her. Nothing about her life is real."

I nearly collapsed onto the next bench I saw and guzzled half of Josh's water. "Okay, maybe we can sit for five minutes."

Josh didn't sit, of course. He kept running in place and I knew that in his mind he was keeping track of every one of those five minutes.

"Turner, stop thinking about it. Do you think anyone even reads that crap? Do you think anyone cares?"

He didn't get it. People would read it. People would care. I cared.

"She made it sound like I had sex with her boyfriend in public. He was the one grinding up against me and saturating me with his tongue, and she made it sound like I preyed upon him."

He leaned down to stretch his hamstring, meeting me at eye level. "None of what she said is true."

"Half of what she said is true." That was all that mattered. Those grains of truth made the whole piece believable. I looked around to see if anyone was watching us, if anyone was close enough to hear. They were on their way to work. They were walking their dogs. They were pushing their jogging strollers. They all had someplace to be and I was on a bench in Central Park, the former queen of the social scene, without a plan in sight. "What am I supposed to do now?"

"What do you want to do?"

I opened my mouth but nothing came out. I'd been a staple in the club scene since I was eighteen. I didn't know how to be anything else. It wasn't like CeCe's tell-all was the gospel. I could have put on a dress, held my head up, and gone back out there, but between her words, and the slimy bouncer who made me wait, and Dyana Wynters calling me Dirty Daisy, and the fact that I didn't even get paid for any of it—I didn't see how I could.

I stood up. "Keep running, I guess. But maybe we could slow down the pace a little."

He patted himself on the shoulder. "Want me to carry you home?"

I almost smiled. The first time I tried to run with him, he actually did give me a piggyback ride halfway to my apartment until we got stopped by mobs of fans. We were sixteen and he was still trying to woo me.

"What do you do with your days when Megan's not around?"

He reverted to his backward run, trusting me to be his eyes. "Morgan."

I could memorize thirty pages of dialogue when I was eight but I couldn't keep Josh's Med Student's name right. Maybe CeCe was right. I wasn't capable of having friends.

"So, what do you do?"

"What do you mean, what do I do? The same stuff I always do. I run."

We could cross that one right off the list because this was something I was never engaging in again. "And?"

"I don't know. Why are you asking?"

Because I wanted to feel less pathetic. Because I wanted to know how he could be so complacent all the time. "Just because."

"I guess I mess around with my music sometimes."

I stopped jogging. He said it so quietly I almost asked him to repeat himself. In the Boyz of the Nation days, when they were selling out arenas singing hit after hit penned by a song factory of writers, Josh would hole up in a hotel room with his acoustic guitar and his thoughts. I hadn't heard him mention it since. "What kind of music?"

He ran his hand down his face, clearly not loving how my constant starts and stops were affecting his run. "Not anything anyone will hear. I'm just playing around, but everyone needs some dumb hobby to keep them sane." He took in the stare I must have been giving him and said, "Come on, Turner, there must be one thing that makes you happy."

I couldn't answer him, because the one thing that ever made me happy only showed up at my door when he was too drunk to stand, and I'd sent him back home to his fiancée. If I'd let Deacon in, he would have been there to hold me when I saw the tell-all, like he had when it was my mother revealing all my broken parts to the world, but instead he was probably home, sleeping off his hangover while Shaunn laughed at the pictures of me standing outside Magic alone.

I pulled out my phone and looked at the blog again. There were now over three hundred comments. Skank. Pathetic. Why is she famous again? The Colonel dodged a bullet.

Josh took the phone from me and put it in his shorts pocket. "What did I tell you when you got one of these things?"

I'd swapped out my beloved pink Razr as soon as the iPhone was released, and I constantly asked Josh when he was getting rid of his flip phone. He said he had no desire to walk around with the internet in the palm of his hand. I hated to admit that he might have been onto something.

"That person she's describing?" he said. "That's not who you are."

I didn't know how he could be so sure. I wasn't.

"Come on," I said. "Let's head home before I change my mind and ask you to carry me."

When we got back to our building, there was a cheerful-looking blonde downstairs talking to Phil. She looked semi-familiar, but I figured I'd probably seen her around the building. That is until she greeted me with a huge smile and a "You're Michaela."

I was afraid this would be like the time some woman showed up at my doorstep claiming to be my second cousin who needed a place to crash. She wasn't, of course, and she didn't, naturally.

Josh stepped toward her, and I thought he was going to ask her to move along, but he gave her a quick kiss and said, "Turner, this is Morgan. Morgan, Turner."

"Josh has told me so much about you," she said. I wondered what. That I was his first under-the-bra action? That I wasn't the mess the tabloids made me out to be? Knowing Josh, he'd probably assured her that everything they wrote was untrue.

"He's told me a lot about you, too," I said, although that wasn't remotely true. "Med school. That's . . . awesome."

I didn't need to look at Phil to know he was rolling his eyes. He was probably annoyed that our chatter was preventing him from enjoying *Days of Our Lives* on his eighteen-inch

TV. If there was one couple Phil liked watching more than Deacon and me, it was John and Marlena.

Morgan rested her hand on Josh's stomach and didn't even balk at his sweaty T-shirt. She'd probably dreamed of touching those abs since she was fifteen. Sure, she seemed nice enough, but there was no way she hadn't been a card-carrying member of the Boyz of the Nation Fan Club.

She looked up at him. "Have you started packing yet?"

My heart, already racing from the run, sped up. He wouldn't move in with her. There was no way he'd leave our building. Every time he was in a bad mood, he'd throw out the idea of packing up and starting over, but he'd never actually do it.

"Where are you going?" I asked—croaked, really.

"We're heading down to Florida to golf," he said, and instantly my body found balance. "But we're not leaving until next week. Morgan doesn't realize I can pack with my eyes closed."

"I'm a little neurotic about these things," she said. "You know how it is when life gets so busy and before you know it, your flight's in twelve hours and you don't even know where your suitcase is."

I could have said I didn't know how that was, but I looked at Josh instead. "I didn't think you still golfed." I couldn't remember the last time he'd mentioned it.

"I golf every Tuesday."

I could feel Morgan's eyes volleying between us, and I knew exactly what she was thinking. *Your alleged best friend doesn't even know you golf? The tabloids are right. How much does she pay you to hang out with her?*

"Wait. Are you visiting your family?"

Josh had bought his mother and stepfather a place on the water when he was eighteen, but he and Morgan hadn't been dating very long. He wouldn't bring her to meet the parents already.

"Yeah, we'll visit them for a little bit." He was trying to play it off as nothing, but I could see the hope in Morgan the Med Student's eyes while she gently fixed his messy hair. Something about the sight of them—two pretty-faced blonds, standing close to each other in a way that didn't appear to be for show—punctured a hole in my gut. Josh was capable of having an actual relationship. With a regular person. I was only capable of having one-night stands with fading rock stars and stabbing my faux friends in the back.

"Well, if I don't see you before you go, have fun." I held out my hand. "Can I have my phone back?"

"You'll see me." He pulled it out of his pocket and hesitated before giving it to me, like he knew as soon as I had it, I'd open up that article. He was right.

As we headed to the elevators, Phil didn't even look up. Golfer Ken and Dr. Barbie didn't give him the same thrill that Deacon and I did, but I was starting to think thrills might be overrated.

I SHOULD HAVE SHOWERED WHEN I GOT UPSTAIRS. I SHOULD have organized my closet, or my cabinets, or focused on finding a hobby, like Josh apparently had with his music and his golf and his running. I should have been doing anything other than scouring CeCe's article looking for one thing that would discredit her story—one quote that could make me feel like the entire tale was bogus.

> "She was jealous of me from day one because I'm close to my family, and she doesn't even have one."
>
> "She's like a praying mantis. She makes a sport out of getting her men, then drops them as soon as she's done. To them, she's just a conquest. To her, they're nothing more than a warm body."

It was almost as if I was reading about somebody else. Some horrible, hateful person whose unforgivable deeds were uncannily similar to my own. I wanted to get on the phone with my lawyer and sue CeCe and the blogger she'd sold the story to, but it wouldn't do any good. She was simply reiterating what the world already knew.

An unknown number flashed on my phone, covering up the article in an act of unintended kindness. Something prevented me from hitting Decline. Deacon did say he was going to call, and it had been two years—it was very possible he'd changed his number.

"Is this Michaela Turner?"

Or it was very possible that CeCe had sold mine.

I should have hung up then. I shouldn't have asked, "Who's calling?"

"I have Caroline Guerra for you."

My heart raced faster than it had on my run. My mother. And the name she took with husband number three.

I managed to keep the phone from sliding out of my hand while I waited to be connected to the woman who had planned my future before I knew the alphabet. The woman who only had me to trap a rich husband, and when that didn't work, used me for every penny she could get. The woman who tossed me aside the second I stopped making her money. It was as if she had some wrong-way maternal radar. *My daughter is hurting. What a perfect time to hurt her more.*

Before she had the chance to say hello, I asked, "Are you in the hospital?"

Her voice, the voice that had guided and misguided half my life, came over the phone, and in her Caroline way said, "Don't be silly, darling girl. Of course not."

I didn't know whether to cry, hang up, or curl up on the couch and just listen to her talk. I wished Deacon was there to take the phone from my hand and tell me what to do.

"Are you in jail?"

"Hardly," she said, so light, so unconcerned, as if we talked every day. "Why would you say such a ridiculous thing?"

Maybe because those were the only two viable reasons for her contacting me, aside from the obvious. I tried to remember every acting technique she'd ever taught me in order to sound calm and in control.

"Well, I guess—I haven't heard from—" I took a deep breath. I was sure she could hear the anguish in my voice. I was also sure she didn't care. "Who connected us?"

"I didn't know if you still had the same number, so I asked the front desk of my hotel to give it a shot. I never meant to alarm you, Gorgeous, I promise."

Gorgeous. That one word made me feel like I was ten again, on the set of the show, with Caroline pinching my cheeks to give them color, fluffing my pigtails to make them pop.

"Why are you calling me?" I knew why. I wanted to believe it was for something else, anything else, but I knew why.

"Does a mother need a reason to call her only daughter?" She sounded as innocent, sweet, and rehearsed as Donna Reed.

I somehow managed a "Yes."

I wasn't being funny, but she laughed.

"I saw this absolutely stunning picture of you," she said, and immediately I thought of my thong and my tongue and Travis. She wouldn't call to gloat. She wouldn't be that cruel.

"What?" I walked over and turned down the thermostat because, clearly, there was something wrong with it.

"With the Colonel." She didn't know. Maybe whatever island she'd been living on thanks to the fruits of my labor was slow to get the gossip columns. For a second, I almost felt relief, until she said, "Twenty million a year. That's my girl."

Her girl. I hadn't been her girl since *Breyer's Town* got canceled and she attributed it to my hitting puberty.

I didn't even recognize my own voice when I said, "Meaning?"

"Meaning I know how grand and fabulous you are now, and I'm happy for you, Gorgeous. I truly am. You never know when that well of yours will run dry. It was smart to find yourself a handsome backup plan."

Hearing her mention Burke sickened me. The idea that she thought I was just like her sickened me. I could have told her right then to Google my handsome backup plan to see how that worked out, but all I could say was, "Why are you really calling?"

I worried something was wrong—that she was sick, or in trouble. I wished I had the kind of mother who called just to talk, who you could just talk to. But I knew it was money. It always was.

"I'm going to be in New York in a couple of weeks. I'd like to see you."

I moved over to the couch because I needed to sit down, but once I got there, I couldn't do anything but stand. "I don't think that's a good idea."

"Come on, Gorgeous. I'm still your mother."

Was she? There were times when I was a young teenager, shortly after *Breyer's Town* ended, when she wanted me to tell people she was my older sister.

"I can't talk about this right now, Caroline. I have someplace to be." A complete lie, of course. I had no place to be. And thanks to CeCe's tell-all, the whole world knew it.

"Just tell me what you've been up to," she said, ignoring my words and my anguish. "I don't even know what's going on in your life."

I swallowed again. "Not really my fault."

Then she actually said, "I'm interested."

I wanted to believe her, but she'd never been interested in my life unless she could benefit from it. "If you're looking for some juicy detail to sell about me or Burke, I have nothing to offer you."

She was quiet. Some delusional part of me thought she might apologize. But what she said was, "We're still on that, are we?" as if I were holding a grudge about her shrinking my favorite jeans in the wash, not about her exploiting everything that was wrong with me in print for the whole world to see. "That was a means to an end. You were struggling and you wouldn't see me. I didn't know how else to get through to you."

"I have to go." I was sweating, I was sick to my stomach, and I knew if I stayed on the phone, I'd fall for it—I'd convince myself that she maybe just wanted to talk.

I hung up and immediately bolted all four locks on my front door. The sound of silence in the apartment only made her words grow louder in my mind. Before I knew what I was doing, I found myself putting on Deacon's first album, sinking down into his Graceland-inspired couch, and closing my eyes, telling myself that the only thing I had in common with Caroline Turner (Martin-Richards-Guerra) was DNA.

CHAPTER EIGHT

When my mother first came asking for money, I was twenty years old and hadn't heard from her in over three years. She called to say that she was divorcing Tyler Richards, her second of three failed marriages, and when she said she was coming to visit me, I naively thought she wanted to reconnect. Then she sprung the money thing on me. Wasn't she the reason I was the highest paid child star of the '80s and '90s? Wasn't it a surprise when I turned eighteen and realized just how much was in my Coogan trust? When I told Josh I'd given her a check, he said, "I get it. It's Caroline." And when I told him she took off with the money and I hadn't heard from her since, he didn't seem surprised.

I didn't see her again for another four years, when her marriage to Franklin Guerra—a *gorgeously* successful financier—ended. When she called and left me messages, I ignored them. Deacon was still living with me at the time, and for a solid week, I didn't mention it to him, either. When she finally arrived in New York and called, inviting me to high tea, I refused to skirt around it any longer. I asked how much she needed.

I'd expected her to pretend she didn't know what I was talking about—I didn't think she'd give me a figure right away. "These divorces can be messy," she said. "You know how it is."

I didn't know how it was, and I told her I'd have to think about it. Three days and two sleepless nights later, I found myself sitting at my kitchen counter at 3 a.m., unable to think of anything but Caroline's frequent mantra when I was growing up—*You're the only family I've got, Gorgeous, and I'm the only family you've got.* It wasn't my fault she'd gotten herself into her third divorce. It wasn't my fault she thought latching on to a man would solve all of her problems, and it wasn't my fault she was wrong. I hadn't asked her to devote fifteen years of her life to my career, but if I didn't help her, who would?

I heard the key turn in the lock, and Deacon looked surprised to see me when he came in. He'd been working on a new album and hadn't made it home before 2 a.m. in weeks. I wondered if he was cheating again.

"You're home early," he said. We'd fought a few days before about my going out too much. When I asked if he was jealous, he said I was the one with trust issues, not him.

"I stayed home tonight," I told him.

He kissed the top of my head before crossing over to the fridge and taking out some leftover Chinese food. "This isn't from last week, is it?"

"No," I said. "That's the one from Tuesday."

He sniffed it to make sure, then took a seat next to me at the counter. "Want some?" He offered me the box and I shook my head. I wasn't completely positive it was Tuesday's.

"They asked me to be part of a Willie Nelson tribute at the Grammys," he said. "I'm gonna play 'Funny How the Time Slips Away.' Can you believe it?"

I tried to muster some enthusiasm. Deacon was obsessed with Willie Nelson. "That's amazing. The whole band?"

He shook his head. "They just want me. But the guys are happy about it. It'll be great exposure for us."

I couldn't imagine Reign would be thrilled about their leader veering off, but I was too tired to get into it with Deacon over loyalty and morality. "I'm excited for you."

"Me, too." He bit into a cold spare rib. "So, how much does she want this time?"

My chest contracted. "How did you know?"

"I've been busy, Mickie, not blind. How much does she want?" I didn't answer. "More than last time?"

I nodded.

"I hope you're not thinking about giving her anything. She doesn't deserve it."

"I know she doesn't deserve it, Deacon, but maybe she needs it."

"If there's one thing I've learned about your mother, it's that she can take care of herself," he said. "She didn't worry about what you needed when she left you for Barbados or wherever the hell she went, did she?"

"I was an adult," I said. "I managed."

"You were sixteen, Mickie. You shouldn't have had to manage."

Four days later, when Caroline came to the door to pick me up for tea, I made Deacon answer. I knew if I had to face her, I'd write her a check, and then a year later, or a year after that, I'd be in the same position again.

I stayed stationary on the couch, listening to the entire exchange, praying that Caroline wouldn't pop her head in a bit too far and uncover me.

"Deacon," I heard her say with surprise. "I didn't realize you were still in the picture." They'd met the first time Caroline came to cash in, before Deacon King became a household name. At the time, Caroline told me musicians were the most unreliable men you could find, and I shouldn't let some boy who wrote a few songs about me interfere with my intelligence.

"Some of us stick around," he said. Little did Caroline know this was our second go-around.

"Is she ready?" She must have tried to come in, because Deacon shifted his weight on the doorframe, blocking her view.

"She's not here," he said. I tried to ignore how naturally he could lie.

"We both know that's not true."

"She's not, and I think you should leave." He lowered his voice, and I'm sure he didn't think I could hear when he said, "Come on, Caroline. Don't do this to her."

She matched his whisper. "I taught my daughter to fight her own battles."

"We both know why you're here, but you're not getting it, so let's make this easy on everyone." He closed the door partially, and I knew he didn't think I could see him pull out his wallet. "Here. This should pay for your plane ticket and hold you over for a while. But that's all you're getting."

For a long time, I heard nothing. Finally, Caroline spoke. "My daughter is brilliant, you know. She'll come to her senses. About a lot of things." There was another pause, followed by, "Tell my gorgeous girl I'll be in touch."

I heard her heels clacking down the hall, then Deacon wordlessly came in and shut the door. He pulled out a cigarette and sat down at his piano. I should have thanked him, but he was already scribbling notes and messing with melodies.

Two weeks later, I was coming home at dawn after another late night at this club called Sevens, my home away from home since Deacon had been living and breathing Grammys, Grammys, Grammys. I was passing a magazine stand when I saw it: *The Juice*—the world's trashiest tabloid—with a split shot of me on the cover. On the left, there I was at seven as Daisy Breyer. On the right, me at twenty-one, dancing on a bar. I wondered how much I'd had to drink, because there was no way this could be real—until I read the headline:

Daisy Lost—A Mother's Heartbreaking Story

CHAPTER NINE

Within a couple days, every gossip site had picked up on CeCe's tell-all. Pictures of me outside Magic alone, waiting to be let in, were everywhere. My reign as Queen of the Social Scene had officially ended. Caroline's prescient words about what I was going to do when my grand and fabulous well ran dry echoed through my mind. It didn't help that I hadn't left the apartment since hearing from her.

Anytime Daisy was in a rut, Dr. Breyer would take her out for the most over-the-top mint chocolate chip sundaes, she would spill all her problems, and instantly, everything would be better. Daisy's troubles were usually limited to things like borrowing a sweater from Veronica without asking and staining it with grape juice, so they were a little easier to solve with dairy. Whenever I was struggling in my own life, I'd read a biography of another former child star. It wasn't like I thought Natalie Wood or Shirley Temple or Margaret O'Brien could offer guidance—it's just that sometimes, it was nice to compare notes.

After days spent obsessively reading CeCe's hit piece and waiting for Caroline to knock on my door, I knew I had to get out of the apartment. I threw on a baseball cap left behind by some guy whose name I couldn't remember and made my way to the nearest indie bookstore, hoping I could get in and out without being noticed.

Every other customer seemed to fit perfectly in this environment—the chatty cliques in the café sipping fragrant coffees and discussing their favorite authors; the loners who sat in chairs or stood in the aisles, quietly reading to themselves; the two men by the vinyl records having a hushed yet heated dispute over who was the better jazz singer, Billie or Ella, as if they couldn't both have a seat at the table. I wished that I was one of them—that I wasn't some kid everyone felt they knew, that I wasn't some woman everyone thought was worthless.

There were a few people by the biographies, so I kept walking, trying to match the lackadaisical pace of the others around me. I didn't need their eyes on me. I didn't need to hear their restrained snickers when they saw me as some airhead who had stumbled into the wrong store. I definitely didn't need one of them to spot Daisy Breyer looking to Elizabeth Taylor's memoir for advice.

On an endcap was a CD display of the Billboard Top 10, and there in the number two spot was *Midnight Moonlight* by Deacon King. The Deacon I knew never would have named his album something so eye-roll-worthy. Then again, the Michaela I knew never would have sent him away in the middle of the night.

I picked it up and read through the track listing, each song with a name more ambiguously vanilla than the one before it. "Ever After." "Since You." "Mine to Hold." "Steady as My Heart." I wanted to throw it on the ground and stomp on it. Especially when I studied the picture beneath the song titles. A hand—his hand—on top of another hand—hers. I could hear his voice at my door, asking me to listen to it, promising to call, so despite my better judgment, I held on to the CD and kept walking.

Someone had discarded a piece of paper on one of the display tables, and I went to move it aside before noticing it was a college syllabus. Women's Lit. My heart pinched when I saw the purple-inked checkmarks of its long-lost owner, remembering how earnest and optimistic I felt about my first college lit class, before the fear of speaking up and humiliating myself paralyzed me. "Your essays show that you understand the material," the professor had said, "but you need to participate in class." He didn't understand that everyone was waiting for me to say something ridiculous so they could tell all their friends what a fool Daisy Breyer was.

Whoever this syllabus belonged to was long gone. I'd come all this way to get a book, so I grabbed the first title from the list, *The Collected Poems of Edna St. Vincent Millay*, and tucked the paper in my bag for later.

The sight of the books almost soothed me, almost let me imagine that the events of the past week had happened to someone else. I couldn't help but think of when I was a little girl, when Katrina would bury her nose in a book between takes. I never had time to sit on the sidelines and read *Little Women*. I was in almost every scene, and if I wasn't, Caroline was making me run lines, or marching me into the executive offices, threatening everyone that if they didn't beef up my contract, I could find another show in minutes.

I headed over to the *A*'s, and when I saw Louisa May Alcott, my fingers were drawn to the spine of *Little Women*, imagining what my life would be like if I were Katrina Wilder. If I hadn't been in the spotlight, but had merely been a minor player on *Breyer's Town*. If I read more, and finished college, and had other interests besides being Daisy.

"There you are."

My fingers immediately retracted. I couldn't even look for a damn book without being harassed.

I pulled my cap down, assuring myself that if I kept my vision lowered, this man would forget he ever saw me. My hope was that he'd turn around and walk away, resuming his reading or his latte.

Out of the corner of my eye, I could see his slightly chapped hands pull the book from the shelf. "Is this what you're getting? Oh, yeah, my sister used to love this book when we were younger, remember?"

I was used to people approaching me like they knew me, but his tone was so unassuming that I wondered if this man had actually confused me for someone else. I finally looked up at him, waiting for the recognition or embarrassment to register. I knew the minute he saw these famous green eyes, he'd call me Daisy or cringe.

He didn't blink.

"I don't want to freak you out." His quiet casual tone was in direct contrast with his words. "But a guy has been following you around the store for the past five minutes."

I looked behind me and sure enough, some dude by the cookbooks was watching me through the screen of his iPhone. Maybe the paparazzi needed to start worrying about their jobs, now that everyone was walking around with a camera in their pocket. Realizing he'd been caught, the creeper turned around and made a beeline out the door, undoubtedly off to sell whatever pictures he'd snapped. I could see the headlines now.

Dirty Daisy Can Read! (Or Can She?)

I turned back to my would-be hero and said, "Thanks for the tip," before redirecting my attention to the books. They seemed a little less magical now.

I could feel him still standing there, but I didn't look up. "What, do you want some kind of reward?" I asked.

"I'm sorry?"

"Go ahead and take a picture if you want, but I'm not going to smile."

I waited to see if he'd take out his phone. He didn't. He started to walk away, but then turned back.

"Are you okay?" he asked. "That guy was *following* you. Do you know him?"

Here's the thing: I realize I wore the baseball cap as a disguise, but I didn't think it would actually work. It certainly hadn't fooled the wannabe stalkerazzi who was probably still loitering on the sidewalk. It wasn't possible that my knight in shining chinos didn't know who I was.

"Of course I don't know him," I said, "but I don't know you, either, so for all I know this could be some charade the two of you cooked up together."

I had to hand it to him. His face told me he was either completely innocent or in the running for Best Supporting Actor in a Former Celebrity Sabotage.

"That's fair." He put his hand on his heart like he was pledging allegiance. "I don't know that guy. My name is Ben English. I teach high school English across the street—no, I'm not kidding. Make whatever jokes you'd like. I come here at least three days a week because that's just who I am, and the whole staff can vouch for me. I have two sisters, and if some creep were following them around, I'd hope someone would step in and help them out." He held out the copy of *Little Women* as if it were a peace offering. "And my sister really did love that book when we were younger."

I didn't know how to respond. I certainly didn't have anything to add about *Little Women*, so I said, "Your actual last name is English and you decided to teach English?"

He smiled. "Imagine if my name were Trigonometry."

He was probably waiting for me to laugh. I gave him a blank stare. "Well, thanks for—you know. The help."

He shoved his hands in his pockets. "It's the least I could do." I waited for the rest—the least I could do for Dr. Breyer's little girl, the least I could do for the Colonel's former flame, the least I could do for someone who's no longer in the running for hottest party girl in New York. Nothing came except, "Take care, okay?" He walked away, so unassuming yet so comfortable that this was a space where he belonged, in a store where the staff would vouch for him, in a world where if a person needed help, you helped them.

Thinking I could blend in with normal people buying books on a Thursday afternoon was obviously too much to ask. I needed to get out of there. I returned Louisa May Alcott to the shelf and looked down at the CD in my hand, wondering if I should put that back, too. I didn't owe Deacon anything. I didn't want to support his collected odes to someone else, but when I thought of his bloodshot eyes at my door, asking if I was okay, I tucked it under the poetry of Edna St. Vincent Millay and paid for both.

As I walked out of the store, I stole one last glance at the customers and employees. I wondered if a single one of them, even for a moment, felt like they weren't good enough to be there.

CHAPTER TEN

When Deacon and I first got together, he wrote the most beautiful songs I'd ever heard. They were gritty and passionate and told stories about how hard it was to love someone, how difficult it was to make it in the world, and how painful it could be to figure out what you wanted in life. His new album made me question whether he'd written those songs.

I didn't listen to it right away. For days, I didn't even take it out of the shrink wrap. I convinced myself that I could return it—or maybe throw it in the trash where it belonged—but after nearly a week of not talking to a soul, with nothing but a stolen syllabus, my mother's words, and the ever-growing comments on CeCe's tell-all to keep me company, every fiber of my body craved relief. I ached for his voice. Hearing it only made me ache more.

The songs he had played at Intuition were a mere taste of the ninety-seven minutes of fluff I subjected myself to now. The whole album was filled with techno beats and booty-shakers and the sappiest love songs imaginable. It was clearly meant to be a feel-good album, but all it did was make me angry. And sad. Shaunn with two *n*'s and Tight T-Shirt Jay didn't have the guts to tell him the truth. There was no trace in these songs of the man who'd sent my mother away two years before, the man bouncing with excitement over a Willie Nelson tribute, the man who knew what I needed when I wasn't even sure. The real tragedy was that he was as lost as I was, and I couldn't even talk to him about it because he was marrying someone else.

I'd held up my end of the bargain. I'd listened to it. I wasn't surprised that he didn't follow through on his promise to call. The memory of his late-night visit probably disappeared with his hangover, if he ever remembered it at all. I should have let it go. I should have reminded myself that he wasn't my problem anymore, but all I could think of was the shape of his back blocking the door, sending Caroline away, begging her not to do this to me again.

I picked up the phone and my thumb hovered over the number I'd never had it in me to delete. I almost pressed down, but then I imagined my name flashing on his screen while he enjoyed a vegan lunch with the fiancée who could confidently say that her thong hadn't been splashed across every gossip rag in the country. Shaunn with two *n*'s probably had the perfect mother—Linda with one *a*—who Deacon never had to protect her from. No wonder his music had become so bland. His life was free of drama—save for a Day-Glo–laden visit to the hurricane he'd escaped.

I stuffed my phone between the couch cushions. Josh was right. It wasn't doing me any good. He was likely on the golf course at that very moment with his happy, normal girlfriend, with no reception on his flip phone and exactly zero concerns about it. *And what are* you *doing?* I could hear Caroline ask. If she knew I was sitting on the couch at 2 p.m. in my pajamas, with *The Collected Poems of Edna St. Vincent Millay* beside me instead of a handsome backup plan, she'd probably change her mind about needing to see me.

She could be doing so much more with her life, Caroline's tell-all in *The Juice* had read. *As a mother, it pains me to say that I don't know if she'll ever get back on track.* I'd memorized the entire article two years earlier, and not a day went by without me thinking about it. She was right. I could have been doing so much more, but I didn't know where to begin. The best I could think to do was drag myself to the Bookery to get more assigned readings from the syllabus. At least that was laid out for me.

IT TOOK ME NO TIME TO FIND VIRGINIA WOOLF'S *A ROOM of One's Own* and Zora Neale Hurston's *Their Eyes Were Watching God.* The store was a lot less crowded than it had been on my previous trip, so I skimmed the titles in the biography and memoir section as I'd planned to do days earlier. There wasn't a single book on a former child star I hadn't read. Apparently, they'd taught me all they could. Traitors.

Since I had nothing to rush home to—and since I didn't see anyone following me with their phone—I moved into the bookstore's café and ordered a large black coffee with six sugars. The barista's wide eyes were a sure sign that she recognized me, but thankfully, she said nothing. I gave her a big tip for not making a scene.

I grabbed a fistful of sugar packets, because six sugars often meant six minuscule sugars and not six lumps. I could almost hear Caroline from two thousand miles away, telling me what a toxin it was. I settled into the corner table with my coffee and new books. A guy seated at the table next to mine did make me hesitate, but he had his head down, earbuds in, and was focused on his scone and the stack of papers in front of him. It seemed like a safer option than being spied on through the window.

I tasted my coffee, added two sugar packets, and was about to crack open one of the books when he said, "Hey, it's you."

Maybe a seat by the window would have been better, after all.

I looked up, dreading a walk down Daisy's memory lane, when I realized I'd seen that smile before. He pulled out one of his earbuds. "Ben."

"Ben English, high school English," I said.

He smiled wider. "Hey. You remembered."

I couldn't believe I did. I never remembered people's names. Take Med Student, for instance.

He extended a hand. "I don't think I got your name."

He couldn't be serious.

"It's Michaela."

I waited for him to blush and say, "Of course it is," or confess, "I only know you as Daisy." He didn't say either. He took his second earbud out and said, "It's nice to formally meet you, Kayla."

He must have misheard me with whatever had been playing on his iPod. I almost corrected him, but there was no harm in letting him think I was someone named Kayla. Kayla was probably far less of a wreck than I was.

I wasn't a monster. I shook his hand, said, "It's nice to meet you, too," and looked down at my book to signal an end to the conversation. Not that Ben didn't seem perfectly nice, but if there was one thing Caroline had taught me, it was don't talk to strangers—unless they can be useful in some way.

"I'm glad to see you're doing okay," Ben said. His parents clearly hadn't taught him the same lesson. "That thing the other day with that guy following you—that was creepy. I kind of couldn't get it out of my head. I kept feeling like I should have done more."

I looked around to see if anyone was watching us. No one

was. It was almost like by sitting there, talking to this ordinary guy, I was ordinary by default. I didn't hate it.

"You did plenty. It was nice of you to step in. I'm sorry if I was kind of a bitch."

"You weren't." He said it like he meant it, not like he was being polite. "So, what are you reading?"

I thought this was a place of quiet respite. I certainly wasn't equipped for any kind of literary analysis, although an English teacher like him would probably at least respect my choices. Respect wasn't something I got very much of these days, so I held up the covers, and sure enough, he nodded.

"Into the classics. Did I see Millay in your hand the other day? Not being nosy. I just always have to see what people are reading. It's a hard habit to break."

"You did," I said. "I—I like her." Somehow, over the past week, that had become the truth. If I'd actually been in the class the pilfered syllabus was from, I could have written an entire essay about how beautifully she captured fleeting love, and life, and the candle burning at both ends not lasting the night.

"Me, too. What is it you like about her?" He looked at me like he was interested in my answer, like I could come up with something of substance. He must have been a good teacher.

I stared down at my coffee, like it would tell me what to say, or give me an easy out of the conversation. But Ben didn't know who I was. If I said something off base, he wouldn't tell the world that Dirty Daisy was illiterate. Kayla from the Bookery was the only one who had to worry about what he thought.

"I guess I like how simply she captures the complexities of being human. In so few words, she says so much." It was the same thing I'd praised Deacon for, before he ruined it all. "I don't read a lot of poetry, so maybe you could say that about anybody."

I waited for him to say that yes, you could say that about anybody, or tell me why I was wrong. "I agree with you completely," he said, and something about his grin of approval made me feel far better than it should have.

The front entrance jingled open and a woman in her early twenties walked in talking on her phone. "No, he was dating that girl from Breyer's whatever, but she cheated on him with that gross dude from Soul Infusion. Maybe he was hot like five years ago, but have you seen him lately? Compared to the Colonel? How much of a slut do you have to be?"

My stomach burned. It was one thing when someone spewed vile things about you to the press or to your face, but it was somehow worse when they did it in the wild, not even realizing you were sitting right there just trying to drink a cup of coffee. My first instinct was to bolt out of the store, but then she'd see me. My only other option was to turn my chair toward Ben English, shake my hair to the side, and prop my face on my hand like I was merely flirting with a cute guy and not hiding in plain sight.

"What are you reading?" I asked him. The sudden shift in my body language and soft dip in my tone made him blink, but then he sat up straighter.

"Pop quizzes on *Othello*," he said. "Somehow I think your books are a bit more enjoyable."

Jackpot. I had memorized Desdemona's monologue for my freshman year acting class and nine years later, I could still dredge it up. "'Alas, Iago, what shall I do to win my lord again?'"

His eyes filled with warmth. "That's pretty good."

I shrugged, embarrassed that his polite appraisal made me feel better, terrified that he would follow up with a remark I couldn't answer. I took a sip of my coffee and said, "RIP, Desdemona."

The walking, talking critic of my dating history hovered near us by the magazines, still chatting away on her phone. "Yeah, the Colonel has moved *on*. *Queen of the Social Scene* posted pictures of him out with two different models. No, not at the same time, but he can obviously take his pick."

I waited for it to sting. Of course I'd been replaced. I wondered if the same publicist who'd set us up had those models waiting on a list, and as soon as I was ousted, they moved up.

"You said the school you teach at is right across the street?" I asked Ben. I needed to keep him talking. I needed to stay perfectly still until the gossip maven with the fake Dooney & Bourke bag moved along. I almost felt bad about keeping him from his papers, but he didn't seem to have any issue with the attention I was giving him. He seemed encouraged.

"That's why I always choose this spot," he said. "These are the only two tables you can't see from the street, and as much as I love my students—after a long day I just need a break, you know?"

I nodded like I did know. "Do you like your job?"

"I do." He hadn't even hesitated. "It gets tiring, but most days I feel like I'm pretty decent at it, and it makes me happy. I guess that's the most we can hope for, right?"

I tried to think of one thing I was decent at or one thing that made me happy, but came up with nothing, so I said, "Sure."

Phone Girl made her way to the back of the store, dishing about some celebrity accused of shoplifting. I knew I only had a minute to make my escape, so I tossed my books in my bag, grabbed my jacket, and told Ben, "It was really nice seeing you again. I have to run."

He looked thrown by my abrupt departure. "Were you afraid I was going to ask you to help grade these? I wasn't. I mean, unless you want to." His smile was so goddamn genuine.

"I just didn't realize the time," I said, shooting a glance over my shoulder to make sure Chatty Patty was still out of sight.

He stood up, shaking the scone crumbs from his khakis.

"Hey, I hope this doesn't sound too forward but . . . would you like to meet up sometime? We could go for a dinner or a coffee." He picked up my cup from the table and handed it to me. I'd almost left it in my rush. "Another coffee, I should say."

I stared at him. No normal guy had ever asked me out before. They never had the guts. But Ben wasn't asking *me*. He was asking Kayla who hung out in bookstores and read Edna St. Vincent Millay.

"I'm sorry," he said, obviously taking my silence as a rejection. "You must be with someone. Of course you are."

"I'm actually not," I said, and his kind eyes became resigned with the realization that I wasn't turning him down because I had a boyfriend; I was turning him down personally. If he only knew that saying no would be an act of kindness. A guy like him should want nothing to do with someone like me. Kayla would have been fine for him, but Kayla didn't exist.

I could have given him a fake number to let him down easy, but it was kind of nice talking to someone who didn't know who I was. "Why don't you give me your number and I'll call you?" I asked, and he pulled a gum wrapper out of his pocket so fast I almost laughed.

He grabbed a pen from his table, scribbled his number, and handed it over. "The Mets might be headed to the playoffs this year. Maybe we could get together at a bar and watch a game."

I almost dropped the gum wrapper right on the floor. A baseball game. He thought I'd be interested in watching a baseball game. Because I had a thing for ballplayers. "What would make you think I'd be into that?"

I had to hand it to him. He looked genuinely confused. "You were wearing a Mets hat the other day. It was just an idea. I'm sorry—did I offend you in some way?"

The hat. I hadn't even realized it was a Mets hat. It was just there and it seemed like a convenient disguise. Apparently it worked. He still thought I was just a normal girl.

"No, I'm sorry," I said, and I actually meant it. "I— Pretend I didn't say that."

I folded up the paper and stuck it in my pocket, although given my reaction to his innocent suggestion, I wouldn't have blamed him for asking for it back. "It was good talking to you, Ben."

"I really enjoyed talking to you, too, Kayla."

When I got home, my first instinct was to stop by Josh's to tell him how I'd succeeded in remaining incognito, but then I remembered he wouldn't be back for a week. He had Morgan now, just like Deacon had Shaunn and Burke had his models. It seemed everyone had someone, and I had nothing but a blemished reputation and a phone number on a Juicy Fruit wrapper.

CHAPTER ELEVEN

I can't say I planned on calling Ben. He wasn't my type, and it didn't seem fair to him that he didn't even know my name. But days passed, and I didn't have anyone to talk to, and I kept thinking about Caroline commending me for finding a handsome backup plan. I didn't want a backup plan. I just wanted to be a person. Ben looked at me as if I were a person.

If grown-up Daisy Breyer were going on a first date, she would have come up with a list of ideas so magical, the guy would immediately fall for her. They'd probably start with a walk through some hidden gem of an outdoor market where she'd make an offhanded comment about this funky necklace that would then show up under her Christmas tree six months later. They'd go to a basketball game where her date would be starry-eyed over how real she was, before they were coaxed into locking lips with the encouragement of the crowd and a kiss cam. Maybe they'd even round out the night with a carriage ride, and Daisy would drop some little-known fact about the city that would show just how remarkable she was.

I suggested Ben and I go to a movie.

To his credit, he didn't say it was a terrible idea—that we

wouldn't be able to talk, that we wouldn't even be able to see each other. That was the whole point. The less conversation we had, the less likely he'd be able to see the cracks in my armor, and in a dark theater, the chances of me being recognized decreased significantly.

We met at this tiny cinema that played old movies every night. When I saw him standing there, all I could think was how average he looked next to everyone else I'd gone out with.

I don't mean that in a negative way. It's not that he wasn't cute; he just looked normal. I was used to Burke, who was tall, beautiful, and carried himself like he was somebody; and Deacon, who was intense, oozed sex appeal, and may as well have had *Rock Star* tattooed across his forehead. Ben stood there in jeans that he likely bought at a department store, wearing his wire-rimmed glasses and a button-down. This was what it would be like to be a regular girl going out with a regular guy to a regular movie.

"You look incredible," he said. In my attempt at normalcy, I'd worn my most common outfit—jeans, UGGs, and a thin olive-green off-the-shoulder sweater. I was trying to blend. I wanted to make this night as easy as possible on the both of us.

"Thanks." I wondered how a few weeks earlier, a compliment like that would have rolled off my back, when now, it actually made me feel good.

"It looks like we have two choices," he said, looking up at the marquee. "*Superman II* or *Jailhouse Rock*. Thoughts?"

My semi-hungry stomach did a little flip-flop. *Jailhouse Rock* was Deacon's favorite. We'd watched it anytime it was on TV. I'd get up to use the bathroom or get a drink, and every time, without fail, he'd call to me from the couch, "Mickie, they're about to find out if he can still sing. You have to get in here!" And I would. I'd rush back in to see Elvis in his paisley robe, holding his throat, tentatively singing "Young and Beautiful" while everyone surrounded him all teary-eyed.

"*Superman II*," I said. I wondered if it mattered that I hadn't seen *Superman I.*

"Perfect. Clark Kent is a man after my own heart."

The bookish type. Of course. Ben was a total Clark Kent—with thinner glasses.

There was a note on the ticket window that read, *Projector being repaired. Movies will now start at 9 p.m.* It wasn't even seven thirty. I wondered if the sign itself was a sign that this had been a mistake. Maybe this was my chance to turn around, go home, and let Kayla fade into oblivion.

"We could grab something to eat while we wait," Ben said, not nearly as fazed as I was. "Have you had dinner yet?"

"I'm not sure we have time." I looked at my wrist like a watch would magically appear.

"There's always time for quick pie."

"Pie," I repeated. Was that some new code word for sex?

He pointed to a brightly lit diner across the street with a neon sign in the window flashing, **PIE PIE PIE.**

It was probably a terrible idea. Walking into a busy restaurant was the easiest way to ensure I'd be recognized, but maybe my ordinary outfit and ordinary Ben would shield me. If anything, it was better than sitting home alone, waiting for Caroline to call.

"Let's give it a shot," I said. I hoped I wasn't setting myself up for disaster.

The diner was filled with tourists, college kids, and theater patrons with playbills. The door actually jingled when it opened. I didn't know when my life had turned from Day-Glo necklaces at Magic to pie à la mode at a tourist trap.

"How many?" a waitress in a straight-out-of-a-sitcom uniform barked.

"Two," Ben said. The waitress eyed me. I swore if she said the word *Daisy* I would turn around and leave.

Luckily, all she said was, "Right this way," and led us to a tiny table squished between an older couple with *Phantom* playbills and some sorority girls who definitely would have called me out if they weren't half in the bag.

"I hope this is okay," Ben said.

"It's fine." I tried to convince myself it would be fine.

"Coffee?" the waitress snapped, and we both said yes. She flipped over our mugs and filled them from a tarnishing silver pot. This was so not what I was used to.

She left us to the menu—a list of desserts, mainly pies—which meant we were alone, forced into actual conversation. Ben started.

"So, Kayla, I haven't even asked what you do."

It felt like salt in a paper cut.

"Do?" I could play dumb just as well as I could play smart.

"For a living."

I hated how that was the first thing everyone always asked, as if your job were the most interesting thing about you. I couldn't very well tell him I hadn't *done* anything since a made-for-TV movie called *Shepherd's Sister*, which nobody saw. What did I do? Lately, I listened to my ex's music and came up with a mental list of all the ways he'd gone astray.

"I'm a consultant," I said.

He sat back. "Oh, wow. That's so cool. What firm do you work for?"

I thought about Daisy Breyer, and how her half-truths saved her in any situation. "I'm not with a firm. I'm an independent contractor." It wasn't a lie. I once put this actor named Trent on the map by making out with him at a few clubs and convincing him to get rid of his ponytail. He gave me a monetary token of his appreciation and I agreed to not kiss another guy in public for two months. In retrospect, I should have bargained for more. Trent went on to become one of *People*'s Sexiest Men Alive the following year.

Before Ben could ask, I added, "I'm an image consultant."

"That makes sense," he said. "I mean, look at you."

It was nice that he thought so. Maybe in another life, I could have been this person. I stirred six sugars into my coffee, and his eyes followed my swirling spoon.

"Bad habit to break," I explained. "It keeps me going when I'm burning the candle at both ends."

"No judgment here," he said, although I wondered if my quoting Millay softened whatever judgment may have been forming. "Do you travel a lot for work?"

That one stung. I wished I could have rattled off a list of unforgettable places I'd been, but even when I was acting, I rarely left New York. *Breyer's Town* was one of the few shows that didn't film in LA, and anytime I shot something on location, I didn't have the chance to see anything other than the set I was working on. I could have made something up, but then Ben would ask questions I couldn't answer, so I said, "Not as much as you'd think. New York has everything I need."

"Did you go to school here?"

He assumed I went to college. Of course he assumed I went to college. And I did. For four months. "Mm-hmm. NYU."

"I wonder if you know my friend Reggie. You probably graduated around the same time."

"Probably not. Big school. And I didn't spend much time on campus." Nothing in that statement was untrue.

The waitress saved me from further interrogation by taking our pie order. Ben got apple, and I went with grasshopper—it seemed like my only option. On *Breyer's Town* they were always surrounding Daisy with green to complement her eyes. She'd be eating a green apple, or wearing a green dress, or sitting in her pink-and-green bedroom. Surrounding myself with green was a habit I hadn't broken.

Before Ben could ask any more personal questions, I flipped the script. I learned that he was born and raised outside of Chicago, that his parents were still together, and that he had one older and one younger sister. He went to undergrad at Penn, came to New York at twenty-five to get his master's at Columbia, and had tried—unsuccessfully—to write a novel for two years.

"Why unsuccessfully?"

He shrugged and took a bite of his pie. "I don't know. I guess when I started, I wanted to make my mark on the world, you know? But now it doesn't seem so important. Now I feel like I'm making a bigger mark on those kids."

He sounded so unlike everyone I had ever known. "You're pretty wise for someone so young."

He laughed. "Try telling that to my students. How about you? Where are you from originally?"

"Manhattan." Whole truth.

"So you're a native New Yorker."

I didn't answer. I mean, it wasn't really a question. Replying would only lead him to ask something unintentionally but equally intrusive.

"Does your family still live around here?"

Like that. I could tell he was just trying to be nice—politely asking the kind of things I suppose people ask on normal first dates. Travis never talked at all. Burke only talked about baseball. My past relationships may not have been perfect, but at least they didn't make me feel like I was in the hot seat.

"I don't really have much family," was all I said, hoping that would close the subject.

"No brothers or sisters?"

"Nope." Not that I knew of, anyway.

"What about your parents?"

I have this tiny scar on my chest from when I was eight and fell on the granite by a network executive's pool. When he asked that question, it felt like Ben had grabbed ahold of that scar and ripped it off.

"My mother moved years ago." That was the most he was

getting out of me. The only person I ever laid everything out for was Deacon, and look how that turned out.

I think he got it, because he didn't ask any more questions. He just looked at my barely touched plate and asked, "How was the pie?"

"It was good."

"You didn't eat much."

I indicated his dish, which was empty. "We're not all members of the clean-plate club."

He raised an eyebrow. "You think you're pretty cute, don't you?"

I forced a little smile. "I am pretty cute." And so was Ben, when he kept the conversation to things like pie and his own nerdiness. I wished he didn't have to be so invasive with his questions. I wished I could let myself like him more.

AT THE MOVIES, BEN WAS THE PERFECT GENTLEMAN. HE opened doors. He bought the tickets and the popcorn. He asked if I preferred the back, middle, or front. Shoulder to shoulder in the theater, I couldn't help but notice that he even smelled great. Clean. Fresh. Like a guy you could bring home to your mother, if you had the kind of mother to bring a guy home to. A normal person would have loved that. A normal person would have thought, *What a great guy.*

But watching the movie, I had to remind myself that even Lois Lane didn't go for Clark Kent. She wanted Superman—the sexy guy who flew in and out of her life, giving no indication when he would come and when he would go. Though my man of steel was a newly commercial rock star and not a superhero in tights, I could see where Lois was coming from.

I needed to stop thinking about Deacon, but with my eyes glued to the screen, my mind couldn't stop racing as the scene played out before me. There was Superman, demanding that Lois tell him she loved him. Instead, she took his hands and kissed them, and he knew. *Love* was just a word. I only used it when I really meant it—or thought I meant it. When I'd tell Deacon I loved him, he'd look me in the eye, give me a firm kiss, and say, "Good." That four-letter word was enough for me.

"I have to run to the restroom," I whispered to Ben. "I'll be right back."

Once inside, I stood in front of the sink, running cool water over my wrists, practicing the breathing exercises my mother taught me. I could pretend that I had my act together for another hour—say the right things, be the right way. I could be with a smart, nice guy, and show Caroline and Burke and CeCe and all the others that I was so much more than—

"Holy *shit*, it's Daisy Breyer!"

Who was I kidding.

I pretended I didn't hear the woman's booming voice and leaned forward, checked my eyeliner, and started out of the bathroom. It wasn't in my contract to be nice to people.

"What a little bitch," I heard her say to her friend. "She looked smaller on TV."

I wanted to say, *I* was *smaller, asshole, I was twelve*, but I was too drained to bother.

When I sat back down, Ben shot me a smile so kind that I placed my still-damp hands on either side of his face and kissed him. It wasn't some romantic gesture. I just wanted to feel better. I wanted to feel something. But though his kiss was warm, gentle, and tasted slightly of buttered popcorn, it didn't give me enough butterflies to sew up my increasingly gaping wounds.

"I'D LIKE TO SEE YOU AGAIN, KAYLA."

We were standing outside the theater, and with the moonlight reflecting off his glasses, it seemed like the last opportunity for me to tell him that Kayla was nothing more than an alias. Maybe Ben wasn't Clark Kent, after all. Maybe I was. It wasn't like Clark was lying about his identity, and I wasn't, either. We were both just living a different version of ourselves, trying to assimilate in a world that couldn't understand we'd come from another planet.

The woman who'd spotted me in the bathroom emerged from the theater with her friend and shot a look my way. I held my breath, moving slightly behind Ben, praying that she'd just keep walking and not cause a scene.

"I don't think that's her," the woman's friend said to her.

I could feel them both staring at me, and staring at Ben, the ordinary guy who was patiently waiting for me to respond about seeing him again.

"You must be right," the woman said. "It can't be."

I could feel my body start to relax as they walked away. Poor Ben was standing there without a clue of how easily he'd been disregarded.

"I'd like to see you again, too," I said.

That awkward end-of-the-date moment lingered in the air, even though I'd already gotten the kissing part out of the way. This time, Ben took the initiative. He placed his hand under my chin and graced me with a tender, sweet little kiss. There were no fireworks, but it was pleasant. A normal person probably would have loved it.

When I got into the taxi, the cab driver asked, "Do I know you from somewhere?" and I wished I still had the cover of Ben as a disguise.

"I think you've given me a ride before," I lied, which satisfied him enough to finish the trip in silence. As I approached my building, I pulled out my phone to see if I had any messages from Caroline. I didn't, but when I saw the time, I realized that in twenty-four minutes, *Breyer's Town* would be on, and I could watch it in bed.

Then I reached my stoop, and my heart stopped.

"Hey, Mickie."

Deacon was sitting on the front step, looking even more beautiful than I remembered, smoking what had to be a freshly lit cigarette.

All I could manage was, "Hi."

CHAPTER TWELVE

After the longest moment of silence in history, I asked, "What are you doing out here?"

Deacon ran a hand over his hair. It'd grown out a little since the last time I'd seen him, and the tufts of curls I'd once loved were starting to come through. "Phil wouldn't let me up," he said, as if that explained everything. "He said you were out."

With those first ten words, I knew he was sober. This wasn't like the night he showed up after too many Jack and Cokes, covered in Day-Glo necklaces, when I'd sent him away and told him to come back when he wasn't drunk and wasn't engaged. I didn't dare ask about the second part of that equation.

"Where were you?" he asked.

I folded my arms across my chest, hoping he'd think I was closing myself off. Knowing Deacon, he'd see I was just cold. "I was on a date."

He drew the cigarette back to his lips—his way of acting like he didn't care about something when he did. "Burke have a change of heart?"

"You wouldn't know him."

He nodded and rolled the burning nub between his fingertips, studying it like it was the most fascinating thing on the planet. He was wondering who my date was, where we went, and why I was coming home alone. Deacon thought every date should end by coming upstairs—and usually mine did—but I needed something different now, and he couldn't possibly understand that.

He stood up, surrounded by fizzled-out cigarette butts. I hated myself for wondering how long he'd been waiting.

Deacon had never needed an invitation to come up, and this night was no exception. I could feel Phil's eyes burning into me as he let us inside, but I couldn't bear to look at him and see the questions in his stare—*What's he doing here? What are you getting yourself into?*—because the same things were weighing on my own mind.

Some people walk into a room like they own it. Deacon always walked in like he built the place. When he pushed the elevator button, it was like he'd laid every last brick of that building with his own bare hands. We had the elevator to ourselves, but I stood in the opposite corner, fearing that if either of us stepped an inch closer, I'd take hold of him and never let go.

"I like that sweater," he said, daring to look me square in the eye. My fatal mistake was staring back.

"Thank you."

"I've always loved you in green."

I tucked my fingers into my sleeves. For the first time in a long time, I let myself feel how much I missed him.

"I know."

The second the elevator doors opened, I stepped out and tried to breathe. I couldn't stay in a confined space with him for another minute without doing something I'd regret. I didn't know why I thought letting him into my apartment would be any different.

He followed me inside, taking in his surroundings as I took

him in. He hadn't set foot in there in over two years. Instantly, the place felt right again. The only time I didn't feel lonely was when he was there.

"The place hasn't changed much," he said, walking through the living room as if he'd never left. I didn't need Deacon to point out the lack of change. Everything was so very much the same that it was almost embarrassing. The couch he'd picked out. The ashtray I'd made him during my two-week pottery kick, sitting on the piano. It was like it had been frozen in time, waiting for him to come back. He probably wouldn't have been surprised to find a pair of his shoes sitting by the door.

He caressed the top of the piano. "You still have 'Cilla." He christened it after the former Mrs. Presley. He thought Elvis and Priscilla had the most tragic love story of all time, and always said that after the divorce, Elvis's music was never the same. "I thought you would have tossed her. Thrown her out onto the street with all my clothes."

"I thought about it." Thought about it on several occasions, but it was a part of Deacon, right there in black and white. If I couldn't have him, I could at least have that.

He took off his charcoal gray car coat and slung it on the couch, revealing a formfitting black sweater that made me long to see the newly toned body underneath. He pushed up his sleeves, sat down at the piano, and brought his fingers to the keys, but he didn't play. He just sat there, pretending he wasn't watching me watch him.

His fingers slid back and forth silently over the ivory until he finally pressed down on middle C. "She's out of tune."

I stood still, unable to move from my position across the room. "Nobody's played it for two years."

The last time he played it was two days before he broke up with me for the second time. He was smoking like a fiend and wearing a white T-shirt that was so threadbare I could see every crevice of his body through it. I knew he was trying to write, but after the third hour of him not moving from that spot, tinkering with the keys when I was waiting to go out, I grew so frustrated that I threw a shoe at him. I thought he'd be furious, but he stood up—completely straight-faced—marched over to where I was, flung me over his shoulder, and carried me into the bedroom where he finally made me feel seen. Afterward, he asked, "You still want to go out?" When I told him no, he resumed his position at the piano.

"Why are you here, Deacon?" As much as I wished he just wanted to see me, I needed to know the truth.

He scratched his elbow, Deacon-speak for unease. "I can't write."

"Of course you can write." It wasn't like him to fish for compliments, and on top of that, he knew it was untrue. His ex-drummer—and probably now ex–best friend—Petie used to make bets with him like, *I'll pay you fifty bucks if you can write a hook that contains the words* cotton candy, Texas, *and* Tuesday afternoon. And not only would Deacon do it in a matter of hours, but the song would be painstakingly beautiful.

"Did you listen to it? My album?"

I swallowed. "I did."

"It's shit, right?"

Deacon could be the most confident, self-possessed person in the world one minute, then seconds later, when you least expected it, you'd catch a glimpse of the self-conscious, insecure side you didn't know existed.

"It wasn't you," I managed.

He didn't look up from the keys. "Yeah. Well, not me will have the number one album in the country tomorrow." There wasn't a trace of pride in his voice.

He played the first few notes of "Tears Me to Pieces," his apology song about how it killed him to constantly break the heart of the only girl he ever loved. Somehow, when he put his terrible deeds to music, it made them forgivable. I closed my eyes and imagined him singing.

Pretty wild child with the daisy tattoo . . .

"Do you remember the first time I played this for you?"

I tried to sound in control. Tried to pretend he wasn't getting to me. Still, my hand drew to my stomach, where I had a tiny daisy inked on my nineteenth birthday.

"Yes."

"Do you like this song, Mickie?"

He knew I did. It was what made me take him back, after all.

"I love this song," I said.

I hated that I loved it. I hated that he could take sleeping with other women while we were together and turn it into poetry.

"Why are you here?" I asked again, wishing I didn't sound so desperate.

"Honestly?"

"Honestly." I tried to ignore the fact that neither one of us were ever very honest.

He took a deep breath and rubbed his nose. I wondered if his nervous twitches bothered Shaunn, or if his being here meant she wasn't around to bother. "I think I'm lost, Mickie. I don't know what I was thinking with that album. I don't know what I was thinking with any of it."

I wondered how much *it* covered—if he meant the veganism or the new look or Shaunn.

"My life has been all interviews and talk shows lately. All the stuff I'm no good at. And every time I sit there, giving scripted answers to questions no one should care about, all I keep thinking is how I have no idea how I got here. I have no idea what I'm doing or even who I am." He looked down at the piano keys like they were speaking to him. "I was so afraid you wouldn't come to my show. And then there you were, on the fire escape, ready to tell me everything I was doing wrong like no time had passed."

Something squeezed inside of me. "You put me on the list?" I thought about CeCe telling me that a VIP had dropped out last minute, and how Deacon had said, *I'm glad you could make it,* like he wasn't surprised I was there. When everyone in the world wanted to write me off, he was seeking me out.

"You didn't know?"

I shook my head. "Why did you do that?"

"I needed to be with the only person who knows me." He turned to me with eyes that made me feel like I was the only person in the world. "I needed to be with you."

I was sure he saw the remains of my makeshift facade melt away. All I could manage was, "Oh."

"Come here." He didn't move from the bench. I hesitated for a half a second, but didn't allow myself time to think. I moved my feet, one before the other, in a direct path to my past.

He slipped his fingers under my sweater and pulled it up just enough so he could see the daisy tattoo on my abdomen. When he gently traced his hand across it, my body whispered, *You're home.* He leaned in and kissed the tattoo, and my eyes filled with tears. I'd been waiting so long, craving his touch for what seemed like eternity—and there it was, in the living room we once shared, when life was messy but at least made sense.

He stood, pulled my shirt over my head, and moved his kiss to my mouth. If I could have, I would have lived in that moment forever. I should have asked if he was still engaged. I should have thought about the days after he broke my heart, when I couldn't even pull myself out of bed, but with his lips on mine and the softness of his sweater against my bare skin, my body sang. I was right back in the only place I ever felt I belonged.

EVERYONE KNOWS I'VE HAD A LOT OF MEN IN MY BED. DEACON was the only one I've ever loved waking up to.

The early-morning sun cast a glow on his face, and all I could think about was the first time he stayed over. It was the night we met. I was nineteen, not so disenchanted by life, and enamored of Deacon King. I remember lying there while he slept, staring at his longer-than-possible eyelashes, studying his rumpled, messy hair, wondering what was going on in that beautiful head. I couldn't believe that out of all the people in the world, this brilliant man was choosing to be with me. Eight years later, I felt the same way.

I snuggled closer to him, breathing in the scent of the coconut soap I was so glad he still used. Gently, I traced the tattoo on his right upper arm. It was a vine that wrapped around his bicep leading to—what else?—a daisy on his shoulder. He'd gotten it midway through our first relationship, after a fight that felt like the end of the world. He went away to play a few shows, and I hadn't seen him for a week. The day he came home, he cuffed up the sleeve of his T-shirt, revealed the fresh ink, and said, "Don't ever say I don't love you."

He shifted under the covers, so I pressed my lips to his shoulder, then slid out of bed to pee and freshen up, pulling his sweater from the trail of strewn clothes. He'd told me years ago that he found nothing sexier than when I'd walk around the apartment in nothing but one of his shirts. And wearing it now meant he couldn't get dressed and sneak out.

He was awake when I climbed back into bed. I was terrified he'd say, *Last night was a mistake*, but he wrapped one arm around me and picked up the book on my nightstand with the other. "You reading poetry now?"

"Just something I'm trying out." I considered telling him more—about the awful things the tabloids were saying about me, about wondering where I'd be if I'd stuck with college for more than four months, about Caroline resurfacing—but for now, I needed to pretend the outside world didn't exist, that it was just me and him and the cocoon of our bed.

He caressed a strand of my hair and murmured, "A tome of revelations with every page you turn."

It was a line from "The Queen." He was the first person who thought of me that way, the first person to see me as more.

"You hungry?"

I shrugged. He always used to make me omelets. It was the only thing he knew how to cook. Now omelets didn't fit into his vegan diet, which worked out because I didn't have any eggs. Besides, he was nourishing me far more than food ever could. I just wanted to lie with him for a while.

"Well, I'm starving." He rolled out of bed, and when I knew he was gone, I rested my head on his pillow, inhaling the scent of him. I'd always slept on the right side of the bed, except when I was with Deacon. He insisted he physically couldn't sleep on the left, so I always did. As long as I was with him, nothing else mattered.

I could hear him opening and closing cabinets in the kitchen, so I decided to follow him out. I didn't love that he had his jeans back on, but barefoot and shirtless, he couldn't escape too easily. His daisy tattoo was on full display, and I had to wonder if Shaunn knew the significance of it and whether it bothered her.

"Mickie." He closed one empty cabinet and opened another. "Do you eat? Like, at all?"

I hated eating alone, so I rarely kept my cabinets stocked. "I usually go out." I wondered why he was so surprised. Maybe when he lived there, I'd been a little more on my game.

He pulled out a box of Hostess CupCakes. "Glad you have the essentials."

I didn't like prepackaged desserts, and Deacon knew that. Because he was mocking me, and also to see his reaction, I told him the truth. "Burke liked them after sex."

He turned away so I couldn't see his face and tossed the box in the trash. "Well, bye-bye, Burke."

I walked over to where he stood. "How do you know I wasn't going to eat those?"

He shot me the slightest grin. "Were you?"

I tried not to smile. As far as I knew, he was still engaged, and until he told me otherwise, I couldn't let myself get attached.

He turned his attention back to my cupboards. "Christ, Mickie, you don't even have any coffee?"

He'd never had an issue with any of this when we were younger. The kitchen he shared with Shaunn was probably perfectly stocked and organized. "I didn't realize my lifestyle was such a problem for you."

I started to turn away, but he wrapped his bare arms around my waist, pulled me in, and kissed the top of my head. "I'm sorry." He never apologized. With one arm still around me, he reached into the cabinet and pulled out a box of instant oatmeal. "What's this we have here? I do believe it's a breakfast food. Do you have any milk?"

Miraculously, I had bought milk a few days before. "I don't think that fits into your vegan diet."

He smiled a little. "I'm thinking of switching to vegetarian. Vegan is too hard."

A lot of things were too hard for Deacon. Commitment, for instance. I wasn't about to call him out on it, because his dropping the vegan thing got me one step closer to the old Deacon.

As we sat at the counter, eating our maple and brown sugar, me in his sweater, I tried not to let myself be too happy. I tried not to relish in the way I didn't have to put on a show or pretend to be anyone else. I tried to tell myself this was probably a one-time thing. Which was why I asked, "Is anyone going to wonder where you've been?"

He was silent for a few seconds, focusing his attention on his spoon. "She's out of town."

Just like that, I was put off my oatmeal. He might as well have reached into my chest and pulled my heart out, barehanded. "Is that the real reason you came here? Your fiancée's away and you had an itch you needed to scratch?"

I hated myself for asking. I didn't want to know the answer. I wanted to take it back.

"I told you last night." His spoon clinked into the empty bowl. "You're the only person who won't bullshit me. I needed to be with you. I meant it."

That didn't help me forget that Shaunn got to have breakfast with him every day and go to bed with him every night.

"My relationship with her is not what you see in the public eye." I knew a thing or two about that. Maybe Shaunn not being at his CD release show was no different than Burke not being at my birthday party. "I'm figuring things out. But what I can tell you for certain is that ever since that night at Intuition, something has been calling me back here."

I almost told him that something inside of me had been calling for him, too, but I couldn't let him believe that I had been there, stagnant, waiting to be tagged in. "You can't expect me to put my life on hold while you sort your stuff out," I said. "I've started seeing someone, too." Or more accurately had seen someone, once, who didn't even know my real name, and who I hadn't given a second thought to since I arrived home to find Deacon at my doorstep.

All of that must have been perfectly clear to Deacon, who took my hand, pressed his lips to the inside of my wrist, and said, "When we're in here, let's tune out the noise and pretend it's just you and me in our own world, okay?"

It was the same thing he used to say to ease my wounded heart when my mother would steamroll through my life or a tabloid would tear me apart. Back then, I'd believed it was possible.

Deacon looked at the microwave clock and stood up. "Shit, I didn't realize what time it was. I gotta go."

It was enough to give me emotional whiplash.

"I have a meeting with the label at one. I have to go home and get ready," he explained, as if to say, *This wasn't a screw and run*. It didn't make me feel any better.

I walked into the bedroom, slipped out of his sweater, and threw on my robe, breathing in the scent of his shirt once more before returning to the kitchen. He already had his shoes on, jacket in hand. He must have read my concern, because after he finished dressing, he leaned in and kissed me.

"I'm not Travis Howard, Mickie." Deacon-speak for *I will be back.*

ONCE HE'D LEFT, ONCE I'D SHOWERED AND REPLAYED EVery minute of the last eleven hours in my mind, I noticed I had a message. I thought it might be Deacon, already determining that our night had been a mistake, or Ben making sure I'd gotten home all right. But it wasn't either of them.

"Hi, Gorgeous, it's me. I'm flying in tomorrow and I was hoping you could meet me at the airport. It's flight 237 from New Mexico. United. See you then."

CHAPTER THIRTEEN

I read this biography on Natalie Wood once, and I learned that her mother tore the wings off a live butterfly right in front of her so Natalie could learn to cry on screen. I guess in comparison, Caroline wasn't all that bad.

This is what I know of my mother's story: When she was eighteen, she moved to LA—where from, I have no idea—in order to "make something of herself." I asked her when I was young about my grandparents and all she had to say was, "You're the only family I've got, Gorgeous, and I'm the only family you've got." She always believed in speaking to me like I was an adult, even when I was four or five. She tried modeling, and when that didn't work out, she tried acting. When that failed, she did everything in her power to make herself something by marrying someone who was something. She married husband number one, an up-and-coming movie producer, when she was twenty, but that didn't last long because she was still in the market for something better, and he never quite made it to the big time. She moved to New York and got pregnant with me at twenty-two, probably in an attempt to latch on to a more successful second husband—but we all know that didn't happen. When I was three, she got me an agent by "losing" me at a swanky restaurant where some power lunch was going on. When I was four, I got my first job, and you pretty much know the rest.

You'd think with our history, I never would have looked up her flight information, but for as long as I could remember, when Caroline Turner told you to do something, you did it. When she told the directors to shoot me from my left side, they did. When she told Jackson Martin and Tyler Richards and Franklin Guerra to marry her, they did. When she told me she needed money and I owed her, I listened. The first time, anyway.

I told myself that even though I had her itinerary, I didn't have to go see her. I'd never committed to anything. She certainly wouldn't be staying with me, so I didn't know why she'd want me to meet her at the airport. Maybe she needed money so badly she thought I'd give it to her the minute she stepped off the plane. Maybe she had no intention of seeing me again for the rest of the trip. Whatever it was, I knew I had no obligation to her, but that didn't prevent me from losing another night's sleep.

The next afternoon, I was in my closet trying on outfits, trying to gauge which would be the most appropriate. I needed to look important. I needed to show her that she hadn't scarred me for life. I needed to show her what she'd left behind. I needed to prove that I was better than her.

I decided to wear black, because Caroline hated me in black. The winning outfit consisted of a herringbone skirt, a black cowl-necked sweater, and knee-high Jimmy Choo boots. Nothing says "I don't need you anymore" like twelve-hundred-dollar shoes. I opened the mahogany jewelry box filled with gifts from boyfriends past and decorated myself with a bracelet that Gregory the painter bought me before he left me for another man, earrings from Burke, and a cocktail ring Josh had given me for Valentine's Day over a decade before. This was what my life boiled down to. I didn't have any accomplishments to speak of, but remnants of unsuccessful relationships? Those were bountiful.

As I waited for the elevator, I asked myself what I was doing, and I couldn't find one suitable answer. A small part of me wanted to see her, because she was my mother. An even smaller part of me hoped that she had changed, and that the past was the past, and that she missed me. Call me a glutton for punishment, a masochist.

The elevator doors opened, and I was just about to step in when I saw Josh coming down the hall. Only Josh preferred the stairs to the elevator.

"Hey," he said. "I was just coming to see you."

"Welcome home." I tried to sound as normal as possible. Josh never interfered, but there were two people in the world he wanted me to stay away from. It would kill him to know that while he was off golfing, one had invited herself back into my life and the other had found his way back into my bed.

The elevator closed, going on its merry way without me, so I jammed the button again.

"Sorry," I said. I didn't want Josh to think my frustration had anything to do with him. "I was just on my way out. How was your trip?"

He shrugged. "It was okay. I tried calling you last night."

I'd stayed in all day and kept my eyes glued to the phone, waiting to hear from Deacon or Caroline, but I hadn't answered any of my calls. All I got was one message from Josh telling me he was home and one from Ben asking when I wanted to go out again.

"I must have fallen asleep."

He knew it wasn't true, but he didn't push it. "I just wanted to see what you were up to. See if you wanted to grab some dinner later."

The smart answer would have been, *Yes, let's go right now.* "Another night?"

"Sure." He scrutinized my eyes, my face, my outfit. "Where are you off to?"

My insides turned. Josh was the one person I couldn't lie to. "Just out."

"Out?"

"I have errands."

He squinted. "Why are you being weird?"

"I'm not being weird. I'm just late."

"For your errands."

I didn't know how to respond. I was sixteen when my mother left me to marry Tyler Richards, and Josh was the only person who'd been there for me. I hadn't had a job in a year, and Tyler was an investment banker. "It's time, Gorgeous," Caroline had said. "There's not much more I can do for you." I knew she meant there wasn't much more I could do for her, but all I cared about was that my mother was leaving. Josh had the pleasure of being the only person I trusted enough to cry to. Even after I broke up with him and the Boyz went on tour, he'd call me every night so I could spill my guts for hours. I eventually stopped burdening him with my troubles, but he never forgot how hurt I was, and he'd probably have an aneurysm if I told him I was going to see her again.

I desperately needed to change the subject. "How'd your family like Morgan?"

"They loved Morgan," he said. "How could they not? A future doctor going out with this idiot?"

"Hey." I squeezed his face. "Only I get to call you an idiot, okay?"

His attention was drawn to my hand. "Hey, is that the ring I gave you? Let me see that."

I held out the enormous sapphire decorating my finger, aggravated and grateful that he was stalling me.

"I must have really been raking in the dough when I bought that bad boy."

"You were."

"Little did I know I'd be unemployed for five years."

His five was better than my twelve. I wondered what Caroline would say when she found out I hadn't had a job since the last one she'd landed me. I sort of assumed she kept tabs on me and was conscious of my career—or lack thereof—but if she knew that my only source of income was *Breyer's Town* residuals, I highly doubted she'd be contacting me.

The elevator dinged open behind me. "I should go." I hoped he wouldn't ask me again where I was going, because I was close to telling him everything. "You coming?"

He shook his head. "I'll take the stairs. I ate way too much conch in Florida. You sure you're okay?"

I gave him a thumbs-up—a gesture I probably hadn't used since I was ten. I prayed that I looked like a normal human being, but I feared I looked how I felt: like a taped-up mess ready to fall apart at any moment.

I WAS AT A LOSS FOR WORDS WHEN I GOT IN THE CAB.

"Well?" the driver urged. He hated me already. I considered getting out of the car and running back inside, but somehow I managed to say, "JFK."

My entire body tingled, from my baby toes to the roots of my hair, and I thought I would throw up during the whole ride. I told myself it had to do with the driver's erratic steering, but deep down I knew the truth. I tried to remind myself that the minute I told her she wasn't getting any money from me, I'd never hear from her again.

I reached into my purse and pulled out my phone, hoping that maybe Deacon had called while I was talking to Josh. If I got just one word from him, I'd tell the driver to turn the car around and I'd meet him anywhere in the world. I shot him a text, asking how he was doing. I hoped for an immediate response, an I need to see you or a Let's meet up. I got nothing.

It took forever to get to the airport in rush hour, but once we arrived, I considered asking the driver to take one more spin around the city. As I reached into my wallet for the fare, I couldn't help but think of Caroline's words. *You never know when that well of yours is going to run dry.* She was wrong—I knew she was wrong—but my bank account had taken a hit since I'd stopped getting paid to party. A tiny voice kept asking me what I was going to do when the reruns stopped airing and the residuals stopped coming in.

Flight 237 was running on schedule, which was more than I could say for myself. I wanted to be on time. I wanted to show Caroline that despite her, I was a responsible and well-adjusted adult—the kind who dates schoolteachers and goes to bed at a reasonable hour. Not the kind who sleeps with engaged men. I wasn't off to the best start.

Watching families reuniting, couples embracing, and bleary-eyed travelers returning from new adventures, I remembered why I rarely left New York. Airports were the most depressing places on earth. When I couldn't find her, I assumed she'd already left or maybe she'd canceled her trip altogether. But then there she was.

She already had her luggage and was standing, like I was, watching as people met up with their loved ones. In my mind, Caroline had always been stunning, with shoulder-length honey-colored waves, picture-perfect skin, and eyelashes that went on forever. I often told myself it was a case of a girl over-glorifying her absent mother, but when I saw her, she was exactly as I remembered. If anything, she was even more radiant. I was torn between running away and melting in her arms.

She didn't see me, but I watched her for a full five minutes, breathing from the pit of my stomach, just as she had taught me. Trying to work up the nerve to approach her, to say something, anything. If she was the only family I had and I couldn't even face her, what kind of person did that make me? I always thought that when I saw her again, I would be filled with rage, thinking about her revealing every bit of my life to a tabloid, living off my money, choosing rich husband after rich husband over her only daughter. But as I watched her, eyeing the time and twisting her rings, all I could think about was our ritual of going to high tea anytime I got rejected for a job. "They're assholes," she would say, no matter whether I was four or fourteen. "They're not good enough to lick our boots." When I'd tell her I wanted to quit, she'd say I was letting the bastards win.

She took out her phone and I expected mine to start ringing. When it didn't, my chest ached, because she had to be calling a cab or a hotel. She had no right to make me feel that way after everything she'd put me through, but still—she was my mother.

After a minute, she tossed her phone in her bag and made her way through the airport. I lingered around the terminal long enough so that I wouldn't risk bumping into her outside. I probably didn't need to sit there for two hours, but I had nowhere else to go, and I couldn't go back to my apartment in case she tried me there next. I needed a place to stay for the night. I would have hung around the airport until dawn, but once the suspicious looks from airport security started multiplying, I knew it was time to go. There was still no word from Deacon, and I couldn't tell Josh the truth, so I had no choice but to call the only other person who wouldn't reject me.

I TRIED TO GET MYSELF INTO FLIRTATION MODE AS I MADE my way up the rickety steps to Ben's apartment. I liked Ben enough to sleep with him. At least, I liked him more than some of the guys I'd slept with in the past. I didn't know him well, but I did know he wasn't the type to make a girl leave in the middle of the night.

He greeted me with a smile that almost made me feel less horrible about the day I'd had. Almost.

"Wow," he said. "You look beautiful."

I wanted to tell him I didn't deserve his kindness, but if I wanted Ben to let me stay the night, I was going to need to cover up that I was the type of wretched person who'd stand her mother up at the airport. I told myself I was playing a part—the part of a girl who was interested in a guy, a part I knew how to play well. I gave him my best smile, tilted my head, and said, "Thank you, Mr. English," before welcoming him with as much passion as I could force into a kiss. If it were any other day, I probably could have convinced myself that I felt something.

A yellow Lab who looked too large for the apartment stumbled up from his post on the couch and pushed his way between Ben's legs, greeting me with a wagging tail. I was afraid he'd slobber on my boots—dogs and Choos don't mix—but knew I'd better play my cards right. "Cute dog." And he was cute, minus the drool.

Ben gave him a little scratch. "This is Holden."

"As in Caulfield?"

"I should have known you'd get the reference."

Even those of us with on-set tutors had to read *Catcher in the Rye.*

"Want to head down to the bar?" he asked. "I'll grab my jacket."

When I called to ask if he was around, he suggested we grab a drink in his neighborhood. I said that sounded perfect, knowing it would offer a natural opening to an invitation upstairs. I told him I didn't know how long it would take me to get there, so I'd meet him at his apartment, which gave me the chance to walk by the bar and scope it out. As soon as I saw the wall-to-wall mix of hipsters and sports fans through the window, I knew it wasn't an option. Even under the cover of ordinary Ben, I'd get recognized, and I'd have to explain that I wasn't the person he thought I was.

"Why don't we stay in?" I gently caressed his hand.

His eyes sparkled, surprised but happy. "Yeah?"

I shrugged like a dazzling ingenue in a rom-com. "It'll give us a quieter place to talk, don't you think? Do you have any wine?"

"I think so." While he looked in the kitchen, I took my boots off—partially because that was one less thing I'd need to remove once we got started, but mainly because my feet were killing me. Heels never bothered me, but it had been a long day.

He returned with two glasses. "White okay?"

I nodded and resisted the urge to swig it all down in one gulp. Kayla would be all about moderation.

"Did you shrink?" he asked.

I felt myself smile—really smile—for the first time in what had to be days. "My feet hurt." I sat on the couch and glanced at the cushion next to me, hoping he'd take his cue to sit. He did.

"I was really glad to hear from you," he said. "I have to admit, for a minute there I wondered if you weren't interested."

It had taken me three days to return his call after the movies. "It's not you. It's—" I stopped myself from saying the gag-worthy *It's me*, even though it clearly was me. "It's been a crazy week." *You know, between sleeping with my engaged ex-boyfriend and stalking my estranged mother.*

"Everything all right?" His tone was so gentle that I feared he was starting to see through my facade. The only things I'd ever been good at were acting and seducing men, but apparently I couldn't even do those anymore.

"Everything's great." I was determined to make him believe that. Someone sensitive like Ben would never want to sleep with a basket case.

I looked around his apartment. It was small—I could have fit two of them in my living room—but unlike my place, it was cozy and lived in. There was an overflowing bookcase next to the couch, with more books piled on end tables and the floor. His laptop sat on the coffee table with a stack of papers next to it. The TV was on. He obviously hadn't planned on entertaining company, but I had to make him forget that.

"I like your apartment."

"I would have picked up if I'd known earlier that you were coming." His eyes landed on the enormous sapphire I should have remembered to take off. "I'm sure this isn't what you're used to."

I wanted to tell him that I was tired of what I was used to, but I didn't want to talk anymore. Talking led to thinking, and I had done enough thinking. Like Caroline always told me, I needed to dive into something new.

"It's perfect. It's very—you." And it was.

Ben took a sip of wine and puckered. "God, that's terrible." He was cute. He made me hate what I was about to do.

"It's not so bad," I said. "But I have a better idea." I took his glass, placed it on the table, and gave him a kiss that told him wine was the last thing on my mind.

His lips weren't Deacon's lips. His hands, tracing their way down my arms, weren't Deacon's hands. I told myself it didn't matter—Deacon was home with his fiancée, figuring things out and not responding to my texts, and Ben was here, with zero clue of what a mess I really was.

I touched the collar of his shirt, willing myself to start unbuttoning it, but my fingers froze. My entire body froze.

He pulled back and looked at me. "Are you okay?"

I took a breath, assuring myself that this was nothing more than blanking in the middle of a scene. On a set, I'd call for a line. Here, I shook my head, said, "Of course, sorry," and leaned in for take two.

I kissed him deeper this time, willing myself to focus on the job at hand. When I was fourteen and terrified to experience my first kiss on screen—my first kiss, period—Caroline assured me I was overthinking it. "You're not Michaela Turner right now," she'd said. "You're Cassidy Sinclair, and that boy is the next-door neighbor you've been dreaming about since the sixth grade. Stay in the scene."

As soon as Ben's hand touched my thigh, I tensed. He could feel it.

"I'm so sorry," I said. "I have no idea what's wrong with me." The image of Deacon with his daisy tattoo, eating oatmeal in my kitchen, seared itself into my mind. "I just started working with a new client, and I think I'm distracted."

Ben looked at me with those kind eyes. "Kayla, we're not going to do anything you don't want to do. We're just getting to know each other. Why don't we take it slow?"

I thought about insisting, *No, I can do this*, and going in for take three, but then I thought about CeCe's tell-all. *To them, she's nothing more than a conquest. To her, they're nothing more than a warm body.* I couldn't prove her right.

I relaxed into the couch cushion. "That sounds nice." It was then that not eating in two days caught up with me.

"Was that your stomach?"

When I didn't say anything—because, really, how do you respond to that?—he said, "I'm gonna take Holden out. I'll pick something up for you on the way back. What are you in the mood for?"

I wondered what his motives were. He couldn't genuinely be this nice. "You'd really do that for me?"

"Do what?"

"Get me food."

"It's no big deal." He didn't realize that to me, it was. Every guy I'd ever dated was more concerned with himself—and I'd always been okay with that. "I could make you something, but with the contents of my fridge, you'd be stuck with frozen pizza or a grilled cheese."

My stomach let out another cry. When we were teenagers, Josh and I practically lived off grilled cheese. "I haven't had one of those in a really long time."

"What, grilled cheese?" When I nodded, he said, "In that case, you happen to be in luck. Not to toot my own horn, but I happen to make a fantastic grilled cheese."

"Did you really just say 'toot my own horn'?"

"Are you making fun of me?" he asked. "Because I kind of hold the fate of your sandwich in my hands."

"Definitely not making fun of you."

He grabbed the leash, and I saw the sands through the hourglass running down. Ben would come back, and I'd eat a grilled cheese, and then I'd have to go home.

"Hey, are there any hotels around here?" I asked.

He looked up from adjusting the dog's harness. "Hotels?"

"They're painting my apartment." I wasn't surprised how easily I could lie to him, but I was surprised how guilty it made me feel.

He looked doubtful. "At ten o'clock at night?"

"No. This week. They started yesterday and the whole place reeks of paint fumes. I haven't slept." At least the last sentence was true.

I was afraid he'd see through me, but he said, "Why don't you stay here?"

Success. "Really?"

"Of course. You take the bed and I'll sleep on the couch."

Now I really felt guilty. "I'm not going to kick you out of your bed."

"You're not," he said. "I'm insisting. My mother raised a gentleman. She'd be devastated to think I'd let a lady sleep on the couch."

Funny. My mother raised a hot mess. She'd be devastated to think I was out with someone who didn't make twenty million a year.

Before he left with the dog, Ben offered me some of his clothes to sleep in. I didn't feel very sexy in his Columbia T-shirt and the plaid pajama pants I had to roll several times at the waist, but I didn't exactly care. For a minute, I pretended that the T-shirt was mine—that I'd gone to an Ivy League school—and that I lived in an apartment that felt like an extension of me. I'd have no housekeeper to pick up after me, but who needed that anyway? I made my way around the living room, a room filled with furniture that was probably handed down from his family or purchased at IKEA. He had a few framed pictures on top of his bookcase—one of the dog, one of his family in front of the Grand Canyon, and one of a little boy and girl, his sister's kids, no doubt. I wondered what Ben would say if he discovered that the only picture I kept around was in my underwear drawer, and that it was of my ex-boyfriend, who happened to be *the* Deacon King.

I tried to imagine what it would be like to have two parents—parents you could talk to on a regular basis without having to wonder why they were calling you. I wondered what it would be like to know whether you looked more like your mother or your father. I bet Ben's parents never would have taken their daughter to a fancy restaurant, telling her to go up to a table full of suits and pretend to be lost. Ben's niece and nephew appeared to be about five and seven. They just looked like kids—real kids, whose biggest concern was whether the rain would prevent them from going out to ride their bikes, not whether or not their cutesy act would work, because if it didn't, their show could get canceled and a hundred people could be out of jobs.

"Adorable, aren't they?"

I jumped. I'd been so engrossed in those stupid pictures I didn't even hear Ben come in.

"They are. Your sister's kids?"

Ben nodded. "Ethan and Caroline."

I felt immediate pressure on my chest. "Caroline?"

"My brother-in-law is a big Neil Diamond fan."

He had to have noticed that I wasn't smiling. "Weren't you going to make me a sandwich?" I tried my best to sound playful.

"Cranky when you're hungry, I see." He headed into the kitchenette. "You're lucky I like you."

I wished he'd stop saying that. I wished he could have been like Burke, who used to check the league's scores while I was still on top of him.

His TV was paused on a movie—*The Great Gatsby*—and when I took a second look at the papers on his coffee table, I felt even worse about barging in on him. It was nearly eleven o'clock on a Wednesday. He had to work in the morning. His night should have been winding down, and instead he was making me a grilled cheese sandwich.

I picked up the top paper on the pile.

Jennifer Freeman, October 3, 2007

The character of Estella in *Great Expectations* is a victim of the upbringing of Miss Havisham, who teaches her to torment men and break their hearts. Because of this, Estella grows to be cold and manipulative, continually telling Pip that she "has no heart."

The paper had little red check marks and squiggles reading *Good!* and *How so?* I was sure Ben was a good teacher. I wondered how it must have felt to know you were making an impact on someone's life.

I heard Ben's footsteps, followed closely by four paws, and immediately placed Jennifer Freeman's essay back on the coffee table. I prayed he hadn't seen me.

"Pour vous." He handed me a paper plate with a slightly-burnt-on-one-side, slightly-underdone-on-the-other-side sandwich.

"Are you taking up French now?"

"Well, you know, if the English gig doesn't work out."

I took a bite of the sandwich. It was the most delicious thing I'd tasted in weeks. "If the English gig doesn't work out, you should get a job at a diner. I'm sorry I interrupted your night."

"You can interrupt my night anytime," he said, looking straight at me. "I meant what I said. I like you, Kayla."

I wanted to point out that he didn't even know me, and if he did—if he realized that like this Estella character, I only used men and had no heart—he would go running in the opposite direction. But I was too tired to argue, and I was too tired to put on airs and reciprocate, so I just asked, "What were you doing before I came over?"

"Watching a movie. And grading papers. And seriously contemplating doing some laundry."

"A multitasker. What movie?" I asked, pretending I hadn't already seen it on the TV.

"*Gatsby*," he replied "I'm giving my class a quiz on the book tomorrow."

"And you're watching the movie instead? Mr. English, I am shocked."

A small grin graced his lips. "It helps me figure out which kids only watched the movie."

"Have you ever caught anyone?"

"Yes. But I'm such a sucker I always give them another chance."

I pictured him in a classroom, wearing a collared shirt under a crewneck sweater, sitting on one of the desks, getting animated as he talked about Fitzgerald or Dickens. I bet all the sixteen-year-old girls had crushes on him, even though he was a little bit nerdy. He probably made them enthusiastic about reading a century-old book. It probably fulfilled him to go home at the end of the day and read papers like Jennifer Freeman's, smiling at how he got these kids thinking.

"It must feel really good to have found your calling." I couldn't believe I'd said it out loud. The emotional weight of the day and warm food sliding down into my belly must have formed some kind of truth serum.

"My calling." He let out a light laugh before realizing I wasn't joking. "Do you not feel that way about what you do?"

I fiddled with Josh's sapphire on my finger. He had been such a huge star when he gave it to me, and I'd felt like someone who never would be again. "Your future is brighter than that ring, Turner," he'd said, and sixteen-year-old me believed him.

"I think it takes some of us longer to find our way," I said to Ben.

"What did you go to school for?"

I didn't know if he was curious or trying to be helpful. I almost told him something that seemed fitting of an image consultant, like marketing, or psychology, which was what I really wanted to study because I wanted to figure out why I was the way I was. But I didn't have the headspace to keep one more story going, so I said, "Theater."

"No way." He sounded so interested. "Did you act?"

"When I was younger," I said.

"Why'd you stop?"

I focused on the grilled cheese, wishing I'd slept with him so I could have avoided this conversation. "Think about what you were good at when you were a kid. What, LEGO? Or building forts? You get over it. You grow up."

"But you're always you, Kayla."

I almost told him I wasn't even sure who that was. I wished

I could have confessed about Daisy, and how once I stopped playing her, everything that followed became a guessing game. "Why don't we finish watching your movie?"

I only lasted twenty minutes. Resting my head on one of Ben's mismatched throw pillows, breathing in the fabric-softener scent of the oversize T-shirt I was wearing, I dozed off, listening to Daisy Buchanan's lament about girls being beautiful little fools.

CHAPTER FOURTEEN

The next morning, I had that seedy sensation of waking up in a stranger's bed, feeling the desperate need to sneak out before being forced into awkward morning-after conversation. I had to remind myself I hadn't done anything with Ben—I had slept in his bed, and he'd slept on the couch with the dog. The only thing I needed to be embarrassed about was scarfing down two grilled cheese sandwiches while wearing a T-shirt that engulfed my entire body.

He'd already left for work by the time I got up, but he'd left a note on the counter.

Wish I could play hooky with you . . . Damn that Gatsby! Stay as long as you want. I'll call you later.

Ben

He'd left a pot of brewing coffee with a clean mug next to it, and beside it was a bakery bag with a Post-it that read,

It's the most important meal of the day. Have it with some six-sugared coffee.

So he had been paying attention at the diner. I opened the bag and found a chocolate croissant and a blueberry muffin. Options. He was way too nice for me.

I glanced at the clock: 8:15. I'd rarely seen this part of the morning unless it was last call at one of Travis Howard's parties. It was the oddest sensation, knowing I could turn on the TV and catch the *Today* show, or step outside and see commuters heading off to work. I tried to avoid the working people as much as possible, because it only reminded me that while they all had a mission—lives to save, accounts to manage, English to teach—I was just wandering.

I'd done the walk of shame on many occasions. Normally I slid into a cab as quickly as possible, wearing a dress completely inappropriate for the daylight. On this morning, I had less to be ashamed about, but I still felt disheveled as I made my way out of Ben's apartment, having just splashed some water on my face, my only makeup some lip gloss and blush I had stashed away in my purse. I hated that I had to take Ben's key with me in order to lock up. I'd never been one for holding on to anyone's keys but my own. Too much responsibility and way too much commitment.

It was one of those ugly October days with drizzly rain and skies as gray as the tweed in my second-day skirt. Before I stepped inside my building, I wrung out my hair and wiped raindrops from my face, trying to make myself more presentable in case Caroline was there waiting for me.

Phil actually greeted me with a smile. "Good morning, Miss Turner."

I recognized that look. It was the look of a man who'd been in the presence of my mother. "Has anyone been by to see me?" My wool turtleneck was suffocating me.

I swear I saw a sparkle in his eye just thinking about it. "Yes, as a matter of fact. Your mother."

I had expected it. I had prepared myself for it. But Phil saying it out loud made it completely different.

I peeked around in the lobby and only saw some woman in yoga pants coming out of the elevator. "She came by last night," Phil continued. Thank God for Ben English. "She asked me to give you this when you got in." He raised his eyebrows with unabashed judgment. "Which apparently is now."

He forked over a business-sized envelope, and I almost felt a sense of warmth when I saw my name written in her familiar penmanship across the front. Holding the same envelope she'd held the night before was the most physical contact we'd had in almost a decade. I considered handing it back over to Phil, but then I'd never know what was inside. With Caroline, it could have been anything from an apology letter (not likely) to a legal document forcing me to sign over my life savings (much more likely). I thanked Phil and headed toward the elevators.

"Lovely woman," he called.

I turned. "What?"

"Your mother," he said, again with that glimmer-in-the-eye, melody-in-the-tone effect that Caroline had on everyone. "She's quite a woman."

I wasn't sure if he could hear me because I was already halfway into the elevator when I mumbled, "Yes, she is."

OF COURSE I DIDN'T OPEN THE ENVELOPE RIGHT AWAY. I quashed the instinct to rip it open and find out what was inside, then placed it on the coffee table, flipped through my mail, and hit the showers, which Burke always insisted was the best way to clear the mind. It didn't work. Everything festered—what Caroline wanted with me, why I hadn't heard from Deacon, how I was going to get Ben's key back to him.

I came out of the bathroom—fully prepared to face the

letter, or whatever it was—and nearly slipped when I found Deacon in my living room tinkering with his piano. My piano. The piano.

I must have looked as shaken as I felt, because he gave me that amused grin and said, "Hey, Mickie."

I was so startled I hadn't even noticed that Jay was with him, all veins and muscles, sniffing through my cabinets.

"Michaela." His usual distaste for me was evident.

I closed my bathrobe tightly around me, trying to ignore the tingle in my stomach at the sight of Deacon, trying to ignore that Jay was munching on a bag of my pita chips.

"What are you doing here?"

Deacon looked so casual, like we hadn't slept together a few days before, like he hadn't broken into my apartment, like we hadn't been broken up for two years. I didn't know why he thought he could stroll back in here after not calling for days, with his trusty security guard when he'd been the one to make the rule about no outside noise.

"I think you're going to like what I have to say."

"How did you get into my apartment?"

He reached into his pocket. "I found my keys."

"They're not yours anymore," I said, but didn't make any effort to take them back. As much as I hated to admit it, I liked that he'd held on to them.

"Come on, Mickie. Don't be pissy." He laced his fingers through mine and massaged my palm with his thumb. The electricity that man could exude with his touch was unfathomable.

I looked over at Jay, silently asking Deacon what he was doing, because in Jay's mind, Deacon was a faithful engaged man. Deacon just smiled. "We're going shopping."

"Who's going shopping?"

"Us. You and me. And Jay."

Jay looked unfazed, just staring at us, still eating my pita chips. “We have to get going,” Jay said. “They’re expecting us at two.”

I looked down at my silk bathrobe, which was coming undone, at my mother’s letter, which was still unopened, and into Deacon’s eyes, which were unwavering.

“What makes you think I’ll go somewhere with you?”

“Because I need you,” he said, and all it took was those four words.

Twenty minutes later, Deacon and I were in the back of his town car with Jay behind the wheel. I turned to Deacon. “He’s your driver, too?”

Deacon shrugged. “You know I only trust a few people.”

“So you told him about us?”

Deacon kissed my earlobe. I loved the way it felt.

“Jay doesn’t ask questions.”

“Aren’t you afraid he’s going to tell someone?”

This was when Deacon was supposed to say that it was fine if Jay told someone, because he’d sorted through things and broken up with Shaunn.

“He signed an NDA,” was what he said instead. I wondered if he’d ask me to sign one. He wasn’t that heartless. Or so I hoped.

“Why are we going shopping?”

“You were right,” he said. “The clothes I’ve been wearing are shit. All I have are lame-ass blazers and tailored pants. It’s not me.”

At least I was doing something right.

His phone buzzed in his pocket, tickling my thigh. He immediately took it out and looked at the screen. “It’s my manager.” Seeing how quickly he answered, I wondered how he could have possibly missed my texts over the past forty-eight hours. I wasn’t dumb enough to think he hadn’t got them, but I tried to tell myself it wasn’t important—he was there with me now, and that was what I needed to focus on.

I listened as he talked to his manager about some new deal, how much he'd get, and if they should hold out for more. The conversation sounded so uncomfortably familiar that I knew no matter how much I avoided my apartment or how long I left that envelope sealed, I couldn't ignore Caroline forever.

"CHARM EVERYONE, GORGEOUS. YOU NEVER KNOW. TODAY'S waiter may be tomorrow's Scorsese."

It was a Tuesday afternoon, and while every other nine-year-old was in school learning long division, I was sitting with my mother in a hotel lounge, sipping on a Shirley Temple. We had just come from the studio, where she'd met with one of the executives. While she was behind closed doors, I prepared the words I was set to say that day as Daisy, but I wasn't blind to the raised eyebrows and mumblings by the cast and crew. Moments later, she emerged from the office with a no-nonsense look I'd become accustomed to and said, "Let's go, Gorgeous. We're not staying."

Sitting in the dimly lit lounge, her face looked complacent and unconcerned.

"Shouldn't we go back?" I finally asked. "We're supposed to start shooting."

She ignored my question and flashed a smile at the waiter as he brought her a martini, on the house. "What's your name, Gorgeous?"

I tried to ignore the sting I felt, hearing her use the same name on this man that she always used on me.

"Jeremy."

"Well, Jeremy, we're expecting a call from a man named Jack Benson at ABC." She tilted her head, tucked a strand of honey-colored hair behind her ear, and raised just her left eyebrow. I'd seen her do it my whole life and recognized it immediately as the Caroline-Turner-way-of-getting-what-she-wanted. "I gave him the number here. You will tell me when he calls?"

The waiter nodded, the same bewitched look in his eye every man had when dealing with my mother.

"Never drink," she told me, sliding her glass away from her. "It will ruin your skin."

"Caroline." She refused to be called *Mom* or *Mommy*. She wasn't a fan of acting like one, either. "We're supposed to start shooting."

"Nobody's shooting anything until someone gives us our raise."

"Why do we need a raise?"

"Because," she said, "we deserve it. You should always get what you deserve in this life."

"Oh." I didn't want to listen to another one of her theories on life. I wanted to go back and play Daisy and film my scenes and make people laugh. It was tiring, but it was what I knew.

"This show isn't going to last forever," she went on. "We need to build for our future. Always think ahead, Gorgeous."

We must have run through this song and dance four times since the show started two years before.

"What if they don't call?"

"They'll call," she said, as if there was no question about it. "They need you. Everyone else on that show is disposable. *You* are Daisy Breyer. Tell me, what was Katrina doing when you were running your lines?"

"Reading a book." I didn't tell her that I wished, just once, I could have read a book instead of a script.

"Reading a book," she repeated. "Let me tell you something, Gorgeous, about the Katrina Wilders of the world. They may be more well-read than you. They may grow up on a traditional path and go off to school, get married, and have babies, but they will be nothing more than common. They will never be as beautiful as you, or as smart as you, or as talented—

because you were *born* with it. But if you don't take advantage of that, it's worth nothing."

She'd been giving me the same speech all my life. Sometimes she attributed it to my father. He was brilliant, she'd admit, though she'd never tell me his name. Sometimes she would blame it purely on the stars aligning just right on the night I was born. I had *it*, and *it* got us ahead in life.

"Okay, Gorgeous," she said, glancing at the clock on the wall. It'd been one hour since we left the studio. If the other times we'd walked off were any indication, ABC would be calling any minute. "Let's run your lines. We'll be getting back to work soon, and I want them to see you are worth every cent."

"MR. KING, WE ARE SO HAPPY TO HAVE YOU HERE." A young shopkeeper with wide eyes and way too much enthusiasm greeted us when we arrived at STAR, the up-and-coming boutique Deacon had selected to house his new look. *STAR*, the advertisements read. *Sexy. Tantric. Alluring. Raw.* I was skeptical of the place—they were trying too hard—but anything would be an improvement on those blazers.

While the staff waited for Jay's seal of approval that STAR would be acceptable for Deacon, I whispered, "Aren't you afraid someone here will say something to the press about me? Or did you have them sign NDAs, too?"

"Of course I did." I hadn't realized just how Hollywood he'd become. "Besides, I told them you're my stylist. No one will know who you are."

Those words stung, and he noticed immediately. "You know I didn't mean it like that."

I wasn't about to make a scene in the middle of STAR, so I shrugged it off. He was right. Even if someone recognized me as Daisy, they still wouldn't know who I was.

Almost an hour later, Deacon stepped behind a paisley curtain into one of the fitting rooms, loaded with the clothes I'd picked out. I found myself facing Jay, and though I certainly had nothing to say to him, he clearly had something to say to me.

"This should be fun, huh?"

"What?"

"This whole merry-go-round. You and Deacon. It's the same ride every time, but you two just keep getting back on."

I wanted to smack that smug expression right off his face. "I don't know what you're talking about."

"History repeats itself, that's all I'm saying." He shrugged. "Just like the reruns of your little TV show. You can watch it again and again, but it's always going to end the same way."

Nothing about this was the same. Deacon was lost. He was coming to me for help. Before I could argue, Deacon called out from the fitting room. "Mickie, I need you!"

His words said it all. He needed *me.*

When I stepped behind the curtain and saw Deacon, I felt like that nineteen-year-old girl who first met him at the piano bar. In his destroyed jeans and plain white tee, he looked every bit the rock god he was born to be.

"I don't know who your stylist is," I said, "but you should give her a raise."

I waited for him to thank me, but he just took off his shirt and started leafing through the pile of clothes. "My head's all over the place."

The tiny room felt smaller, and I feared his next words would be, *The other night was a mistake.* He pulled out one of the T-shirts I'd picked out. "Queen?"

It had been my proudest find. Vintage-inspired, with the album cover of *The Game.*

"Finish what you were going to say."

"I can't get out of this funk. And I thought about how you said once that sometimes when you're feeling bad, you have to start on the outside and work your way in."

I froze. “When did I say that?”

“I don’t know, a few years ago.” He must have noticed my expression, because he tapped his forehead and said, “I’m a writer. I remember everything.”

It wasn’t his remembering that threw me. It was that I’d heard those exact words from Caroline hundreds of times in my life. I never realized I’d repeated them.

I directed his attention back to the shirt. “Try it on.”

He looked at it. “I don’t know, Mickie . . .”

“What, do you not like Queen anymore?”

Queen was Deacon’s all-time favorite band. He used to sit at that piano, sing “Good Old-Fashioned Lover Boy,” and say that he was channeling Freddie Mercury. He’d gotten into a few drunken debates and one actual fist fight when someone dared to challenge his assertion that “We Will Rock You” was the greatest two minutes and two seconds of rock brilliance ever recorded.

“I do. I just don’t know if it’s me.”

“This is exactly you,” I told him. “People want to see who you really are. They don’t want to see that jackass on your album cover. Trust me.”

“I trust you more than you know.” He fiddled with his zipper. “Do you ever wonder what the little *YKK* on zippers means?”

“Yoshida Kogyou Kabushikkaisha.”

He looked up at me. “What?”

“It’s a Japanese company. They make 90 percent of all zippers.”

I could see the grin in his eyes before he even smiled. “Christ, I’ve missed you.”

He would buy the Queen shirt. I was sure of it.

THAT NIGHT, WHILE DEACON SLEPT IN MY BED, HIS FACE aglow from the *Breyer’s Town* rerun on TV, I tiptoed into the living room and picked up my mother's envelope. If spending the day with Deacon couldn't stop me from thinking of her, nothing would. A part of me hoped that whatever was inside that envelope was so horrible it would finally make me stop wanting to see her. I slid my fingernail along the seal, thinking how disappointed she'd be that I was ruining my manicure.

I can honestly say that what I found inside was the last thing I'd expected from Caroline: A check, made out to me, covering the amount I had given her seven years earlier, plus interest. This had to be some sort of joke. Maybe Phil had rigged it up as a hoax. My mother never would have returned this money to me on her own.

I opened the letter that was attached, hating the warmth I felt from her handwriting.

My Gorgeous girl—

I know you think this is what I want. It's not. So would you be a doll and meet me already? I'll be expecting your call. I'm staying at the Plaza—and no, not at your expense.

Smooches,
Caroline Turner

I almost laughed at the signature. Ever since I was a little girl, Caroline insisted on signing her name that way on everything, even when she remarried, and married again. She said she never did get to sign autographs, so why not take every opportunity to do it right?

I had no idea what to do with the check. I had no idea if it was even real. I slid it back into the envelope and slipped it where no one would think to look: under a Boyz of the Nation CD. Josh would kill me if he knew about any of this.

I got back into bed next to Deacon, wishing he'd put his arm around me. He did, but it didn't wipe away my confusion or make me feel better.

"This is my favorite episode," he murmured, his lips tickling my hair.

"I thought you were asleep."

"No way. Daisy's school Thanksgiving pageant? I love this one." He sat up, and I pretended not to notice that he checked his phone before grabbing a cigarette. I hated when he smoked in my bed, but I didn't say anything.

"Did I tell you when I was in France, they were playing reruns? It was the cutest goddamn thing—you, at like eight years old, with some French girl's voice dubbed in."

"I didn't realize they showed it in France," I said, though I should have remembered since I got paid for it.

"They show it all over Europe. In some places I'm pretty sure they think it's a new show and that you're still a kid in pigtails."

When Deacon first started touring, I loved listening to him talk about the places he'd been. Since I rarely left New York, his stories let me travel vicariously through him. I loved imagining places where I was still a girl in pigtails.

"What's it like there?" I asked.

"Where?"

"Europe."

"What part of Europe?"

"All of it."

There was a time when he would have described in detail every smell, every sight, every sunset. Now all he said was, "Beautiful."

Maybe it was the weight of his arm holding me, or the innocent little girl on TV, but the words that had been bubbling in my mind for days came pouring out. "Caroline's in town."

"What?" He stopped smoking mid-drag and stared at me

to see if I was bluffing. A part of me wished I was. When I didn't respond, he said, "You're not going to see her, are you?"

I thought back to her note, to the feeling I had when I saw her in the airport. "I think I have to."

He flopped back down on his pillow, covering his eyes like he was immediately stricken with a migraine. "Jesus Christ, Michaela."

He never called me Michaela unless he was upset with me. It sounded so strange coming from him.

"You're going to burn my sheets." I tried to take the cigarette from his hand, but he wasn't letting go.

"Why would you see her?"

"I have to see what she wants."

"You know what she wants."

All I could think of was that check, which I had no intention of cashing. "I don't think that's it."

"Of course that's it." His words hung in the air.

"She's still my mother, Deacon."

I'd broken our only rule: While we were inside the walls of this apartment, it was just us, no outside noise, but I had no one else to tell. He must have understood that, because he was calmer when he asked, "Where are you going to go?"

I knew I'd have to take her someplace with a lot of hype, someplace that would make her see I was still somebody without her. Someplace that would show her she hadn't destroyed me.

When I told Deacon this, he said, "Someplace like Glass Orchid."

Someplace exactly like Glass Orchid was what I was thinking, but even I couldn't get my name on that list. "I heard they have a six-month wait."

I hated to admit there was a place I couldn't get into. Had it been a few weeks earlier, and a nightclub, I would have been golden, but an elite celebrity restaurant was an entirely different story.

"I can get you in," he said simply.

My heart ballooned. "Really?" It was that day at the door all over again, when he gave Caroline the money and gave me exactly what I needed.

"Consider it payback. For helping me shop."

"Can you send your car, too?" Glass Orchid just wouldn't work if we had to take a taxi. Besides, as he said, it was payback.

He grinned. "To impress Caroline Turner-Martin?"

"Turner-Martin-Richards-Guerra," I corrected, kissing his cheek, his neck, his lips.

He finally put out his cigarette. "We may be able to work out a deal for that."

CHAPTER FIFTEEN

Preparing for dinner with my estranged mother was sort of like preparing for a date: the nerves, the expectations, the what-to-wear. A date was easier, though—I only had to show a bit of skin, and going into it, we both knew how the night would end. I couldn't say the same with Caroline.

"I am so glad you decided to see me, Gorgeous," she'd said when I called. "Will Burke be joining us?"

It seemed impossible that she still hadn't heard about our breakup, and I didn't have the courage to confess. I had to let her believe I could keep a man like Burke Sanders, and that unlike her, I wasn't simply dating him to get places. "I'm not sure if he'll be able to make it."

"The season's over, he must be around."

It hadn't even occurred to me that the season was over, but it was a good thing she'd mentioned it before I said he had a game. "Oh, he's around. We'll see."

I looked through my closet for an outfit that would fit the role I'd be playing that night: The role of a completely secure Manhattan socialite dating an all-star athlete. I needed to be what Daisy Breyer would have been when she grew up.

I decided on a strapless sea-green dress that I'd always wanted to wear out with Burke because it matched his eyes, but never got the chance to. If I was supposed to be Burke Sanders's girlfriend, the dress seemed like the perfect option. I slipped on Josh's sapphire cocktail ring, too. Caroline didn't know it was ten years old; it was huge, and that was all she'd care about.

My phone rang as I headed out the door, and I wondered if it was a sign—fate telling me not to go. I was afraid it would be Caroline, telling me she'd changed her mind about seeing me—thanks, but no thanks—and could she have her check back? I immediately felt torn when I saw the name Ben English.

I should have answered. He deserved it. He'd been so good to me the night I stayed over, and it didn't stop there. We'd gone to MoMA a couple days later—when I'd happily returned his key—lunch a few days after that, and then there were the flowers he'd sent, which were displayed so beautifully on the piano. A mix of roses, carnations, and lavender. There wasn't a single daisy in the bunch.

His name flashed before me, challenging me to join him for another date, daring me to keep running away from my past. But seeing Caroline was something I had to do, and I didn't have the energy to concoct a half-truth about what I was actually doing with my night. Fighting a stomach bug, I texted him. I'll call you when I'm over it.

When I made my way down to the lobby, I almost expected to see Burke there, ready to make Caroline's dreams come true. I stepped outside and was hit with a burst of cold autumn air that made me want to run in to get a coat, but I knew if I walked back into that building, I'd never leave.

I panicked when I didn't see Deacon's town car, but then I spotted a driver standing in front of a Hummer limo. It was vintage Deacon, always over the top, even just for annoyance's sake. When I'd asked him if he was sure he'd remember our agreement, he'd said, "Baby, I am going to blow your mother's socks off." It was excessive, yes, but I was at least glad he hadn't sent Jay as a chauffeur.

It took no time to get to the Plaza. I wasn't sure if that was a good thing. It wasn't until I noticed a numbness in my lip that I realized I'd been gnawing on it. I dug my lipstick out of my clutch and reapplied it before getting out of the car.

I expected Caroline to still be up in her room when I got there, that I'd have to call her and wait while she put the finishing touches on that perfect wave in her hair. When I saw her standing outside, I had to do a double take.

She was chatting it up with the doorman—apparently, she had a new fondness for doormen—and was tossing her head back with laughter, touching his forearm to express her points. He was enthralled by her. Everyone in the vicinity was. I wondered how close he was to giving her the list of VIPs who were staying at the hotel.

I waited for her to notice me, and when she didn't, I had no choice but to make my way toward her. I didn't know what to say—*Excuse me, long time no see*—and a part of me felt bad about interrupting her conversation. I cleared my throat.

She spun around and looked me in the eye, holding for a beat. Every sensation in my body froze. I was sure she had no idea who I was.

Her face broke into a radiant smile. "There she is, my Gorgeous girl." Despite my better judgment, I felt my heart warming, in part because of the familiarity of her smile, in part because I was still her Gorgeous girl.

On TV we would have hugged, and she would have told me what a fine woman I had become. In real life, she turned to the doorman and said, "Don't wait up, darling."

As if it were a last-minute thought, she gave me a Hollywood air-kiss on the cheek, her eyes glued to the vehicle stretched out before us. She wouldn't say anything to acknowledge it, but I could see the approval in her eyes.

When she slid into the car, I swore I saw her wink at the driver. I certainly saw him blushing. He closed the door behind us, and for the first time in years, there we were, alone—the only family I had, and the only family she had.

I wasn't sure what we should say to each other. In an episode of *Breyer's Town*, Dr. Breyer would have said, "Tell me, Daisy, what did you learn at school today?" I wished I'd consulted Uncle John before leaping into this, but that was ridiculous, because he was only my father on TV.

"So . . ." I began.

"So." She crossed one leg over the other, flashing the red soles of her Louboutins. I wondered how she'd afforded them, and how she'd afforded to pay me back. She didn't look like she was in dire need of money, but then again, she'd never looked that way in the past, either.

"Why are you in New York?" I couldn't believe I'd asked so quickly. The words flew out of my mouth because I had to say something, but when I realized she'd actually have to answer the question, I wanted to take it back.

"Why not?" Her attention was immediately drawn to the size of the sapphire on my hand. "Is that from Burke?"

"Yes," I said automatically. "He gave it to me for my birthday."

I waited for her to recognize that my birthday had come and gone and she hadn't called or even sent a card, but she just nodded her approval at the ring. It didn't surprise me. Caroline hated birthdays. "If you don't celebrate your birthday," she always said, "you won't really get any older."

"Good for you," she said, as if dating Burke Sanders was my greatest accomplishment. "Remember what I told you, Gorgeous. It's always good to have a backup plan, but never let him forget that he won the lottery on you, too."

I twisted the ring, thinking how Burke wouldn't even know my birthstone. If he was a backup plan, he wouldn't have been a very good one.

"Will he be meeting us at the restaurant?"

"No," I said. "He's . . . totally swamped."

I couldn't tell if she was disappointed when she tossed her hair and said, "Ah, well, comes with the territory, I suppose." She smiled with her blue eyes, which were so unlike mine that I told myself, as I had so many times in the past, that I must have gotten mine from my father, whoever he was. "It'll be nice. Just the two of us." It was the same thing she used to say when she'd take me to high tea, or to an audition, or to an agent's office, back when I still thought this was how all mothers were.

I almost told her that I missed those days, and that I'd missed her. I wanted to tell her how beautiful she looked, and tell her that despite everything, I was happy to see her. Instead, I said, "I hope so."

IF I HADN'T KNOWN GLASS ORCHID HAD JUST OPENED THAT week, I would have guessed it from the outside. There were people clamoring for tables or hoping for a peek inside, and clusters of photographers waiting for a money shot. The same guys who couldn't get enough of me when I was dating Burke and reigning over the club scene lined up in front of the Hummer, but only a few flashes went off when I got out of the car.

A willowy girl—definitely an aspiring model—stood at the podium. "No tables," she said, not even looking up from her digital screen.

"I have a table. Michaela Turner."

She still didn't look up from her list. "I have nothing under that name."

I started to feel hot, despite the cold weather, and lowered my voice so Caroline couldn't hear. "Try Deacon King."

Little Miss Attitude finally looked up and gave me a once-over. "Pardon?"

"Deacon King. Or maybe Freddie Mercury." It was just the kind of unfunny joke Deacon would pull.

She turned away and started talking into her headset. I glanced over at Caroline to see her reaction, but she didn't seem to notice. She was busy texting.

"I have nothing," the girl finally said, her snooty voice grinding on my last nerve. "I suggest you step aside. We're quite busy, as you can see."

There was no way I was stepping aside. How could Deacon have remembered the Hummer limo but forgotten Glass Orchid? I wondered if Shaunn with two *n*'s had anything to do with it. Whatever the reason, I wanted to kill him.

I finally had to ask the girl the question I hated most. "Don't you know who I am?"

She stared back at me with dull, expressionless eyes. There was no way she'd make it as a model.

"No."

"They're with me," an all-too-familiar voice said from behind. I swear to God, I could have sunk right into one of the cracks in the sidewalk.

Podium girl was immediately alight. "Mr. McKenzie!" She didn't dare look down at her screen this time. "I thought we had you for a party of two?"

I could feel myself turning candy-apple red, which was really unfortunate, because with my green dress, I must have looked like a Christmas card.

"No. It was four." I could hear the agitation in Josh's voice. There was no way I could bring myself to face him.

What the hell was Josh doing at Glass Orchid? How did he even get a table? Okay, so he had been a pretty huge name in his time, and people everywhere were still completely in love with him, but still. What the hell was he doing at Glass Orchid?

Caroline slipped into one of her phoniest smiles. "Joshua."

I didn't need to see Josh's face to know he had the same toothy grin plastered on his. I called it his you're-an-asshole grin, because that was what he was always thinking when he used it. "Caroline."

I couldn't force myself to turn around. Maybe if I stood completely still and closed my eyes, I would wake up in my bed and this whole thing would be some ridiculous dream.

"Uh, Michaela?"

Josh calling me Michaela was as strange as Deacon calling me Michaela. I'd been "Turner" since we were sixteen—whether he was making fun of me, feeling me up, or listening, fittingly enough, to my mother troubles.

I turned to face him, and there it was, his you're-an-asshole grin, which I really hoped was directed toward Caroline and not me. His blue eyes screamed, *We are so going to be talking about* this *later.*

"Josh."

"Hi, Michaela." Morgan. I hadn't even noticed her standing there. She didn't look at all intimidated by the freak show the three of us were creating, but she should have been.

"Morgan." There really must have been something wrong with my brain to finally get her name right.

"Morg," Josh began. "*This* is Michaela's mother. The famous Caroline Turner-Martin-Richards . . . Guerra. Sorry, I always forget the last one."

I would have stepped on his foot if I didn't think my spike heel would endanger any chance of him making a boy-band comeback.

Morgan shook my mother's hand. "Nice to meet you."

"Mr. McKenzie?" the once-bitchy-now-googly-eyed hostess interrupted. "Your table for four is ready."

Caroline headed in first, with Morgan straight behind. Josh leaned his head close to my ear as he passed by. "You're doing that thing."

"What thing?"

He nonchalantly gnawed on his lower lip. I didn't know whether to punch him or thank him, so I made a conscious effort to pull my lip from its position between my teeth and walked into Glass Orchid, refusing to make eye contact with anyone. I could feel Josh's eyes drilling into me during the entire route to our table.

Glass Orchid was designed to be a Thai paradise. Flowers (oddly, no orchids) hung from the walls and glass lanterns hung from the ceiling. We were supposed to take off our shoes and sit on the floor, but with what this clientele was wearing, no one followed the first rule.

Morgan had an early-morning shift the next day, so she started with a water. Caroline had the same, "But with a lemon and a lime, darling, and maybe just a splash of cayenne pepper?" I ordered the sake, and so did Josh. I knew what Caroline would say about alcohol and the skin, but I needed something to get me through the night.

No one said anything for about a minute and a half, which is really a long time when no one is talking. Josh picked up his fork and put it back down three times. He and Caroline were still competing over who could show more teeth in their grins. Morgan was still clueless.

Josh finally spoke, but I couldn't decide if that was a good thing. "So, Caroline, what brings you to New York?"

"Do I need a reason?" she asked. "Everyone needs a taste of the city once in a while, don't you agree?"

"There's no place like it," Morgan piped in. She was probably trying to be polite and cut the silence, but if she knew what was good for her, she would have kept her mouth shut and escaped out the back entrance unnoticed.

"It's great that you managed to squeeze a visit with Michaela in," Josh said, taking a sip of his wine and giving me a look. I was going to kill him.

Caroline turned to Morgan. "And what do you do, lovely?"

Morgan looked from Josh to me, like she was wondering how she'd been put in the hot seat. If she only knew Caroline was acutely aware that neither Josh nor I did much of anything worth asking about.

"I'm in medical school," she said.

"Fascinating," Caroline said. "What area of medicine?"

"Cardiology."

"Such important work." Caroline placed her hand on her chest as if she were feeling for her own questionably existent heart. "Brilliant girl you've got there, Joshua."

Josh took another gulp of wine. "Yes, I know."

Morgan smiled at him. "I think I'm the lucky one."

Of course she did. She was dating her teenage dream.

"So fitting that you're dating a cardiologist," Caroline said to Josh. "Didn't you Boyz do that music video where you dressed as shirtless heart surgeons? Funny how everything comes full circle."

Josh was silent for a second. I thought he might get up and leave. "It is truly always a joy to see you, Caroline."

Things didn't get much better once we ordered, or after the food came. I had hoped that once Josh had something to put in his mouth he'd be forced to stop talking, but with dinner came more wine.

"How long has it been since you were in the city, Caroline?" he asked. "I mean, I feel like it's been years. Years. It can't have been that long, right?"

Caroline sipped her water-with-the-works. "Life is short, Joshua. And there is civilization outside of Manhattan."

Josh snapped his fingers. "True. That is so true. Actually, Michaela used to say that all the time when we were younger.

Remember, Turner? She always wanted to go places, see things. Maybe one day move out to the West Coast. San Francisco, I think." He elbowed me. "You were going to go to school out there, remember? Guess she never got the opportunity."

I seriously considered tossing my wine in Josh's lap, but I just looked down at my jasmine rice. Coming here was a mistake. I didn't even like Thai food. Come to think of it, neither did Josh. He had too many allergies and a sensitive stomach. This place must have been Morgan's idea. She'd already mentioned twice since we arrived that she wanted to practice medicine in Thailand for a year.

"This meal is divine," Caroline said with flourish. "Don't you think, Gorgeous?" Before I could answer, she took my hand in hers. At first I thought it was a sign of affection, until she grazed my cocktail ring and said to the table, "Did you see the ring Burke bought Michaela? Have you ever seen anything so stunning?"

Josh looked from the ring, to me, and back to the ring, a flash of something resembling hurt in his eyes. "Burke bought you that." He toasted his glass to no one in particular. "What a guy."

"It's a shame he couldn't make it tonight," Caroline said. "I was looking forward to meeting him."

Josh raised his eyebrows and looked at me. I knew he'd never blow my cover, but I still feared what his next words might be. "That is a shame. I love the Colonel. He's awesome. Great guy." He took a bite of his pad thai and chased it down with sake.

Caroline looked at him with obvious distaste. As much as Josh despised my mother, she disliked him just the same. She blamed him when I wanted to put acting on the back burner so I could try to have a somewhat normal life. It never occurred to her that I was tired of getting rejected, tired of being offered horrible after-school specials, tired of gross websites counting down to my eighteenth birthday, and tired of working, period. She thought I was just a hormonal teenager who wanted to spend all my time with my teen heartthrob of a boyfriend.

"And what about you, Joshua?" she asked, clearly baiting him. "What are you up to these days?"

Josh shrugged. "Absolutely nothing. Just sitting on my ass and living off the millions I made shaking my teenage butt. I mean, *I* worked for it, right?"

"That's not true," Morgan chimed in. "Tell them about your show."

Caroline arched a perfectly groomed eyebrow. "What show?"

"Yeah, what show?" I heard myself ask. I prayed to God that Josh hadn't caved and signed on to one of the reality series he was constantly being offered.

Josh shot Morgan a look that she clearly missed, because she prattled on. "Josh is performing at the Burgundy Palace."

"You're what?" I asked.

"Performing what, exactly?" Caroline said.

"Just some music," he said. "It's really not a big deal."

A smile played on Caroline's lips. "Don't tell me the band got back together."

"No," he replied, not daring to look at me. "It's just me."

The table fell silent. I had so many questions, but I could see that Caroline had so much judgment she wanted to pass. Morgan cleared her throat. "Caroline, that dress is stunning. Is it Diane von Furstenberg?"

Caroline didn't take her eyes off Josh. She looked like she wanted to make another comment, but she put down her water glass and said, "Naturally. They're the only wrap dresses worth investing in." She stood, and her investment of a dress fell around her effortlessly. "Excuse me for a minute. Just need to use the ladies'." I was reminded of a time when I was eight and someone offered to show us the "little girls' room." Caroline told them not to patronize me.

"I have to go myself," Morgan said, standing up. "Do you mind showing me where it is?"

Once they were out of earshot, Josh wiped the practiced smile off his face and turned to me. "Okay, *seriously*?"

I wouldn't make eye contact. "What?"

"Don't give me *what*. Your *mother*? Your *mother*, Turner? What the hell is she doing here?"

"You heard her. She has things to do."

"Oh, come *on*. Do you honestly think this was a good idea? You had to tell her you were still dating Burke. What does that tell you?"

"I know what I'm doing," I lied. "And what about you? When were you going to tell me you're coming out of retirement?"

"Oh, I am not coming out of *retirement*. It's barely more than an open mic night. And don't change the subject."

"When did you stop talking to me?" I asked, but it was probably the wine speaking. "You used to tell me stuff."

He let out an emphatic "Ha. *I* used to tell *you* stuff. Classic."

"Why are you even here tonight? You hate trendy places. And you hate Thai food. And you hate getting dressed up." As the words came out of my mouth, the pieces clicked. "Oh my God. You're going to propose?"

He started choking. *"What?"* He took a long drink of Morgan's water, his eyes watery, his face purple. I took that as a no.

"You know, a person can date," he said once he regained his breath. "You don't have to marry everyone who turns up, contrary to what your mother may think. And why are *you* here? I mean, aside from Caroline wanting to show off her new rack."

My jaw dropped. "Do not look at my mother's chest." Though, now that he mentioned it, I hadn't quite been able to put my finger on what was different. He may have been right about the implants.

Caroline and Josh's non-fiancée returned to our table, and I was almost relieved, until Morgan said, "Your mother was just telling me about your days on TV. Could you really memorize an entire script in a day?"

I wondered why Caroline had chosen to wait until I was out of earshot to tell that story. I had to wonder how much of the truth she'd embellished. "People would marvel," she said. "They couldn't believe she was only a child."

"Really, Caroline," Josh said, all faux-polite airs out the window, "why are you here?"

Caroline looked from Josh, to Morgan, to me. "I didn't really want to do this in front of an audience." Who was she fooling—she wanted to do everything in front of an audience. "I'm getting married."

Josh took his napkin, folded it, and placed it on the table, as if his work were done.

"What?" I could hear my shock coming through, in spite of myself. "Marrying who?"

"His name is Peter Jacobs," she said simply. "He's a television producer. I had hoped you'd be able to meet him tonight, but he had a meeting, so some other time."

Nothing Caroline did or said should have surprised me, but even after three husbands, I hadn't seen this coming. "How did you even meet him?"

"On vacation. Whirlwind romance. You know how it is."

"And you're marrying him." Maybe I'd heard wrong, because she'd been so matter-of-fact about it. There was no emotion, no stars in her eyes, not that there ever had been in the past.

"Not until next year," she said. "But yes."

It didn't make sense. If she was getting married to another wealthy fool, why did she need to see me? I was usually her last resort, her backup when they left her.

"So how long will you be in New York?" I asked. "Are you moving here?"

"Possibly," she said. "We haven't ironed out all of the wrinkles."

I wondered if I was one of the wrinkles. Or maybe the only wrinkle. How was I going to function in New York with Caroline living around the block? Did she expect she would marry Peter What's-His-Name and we would all be one big happy family?

The bill came, and I somehow managed to compose myself enough to reach for my purse. Josh pushed my hand away under the table and handed the waiter his credit card. I wasn't sure if Caroline witnessed it, but if she did, she never said thank you.

Once we were back in the limo heading to the Plaza, just the two of us, she started in on Josh. "Can you imagine? He used to sell out stadiums, now he's playing a no-name nightclub. Not that that band of his had much substance, but this is what happens when people squander their talent."

That was when I heard myself ask, "There's more to this engagement, isn't there?"

She looked at me. "What do you mean?"

"What aren't you telling me?"

Her smile was almost proud as she touched my cheek. "You've always been too smart for your own good, haven't you?"

"What is it." It didn't come out as a question. I was tired of questioning everything with her.

"Peter is producing a new soap opera," she said. "It's going to be very cutting-edge, very borderline for daytime TV. And it will be a steady paycheck."

"For who?"

And then I saw the look in her eyes. It was the same look she gave me when I was five, when she told me how much fun it would be to be on TV instead of going to school.

"For you, of course."

I should have known. I should have known she didn't want to just see me.

"I don't act anymore."

"Darling girl, of course you do," she said. "You haven't acted in a while. You'll always be an actress."

"So *you* decided." My skin grew hot. She'd decided when I was four years old how my life was going to play out. None of it had been my choice.

"You're being ridiculous," she said. "You can't go on doing nothing. You're twenty-six years old."

I would not let myself cry in front of her. I would not let her see how she had ruined both that night and who I had become.

When the driver let her out at the Plaza, I refused to look at her.

"Call me once you've thought it through," she said.

The only thing I said in response was, "I'm twenty-seven."

And that was it. She went up to her room, without a care in the world, off to go to bed with her powerful TV producer. And I was left in the back seat of a stupid Hummer, provided by my engaged ex-boyfriend, wearing the dress I selected because, if I was being honest, it was my mother's favorite color.

CHAPTER SIXTEEN

It took Caroline exactly twelve hours to get the audition sides for *Crescent Grove* to me. The envelope had come by courier service, and inside were ten pages of a script highlighting a character named Foster Greene. I only read the first line—"Miss me, bitches?"—before stuffing the whole thing under *The Bluest Eye*, my latest purchase from the women's lit syllabus. If I took the role, I could kiss my education-by-proxy goodbye.

Deacon's name flashed on my phone for the third time that morning. "Mickie," he'd said in his first message. "I need you to call me back." I didn't. Whatever excuse he had for humiliating me in front of my mother, I didn't want to hear it. If he cared that much, he would have explained in his voicemail, or showed up and begged forgiveness. If he really cared, he wouldn't have forgotten the reservation in the first place. I shoved my phone under a couch cushion and headed downstairs to the gym.

I wasn't doing the show—I couldn't do the show—but the idea of prancing around in lingerie on TV was enough to get me on the treadmill. When a punching bag opened up, I gave that a try, hoping to channel some of my frustration over Deacon and Caroline. All it did was batter my hands, but I kept at it until someone tapped my shoulder and I almost slugged him—accidentally, of course.

"Jesus, Josh. Do you want a black eye?"

His pale skin and scowl revealed how hungover he was. "Don't worry, Turner. You're not exactly a heavyweight." The casting directors of *Crescent Grove* would be elated to hear that.

"You kind of messed up my flow," I told him, because now that I'd stopped, I sort of felt like collapsing.

"Sorry. How are you holding up?"

"From the looks of it, better than you."

"You know what I mean, Turner." He leaned on the equipment.

"If you want to know what happened with Caroline, just ask."

"It's none of my business if you don't want to talk about it." He took a long drink of water. He was in no shape to be working out. I didn't think he'd had any more sake than I had, but I guess he had a lower tolerance—which really said more about me than it did about Josh.

"She wants me to do a soap opera," I spilled, because I had to. "The guy she's marrying is a producer. That's why she's here, and that's the only reason she wanted to see me."

All he said was, "Christ, she sucks," and I was so thankful that he didn't ask if I was planning on going for it. I'm sure the thought didn't cross his mind. Then again, he wasn't the one who had to hear Caroline's speech about how I couldn't go on squandering my talent and doing nothing with my life.

My knuckles were already starting to turn purple. "I probably shouldn't have punched this thing without gloves, huh?"

"I didn't want to be the one to say it." He bit the skin around his thumbnail. "Hey, if you don't end up in the hospital with a broken hand, I didn't know if you maybe wanted to come to my thing tomorrow night."

"What thing?"

"At the Burgundy Palace."

"That's tomorrow night?"

"Yeah."

His nonchalance made me want to scream. "You need to tell me what the deal with that is right now."

He scratched his five-o'clock shadow. "It's not a big deal."

"So you keep mentioning."

"I'm just playing a short set. Like eight songs. I thought it might be good to get my feet wet again. Get my music out there. See if I still feel like doing it."

If that was the case, maybe Josh wouldn't think it was so bad if I auditioned for what's-his-face's soap opera.

"Are you going to do Boyz of the Nation songs?"

"God, no," he said, which made me a little relieved. I wasn't sure "Girl, Hit Me Up with a Page" would have the same effect it once did. "It's just some stuff I've been working on. It's not a big deal."

The fact that *it's not a big deal* was becoming Josh's mantra made it clear it was a big deal. "Of course I'll be there. But I think you should shave first."

And then Josh did something he'd been doing since we were kids. He gave me a little flick on the nose, thankfully leaving out the noogie that normally followed. "You're all right, Turner."

A petite blonde in a hot pink sports bra approached us with a scowl that didn't quite match the rhinestone Sassy scrawled across her ass. "Are you guys done with this? You really shouldn't hold up the equipment if you're just going to chat."

"It's yours," I told her, stepping away from the coveted punching bag. It had nothing to do with her attitude; I was way too tired to keep going. I obviously wasn't much of an exerciser.

As we made our way out of the gym, I asked Josh, "Do you know what you're going to wear?"

"Where?"

I almost hit him. "To your show."

"Oh." He'd known very well what I meant. "No, I'll figure something out tomorrow."

"Joshua Thomas McKenzie—"

"Here we go."

"This is your first public appearance in—" He shot me a look. It was a sensitive subject. I got that more than anyone. "In a long time. I'll help you. But with the contents of your closet, we're really going to have to reach."

IF JOSH WAS GOING TO MAKE A COMEBACK, THE BURGUNDY Palace was a good place to do it. It was a decent-sized club—not too big, but not a hole-in-the-wall, either. I couldn't help but compare it to the last Boyz of the Nation show I'd been to, when they played three consecutive sold-out nights at Madison Square Garden. I wondered if starting so high, so young meant the only way to go was down.

The club was starting to fill in by the time I got there, mostly with girls about my age and younger who were obviously Boyz of the Nation fans. Some of them wore their old T-shirts with Josh's seventeen-year-old face on them. I didn't know if I wanted to cringe or smile.

The VIP section wasn't really a section at all—it was one table off to the side, where Morgan was already standing, flagging me down as I walked in the door. I was almost coming around to Morgan—she certainly handled the freak show that Caroline, Josh, and I created better than most—but we had nothing in common. I wished I could have brought Ben along as a buffer, but within five minutes he'd have figured out that I wasn't an image consultant, that my name wasn't Kayla, and that the girl he thought he liked didn't even exist. Besides, I'd canceled our date the night before, maintaining the feigned stomach-bug story. Between Caroline and Deacon and those audition sides, I couldn't find the energy to be someone else.

"Your outfit is incredible," Morgan said, taking in the suede booties, lace-up miniskirt, and sheer white tee I'd paired with a black bra. "Your closet must be to die for."

It was. Only these days, I had very few places to wear any of it. I supposed that would all change if I went back to work, between talk show appearances, and press junkets, and cast parties. The idea of rehashing my Daisy days in interviews, recounting scripted stories that were meant to sound endearing and off the cuff, was enough to exhaust me, even if the on-set camaraderie and steady paycheck did have some appeal.

"You look great, too," I told her, pushing the possibility of *Crescent Grove* from my mind, at least for the night. "How's Josh?"

She let out a sigh. "God, he's been a nervous wreck all day. He even snuck in a third run this afternoon. I told him there's nothing to worry about. Look how excited these people are."

I looked around the club. It was still sparse enough to see that people did seem excited—doing Boyz of the Nation dance moves and squealing how they'd soon be seeing Joshie Mac.

"What do you mean a third run? Has he been going for multiple runs a day?" Josh never skipped a morning run, but I'd never seen him do more than that.

"Usually two. I got him a pair of running shoes for his birthday and he's already wearing through them."

I waited to see if she thought that was concerning. She was studying to be a cardiologist. She should know. "Is it okay for someone to run that much?" I asked.

"Sure. If they're healthy and active." She shrugged like it was nothing, so I told myself it was nothing.

My phone started buzzing—Deacon again. He hadn't left a message since the day before, but he had called again that morning, and several times that afternoon. It took everything in me not to pick up that phone, to hear what he had to say for himself, but if he was really that sorry, he wouldn't have screwed me over in the first place.

I stood up. "I'm going to check on Josh."

"He'd love that," Morgan said. "It might help with his nerves."

I couldn't remember the last time I'd seen Josh nervous. He usually walked through life like nothing bothered him. But when I got to the tiny backstage area, I could see Morgan was right.

He was pacing back and forth, dressed in the white button-down shirt and jeans I'd helped him choose the day before, tapping his stomach with one hand, gnawing on the thumbnail of the other. I hadn't seen him like this since he presented at the Teen Choice Awards for the first time.

"Looking good, McKenzie."

Josh turned and faced me. He looked a little nauseated. "Did Morgan send you back here to check on me?"

"No. And hello to you, too."

"I don't want a pep talk. I just puked." Yep. Definitely like the Teen Choice Awards.

"Were you at the sake again?"

"Turner . . ."

"Are you pregnant?"

Still no smile. He only asked, "Why the hell am I doing this?"

I didn't know how to answer him, so I said, "You tell me."

He jiggled his knee back and forth. "I needed to do something. Try something. I'm twenty-seven years old and haven't worked in five years."

I'd never seen Josh act like this before. I thought he enjoyed spending his days watching *Godfather* marathons and hanging out at the gym. For the first time, I saw fear of failure in his eyes, and I completely understood.

"Remember what I always told you," I said. "Breathe from the gut. Annunciate, articulate, exaggerate. Do it for the girls in the back—"

A smile started to surface when he finished, "Just don't do it with them."

It was our shtick when we were sixteen, when Josh was starting to look like somebody really successful, and I was starting to look like someone who once was.

He let me hug him. "Thanks for coming," he said. "Really. I wasn't even going to tell you I was doing this. I thought you'd think it was stupid."

"It's far from stupid." I wanted to tell him I was proud of him for putting himself back out there, for taking a risk and trying something. If Josh could pull this off, maybe I wasn't as stuck as I thought.

Before going back out in the club, I told him, "You're going to be great, McKenzie." And he would be. He had to be.

The club was still half empty when I got back to the table. Josh would be going on shortly. There had to be more people who cared about seeing him. He'd been the star of the biggest boy band in the world.

"Where do you think everyone is?" I asked. I didn't know why I was so nervous. Josh was always okay. But I needed this night to be triumphant for him.

Morgan didn't look as concerned as she should have. "I think this might be it. But that's okay. This is his first show in a long time."

"What did the venue do to promote it?"

"I have no idea." She looked surprised that I'd ask such a thing, but someone should have been asking. "I'm sure plenty."

I wasn't so sure. I couldn't begin to imagine how fast Josh's gut would drop when he walked out and saw so much empty space. He'd only ever played amphitheaters, arenas, and stadiums. Performing for less than two hundred people would be a very different experience, and he didn't even have his four bandmates there to lean on.

My phone again started buzzing in my purse. Deacon. According to my missed call list, he'd tried me twice while I was talking to Josh. He always did have the worst timing imaginable.

The lights dimmed and the sound system started playing Van Halen's "Jump," Josh's warm-up song. He used to have the sound guys play it before every one of the Boyz' performances. I'd forgotten how superstitious he was.

"You really think this is everyone who's coming?" I asked again.

Morgan looked around. "It's not that bad."

It was that bad.

Another missed call signal flashed on my phone, then it started ringing again almost immediately.

"I have to run to the restroom." I snuck down a semi-quiet corridor and finally whipped out my phone. "What?" I couldn't wait to hear it. I couldn't wait to hear his excuse for Glass Orchid, and why he had called me a total of eighteen message-less times in the past twenty-four hours.

"Michaela? It's Jay."

My chest clenched. "What's wrong?"

I couldn't hear him all that great, but I could tell he was in the midst of some kind of chaos. I tried to tell myself that if something had happened—if something was seriously wrong—it would have been on the news. Okay, so I didn't watch the news. But I would have known.

"I suggest you get to your apartment as soon as possible," Jay said, so goddamn cryptic I wanted to scream.

"Is he hurt?"

"No one's hurt," was all he'd say. "But you need to get home." And then he hung up, or was disconnected, or something.

"Jump" was about halfway through when I got back to the table. The crowd hadn't gotten any bigger. "I think I need to go. I'm starting to feel really sick." Half-truth. My pulse points were exploding and the room was definitely closing in on me.

Morgan stood up. "Oh my God, are you okay?"

"It's just a stomach thing." I grabbed my coat. "Tell Josh I'm sorry." Before I could even get her reaction, I bolted across the floor and out of the club. I could not let Josh see me leaving as he walked onstage.

I was in a cab before I could even button my coat, and when I got home, I breezed past Phil and caught the look he was giving me, like he was the keeper of some guarded knowledge of what I'd been up to, even though I had no idea.

The elevator up to my apartment had never seemed so slow. My heart was still beating heavily. I was sure the Burgundy Palace had filled up by now. It must have. I felt bad leaving Josh, but he'd understand.

When I stepped off the elevator, the sensation from my pulse was replaced with the vibrations of pulsating music. As I made my way toward my apartment, the sounds grew louder, and the worry and concern I felt for Deacon was blanketed by absolute fury.

A thick cloud of smoke hit me when I opened the door, and I choked back the stench of cigarettes, pot, and tequila. There were spilled drinks, stubbed-out cigarette butts, and tipped-over ashtrays. The vase containing Ben's flowers was knocked over, the stems and petals scattered and broken all over the carpet. Deacon's horrific new backup band—that jackass Douglas included—infested every corner of my apartment. They were all strategically seated—some of them drunk, all of them stoned—holding their instruments lamely in their hands like some poor excuse for a jam band. The music, instead of coming from them, was coming from my speakers, and their fearless leader was sprawled on my couch. That terrible leather couch I'd never wanted, that he'd insisted on, that I'd kept all these years only for him.

Jay stepped forward, as if he was the responsible one. "Thanks for coming down." To my own apartment. "He started dialing the wrong numbers after a while, so he wanted me to call."

I couldn't speak. I was seething.

Deacon's eyes slid open and he grinned a wide drunken smile I knew so well. "There she is, my Queen."

He held out his arm to take my hand, but I wouldn't go near him, despite how pitiful he looked. "You look pretty, Mickie Mouse." He stretched his fingers, as if that would help him reach me.

I knew his patterns, and as furious as I was, a part of my heart broke for him. Something had to have triggered this drunken stupor. Looking around at all the sponges latched on to him, though, all the sponges he had hired to do just that—Douglas, *Douglas*, who had the nerve to show up here after the whole scene with CeCe—made the anger outweigh the pity.

I finally managed four words. "Jay. Get everyone out."

If he contested it, if any of them did, I would lose it. They must have sensed it, because one by one, Deacon's hangers-on filed out of my apartment, guitars and tambourines in hand.

Jay started toward Deacon but I managed to block him. "Leave him here."

He looked like he might put up a fight but was afraid of how I'd react. "You can't very well bring him home like this," I said, and he knew I was right. I wasn't the girl he was marrying, but I was the girl who would make sure he didn't get into any more trouble that night. I was the girl who would roll him on his side so he could sleep, and clean up his vomit every hour. Wordlessly, Jay left us alone.

"I've had a bad week, Mickie Mouse," Deacon said, his voice bordering on a moan. He only called me Mickie Mouse at his absolute highest level of inebriation.

"Have you." I wasn't going to lecture him or fight with him. He wouldn't even remember it if I did.

"They made me write a song for a cartoon. A cartoon movie. And I did it."

I went into the kitchen and poured him a tall ice water in a plastic cup. I'd learned my lesson a few years back after he shattered a glass, slicing his hand the night before a show.

"Drink this," I said, putting it in front of him. "And go to sleep." He'd probably spill it in a matter of minutes, but with the state of my apartment, what was one spilled water?

"It's called 'Believe in You.' The song. That's what it's called. Can you believe I wrote a song called 'Believe in You'? It's such a piece of shit."

"I'm sure it's beautiful," I said, and I was sure it was. Every song he wrote was beautiful, even the terrible ones.

"Guess how long it took me to write it?"

"I have no idea, Deacon."

"Nine minutes and forty-two seconds."

"Wow," I said, trying to remove his shoes.

"I made a bet with myself I could do it in under ten. And I did."

I thought of the bets he used to make with Petie, or any of the guys from Reign. They made bets to challenge him. These new guys just wanted a buck and a line about Deacon King on their résumés.

I started picking up the cups and crushed flowers. My housekeeper was going to hate me. "Is that why you forgot about Glass Orchid?" I didn't know why I asked. I should have waited until he was more coherent, but it's not really a question when you already know the answer.

"What?"

"Nothing, Deacon."

"Shit." He rubbed his face. "The restaurant. Shit." He put one foot on the ground like he wanted to get up but couldn't.

"Just forget it," I said, and he already had, because he was now passed out. I put a blanket on him, even though he'd probably puke on it, and moved his leg back up on the couch so he wouldn't have a cramp in the morning. I removed my heels and looked at the clock. Josh was probably halfway through his set. I'd catch up with him the next day, and he'd tell me how great he did, and that everyone loved him, and he wouldn't even mind that I had to leave. Maybe I'd take him to breakfast and explain. Of course, I'd have to think about what I was going to tell him. But for the moment, all I could do was open up a trash bag and attempt to clean up the mess.

CHAPTER SEVENTEEN

I've been known to stay in bed to avoid facing reality. Take the week Caroline's tell-all was published, or that time they printed pictures of me taking a nasty drunken spill outside of Club Indigo, or really, after any one of my encounters with Travis Howard. As long as I could stay under the protection of my sheets, I could pretend that whatever was going on beyond my bedroom door never existed. On this morning, I could pretend that Deacon hadn't trashed my apartment, that I hadn't abandoned Josh. If I really wanted to, I could even pretend that Caroline was still in Fiji, or wherever the hell she'd been living last.

I expected Deacon to be gone by the time I got up. I expected to find a vacated couch—spilled drinks, cigarette butts, and the after-party stench of liquor and vomit the only hints he was ever there. I didn't expect that after I pulled myself out of bed, after I showered and thought about what I was going to say to Josh, that Deacon would still be face down on the white leather sofa.

I thought about throwing something at him—a shoe or a book—as I would have in the old days. I thought about slamming doors and cabinets to shake him from his sleep. Of course, even that wouldn't work. His hearing was shot from years of touring. As angry as I was, I decided I'd better check that he was still breathing. I stepped closer and could see the slow rise and fall of his back under his thin gray T-shirt. As if he knew I was watching him, he turned so I had the perfect view of his daisy tattoo. I swear I could have smothered him with a throw pillow, but then I would have had to explain what he was doing in my apartment in the first place.

In the name of damage control—and also to prevent myself from inflicting any physical harm on Deacon—I headed down to Josh's apartment. I knew if I didn't take care of this first thing, I'd be thinking about it all day. I had that sick sensation in my stomach I used to get before an audition. Back then, Caroline always told me the only way to get rid of it was to practice, practice, practice, so in the elevator, I went over exactly what I was going to tell Josh. I'd stick with the same thing I told Ben nights earlier: stomach bug. No one asks questions when you tell them you have a stomach bug.

As I knocked on his door, I wondered if I was making a mistake. He'd had a big night. Maybe he and Morgan were still celebrating. Besides, my stomach bug story needed work. I was about to turn away when he opened the door.

He greeted me with the same look he'd given me when we were sixteen, when I told him that Caroline wanted me to see less of him. One part disheartened, one part defeated, and one part pure disappointment in me. He also looked like he'd just rolled out of bed.

"Did I wake you?" It was almost noon. Normally, Josh had already had his morning run and daily visit to the coffee shop.

"No," he said. "I've been up."

His tone matched his expression, and I wanted to tell him that I got it, that he was mad at me, that I was mad at myself. "Can I come in?" I asked.

He shrugged and headed wordlessly back inside. His TV was turned to some badly acted action movie, and the clothing options we'd gone over two days before were strewn on his furniture. In spite of it all, his place was in better shape than mine.

He kept his back to me as he pulled a box of Fruity Pebbles from one of his cabinets. To his shoulder blades, I said, "I'm sorry about last night."

"Don't worry about it." I could tell he wanted me to worry about it.

"No, seriously, I'm sorry," I said again. "I wasn't feeling good. It's no excuse—"

"You want some?" he asked, pouring himself a bowl of cereal.

"What?"

"Cereal. Do you want some?"

"No, thanks," I said, but wondered if I should have taken him up on it as a peace offering. "Where's Morgan?"

"Working," he said. "Unlike you and me, most people go to work every day."

It was a gut punch, and I deserved it. "I came over to apologize about last night. Really, I didn't want to leave."

He finally turned toward me, taking a bite of his cereal. "Then why did you?"

My mouth opened, but it was hard to find my words. "I just told you. I felt sick."

He nodded. "Stomach bug?"

Now I really was nauseated. I'd never used that excuse on Josh. I'd never needed to. He couldn't have known it was a lie. "Yeah."

He didn't look right at me when he said, "Yeah, well, you didn't miss much."

"Don't be ridiculous. I'm sure you were great. I want to hear all about it."

He didn't say anything. He moved over to the couch and focused his attention on his giant TV, sloshing milk over the side of his bowl when he sat.

"Look, I know you're mad at me," I said. "But I don't know what you want me to do."

He finally looked me in the eye. "You may find this hard to believe, Turner, but everything is not always about you."

I swallowed. I deserved what he was saying, I knew that I did, but this was Josh. He couldn't stay angry at me. I waited for him to say something, to tell me what I could do to make it up to him. He just sat there, eating his cereal.

"I'll be at your next one," I told him, then added a phrase I rarely said. "I promise."

He snorted into his Fruity Pebbles and one went flying out of the bowl. When we were teenagers, Josh lived off cereal. I didn't realize he still did.

I sank into the couch next to him, pulling a blue button-down shirt out from underneath me. "Please don't be mad at me. I really mean it. I'll be at your next show. I can't help it if I was sick." I'd said it so much I was starting to believe it.

"There's not going to be another show."

I'd forgotten how he used to be after his concerts. In his Boyz of the Nation days, he would harp for hours on end about one flubbed dance move, one no one noticed but him. "What do you mean?"

"The show sucked. You missed nothing. The end."

I thought back to the half-empty club and had a feeling it was time to stop apologizing. "What happened?"

He put his bowl down on the coffee table and leaned back, scratching the blond stubble that, despite my advice, he had refused to shave. "Where should I start? With the fact that I had to sing to a sea of my own face on everyone's T-shirts? Or that they had absolutely no desire to hear my music? They just kept throwing roses at me, and begging me to sing 'Only for

You, Girl,' and asking where Jesse was." Jesse was Josh's biggest competition in BOTN, the second most popular member according to poster and button sales. After leaving the band, he had a successful career on Broadway and a few solo hits. We hated Jesse.

"One girl kept shouting for me to do the dance moves," he said. "I was so desperate up there I almost did."

"You should be flattered," I tried to convince him. "You probably remind them of their childhood. It was probably such a thrill—"

"Bullshit," he said. "If you really felt that way, you'd be at every *Breyer's Town* reunion you're offered. I never should have done it. It was stupid to think I could try something without being thought of as Joshie Mac."

"But you *can*," I told him, needing it to be true.

"How would you know? You weren't even there. And you know what, I'm glad. I really am. The fewer people who witnessed it the better."

I didn't know what to say. I wanted to find the right words, to tell him that he couldn't give up, that he would find his way if he only kept trying. But he was right, I hadn't been there. I couldn't tell him how great he'd been if I wasn't even there to see it.

"Josh—" I began, having no idea what to follow it up with. Josh always knew the right thing to say to me, when my mother left, when I dropped out of school, when Deacon broke up with me—always. Now, when he needed me, I came up empty.

"Just get out of here, Turner. Seriously. I need you to not be here right now."

I stood, wishing he could have yelled at me, been outright angry with me, something. I'd been prepared for an argument, but I didn't know what to do when he shut me out.

"I'm going to go get breakfast," I said. "Do you want to come with me? Breakfast in the afternoon? My treat."

He held up his bowl. "All set."

I stood there for a minute, then headed toward the door. "I'll call you later?"

He didn't respond. I told myself he didn't hear me, but I knew that was just another of my half-truths.

I NEEDED TIME TO THINK, BUT I COULDN'T GO HOME, SO I went to the coffee shop down the block. Josh's coffee shop. I wondered if the employees were missing their favorite customer.

I ordered my coffee and took a seat in one of the booths. The sick part was that I considered ordering one for Deacon, too. I definitely wasn't ready to forgive him, but I knew he'd have a monstrous headache when he woke up, and I didn't have any coffee back at the apartment. Then again, I was sure he'd be gone the minute he got up. He had a fiancée to get home to.

My phone rang and I started to relax, certain that Josh was ready to talk. I'd go back and I'd apologize again and maybe he'd say something curt, but then everything would be fine. When I saw it was Katrina Wilder calling, I felt nothing but guilt.

Her wedding invitation had been sitting on my counter for weeks. I didn't want to go, but I also knew it would be wrong not to, so I kept telling myself I'd think about it tomorrow. I hated going to these things. I hated being the non-well-adjusted Breyer. I hated being reminded again and again of how stagnant my life was. But I also hated that I hated going. I wanted to be able to show up and be all smiles for Katrina and enjoy the company of the people who'd known me since I was seven and claimed they loved me as family. I wanted to believe them, especially since they'd treated me better than my own family had.

"I'm sorry I didn't RSVP sooner," I told her after we'd

said our hellos. "I'll be there. I've just—I've had a lot going on lately." Because I've been known to be insincere, and because I needed her to know I was telling the truth, I said again, "I'm really sorry I didn't RSVP sooner."

"It's okay," she said, still cheerful. "I know how busy you are."

I looked around the coffee shop, at the people rushing in and out, all with someplace to be. I wasn't all that busy.

The main thing she needed to know was if I'd be having the chicken, beef, or fish, and I said the chicken would be great, please. Maybe this chat wouldn't be as bad as I thought. Maybe this would be the easiest conversation I'd have all day.

"And Josh? Do you know what he'll want?"

My throat went dry. Of course she thought Josh would be my date. Ever since we were sixteen, he'd joined me at every "family function," mostly because I needed someone in the cab with me, convincing me to go in when I wanted to back out. He'd chat with everyone at the party, pose for pictures with Uncle John's daughters and nieces, cover for me if I needed to disappear for a while, and he always, always had a great one-liner about Mrs. Wilder's jazzy outfits.

"Um, I'm not sure if he's going to make it. I know he'd love to, but he might not be around."

Love may have been an overstatement, but he'd always liked Katrina and Uncle John, and they adored him. At Uncle John's twenty-fifth wedding anniversary, he put one arm around Josh and one arm around me, and in that fatherly tone he always took, said, "Thanks for looking out for our girl all these years." Josh simply replied, "Don't worry about her. She takes care of herself."

"But Josh is always there," Katrina said.

I wished I could have said the same for myself. Maybe she was right, though. This was Josh. We'd get through this in a couple days, and by the time Katrina's wedding rolled around, everything would be back to normal. Katrina believed it. I had to believe it. "You're right. He'll have the chicken."

After hanging up, I sat there, thinking about the last time I'd been to the coffee shop with Josh. That day, he'd seemed so content, reading his paper, drinking his coffee. I hated to see him hurt. I hated that I had hurt him. I wanted to go back and apologize, to make things right, but I knew Josh. He needed time to cool off.

It was nearly 3 p.m. Deacon was either still passed out or back home with his fiancée like nothing had ever happened. I wasn't ready for the possibility of facing him, or the idea of dealing with my trashed apartment. I wished I could be someone else, at least for a little while. Someone with a normal mother and a clean home and a life not ripping apart at the seams.

And then I remembered that I could.

I KNEW TWO THINGS ABOUT BEN ENGLISH—WHERE HE taught, and that he worked until three thirty every day. I got there at quarter past and sat on a bench outside, waiting like a schoolgirl with a crush. Although school had been out for an hour, students milled about in clusters. There were girls with fake tans who looked like miniature versions of CeCe and every other faux friend I had before her, jocks with their assorted jackets and jerseys, kids dressed in black with piercings and eyeliner, studious types talking about college apps and National Honor Society. I had never been to a normal high school, but these kids looked straight out of every after-school special I'd ever done. Except on TV, kids who were different migrated toward each other—the star quarterback hung out with the class clown, the editor of the newspaper, and the homecoming queen. These real-life kids had already learned to separate. They knew where they fit. As pathetic as it sounds, I felt like they had a better sense of who they were than I did.

At three thirty-five, Ben emerged from the building, looking every bit the attractive young teacher on said after-school specials. The AP kids waved at him, two girls blushing as they called, "Bye, Mr. English!"

Ben waved back. "See you tomorrow, guys. Nicole, I'll have your recommendation ready in the morning. I promise."

I couldn't help but notice that when he promised something, there was no question he meant it.

He started to walk the other way and I scrambled off the bench. "Ben!"

To say he looked surprised would be an understatement. "Kayla, what are you doing here?"

The paper cup felt tepid in my hand. "I brought you a coffee. But I think it's cold now. I didn't really think it through."

He took it and smiled. He was the first person all day who looked happy to see me. "Thank you. This is such a nice surprise."

"I didn't know how you took it, so . . ." I pulled the sugar and cream packets out from my coat pocket and held the handful out to him.

"Thanks." He took them all, but didn't do anything with the coffee. "You're feeling better?"

I almost asked what he was talking about before remembering I'd canceled our last date because of the feigned stomach bug. "Yes. Much. It must have been a forty-eight-hour thing."

"Yeah, there seems to be a lot of that going around." The way he so easily believed me was a comfort. He had no reason to suspect I'd be anything other than honest.

He stood there like he was waiting for more on why I'd come. On TV, the girl would have surprised the guy, he would have been happy, then the show would cut to commercial, leaving you to infer they were about to have a great day. I hadn't thought past the coffee.

"Are you busy?" I asked. "I was wondering if you wanted to hang out. We could go to the bookstore. Or another art gallery." I tried to think of something a normal person might suggest. "Mini golf?"

"Are you not working today?" He asked it so innocently, and I hoped my face maintained some composure. Of course he thought I'd be working. Of course I should have been. My mother would agree.

"My afternoon's wide open," I said.

"The beauty of being self-employed," he said, like he should have thought of that in the first place. "I'd love to hang out, but we have parent–teacher conferences starting in an hour. I was just going to meet up with some of the other teachers for a coffee while we wait. Not that I don't appreciate this one." He added the last part quickly and took a sip to prove his point.

"No, right, of course." I felt like a fool for just showing up, for assuming he'd be free. "I was just in the neighborhood meeting a client and was about to pop over to the Bookery and thought, Hey, why don't I see what Ben's up to? But I should have texted."

"No, I'm glad you came."

He looked like he was about to say something more, but then a woman around our age came over and asked, "Hey, Ben, you ready?"

"Yeah, one second, Rachel."

"Sure. So sorry to interrupt." Rachel turned to me like she expected me to be another teacher, then stopped short. "Oh! Oh my God."

My coat immediately started itching my skin. I prayed that she was just embarrassed for barging into a conversation, but I knew that look. I'd known it since I was seven years old.

"It's you," she said, like she was telling me. Like I wasn't desperately aware.

"You guys know each other?" Ben asked.

I didn't say anything. I wished I could have said she had me mistaken for someone else, but Rachel was already shaking her head.

"No, no, of course not," she said. "I was just a big fan. I mean, I still am! I shouldn't have said *was*. That was rude. *Holy cannoli!*" She laughed awkwardly, like she almost couldn't believe she'd just said Daisy's catchphrase to my face.

"I am so confused by what's happening right now," Ben said. If there were an inkling in the recesses of my mind that he might have been onto me this whole time, his baffled expression was enough to wipe it away.

"Haven't you ever watched *Breyer's Town*?" Rachel asked him before turning back to me, face flushed. "Not that you didn't do other things. Um . . . there was that movie."

Another guy approached, a messenger bag slung over his shoulder. "You ready?" he asked Ben and Rachel before turning to me. "Holy shit."

It was better than *holy cannoli.*

"It was nice meeting you," I said to them both with a hurried wave. I nodded to Ben. "I'll see you around, okay?"

"Kayla," he said, following after me. I almost didn't stop, but I owed him that much. "What was that about?"

"Nothing." I could have left it at that and let his friends explain, but he was looking at me so perplexed I had to give him something. "I used to be on TV. So sometimes people recognize me and it gets awkward." I flashed him jazz hands, as if that didn't make it more awkward.

"Oh." He looked like he didn't know what to make of it. I couldn't blame him. It wasn't the kind of information anyone would expect on a random Thursday afternoon about the person they were maybe sort of dating.

"Yeah. So. Anyway. You go have fun and I'll talk to you sometime." I turned around and walked away without looking back. It wasn't until I was halfway home that I thought maybe I should have given him one last glance. I knew his friends would tell him over coffee about my entire history—not just Daisy, but Dirty Daisy, too. Maybe I should have savored a last look from the one person who believed I could be somebody else.

WHEN I GOT BACK TO MY APARTMENT, I EXPECTED IT TO be empty and torn apart, but someone had cleaned up. It wasn't perfect by any means, but it was better than the night before, and the entire place smelled distinctly of cleaning products instead of pot and alcohol. There was still the aroma of burning cigarettes, but it wasn't day-old. It was coming from Deacon.

He had the top of the piano open and was leaning over it, messing with the strings. He was concentrating so hard I almost felt like I was interrupting him.

"Where have you been all day?" he had the nerve to ask.

All I said was, "Out."

He nodded, and I couldn't tell if he was nodding in response to what I'd said or nodding out of distraction.

"What are you doing?" I asked.

"Tuning the piano."

"Do you even know what you're doing?"

He finally looked up, hurt. "What kind of question is that?"

I knew he knew what he was doing. When we first met, before he got his band off the ground, he repaired and restored pianos. What I meant was he had no business being there, he had no right to be tuning the piano as if nothing had happened. What I meant was, *Do you even know what you're doing to me?*

He abandoned his work and faced me. "I'm an asshole."

I crossed my arms. "I know."

Obviously, that wasn't the reaction he was looking for, because he threw up his hands. "Mickie, I said I was sorry!"

"No you didn't. You said, 'I'm an asshole.'"

He looked down and rolled his little wrench around in his fist. "I'm trying to apologize. Last night got out of hand. It's been a rough week."

"I know, Deacon." I unraveled my scarf, resisting the urge to strangle him with it. "I know all about your rough week. You told me last night."

He stayed quiet. "They're coming tomorrow to clean your carpets."

I made every attempt not to look directly at him. I needed to be angry, and if I stepped any closer to him or caught one vulnerable stare, my resistance would falter.

"Good."

I didn't say anything for a minute, and neither did he. If he wanted to dig himself out of this, I wasn't going to help him.

"Do you remember that night on the fire escape? When you told me this new music wasn't me?"

I didn't reply. I didn't need a reminder of the night that invited him back into my life.

"You were right," he said. "Every song I've written for the past year has had absolutely no substance."

After the day I'd had, I was in no mood to boost his ego. I headed over to the counter and pulled out my take-out menus, realizing I hadn't eaten all day. "Isn't your fiancée going to wonder where you are?"

He didn't answer. I wondered what that meant. I hated that I wondered what that meant.

"Who's Ben?"

I suddenly wasn't hungry anymore. "How do you know about Ben?"

"I found his card." He wiped his nose, which meant he was trying to conceal whatever emotion that card incited.

"Don't go through my things."

"I wasn't going through anything," he said. "It was on my piano."

"It's my piano." I finally turned and looked straight at him. "Is that why you destroyed my flowers?"

He went back to the piano but didn't touch it. "Why does he call you Kayla?"

"Why do you call me Mickie?"

He looked up, as if he couldn't believe someone else would be worthy of giving me a nickname. "Is he your boyfriend or something?"

At that very moment, Ben's friends were probably showing him clips from *Breyer's Town*, or worse, the photo of Travis and me. He wasn't my boyfriend, and now, he never would be.

"He's a really great guy. A great guy who wouldn't expect me to drop everything and rush home to make sure he didn't choke on his own vomit. That's who he is."

He laid his finger down on middle C and started pressing it repeatedly. "I know I screwed up with the restaurant. I called for the car, but then this stuff happened with my song and I just forgot. I'll make it up to you, I promise." After all these years, I'd come to realize that his promises meant nothing.

"I got into the restaurant." I omitted the part about Josh and how I embarrassed myself completely in front of Caroline. "What possessed you to come here last night?"

"I need to get back to where I was," he said. "I need to get good again, and the only place I can do that is here. I wrote my best songs here, with you. On 'Cilla."

"You're in charge of your own career," I told him. "You didn't have to write this cartoon song. So why did you?"

"Because my team said I should."

"Your team has always told you what you should do, and you always did what you wanted. Why did you write the song, Deacon?"

He sighed and pulled out a cigarette.

"Don't light that. Why did you write the song?"

He stared at me for a second. "Because they paid me a shitload of money."

"Maybe that's your problem. You have no idea how lucky you are to actually know what you want to do with your life. You have this passion, this gift, something you love. And you're brilliant at it. You have the opportunity to do something that fulfills you every day. There are people who would die to be in that position, and you're blowing it." I shouldn't have been lecturing him when I'd wanted to wash my hands of him, but for the first time that day I felt like I was accomplishing something. "Do you talk to any of your friends anymore? Anyone from Reign? Petie?"

He scratched the side of his neck. "They're not really speaking to me right now."

"Because you leave people behind," I said. "They were your best friends. Petie was your best friend. You abandoned them. You can't do that to people."

"I was an asshole last night," he said again. "And if you want me to leave, I'll go." He took a look at the piano and started putting the top back down. "I know you're pissed about the restaurant, and you should be, but I thought you could help me. I thought you'd understand."

He headed toward the door and started putting on his shoes. My head said, *Let him go*, but my heart only saw him in that very spot, pleading with my mother not to hurt me. I didn't know what was going on with Josh or Ben or Caroline, but here was the one man who'd loved me for me—not some person he saw on TV and not some identity I made up. All he needed was for me to love him for him. And despite everything, I did.

"You can write here," I said. "I'll help you get over whatever you need to get over. But no more parties. And no more going through my stuff."

He turned toward me, and I waited to see appreciation in his eyes. I expected a *thank you*, and hoped for an *I love you.* He took me in his arms, kissed me, and said, "I knew I could count on my Queen."

I waited for something more. For him to ask what happened with Caroline, for him to say something, do something that would show me that what I was doing was right. I waited, then watched as he walked back over to his piano, propped open the top, and returned to his work. As I listened to 'Cilla's sounds, I tried to ignore the voice inside asking if I had any clue what the hell I was doing.

CHAPTER EIGHTEEN

For the next week, Deacon was on his best behavior. He wrote at 'Cilla, he made me omelets, we watched *Jailhouse Rock*, and we never once uttered the names Ben or Shaunn. It was almost as if we were that couple who'd lived together years before, except that couple fought; we weren't fighting. That couple shared a bed every night; Deacon was now usually gone by dinnertime. That girl would have told him about her mother and the soap opera. I wasn't ready, not yet. Still, it felt good to know that I was helping Deacon, that I was fixing him, that I was fixing something.

I hadn't heard from Josh. I called; he didn't answer. I stopped by; he wasn't there. Ben was a different story. He texted and left messages, but I couldn't return his calls. The person he thought he was dating didn't exist. He had to have seen that by now. He was so much better off without me, and when his attempts to reach out stopped, I figured he understood.

Believe it or not, the only call I did answer that week was Caroline's.

When she called, I expected her to immediately ask me

about *Crescent Grove*. She didn't. She actually said she was sorry the other night hadn't turned out as planned, and asked if I'd meet her for high tea. "You always loved it," she said, but she didn't need to remind me. It was the closest thing we had to a tradition when I was a kid, the one semi-maternal thing Caroline ever did. Despite the voice warning me there was more to her agenda, I found myself saying yes.

The first time Caroline took me to high tea was after the first time I was rejected from a job. I was eight years old, on summer hiatus from *Breyer's Town*, and had just lost the lead role in *Nine's a Charm*, a miniseries about a family of adorable adoptees. We went straight to the Ritz, stuffed our faces with clotted cream, cucumber sandwiches, and petits fours, and Caroline gave me one of her famous speeches. "Put it behind you and don't give it a second thought. If there's one thing you have to learn in this world, it's to put the past in the past. If you don't, you'll never move forward, and if you never move forward, you'll never grow up." She'd made it sound so easy, and that eight-year-old girl who'd just experienced rejection for the first time believed her. Nineteen years later, I wished I still could.

She was already sitting at a table when I arrived, chatting it up with the waiter. "There she is," she said when I approached. "Didn't I tell you she was gorgeous?"

"Like mother like daughter," he replied. Nice to see she'd already worked her charms on him.

"Gorgeous, this is Alex," she told me, actually caressing his arm. "He's from Australia."

"I adored your show as a kid," he said, looking a little bit shy. "Sometimes I still catch the reruns."

Caroline raised an eyebrow at me. I wondered if she put him up to it. All I could deem appropriate to say was, "Thank you."

"You do still like cranberry tea, don't you, Gorgeous?"

Caroline had been talking about the benefits of the antioxidants in cranberries for as long as I could remember. I didn't feel like hearing it again. "Sure."

"Brilliant. That's what Alex will bring us, then."

Australian Alex sauntered off and Caroline and I were left in silence, save for the harp playing nearby. The minute we were alone, I wondered why on earth I'd said yes to this. Especially when she asked, "How's Joshua?"

"Meaning?"

"I read about his little blip."

"You read about it?"

"Scathing review," she said. "'Man Without a Nation.' Gorgeous, you should really start reading the news."

I'd had no idea about the review, but leave it to Caroline to make me feel even worse. "Since when do you care about Josh?"

"Contrary to what you may think, I do have a heart. To put yourself back out there only to get rejected—that must be hard." She picked up her empty teacup, examining the intricate design. "Remind me to ask where they got these. I love this china pattern."

I couldn't pay attention to what she was saying. All I could think about was "Man Without a Nation." The critic was probably some sloppy jerk who was jealous that Josh still had his hair. If I'd stayed to witness the show, I could have told Josh how great he was, but as it was, I didn't have any authority.

"Josh is fine," I told her. And he would be fine. Josh was always fine.

"Good," she said. "I don't want this affecting you."

Before she had a chance to elaborate, Alex came back over with the cranberry tea and tiered tray of treats. The little sandwiches didn't look as exciting as they had when I was a kid.

"When we first used to come here, no one could believe

how eagerly you dove into these things." She took a tiny sandwich from the top layer. "Not many children like watercress."

"Affecting me how?"

"I'm sorry?"

"This thing with Josh," I said. "You don't want it affecting me how?"

"I know you two have always been . . . close." She said the word as if it were infectious. "But you're not the same person. Just because he failed doesn't mean you will. They discovered him at a *mall*. He fell into all of this. You were born for it."

I could feel my defenses heightening, for both myself and Josh. "Josh is a talented musician." It all sounded so familiar, like the fights we had when I was a teenager.

Caroline could feel the déjà vu, too. I could tell. She put down her teacup and said, "All I mean is don't let this hold you back."

It would have been the perfect opportunity to tell her I wasn't doing *Crescent Grove*, but just for one day, I wanted to pretend I was a girl out for tea with her mother.

"So you know the little thing I sent you?" she asked.

"Don't worry," I said. "I didn't cash it."

"Gorgeous, why? That's your money. I always planned on paying you back. I just had to wait for Franklin's settlement to come through. But I was thinking, you know what you could use some of it toward?"

I couldn't wait to hear this one. "What?"

"New headshots. When was the last time you had them done?"

The last time was when I was sixteen, before she left me to marry Franklin's predecessor, Tyler. I should have known she had ulterior motives behind that check.

"I don't need new headshots."

"Look, Peter has basically guaranteed you the role. It's

yours. The audition is a formality, but you'll still need to give them something."

"I never said I was doing the show," I told her, but I never said I wasn't doing it, either.

She remained silent for a moment. It was something she always did when I was younger, when she wanted me to rethink the last thing I'd said. "It's your decision. Just promise me you'll take your time with it. Peter needs to know in a couple of weeks. Of course, the sooner you decide the better."

I wanted to tell her I didn't know what to do—that I was afraid if I said yes, I'd hate it, and I was afraid if I declined, she'd take off again and I wouldn't see her for another five years.

As if by cue—and knowing Caroline, it probably was a cue—a tall handsome man with Clooney-gray hair approached our table. He was a little older than my mother, dressed in an Armani suit, and looked like the kind of man who knew how attractive he was. All eyes were on him when he entered the room, but it was only because he was talking so loudly on his Blackberry. He also smelled vaguely of alcohol, even though it was quarter to three. I knew instantly this was my future stepfather.

"Peter!" Caroline stood to greet him. I couldn't help but think how she remained seated when I came in.

He didn't acknowledge her. He just took a seat, spun around the tray of snacks, and continued with his phone conversation for four and a half minutes, while the two of us sat there and watched him.

"I didn't think you'd be done with your meeting so soon," Caroline said once he hung up. She adjusted her blouse, and I swore she almost looked self-conscious, if only for half a second.

"Can't stay long," he said, looking at the tray.

Caroline glanced from Peter to me and put her hand on his arm. "Darling, this is my daughter."

He ripped off a piece of scone before turning to consider me. I felt like I was auditioning for him already. He looked me over and said, "Perfect."

I didn't know what to say or do. Part of me was furious at Caroline for setting me up this way, part of me was embarrassed that I'd actually hoped she just wanted to meet for tea, but most of me wanted to shake her because despite the kind of woman she was, despite what kind of mother she turned out to be, she deserved better than this asshole.

"Your mother told you about the show?" he asked, typing into his phone.

Caroline appeared calm on the outside, but I knew my mother, and I knew she was panicked about what I might say. "I told you. Michaela's weighing her options right now."

Now that I'd seen him, I wanted to tell him there was no chance I'd do his show, but even after everything Caroline had put me through, I couldn't do that to her. I was sure that was her plan all along.

"I'm weighing my options," I repeated. There was a flash of relief in Caroline's eyes, and as crazy as it sounds, it felt good to have her approval.

"Let me give you a little insight into what it's all about," he said, finally coming alive at the discussion of his creative brainchild. He explained with a dose of arrogance how this show would change the face of daytime TV, but the premise—the trials and tribulations of the wealthy inhabitants of a cul de sac called Crescent Grove—sounded like every soapy drama I'd ever seen. Foster Greene, the character they had in mind for me, was the resident vixen: backstabber, husband-stealer, manipulator. Lovely that this was the role my mother would offer me up for.

"Would certainly get rid of that Rosie image," Peter said. "Am I right?"

I wanted to throw my tea in his face. "Daisy."

He looked offended that I'd corrected him. Like maybe I was wrong, that maybe her name actually was Rosie. I had to stop myself from telling him about the Daisy dolls and Daisy necklaces that stores couldn't keep on the shelves at Christmastime, from telling him that the year the show premiered, *Daisy* surged on the lists of top baby and pet names. I didn't know why I was so angry, when all I'd ever wanted was not to be called Daisy, but you'd think he would have done a little bit of research. Clearly, he hadn't done any at all, given the next thing he asked.

"What's the last thing I would have seen you in?"

It surprised me that Caroline hadn't debriefed him on my lack of employment for the past decade. I thought she might have tried to spin it as "Daisy Breyer's return to TV! Like you've never seen her before!"

"I told you, Peter," Caroline said. "Michaela's been very particular about the choices she's made over the past few years. She took a break from acting to go to college, and she wants to make sure that when she puts herself back out there, it's for the right project."

"Well, if she waits too long, the right project might pass her by." He made me feel like I was ten again, when executives would talk to my mother right over my head. "In this business, twenty-five isn't all that young." He looked at me as if we were comrades and asked, "Am I right?"

I stared at Caroline, but she didn't flinch. I couldn't believe she lied about my goddamned age.

I placed my napkin on the table and stood up. "I'm late for an appointment. Thank you for the information. I'll think about it." I threw on my coat and buttoned it at the table, knowing very well that Peter would look at my ass on the way out.

I was halfway down the staircase when Caroline caught up with me. "You were very rude to Peter. He's trying to help."

"I was rude? He had raspberry preserves on his chin when he basically told me I'd be perfect for playing a whore."

"It would be a challenging role. Think of the fun you could have with it."

"You lied about my age."

"One year—"

"Two years." I wondered when it was going to finally sink in.

"Everyone lies about their age in this industry. You know that."

"I don't want to have to lie about who I am." I waited for her to react, but she had nothing to say. As angry as I was with her, I was angrier at the situation, why she thought she had to live her life this way, why she'd taught me to live my life this way. "Are you seriously going to marry that guy?"

She made a gesture of checking her skirt for crumbs, but I could tell she was really making sure there were no witnesses around. "We all make our choices, Gorgeous."

"And you can choose not to marry him." I didn't understand her at all. She was as stunning at forty-nine as she had been at nineteen. She commanded the attention of every person in every room she entered. She had a better mind for business than any studio head I'd ever met, yet she clung to men well beneath her in exchange for money and status.

"Not everyone is blessed with the same talents as you," she said, her voice lowered. "We all do what we have to do to survive. That's life."

I thought of Peter, probably devouring the tea sandwiches and desserts. I thought about the pot of cold barely touched cranberry tea and our half-filled china cups. Even though the afternoon teas we'd shared twenty years before always followed rejections, they were worlds more satisfying than this one had been.

"You will think about the show, Gorgeous?" she half asked, half stated. "I think you'll regret it if you don't. You don't want to be thought of as Daisy your whole life."

I didn't answer. I don't think she really expected me to. I just turned and headed down the stairs, leaving Caroline to finish her antioxidant-filled tea with her soon-to-be-fourth mistake.

PHIL GREETED ME WITH A SEMI-SMIRK WHEN I RETURNED to my apartment. I was sure he was loving that his favorite soap, *The Saga of Michaela and Deacon*, was back from hiatus. Maybe Peter should have come over to bounce some *Crescent Grove* ideas off him. Phil would have been the ideal test audience.

I was waiting for the elevator when I spotted Josh coming down the stairs in a sweatshirt and running shoes. I knew he was still mad at me, but I had to tell him about Caroline and ask if he thought she was right—if the only way to not be Daisy Breyer was to be someone named Foster Greene.

I called out but he didn't look up. He just headed toward the front door, engrossed in his music. "Josh!" I said again, this time following him and grabbing his shoulder.

He finally turned to face me, pulling out one of his earbuds. "Sorry. Didn't hear you." His tone didn't imply he was sorry or that he in any way wanted to hear me.

"Where are you going?"

"Running."

Normally, I would think nothing of it, but now that I knew about the article, I could see he wasn't just running. Ever since we were kids, anytime he was upset or insecure, he'd work out obsessively. Back then, I thought it was because he was expected to have the world's finest six-pack. Now, all I could think about was Morgan saying he'd already worn through the shoes she got him in July.

"It's raining," I told him.

He looked through the glass door. "So it is." With that, he put his earbud back in and started out again.

"Josh," I said, holding on to his arm. He faced me, and I realized I had a million things I wanted to say to him. Not only did I want to tell him about my mother and Peter and the role they had in mind for me, but I also wanted to tell him not to let that article bother him, that he was talented, that I was proud of him for putting himself back out there. I wanted to tell him I was sorry. But the look he was giving me—this disinterested look I thought he saved for overzealous fans or hecklers—only allowed me to ask, "Where have you been?"

"Around." He didn't bother to take his earbuds out this time.

"Where were you last night?" I asked. "I came by."

"I was out."

"With Morgan?"

"Nate." I couldn't remember the last time Josh had hung out with another Boy of the Nation, especially the one who'd remained in the headlines through his partying, womanizing, and failed attempts at rehab.

"Why were you out with Nate?"

"Why do I need to run that by you?" He turned away once more and I grabbed his hood. I could tell from the look he gave me that the next time I grabbed him he would lose it.

I felt pathetic—even more so in front of Phil and the two other residents coming out of the elevator—but I had to ask, "Are you mad at me?"

His expression didn't change. "I'm going for a run." Before

I could stop him, he turned his music up, brushed past Phil, and headed out into the rain.

Deacon was gone when I returned to my apartment, which allowed me to search the internet for Josh's review uninterrupted. I found "Man Without a Nation" right away, but after skimming it, I wished I hadn't. Highlights included: *Josh McKenzie hung up his dancing shoes five years ago, and his attempt to resurrect his career at the Burgundy Palace only confirmed he should have stayed in retirement*; *Fans wanted to hear Boyz of the Nation songs—which would have been bad enough—but McKenzie made things even worse by subjecting the crowd to his original (yet unoriginal) material*; and *If you're wondering where the Boyz have been since they left the Nation, Jesse Branford has had a highly successful solo career, Nate Hunter has been in (and out) of rehab, and Josh McKenzie has apparently been writing crappy music. Whoever told this guy that making a comeback was a good idea should get their head examined.*

I was furious. I wanted to go down to this Bob Danvers's office and give him a piece of my mind. I searched for another review, something positive I could bring to Josh so he'd forgive me, but I could only find fan stories, which would probably make him feel worse. Some were positive—*The thrill of seeing Josh McKenzie in person made me feel fourteen again. His eyes were bluer than I remembered!!!!!!*—while others were less than glowing—*I've waited five years to see Joshie Mac again, and he didn't even sing "Alwayz in My Heart!"* If only I'd seen him, heard his songs myself, I could have told him to screw what the critics had to say and it would have meant something. He knew I wasn't the kind of person to sugarcoat things, and I knew Josh. I knew how heartfelt he was, how smart he was. I was sure his songs were great.

After a solid hour of searching, there was a knock at my door. I was relieved to see it was him.

I opened the door and his first words were, "You know what, I am pissed at you."

He was soaked with rain and sweat, and it was clear he'd been running and thinking that whole hour.

"Josh—"

He stormed in, bringing a muddy puddle on my freshly cleaned rug with him. "Why did you leave?"

I wanted to tell him the truth. I was sick of lying. But I couldn't let him grow any angrier than he already was. "I told you I was sick."

"Bullshit." His chest was heaving and his face was moist with rain. "I have been your friend for over ten years and I am always there for you. Once, just *once* I needed you to be there for me." He wiped his face with the arm of his saturated sweatshirt, which only made things worse.

"Let me get you a towel," I said, escaping to the bathroom. As he said, we'd been friends for over a decade, but never once had we fought. We'd had our tiffs—he'd call me a brat, I'd call him an old man—but we never fought. I didn't know how to react.

I wasn't sure if he'd accept the towel, but he did, wiping the rain from his face and hair. He seemed to have regained his breath, and I hoped he'd calmed down.

"If you thought it was a bad idea, you should have said so." He rubbed the tiny scar above his right eyebrow, the one they used to cover with makeup. "Did you really think I wouldn't notice if you left?"

"I didn't know it was such a big deal. You weren't even going to tell me about it."

"You knew it was a big deal. Why did you leave?"

"I just had to leave—"

"Why?" he asked. "Did you think it was going to be so horrible you couldn't sit through one hour-long set?"

"No—"

"Then why? What could have been so important that you had to leave before it even started? And why does it reek in here?"

I didn't say anything. I didn't have to. His eyes turned to the piano and sitting on top was an overflowing ashtray.

"That's real nice, Michaela," he said, his tone dead as he turned to leave.

"It's not what it looks like."

"Oh, really? What, are you going to tell me you took up smoking and finally learned to play the piano?"

There was literally nothing I could say. I hated the way I must have looked to him. His tone revealed everything when he said, "I cannot believe you."

"He needed me." I barely recognized my own weak voice.

"He *always* needs you. He needs you for his own sick purposes and when he gets what he needs, he's done."

I could feel tears coming on, but I refused to let them through. Josh was the only person I ever let see me cry, but he'd never been the one to provoke it.

"You don't understand," I said.

"You're right, I don't understand. Your mother—your mother was one thing. I didn't get it, but she's your mother, okay. But *this* asshole? He's *engaged*, Michaela. I realize to someone with the strong moral high ground of Deacon King that probably doesn't mean a lot, but come on."

Something about the way he was standing in my living room in his sweatshirt and sneakers reminded me of the day he helped me move in. He'd found the apartment for me right after I dropped out of college, and even though he had just been on a publicity tour, he flew all night to come help me move. I'd had no furniture and he helped me shop, let me stay at his place until I got a bed, then put the bed together for me when it arrived. When I asked him if he'd rather be out with the Boyz, wooing some pop tarts, he said no—"This is just the kind of stuff we do for each other." Now, as he stood before me, soggy and muddy, he looked at me like he had no idea who I'd become. I couldn't blame him. I didn't know, either.

"I've always stayed out of your life," he said. "Never commented on your bad decisions, your mistakes. I defended you. But after everything we've been through—after everything *he's* put you through—for Christ's sake, Michaela, do you not remember how you couldn't even get out of bed when he left?"

"This time is different." I knew how it sounded. "I'm helping him."

"You're a shitty friend."

I'd heard that so many times from other people, people I didn't care about, people like CeCe who didn't actually matter to me. But hearing it from Josh made me dizzy with nausea. Over the years, I thought I'd come to know every expression his face could make—how he'd look when he was hungry and irritable, or when he was excited but trying to act like he wasn't excited, or when he thought I was being stupid about something but would humor me anyway. But this look he was giving me now was a look I hadn't known existed. I wouldn't let him walk out of my apartment. I couldn't. That tone, that look, told me that once he was on the other side of that door, we would be beyond repair.

"Can we please sit and talk about this?" I asked, moving toward the couch. He didn't budge.

"You've only ever cared about two people in your entire life," he said. "Yourself and him. And he does not care about you."

"That's not true."

"If he cared about you, he wouldn't string you along. If you care about someone, you don't treat them like a piece of shit."

"He doesn't treat me like that," I said.

Josh shook his head and the next words he spoke were like a fist to the stomach.

"You're never going to change."

He looked around the apartment and then at me—the girl he told at seventeen he would always be there for—and said the only thing that could have hurt worse than what he'd said already. "I'm done."

I could feel my insides falling apart. He tossed the damp towel on the white carpet, and just like that, my best friend—the closest thing to family that I had—walked out, leaving nothing behind but a trail of muddy footprints.

CHAPTER NINETEEN

There was an episode of *Breyer's Town* when Daisy got into a fight with her best friend, Marcie Glick. They fought because Daisy went to a pool party that Marcie wasn't invited to, and if they were *really* best friends, Marcie said, Daisy wouldn't have gone. Dr. Breyer took Daisy out for pizza and told her that she and Marcie had been best friends their whole lives, and that they would patch things up. In twenty-two minutes (excluding commercials), they did. It had been five hours and twenty-two minutes since my fight with Josh. There were no signs of reconciliation, and I had no bright ideas of how to fix things.

I'd only hurt Josh one other time in our twelve-year friendship. He'd been on a worldwide tour, a tour that seemed to last an eternity to two teenagers in lust. While he was gone, we planned all the things we would do once we were finally in the same city again—real dates we could go on, which took a lot of creative thinking, considering that he was the biggest teen sensation in the world, I was his semi-famous girlfriend, and to the public eye, he was "single and looking." (Something Caroline pointed out every chance she could.) Josh's favorite ideas included a 3D film festival—who would recognize us behind the glasses?—and comic book conventions—we could go as Batman and Catwoman, who cared that neither of us read comic books? Caroline didn't like that I was making so many plans that didn't include casting sessions, told me I spent way too much time waiting for his calls, and implied not so subtly that Josh was less than faithful on the road. "He has girls hiding in laundry carts to get backstage," she'd say. "Do you honestly think it ends there?" Of course, me telling her I wanted to take a break from acting to try being a normal teenager for a while didn't help matters.

With two weeks to go until Josh's big arrival, Caroline sprung the news on me that she was leaving to marry Tyler Richards. Our lease ran out the next fall, conveniently coinciding with my going to college, but Caroline didn't plan on staying that long. I was perfectly capable of taking care of myself, she said, and ten days after she told me of her engagement, she was gone. I couldn't stand sleeping in that empty loft alone, couldn't accept that my own mother dumped me for an investment banker just because he was more lucrative, so Josh stayed up with me every night—first on the phone, then once the tour was over, at either my place or the Four Seasons, where he was staying. I couldn't bring myself to cook or buy groceries, so every day at noon we'd meet for lunch at this greasy diner called Bennett's that was so off the radar no one ever caught on to our game. I'd get a grilled cheese and tomato, he'd get a turkey club, and we'd share both. He'd listen to me if I wanted to talk about Caroline, and if I needed to take my mind off it, he'd tell me crazy fan stories from the road or talk about the dumb things his bandmates would do. It was a lot to ask of a seventeen-year-old kid.

It was about two weeks into this routine, and I was pretty quiet through lunch, so Josh told me a story about how their tour bus broke down in Japan and they didn't know what to do because the only things anyone knew how to say were *hello, we love you*, and *good night*. After we ate, he asked if I felt like hanging out and watching a movie. We went back to the hotel, and ten minutes into *Ferris Bueller's Day Off*, I told him I couldn't see him anymore.

He didn't need a girlfriend, I told him. He had enough on his plate, and neither of us could claim this was some great romance. Besides, maybe my mother was right. Maybe I should have been concentrating on my career and not some puppy love.

He paused the movie and sat in silence. "Your mother?" he finally asked. "Your mother who left—who you haven't spoken to in weeks—you want to listen to her."

I had never broken up with anyone before, unless you counted that after-school special *Bleecker High*. I couldn't look at him, so I focused on the TV, on Cameron Frye in his hockey jersey, sitting frozen in his car. "You have your own thing going on," I told him. "Pretty soon you're going to be recording your new album, and then you'll be touring again. I can't be one of your hangers-on."

He sounded genuinely pained when he asked, "When have I ever treated you like that?"

"I'm just saying. That's what you should be focusing on, and I should be focusing on what I need to." I tried to sound like the rational adult Caroline wanted me to be.

"You're going to college next September," he said. "You finally get to lead a normal life. That was going to be your focus, remember?"

I didn't know what to say to him, and after another minute, he said, "Breaking up with me isn't going to make her come back. I'm not the reason she left, and neither are you." When I didn't respond, he said, "Come on, let's forget this whole conversation and watch the movie, okay?"

I wanted to listen to him, to believe what he was saying. I was so desperate for him not to hate me that I almost sat back and said all right. Instead, I stood up, collected my shoes, and told him he was still my best friend. He didn't say a word.

Before leaving, I turned to face him. He wouldn't look at me, or at the TV screen, which had turned black because the movie had been on pause for so long. He was staring at his socks, playing with a tiny thread hanging from his left heel, his face a mixture of anger and sadness. Something in his resigned dejection made me feel like he'd known this was coming, but it didn't seem to help. Millions of girls across the country—around the world—had his poster on their walls, dreamed of seeing him on the street, meeting him, marrying him. He wasn't on a pedestal to them; he was on a throne. But that day, he was just a teenage boy, hurt by a girl for the first time.

Even then, I hadn't hurt him as much as I had now. Back then, I still went to Bennett's the next day because my stomach hadn't received word of the breakup. When I got there, I found Josh at our regular booth with two plates in front of him. He didn't say anything when I sat down, just put half his turkey club on my plate and took half my grilled cheese for himself. We ate in silence, but it wasn't uncomfortable, because, like I'd said the day before, he was still my best friend. After we ate, after he paid the bill and finished my soda (he hated seeing it go to waste), he pulled his hat down over his eyes and said, "What can I say, Turner? You've grown on me. I think I'm stuck with you for life." From that moment on, everything was fine. He had never before said he was done with me, that I was a shitty friend, that I was never going to change. Our fight now had so much finality I knew a grilled cheese and tomato would never fix it.

The image of that look he'd given me wouldn't go away, nor would his words. *You've only ever cared about two people in your entire life, yourself and him, and he does not care about you.* Josh may have been on target with our first fight—maybe my breaking up with him did have something to do with Caroline, maybe

I did think it was my relationship with him that made her run in the first place. But this time he was wrong. He couldn't get past two years earlier, when Deacon left me in my bed and told me it was never going to work. Josh didn't get that Deacon was the only person who actually saw me for who I was and loved me for it. Yes, Deacon and I had hurt each other in the past, but this time was different. I had to believe that was true. Otherwise, I'd hurt Josh—I'd lost Josh—for nothing.

I dialed Deacon's number and waited for him to pick up. All I needed was to hear his voice and everything would be all right. When Jay answered, I felt sick.

"Why are you answering Deacon's phone?"

"He's busy."

"Is she there?"

I couldn't believe I'd said it. For the most part, I tried to pretend she didn't exist, or if she did, that I didn't care. Now I sounded like I did when I was twenty-two, when Deacon broke me for the first time and I'd call him after too much thinking or too much drinking. Except this time, I didn't have Josh to take the phone from me, to put me to bed, to listen to me cry.

Jay was silent for a long moment. I swore I could almost hear pity in his voice when he asked, "Why are you doing this?"

I didn't answer. For a minute, we both waited for the other to cave.

Finally, he said, "She's out of town."

DEACON'S BUILDING WAS DEFINITELY SUITED FOR A KING. The lobby alone was four times the size of mine and the security twice as tight. I couldn't imagine why he'd need to spend so much time at my place when next to his, it looked like a studio.

Jay had already called down to let them know I was coming, and I had to show ID to be let up. An elevator attendant had to allow me access to Deacon's locked floor, and after all this—after his housekeeper let me in—I still had to wait for him in the foyer for six minutes.

His front hall was just as elaborate as the rest of the building. I could only imagine what the rest of the apartment looked like. I could have blamed the enormous mirrors that lined the walls on Shaunn, but they were quintessentially Deacon. When we lived together, if I ever got mad about his narcissism, he would make me laugh by playing "You're So Vain" on the piano. It became a long-running joke. I even got him an apricot scarf for his birthday one year.

I didn't want to look in any of the mirrors, though they were nearly impossible to avoid. I didn't want to see how pathetic I looked. I focused on my shoes and the tiny blister they were forming on the top of my left foot.

"Mickie, what are you doing here?"

Deacon looked like he was just passing through, not expecting to find me.

"Jay didn't tell you I was coming."

His face softened a little. "He did. I just didn't realize you were already here."

"Why can't you ever answer your own phone?"

A defensive arch lifted his left eyebrow. "I had press all afternoon. Then I had a meeting, and I just got out of the shower. Is there anything else you need to know?"

I knew he was telling the truth. His hair was still damp—which only reminded me of Josh—and he hadn't bothered putting on his T-shirt; he was still holding it in his hand. He had, however, found time to light a cigarette.

"So what's up?" he asked. When I didn't answer, he said, "You really can't be showing up here. I mean, Shaunn's out of town, but—"

I couldn't listen to him acknowledging her existence. "I called," I said. "I called and told Jay I was coming." I wanted to tell him that he owed me this much—that he could throw parties at my place, write there at all hours, watch movies, and show up whenever he felt like it—that I should have been able to see him when I wanted to. "I couldn't be alone tonight."

He considered me through a stream of smoke, probably debating whether he should ask me what was wrong or kick me out on the street. He stubbed out his cigarette in a nearby ashtray and held his hand out to me. "Come on, then. I'll give you the grand tour."

We'd lived together for a combined total of two years and eight months, and everything was ours; now, it was his and someone else's. I tried not to think about it, tried not to think which of them picked out the red velvet couch (obviously Deacon) and who put the little touches here and there that made it a home, like the candles on the mantel or the little scarves on the end tables. I made my living as a child pretending to be someone I wasn't; I could pretend, just for one night, that Deacon lived alone.

"Where's Jay?" I asked.

"He left. He's not around all the time, Mickie."

I almost pointed out that evidence indicated otherwise, that maybe Jay and all the others like him had something to do with Deacon's writing problems. Then, through a doorway, I saw something that should have helped him overcome any troubles he might have had.

"Deacon." I made my way into the room uninvited so I could inspect it further—a white grand piano that was so pure and pristine it had to have been brand-new. "This is unbelievable."

He stood in the doorway a safe distance away. "It was custom-made."

I didn't touch it. It didn't look like it had ever been touched.

There weren't even any ashtrays nearby. "Why do you need to write at my place if you have this?"

He shrugged. "It's not 'Cilla. This is the third one I've tried. I wrote my solo album on the last one, and that was shit. So I'm trying this one."

It didn't look like he'd tried it at all. Hard evidence of his success lined the walls: eight Grammys, multiple Gold and Platinum records, one Diamond award. I knew he couldn't honestly believe he owed it all to a piano I'd bought him eight years before. All his album covers were framed and mounted, and even though I didn't want to think about her, I found myself wondering if Shaunn knew that it was my back on *The Queen*, if she knew that every song on that album was just as much mine as it was Deacon's.

That album wasn't my only contribution to the room. Hanging next to it was a framed black-and-white photograph I had taken during my three-week photography phase. I took it in the recording studio when Reign was working on their first album, and it was hands down my favorite picture of Deacon. He was standing with Petie, and they both had that glow of finally getting everything they'd ever wanted. Petie had this smug expression on his face because he'd just cracked a joke he thought was mildly funny, and Deacon was flat-out laughing, the kind of laugh you can only experience when you have complete contentment.

"I love this picture of you," I said, wondering when the last time Deacon laughed like that was.

"You captured a good one."

"Don't you miss him?"

Deacon sighed. "Come on, Mickie. You didn't come over to talk about me and Petie."

"I'm just asking a question," I said. "He was your best friend for half your life, and you hurt him. Doesn't that bother you?"

I tried to read him, to see if he cared about any of the things he used to. He pinched the bridge of his nose, which he always did when I burdened him with questions he didn't want to answer, like "Where were you last night?" and "Whose number is this on your phone?"

"Yeah," he said. "It bothered me for a while. But you have to make certain choices to get where you want to be. Breaking off with the guys was business, it wasn't personal."

He sounded so much like Caroline. I wondered how much of his life was controlled by his business, by this image he'd created for himself. I wondered if there was a single part of his life that was strictly personal, or if maybe Josh was right—if maybe everything he did was for his own purposes, and once he got what he needed, he was done.

"Do you think he'll ever forgive you?" I needed him to say yes. I needed him to say that even though he'd hurt his friend in the worst way imaginable, they would find a way through it.

"Come on, Mickie. Tell me what's up."

It seemed so much later than it was. Between Caroline and Josh, it had been the longest afternoon of my life. "I'm just having a bad day."

I wanted him to ask me what was wrong. I wanted him to give some indication that he still cared about me, that he'd ever cared about me. As if he knew what I needed, he came toward me, gave me a hard kiss, and said, "I'll fix it."

He always kissed me that way, urgently, passionately, as if one kiss could erase all the pain I'd ever felt. When I was younger, I actually thought it worked, then I eventually came to realize that all it did was mask things for a while. Now I would have taken even that temporary relief but as I kissed him deeper, as I touched his bare skin, as he undressed me, I only felt those wounds widening. I only felt more broken.

As we made our way to the bedroom, I said the three words we hardly ever used. I knew he didn't believe in them. I knew he'd always said they were only words, but sometimes, when

I needed it most, he would come through. I needed him to know that even though things were different this time, I still felt the same way. I needed to hear it back.

When I said it, he smiled, revealing that tiny chip in his eye tooth I once loved so much, and I was sure he was going to repeat the words back. Instead, he looked me in the eye, pulled me onto the bed, and said, "Good."

LATER THAT NIGHT, I WAS LYING IN THE BED MY VEGAN engaged ex shared with his fiancée, eating Chinese food. As he popped a spare rib into his mouth, Deacon said exactly what I was thinking:

"This is so wrong on so many levels."

Only Deacon seemed amused by it. I wasn't.

The rain was hammering on his bedroom windows, and every once in a while, I could hear the crack of thunder. When he was a kid, Deacon was petrified of storms because his neighbor's trailer was struck by lightning. It soothed me a little to see him flinch at the louder crashes, knowing he was still the same man who told me that story years before.

"More soy sauce?" he asked, opening another packet and squirting it onto his pork fried rice.

I shook my head. I had to breathe for a minute. I had to tell myself that what I was doing wasn't wrong. I wasn't a woman who was sleeping with someone else's fiancé. I wasn't in someone else's bed, in someone else's home. I was just a woman with the man she loved, the man who'd never had to tell her he loved her in return for her to know it was true.

"Hey, just so you know," he said, "I'm not going to be around for the next few days."

I tried not to let those words hurt, but I had to wonder if it was something I'd done, with the sex or what I'd said or just by showing up. All I could manage for a response was, "Oh."

"I have some shows on the West Coast. I'll be back next week."

I wanted to let myself feel better. I wanted to believe he'd be traveling to those shows alone. I wanted to believe he'd invite me along when I asked, "Where are you going?"

"Seattle, LA, and San Francisco."

I felt a pang at the last one, because it made me think of Josh. When we were kids, we always said we wanted to live there, side by side on the beach. I'd wanted to go to college there, but decided to stay in New York in case Caroline came back. "I love San Francisco."

"Yeah, it's beautiful." I waited for him to mention the picture he bought me of the Pacific Ocean, the one that still hung above his piano. But he just took a bite of rice. "I forgot how much I loved Chinese food. We used to practically live off this stuff, remember?"

Of course I remembered. That was the reason I'd suggested it. My hope was that he'd be reminded of the days he'd come home from the recording studio ridiculously late, and I'd be waiting up for him, and we would eat leftover Chinese and just talk.

"Deacon, what we had back then—"

He looked at me, waiting for me to finish, and I found myself wishing I hadn't started at all because I didn't know how he'd react.

"What we had was good, right?"

He kissed me. "Do you remember when we went to Cabo?"

"Do *you* remember when we went to Cabo?" Clearly, his recollection was a little different than mine. He probably remembered writing "'Til the Moonlight Fills Your Room," a song that won him two Grammys. I remembered that he wrote it after the huge screaming match we had because I found him pants-down with a spring-breaking groupie. Every time he played it live, the moment he'd sing the opening line—"I'd swallow you whole if it meant you would stay"—the crowd would go wild, without the slightest idea that while he was writing it, the girl he supposedly loved was packing her suitcase in tears, on the phone with her only friend, who was trying to find her a flight back to New York.

"I'm trying to say that I never wrote like I did when I was with you," he said. "No one else has ever inspired me in the same way."

I tried to ignore that it wasn't really an answer. Then again, everything with Deacon related back to his music, and if he said he was at his best when he was with me—which was the truth—that had to mean something.

"Do you remember CeCe? She was with me that night at Intuition."

"Remember her? She's still with Douglas. She's a pain in the ass."

"She's still with Douglas?" I couldn't believe it. She went to the tabloids because of my betrayal, but had no problem with Douglas's infidelity. Classic.

"Why are you thinking about her?"

"I was a shitty friend to her. I'm a shitty friend in general." He knew me enough to know there was more, so he didn't say a word until I elaborated. "I had a fight with Josh today."

Deacon snorted. "Don't worry about McKenzie. He's just pissed about his show."

"How did you know about that?" I knew I hadn't told him about my leaving Josh behind to clean up his vomit.

"Everyone knows. It was a flop. I'm sure he's just taking it out on you."

I didn't go any further. If I told him that Josh knew he was back in my life, he'd freak out and think Josh was going to tell somebody, blow our cover.

"That's why you're having such a bad day? Because you fought with McKenzie? Christ, Mickie, consider that a blessing."

I wanted to defend Josh. Deacon had never been fair to him, and now I'd given him more ammunition. I shouldn't have brought it up, but I needed to feel that way I once felt, that I could tell Deacon anything, and he would care.

"You never asked how things went with Caroline." There was a time when it would have been the first thing he asked.

"I didn't know if you wanted me to, after I blew it with the reservation." I wasn't sure if that was the truth or an easy excuse. "I figured if you wanted to tell me, you'd tell me."

He put on his "listening face," as he used to call it, and kept his views impartial while I spilled the whole story—the tea, the fake breasts, Peter's eating habits, *Crescent Grove.* In the old days, he would have reiterated how awful Caroline was and asked if I was okay. Now he asked, "Are you going to do it?"

"I don't know," I said, though if I was going to, maybe a second egg roll hadn't been the best idea.

"How much are they paying you?"

"I don't know," I said again.

"Jesus, Mickie, that's the first thing you should have asked."

"I think you're missing the point."

"I'm not missing the point," he said. "Caroline's involved. That's bad news right off the bat. I get that. But this is an opportunity. You have to weigh it out. Is it worth it? If the price is right, it might be."

He sounded so straightforward, so sure of what he was saying, like he wasn't at all considering the person behind the question. "I need you to answer me not in terms of this being a business decision," I told him. "I need you to answer me as someone who knows me."

"But it is a business decision." My anxiety must have been all over my face, because he softened a little and added, "And I think it might be good for you to, you know, do something."

I wanted to be insulted by that, but deep down, I knew what he meant. Watching him this past week, seeing him get so wrapped up in his art, seeing that light in his eyes when he hit just the right note, I was envious. He had such purpose, such fulfillment, even when he was tortured by it. More than anything, I wanted to feel that way about something, but acting wasn't it. I wanted to explain that to him, to remind him acting was something I'd tried to get away from for half my life. I wanted to tell him I didn't think being known as Foster Greene would be much better than being known as Daisy Breyer. I wanted to ask him if doing something just for the sake of doing something was really any better than doing nothing at all. Then his phone started buzzing and he leaned over and looked at the screen.

"Shit. I gotta take this."

I wondered how his phone was always so accessible when I was with him but not when I was calling him, but I tried not to think about it. As he rolled out of bed, some chicken chow mein slid off his plate onto the sheet.

"This is why we shouldn't have eaten in your bed."

"Screw it," he said. "If I'm gonna be bad, I'm gonna be bad, right?"

He escaped to the other room and I was left alone, trying to dab the greasy chicken stain from his silk sheets. I knew he had people to do this sort of thing for him, or to buy him new sheets if they couldn't get it out, but I still felt responsible. I tried not to think about who it might be on the phone, and if it was who I thought it was, how she'd feel about her bedroom smelling like meat.

Don't think about her, I told myself. This was Deacon's room, Deacon's apartment. Glancing around the bedroom, I could almost convince myself of that, because it was clear that Deacon had played a key role in the decor, from the dark red bedspread to the framed picture of Elvis's *'68 Comeback Special.* I'd thought Shaunn was responsible for his being lost, for stripping away what made him him and replacing it with new clothes and music and fake veganism, but he seemed to be holding his own. When we lived together, if Deacon wanted something, he got it. Take the piano, and the white leather couch I was still stuck with. He could persuade me of anything. Maybe things with Shaunn weren't all that different.

I climbed out of bed to check my own phone, to see if anyone had called. He hadn't, but getting up gave me an excuse to examine the nightstand next to my side of the bed. There was a small lamp, a bottle of lavender hand lotion, and a book. *Rebecca*. I hadn't pegged her as a reader, or at least a reader of classics. Judging by the bookmark, she hadn't gotten very far; she was only on chapter three. I wondered if she meant to bring it on her trip with her, and if maybe she was sitting in her hotel room at that moment, looking in her suitcase and realizing with disappointment that she didn't have it. Maybe she was even calling to ask if she'd left it on her night table. Maybe after a long flight, all she wanted to do was sit down and find out what was going to happen in chapter three, and now she couldn't. The book was slightly battered, and I wondered if she'd read it before, or if she'd borrowed it from a friend, if she was reading it for pleasure, or in an attempt to broaden her mind. Whatever it was, it was her book, on her nightstand, next to her bed, where I'd just had sex with her fiancé.

Through the door, I could hear him talking to her, trying to keep his voice down. I recognized that tone from when we were together, when I'd be the one calling to find out where he was, and he'd tell me he was with Petie or Jay or by himself writing. I always knew when he was lying, and sometimes I'd call him out on it, but usually I'd let it go because I knew I was the one he was coming home to. I knew, deep down, I was the one he loved. I was right when I told Josh things were different this time. This time, I was the one who'd have to leave in the morning when the person he shared his life with came back.

"I'm glad you got in okay. I was worried with these storms,"

I heard him say. He let out a half laugh, half sigh. "Yes, Shaunnie. I'm fine."

A sharp pain shot through my chest. She must have known about his fear of thunder, too. I knew I shouldn't have been listening—it was masochistic—but I couldn't force myself to move.

"No, it went great," he said. "At least Nick thought so."

I had no idea what he was talking about. I had no idea who Nick was. But she did. He had this entire life with people and places and events that I not only had no part in, I had no knowledge of. With the exception of Jay, all the people who'd been a part of his life before were gone. Everything was different, except for me, and like Josh said, I was never going to change. I was still holding on to Deacon like I had when I was nineteen, reading his every move, dissecting his every sentence, searching for evidence that I was special to him.

I should have moved away from the door before he said goodbye, but I had to hear if he'd end with an "I'll talk to you later," or an "I miss you," or simply a "Good."

"I'll call you in the morning," he said. "Hey. I love you."

The apartment felt stifling. I wanted to sit down and regain my breath, but I had to get out of there. I didn't know what to believe—the words he'd just said to her, or him telling me they were only words—but I couldn't stick around to find out. I could hear him moving back toward the bedroom, and I quickly gathered my clothes and started getting dressed. When he opened the door, I couldn't quite look at him.

"Where are you going?"

"I can't stay here." I didn't tell him why, or that I shouldn't have come in the first place.

"It's really bad outside." He glanced at the window. The rain was hitting it so hard it was a wonder it didn't shatter.

"Really, no, I should go. I tried to get the chow mein out of your sheets, but I think it might stain."

"I'll take care of it." He sounded thrown. "Mickie, what are you doing?"

All this time, he'd convinced me he was figuring things out, but it seemed like he had his life perfectly sorted. He had the best of both worlds.

"I have to go," I said again.

He didn't ask me to stay, or ask what was wrong. He didn't even offer to walk me to the door, but I didn't really give him a chance to. All I said was, "Good luck on your shows," before slipping out of his bedroom and hurrying down the mirror-lined corridor. Despite my every intention, I caught a glimpse of myself on my way to the elevator. I had no idea who that person was looking back at me.

Josh was right. Not only was I a shitty friend, I was a shitty person. It made perfect sense that he didn't understand me; I didn't understand myself. I couldn't blame him for being done with me, because I wasn't the same girl who'd shared a turkey club with him at Bennett's. That girl might have been a bit frail, a bit of a mess, but she was nothing compared to who I was now. For years, I'd done everything I could to separate myself from Daisy Breyer, but at that moment, I wished I was her. She had a whole team of writers, producers, and supporting characters to help her solve all her problems. I had no idea how to fix any of mine.

CHAPTER TWENTY

Five days after the fight-heard-round-the-building and I still hadn't heard from Josh. He was stubborn, he was upset, and I definitely didn't deserve his forgiveness. I spent the better part of my week debating if I should go to the gym downstairs, where I was almost sure to run into him. Even if he wouldn't speak to me, I needed to know how he was doing. I worried about him exercising too much, hoped he hadn't had any more Boyz nights with Nate. I tried to tell myself he had Morgan, that at least she could be there for him. I was just concerned she didn't know him well enough to get that something was wrong. I even went so far as to change into my gym clothes a couple times, but remembering the look on his face when he told me he was done with me was enough to keep me away.

For the third time that week, I sat down on the couch with the audition sides for *Crescent Grove.* I wanted to hate it, but I had to admit the script wasn't all that bad. The lines were all there for me, laid out. *This is what you need to say. This is what you need to do.* It was almost a comfort. I'd memorized it within the first hour of picking it up. It was the one thing I was good at. Maybe it was the one thing I'd ever be good at.

I looked at my copy of *Ordinary People*, the last book on the swiped syllabus and probably the last opportunity I had to pretend I could live up to its title. I was already starting to miss Kayla, the girl I thought I could be with Ben. She never would have hurt her best friend or told her engaged ex how much she loved him only to hear him turn around and tell his fiancée the same thing.

Ben had likely written me off like everyone else, but I had to give it a try. Unlike Deacon, he picked up on the first ring. He sounded groggy, and I could hear *The Tonight Show* in the background. I definitely woke him up.

"Remember me?" I tried to sound playful, but I could hear the sadness in my own voice. *Give me another chance*, it was saying. *Please don't reject me, too.*

I wanted to believe what I heard was a laugh, but it sounded more like a sigh. "Shouldn't I be the one asking that question?"

He had a point. A normal person would have answered his calls and texts and behaved like a mature adult, but I wasn't either of those things.

I could have made up a story about my phone being broken, or about traveling for work, but I was too tired of the act. "I think I freaked out at your school when your friends told you who I am." It was probably the most honest thing I'd ever said to him.

"Kayla." He still didn't get that I wasn't this person. I didn't know if that was a wound or a comfort. "Do you think I care that you were on TV as a kid?"

When he put it that way, it didn't sound so complicated. He didn't get the pounds and pounds of baggage it came with.

"What did they tell you about me?" I had to know. The idea of his friends showing him the picture with Travis, or CeCe's blog, or my mother's tell-all stung more than it should have.

"Aside from making me feel like an idiot for never hearing

of that show? Nothing." I wanted to believe him. He sounded so sincere. "No offense, but I didn't watch a lot of TV growing up."

I'd never been around someone who didn't know everything about Daisy Breyer, who didn't say things like, "Hey, remember that episode when Daisy got her head stuck in the banister?" or "What was it like having a gumball machine in your bedroom?"

"So that's why you never returned my calls?" His voice, though scratchy with sleep, sounded sympathetic. I didn't deserve it.

"It's just hard," I tried to explain. "You can Google me and find out every embarrassing thing I've done since I was eighteen." Even the tabloids had boundaries around children, but once I came of age, all bets were off.

"I've never Googled you," he said. "I wouldn't. It's you I was interested in."

The *was* struck like a dagger. As soon as he said it, I realized I wasn't ready to lose the one person who'd seen me with a blank slate. "Give me one more chance. Please. I promise I'll be more together."

"I don't need you to be more together," he said. "I need you to let me in a little bit. Return my phone calls. Or it's okay to just say you're not interested."

"I am interested. I've been—" I thought about Burke, and how when we wouldn't talk for more than a week at a time, he'd say, *I've been busy, babe. Doesn't mean I wasn't thinking about you,* before hoisting me up with one arm and carrying me off to bed. This wasn't that. "You said you were okay with taking things slow."

He was silent for a second. He was trying to figure out how to let me down easy. I was about to tell him to forget this whole phone call, but then he said, "You want to do something this weekend?" and my body sank into the couch with more relief than I expected.

"Really?"

"It's not every day you meet someone who can recite Shakespeare on the spot. I want to see what other surprises you've got hiding in there."

I fiddled with my slipper. "I don't know what surprises you'll find. I've shown you who I am." Or, at least, I'd shown him who I wanted to be.

"Okay. You're worried about me Googling you, so how's this? When we go out, tell me three things about you that I couldn't find on the internet if I tried. And I'll do the same."

Three things. Three wasn't too bad. I'd just have to think of three things that wouldn't scare him away, three things that wouldn't hurt too badly when he sold them to a tabloid.

"This sounds an awful lot like a homework assignment," I said, and honestly, I didn't hate it.

"Bad habit to break," he said. "So do we have a deal?"

"We do," I said. "Although I'm not sure how fair it is."

"Why isn't it fair?"

"Because I probably can't even find you on Google."

"Clearly you haven't tried," he said. "Otherwise you'd be fully aware that I was the Illinois state champion of the national book reading competition, grade four."

I couldn't smile, thinking of Josh two floors below me and Shaunn back in her chow mein–stained bed. Still, I tried to sound upbeat when I said, "That's pretty impressive."

"It is pretty impressive. I read more books than any nine-year-old in the state. If it weren't for that kid in Delaware, I could have taken the whole thing. But I heard he had a broken leg. What else was he going to do that summer?"

I didn't want to hang up. I wanted to tell him to come over. "Thank you, Ben."

"For what?"

For being kind to me. For being who he was. "Just because."

I hung up, guilty for my slight relief. I shouldn't have been going on dates when I was messing with an engagement, shouldn't have been cute and jokey when the person whose jokes I laughed hardest at wouldn't speak to me. Maybe calling Ben had been a mistake, but I needed to be near someone who thought there was more to me than I let on, and for some inexplicable reason, he did.

I DIDN'T KNOW WHERE WE'D BE GOING ON OUR DATE. BEN called me the night before to ask if I had any ideas, and I told him, "Take me to your favorite place in the city," anticipating he'd tell me what it was. He only said, "Done deal."

He was supposed to pick me up at seven, but at six fifteen I heard a knock at my door. I knew Phil wouldn't have let him up without buzzing. Deacon, as far as I knew, was still on the West Coast, and he wouldn't bother knocking anyway. It had to be Josh. Maybe he'd want another fight, but the idea of seeing him made me rush to the door. Any relief was erased when I saw it was Caroline.

She looked flawless in her winter white wool coat, burgundy scarf, and matching patent leather heels, and I was reminded of when I was a little girl, how she always used to say I should never leave the house without looking my best. "You never know who you might bump into, or who might have a camera."

When I opened the door, the first thing I asked was, "How did you get up here?"

She smiled and reached out as if to pat my cheek, but stopped an inch away as always. "Is that any way to greet your mother?"

I didn't step aside to let her in. I wasn't going to let her ruin my night with Ben.

"Your doorman let me up," she finally said. "Phil. Gorgeous man."

"He's about eighty years old."

"Age isn't a number, Gorgeous. It's a state of mind. And he's only sixty-eight."

Despite everything, I wished Deacon was there, because I didn't have the strength to send her away. All I could think about was the last time she'd shown up at my door, years before, when he blocked the way and told her to please leave me alone. He still didn't know I saw him give her the money I'd refused. He knew that Caroline's crossing that threshold would have been poison for me, and he did what he had to do to keep her away. "You're a strong girl, Mickie," he'd said, "but when it comes to this power she has over you, you lose all judgment." Which would explain why now, face-to-face with her, I let her in.

"I'm getting ready to go out," I said, watching her take off her coat and scarf. Her dress matched her shoes perfectly.

"Big date?"

"Yes." I refused to go into detail.

She arched an eyebrow and smiled. "How is Burke?"

A sharp pain made me realize I was gnawing on my lip. If Josh were there, he would have nudged me, a sign to come clean. "Actually, Burke and I broke up."

She didn't look surprised. Maybe because she knew how easy it was for a person to walk away from me. I waited for her to tell me to go out and win him and his twenty-million-dollar contract back. "I wondered when you'd tell me."

"You knew?" The thought of her seeing through my lies about his gifts and stories about why he wasn't around was enough to make my stomach burn.

"Darling girl, I'm always telling you. You have to read the news."

If she knew about Burke, she knew about all of it. The Dirty Daisy headlines. My night with Travis Howard. CeCe's tell-all. The rise and fall of the Queen of the Social Scene. If she only knew how much I followed every bit of that news. "Is that why you came back to New York when you did?"

"Pure happenstance," she said. "But don't you see, Gorgeous? This is all a good thing. You're so much better off without him."

She was drawing me right in—we both knew it—but I couldn't help asking, "Why do you say that?"

"People like Burke are fun," she said. "They serve a certain purpose, but there's always an expiration date. Six months tops."

Ben was supposed to arrive in forty minutes. My hair was half dried and I only had mascara on one eye. I needed to get ready, but instead I asked, "What kind of purpose?"

Her eye caught Deacon's piano and she sauntered over to it. "I didn't realize you still played."

"I don't. I never played." She had lied about my talents so much while I was growing up that she didn't even remember the truth herself. "What kind of purpose, Caroline?"

She took a seat on the piano bench but faced away from the instrument. She knew how to play as well as I did. "He's beautiful. He's rich and he's famous. So you date him awhile, get your name back out there, and move on to the next person."

I considered telling her the next person was a high school English teacher with an apartment the size of my living room, and that he was ten times the man Burke Sanders would ever be. "I didn't date Burke because of who he was."

She cocked her head and gave me a look that almost passed as maternal. "Gorgeous . . ."

"I didn't. I dated him because—"

I couldn't finish. Burke wasn't intelligent. We couldn't even carry on a conversation. I saw him once every few weeks and couldn't think of a single thing we had in common or that attracted me to him other than the fact that he was Burke Sanders.

"I cared about Burke." I knew it wasn't the truth. I didn't even care that he broke up with me, only that he made me feel disposable when he did it.

"Whatever the reason, it worked for us." She was trying to placate me, not realizing the word *us* only made me angrier. "It's a little hard to ignore the gap in your résumé, but throw a high-profile relationship in there and it helps conceal it." She popped up and walked over to one of the art prints on my wall. "Paris. God, how I love Paris."

"I'm not using Burke to conceal anything," I said before she could go into her spiel about Europe and all the fabulous times she had there before I was born. "He is a person I dated and it ended. That's all."

"There's nothing wrong with owning the truth. It's like me with Franklin. I knew going into it that it wasn't going to last, but it was the right choice at the time. In the end, I was better for it."

I should have asked why she only cited Franklin, when she'd done the same thing with Jackson and Tyler and now Peter, but I was too infuriated at the thought of her comparing me to herself.

"It's not the same thing," I said. "For starters, I didn't marry Burke."

"Shame. You could have cashed in on that one."

She must have sensed I was ready to throw her out, because she waved a hand and said, "All I'm saying is that every person you meet in life serves a certain purpose. Every person, no matter how you look at it, is a tool that helps you get from one place to the next."

I thought about Deacon, about how quickly I was willing

to believe jumping into bed with him would solve all my problems with Josh.

"I don't believe that's true," I told her. "Sometimes people are just people."

She flashed me the same smile she used when I was a child, when I'd say something far too adult for my age in a room full of executives, and everyone would laugh because it was cute, but no one would take me seriously.

"The person I'm seeing tonight is kind," I said. "And he wants to get to know me. And I'm dating him because I like him and he likes me. That's all."

"Then I'm happy for you. Just remember what I always told you. It's never a bad thing to leave your wall up. If you don't reveal your true self, no one will ever be able to hurt you."

I didn't know why she thought she could reappear after years of not calling and start recycling The Greatest Hits of Caroline Turner's Theories on Life. I didn't want to think about her maybe being right, but the only person I'd opened myself up to was now saying "I love you" to somebody else. Maybe once people really got to know me, once they saw I wasn't Daisy Breyer, they'd always walk away.

"Why did you come here?" I asked.

"I didn't like the way we left things the other day."

"When does he need an answer?"

Relief flashed in her eyes when she realized I still hadn't said no to *Crescent Grove*. "By next week."

"Then I'll let you know by next week."

I should have said no. I should have told her she had no right to come into my apartment—the apartment I had to buy when I should have still had a home with her—and comment on my life. But part of her was right. I couldn't keep doing nothing, and I had to admit, life was a whole lot easier with a script.

"Can I just say one thing?" Without giving me the chance

to respond, she continued, "Before you make an impulsive decision, remember that life only gives you a handful of chances for success. You can have all the talent and brains and looks in the world, but you have to go after what you want if you're ever going to be happy. This show may not be perfect, but it's a stepping stone. It's what we can get right now. It will lead to other things."

She collected her coat, draped her scarf effortlessly around her neck, and took one long look at me. For a minute, I thought she'd assure me if I decided against the show, she'd still support me, but she just unbuckled her high heels and slid them over. "These will go perfectly with that top." I'd forgotten we wore the same size.

I didn't pick them up. "I'm not wearing your shoes, Caroline. What, are you going to walk back barefoot?"

She gave me one of her looks. "Don't you remember anything I taught you?" She reached into her Birkin and pulled out a pair of ballet flats. It wasn't until she was out the door that I remembered one of her many mantras. She never focused on my studies, told me nothing about my heritage, and certainly didn't show me how to become a well-adjusted adult. But when it came to footwear, she had one valuable lesson: Always bring a spare, in case you're on a bad date and need to run.

I WAS ADAMANT ABOUT NOT WEARING THE SHOES. I'D never needed anything from Caroline in the past. I certainly didn't need a pair of burgundy Manolo Blahniks when I had a closet full of every color, texture, and style. Caroline was right, though—they did go perfectly with my top—so I had no choice but to change into a different sweater and throw on my mukluks.

Ben greeted me with a tentative kiss in the lobby, and I did all I could to focus on him and not on what Caroline had said.

I didn't want to think about life's handful of chances or résumé fillers or tools to get from one place to the next. I didn't want to think about *Crescent Grove*. For one night, I wanted to be a normal girl on a normal date with a normal guy.

"Holden would have a field day with those boots," he said, nudging one of the pom-poms with his toe.

"I hope I'm dressed okay for where we're going."

He pretended to mull it over. "I don't know. There's a pretty serious dress code."

"So where are we going?"

"You said you didn't want to know."

"No, I didn't. I said for you to pick."

"Oh, so I guess I just made the surprise thing up myself, then." He smiled, revealing a slight dimple on his left cheek but not his right. He was cuter than I'd let myself realize. Any girl would have been lucky to go out with him. I was lucky to go out with him.

"You ready to go?" he asked.

"Yes." Maybe once I said it out loud, I would be. "But I forgot something upstairs." My last lie. "I'll meet you outside."

I watched him through the glass door, standing patiently on the sidewalk with his hands in the pockets of his wool peacoat. I didn't want to tell him any more half-truths, but if I didn't take care of this before I left, it would be weighing on my mind all night.

Phil was standing behind the door, shielded from the November cold, his TV turned to *Inside Edition*. He knew I wasn't going back upstairs judging by the dry "Yes, Miss Turner?" he gave me.

"Phil, can you do me a favor? From now on, can you not send my mother up without buzzing me first?"

He almost looked apologetic. "I know. Mr. McKenzie already told me. It won't happen again."

Everything in my mind came to a halt and I looked around

the lobby for a sign of him. "What do you mean? What did Josh tell you?"

Any remorse was replaced with annoyance. I was clearly interrupting his show with my he-said-she-said inquiries. "He was on his way out. I asked him how he was doing—you know, he got some terrible reviews on that performance of his—"

"Yes. I know. Continue."

"Well, I happened to mention that your mother was upstairs, that she wanted to surprise you, and since I know you and Mr. McKenzie are close, I thought he'd want to go up and meet her." He raised his eyebrows. "But apparently he already has."

I wasn't sure how much Phil knew. I was certain Josh wouldn't tell him my business. "What did he say?"

"Just that I shouldn't have let her up without buzzing you first. So from now on, I won't."

He acted as if this were a lot to ask, as if this wasn't his job in the first place. "How about from now on you don't let *anyone* up without buzzing me first?"

"Even Mr. King?"

I should have known that was coming. I needed to sort the Deacon mess out, but now wasn't the time. "Mr. King has a key."

"Okay. So Mr. King is okay to go up. And Mr. . . ." He looked through the glass pane. ". . . English, was it?"

Maybe he wasn't asking to be cruel, but it sure felt like it.

"Mr. English doesn't have a key."

Apparently, that was enough for Phil. As he opened the door to let me out, I asked one last question.

"How did Josh seem to you?"

Phil looked surprised. "He said he was doing fine, but if I'm being honest, he looked like he'd seen better days."

I wanted to ask Phil if he could tell Josh, the next time he saw him, that I was asking about him, but that would probably lead to a series of follow-up questions I wasn't quite prepared for.

When I exited the building, Ben turned and looked at me, holding out his hand. "Get what you needed?"

"Yep." I considered his open palm. I'd never been a hand-holder, and it didn't seem right accepting it when I had just given Deacon priority over him to my apartment. My first instinct was to cross my arms and walk alongside him, but my instincts had never done me any good. I slid my hand into his. "Now can you tell me where we're going?"

"I told you to trust me, didn't I? I'm taking you to my favorite place in New York. That's what you asked for. Oh, and by the way, you're going to absolutely hate it. I expect full mockery."

"You're really selling it."

"We'll need to pick up food on the way," he said. "It's kind of part of the whole experience. Something that travels easily. What's your favorite food?"

My mind went to turkey clubs and grilled cheese with tomato, but I couldn't share that with Ben, because then he might ask where I liked them best, and I couldn't open up about Bennett's and the best friend I'd lost.

"I don't really have a favorite food."

"Come on, everyone has a favorite food," he said. "What is it? This could count as the first of the three things you're going to tell me tonight."

I hoped he couldn't feel my palm sweating in his. After Caroline's speech about leaving up my wall, even three simple facts seemed dangerous. "What's your favorite food?" I asked, hoping he'd drop it. Ben was too smart for that.

"Macaroni and cheese, and don't think you can deflect. What, is it something embarrassing like—"

"Like macaroni and cheese?"

"I was going to say like haggis. And PS, macaroni and cheese is not embarrassing."

"Not if you're twelve."

"Okay, what's your least favorite food?"

Ben was nice, and he liked me. I didn't want another Burke Sanders relationship. I didn't want to be Caroline.

"Green apples. I hate green apples." I waited for a reaction, for him to laugh at me, but he just looked at me, waiting for me to go on. "Daisy was always eating green apples on *Breyer's Town*. The directors thought they matched her eyes. So take after take for five seasons, it was one green apple after another. And now they make me gag."

He took me in silently for a second. I thought he might have forgotten what *Breyer's Town* was. "It's interesting how you say that."

"What?" I didn't think gag reflexes were all that interesting.

"You say *Daisy* ate a lot of green apples and they matched *her* eyes. I mean, they're your eyes."

I wanted to disappear. What Ben didn't understand was there were times I didn't know whose eyes they actually were.

"Weren't we talking about getting food?" I asked. This time, Ben allowed me to change the subject.

"I believe we were. What are you in the mood for?"

"What do you normally get when you're going to wherever it is we're going?"

"Hot chocolate and french fries. I'm pretty high-class about it."

It sounded absolutely disgusting but pretty wonderful at the same time. "You're kind of weird, Ben English."

He lifted my hand and kissed it. "I'm not the one with pom-poms on my boots."

THIRTY-FIVE MINUTES LATER, OUR HANDS NOW HOLDING cocoa and fries instead of each other, we arrived at Ben's favorite place in the city. I had no other choice but to say, "You really aren't from New York, are you?"

Only Ben would pick the rink at Rockefeller Center. He

looked proud and somewhat amused by my reaction. "I told you I expected full mockery."

The thought of exchanging my warm and fuzzy boots—my warm and fuzzy pricey boots—for a pair of rented skates made me itch. "We're not going skating, are we?"

"We are not going skating, but glad to know how you feel about it." He opened his hot chocolate and leaned on the railing overlooking the rink. "I like to come here and people watch."

"And no one gets creeped out by that?"

"Why would anyone get creeped out by that? Look at all the people here. No one's paying attention to me."

A pang of envy stabbed my heart. I avoided places as public as Rockefeller Center because I didn't want all eyes on me. With my luck, a group of tourists would spot me and ask me to pose for a picture. Ben would probably offer to hold the camera.

"And this is your favorite place in New York?"

"Sure is. What's yours?"

I opened my mouth to give him my answer. I'd lived there for twenty-seven years. I had to have a favorite place. "I don't know. My apartment?"

He laughed. "Besides your apartment."

If he'd asked me this question a few months before, I would have searched through the catalog of clubs I frequented, even though I wasn't really a fan of any of them. I'd been to every buzzed-about restaurant that opened in the city, and not a single one stuck out as mentionable. Every place I could think of had a lot of hype and little to remember.

"I don't know why my apartment's off the table." I hoped I sounded coy and not as desperate as I was starting to feel.

His smile was beginning to look forced and tired, and we hadn't even been out long. "All right, what makes it your favorite place? It's a stunning building, I'll give you that."

I thought about when I left college and had no idea where to go. I kept imagining Caroline was going to come back and point me in the right direction. It felt like a miracle when Josh said the apartment above his was available, and it was big enough that if Caroline did return, there'd be room for her. Months later, when Deacon moved in, he made it feel more permanent. He even found an 8x10 picture of me with Lionel Richie from the set of *Breyer's Town* and hung it by the door. It was from Daisy's dance recital episode, which they wrote when Caroline let it slip that I was classically trained in ballet. By the time they realized that I didn't know my *tendu* from my *plié*, it was too late. They had already hired Lionel to sing "Ballerina Girl," and I had to take a crash course in order to fudge an arabesque or two. Every time Deacon came home, he'd tip an imaginary hat to the photo and say, "Lionel," before proceeding any farther.

"I guess it's the only thing that's ever been mine," I said, and I swear the fatigue in Ben's eyes turned to pity. I didn't know if I could bear one more question. If I pulled just one thread, the whole together persona I'd created would unravel. "What do you like about people watching?"

He looked like he might push it, point out that I was deflecting again, but he took a breath and looked back at the rink. "I love to try to figure out what everyone's deal is—where they come from, what makes them tick. Like these two—"

He pointed to a couple below. The guy didn't look thrilled with the idea of ice-skating. "Maybe they just got engaged. Or maybe they're on their second date. Or maybe he's married and she's the other woman." That last one definitely turned me off the cold french fry I was putting in my mouth.

"So I come here, or sometimes I sit on the steps of the library, and I people watch. It's kind of my thing."

I homed in on the couple skating. The girl was clinging to her boyfriend/fiancé/secret lover as if just holding on to him was helping her breathe. I knew exactly how she felt, because even though I didn't want to think about him then, that was how I was with Deacon. Caroline could say what she wanted about my having ulterior motives with Burke or the chain of men that preceded him, but with Deacon I had always let my passion lead, and sometimes that passion blinded me. Maybe that led to our downfall, but it was the antithesis of all of Caroline's relationships, and that much I could feel good about, knowing I was with him because I couldn't bear not to be, couldn't stand within ten feet of him without aching to touch his skin. I wished I could have felt that way about Ben.

I put down my hot chocolate and stuck my hands in Ben's coat pocket. "I forgot my gloves."

He rubbed the outside of the wool overlay, warming my hands within. "Better?"

I didn't want to lie, so I leaned my head on his shoulder, hoping that would make me feel more.

"Okay, I've told you my thing," he said. "What's yours?"

"I don't really have a thing."

"Well, I told you three things about myself, and so far you've only said one."

I looked at him. "You didn't say three things."

"Sure I did. Mac 'n' cheese, Rockefeller Center, and people watching."

"Those last two are kind of the same."

"Okay," he conceded. "How about this. The worst gift I ever got was when I was eleven. My aunt from Seattle brought me a Ouija board for my birthday."

"What's wrong with a Ouija board?"

"I was a sensitive eleven-year-old. It completely freaked me out."

I pictured Ben as a kid, probably as polite as he was today, trying to act appreciative to his aunt. The image was adorable, but it also made me envious that this was his biggest concern at that age.

"What was your worst gift?" he asked. "Or your best gift. I'll take either one."

My first thought was the Suzy Surprise doll, the surprise being that you never knew if she was going to speak, cry, or pee. But Suzy Surprise wasn't real—she was manufactured by the team at *Breyer's Town*—and it was Daisy who wanted Suzy Surprise so desperately, not me. The producers were nice enough to let me take the doll home after filming, but she neither spoke or cried, nor peed. It was all fabricated for the show.

"I'll have to think about that one."

I could tell Ben was getting agitated by my lack of answers. "Santa never brought you something you still think about to this day?"

I took my hands out of his pocket, regretting that I agreed to this three-fact pact. "These are silly questions, Ben."

His expression resembled that of a director who, after a dozen takes due to flubbed lines, was no longer able to compose his feigned patience. "I'm just trying for something here."

The truth was that Caroline once told me about Shirley Temple, and how she stopped believing in Santa Claus when she went to have her picture taken with him and he recognized her from the movies. My mother wanted to spare me, so we never did Santa, à la *Miracle on 34th Street*. But that sounded pathetic, so I said, "I really don't remember."

He sighed. Take thirteen. "Do you want to go get a beer?"

I hated beer, but I couldn't have asked for a better escape route. Maybe he'd finally given up on his little assignment. We walked to a nearby bar, and this time when he held out his hand, I was grateful it was still on offer. I didn't even mind the peanut shells on the floor or the somewhat sticky smell of the place. I was determined to stick this thing out—but when we stepped inside, I could feel the weight of people's stares. Maybe the cover of normalcy Ben gave me was fading. Maybe it had never been there at all.

"Can we sit in the corner?" I asked, eyeing the empty table shrouded in the dimmest lighting.

Ben nodded. "Sure. You go get a seat and I'll grab some beers. What do you like?"

I couldn't be bothered to pretend I had a favorite beer when I had to focus on walking across the room alone. "Whatever you're getting is fine."

I kept my head down as I made my way to the table. I didn't want to know how many people had their phones out, ready to capture Daisy doing something that would land her back in the tabloids. I couldn't imagine how many of them at that very moment were texting their friends, asking if they thought it was really me. It felt like an eternity before Ben reached the table with two pints.

"You hungry?" he asked. "This place has pretty good pizza. I know the fries didn't really cut it."

"Okay," I said, although food was the last thing on my mind.

"What kind do you like?"

"I'm not picky."

"Do you like cheese? Veggie? Meat?"

The back of my nose burned. If I were with Burke, we would have had extra pepperoni. Deacon, pineapple. Jordan the chef was always trying something new, and Gregory the painter would only eat pepper and onion. Whatever they wanted, I went with.

"It really doesn't matter," I said.

"Kayla, I'm just asking what you want on your pizza."

The bar felt smaller. I wished he'd stop calling me that. Kayla would know in an instant what kind of pizza she liked. "Plain cheese?"

"Plain cheese it is." His eyes were kind, but something in his tone said, *Was that so hard?* He didn't get that it was.

I wished I could have thought of something to say while

waiting for the food to arrive, but I was too worried about what he'd ask me next. Maybe he was as tired of the charade as I was, because he stayed quiet, drumming his fingertips on the table, watching one of the TVs hanging from the ceiling. A couple around our age approached our table, and I was sure they were about to call me out, but then the guy gave Ben a half handshake, half hug and said, "English! What's up?"

Ben looked relieved to see them. Maybe he was glad to have someone else to talk to, but the fact that he didn't seem overly surprised they were there made me wonder if I'd been ambushed.

Ben introduced me to Greg and Callie, friends of his from Columbia. They seemed nice enough, but I knew people, and I knew they were only being polite for Ben's sake. They were probably thinking, *Good going, English. Bed Dirty Daisy, then be done with her.* Maybe Caroline was right. Maybe every person was a tool, and maybe I was Ben's tool for impressing his friends.

"Mind if we sit for a sec?" Greg asked, and they set down their beers before Ben could nod his agreement.

"So you're the girl Ben's been seeing," Callie said, trying to act friendly, like she wasn't judging me behind her trendy glasses and turtleneck. Just because Ben hadn't seen my thong in the tabloids didn't mean they hadn't. "Where did you guys meet again?"

I didn't know how I'd ended up in this situation. After the round of interview questions Ben had thrown at me, now I had a new firing squad.

"The Bookery." I waited for a snicker. They only nodded, but I knew they were wondering what I'd been doing in a bookstore. They probably thought I stopped in to ask for directions.

"That's cool," Callie said. "Are you a big reader?"

They waited for my answer. I hoped Ben would jump in and save me, but he, like the two of them, continued staring.

"I like to read. But I wouldn't say I'm a big reader." I added the last part quickly, before they could ask me what types of books I liked or who my favorite author was. I blanked on all the titles from my stolen syllabus, and somehow, I didn't think those Natalie Wood biographies I loved so much would impress them.

Ben shot me a confused look. "You're always reading."

Of course he thought that. It was what I'd projected. It was even almost true, but that didn't mean it was real.

The pizza arrived, and I could feel Greg and Callie looking at me. They were probably trying to guess if I would eat, or starve, or eat and throw it up in the bathroom. I took a piece and put it on my plate, but I had no appetite.

I felt like they were all staring at me, waiting for me to perform. It reminded me of when I was a kid, when Caroline would trot me out in front of casting directors, and they'd all wait for me to say something smart and precocious.

"So, what do you both do?" I asked. It was the question I hated most, but I wanted to be the kind of person who could sit with people and talk and be normal. Callie said she was in social work, and Greg was an accountant. I waited for the inevitable *And what do you do?* But it shouldn't have surprised me that they didn't ask. They were probably very aware that I did nothing.

"Kayla's an image consultant," Ben offered, giving me an encouraging nod to elaborate. My lip burned. I was gnawing at it again.

"You don't act anymore?" Greg asked. Callie shot him a look, like she couldn't believe he'd said it.

"Not really," I said, although maybe that wasn't accurate. I could have told them about *Crescent Grove.* I could have told them my whole life was an act.

"How long have you been consulting?" Callie asked.

The bar felt stifling. In the face of two strangers, it didn't feel like a half-truth at all. It felt like what it was: an outright fabrication. "Awhile."

"It must be fascinating," she said. 'I'm sure you're really good at it."

I thought about Josh, and how the carefully curated outfit I'd selected for him didn't stop the press from tearing him apart. I thought about Deacon, and how the weeks I'd dedicated to helping him find his old self left him with nothing but a song he'd gotten into a drunken stupor over. Callie shouldn't have been so sure.

Two beers in, Greg leaned forward and said, "Okay, Michaela Turner, you have to tell us what it was like when—"

From the way the table shifted, I could tell that Ben either stepped on his foot or kicked him in the shin. Greg's eyes widened, and when he took in Ben's look of warning, he let out a laugh. Ben had definitely cautioned them to stay away from any mention of Daisy. Or maybe Greg was going to ask about the Colonel. Whatever the case, it made me more embarrassed than if he'd actually asked.

"Come on, English. I was going to ask her what it was like when she met Holden." Greg looked back at me. "Great dog, isn't he?"

That clearly was not his original question, but I didn't want to make things even worse than they already were, so I said, "Yeah."

"He really is a sweet dog," Callie said, probably trying to smooth things over. "If Ben hadn't rescued him, who knows what would have happened."

"Why do you say that?" I asked.

"I told you his story," Ben said. "Didn't I?"

"You should have seen him when Ben first got him," Greg said. "He hardly had any use of one of his back legs." He clamped his hand on Ben's shoulder in a way he probably wouldn't have if he was sober. "This guy spent months bringing that dog to physical therapy so they wouldn't amputate it. His sister says he's always been like that. Bringing in strays, trying to save them. Lost causes are kind of his thing."

The two sips of beer I'd had fell flat in my stomach. His friends probably thought I was so below their intellectual radar that I wouldn't get what they meant. Ben liked to save things. Of course he did. That explained why he first approached me in the bookstore, and why he let me stay at his place, and why he kept coming back when I'd ignore his calls and texts. Just for a moment, I craved my relationship with Burke. Maybe it was shallow, maybe neither of us was faithful, but at least I didn't feel like I was being analyzed on *Oprah*. I'd met some of his teammates, and they had never asked me a single thing about myself. They hit on me, made inappropriate propositions, and more than one grabbed my ass, but I'd never been humiliated.

"You know what," I said, grabbing my purse. "I'm going to call it a night. It was nice meeting you." Before they could react, I stood up and headed outside. Ben followed close behind.

"What are you doing?" he asked. I was already hailing a cab, and he tried pushing my arm down, but Ben was too gentlemanly to use force, so my position remained the same.

"I don't need your pity, Ben. And I don't need to sit there and be insulted by your friends."

"What are you talking about?" After another unsuccessful attempt at pushing my arm down, he said, "Can you please stop for two seconds and tell me what the hell is going on?"

I turned and faced him. "Lost causes are kind of your thing?"

"They were talking about my dog," he said, as if the thought that I'd take it any other way was absurd.

"Why did you bring me here? To show me off? Parade me in front of your buddies like some kind of spectacle?" I should have known that the minute he found out I'd been famous, everything would change.

"I had no idea they were going to be here—"

"Well, you didn't seem too surprised to see them."

If this was a Deacon fight, he would have kicked a nearby trash can, told me to leave, then just as I was about to get into the taxi, captured me with a blazing kiss. Ben just looked defeated, like he had no idea how we got from my hands in his pocket at the rink to fighting in the street. To be honest, I had no idea how it happened, either.

"They come here a lot," he said. "*I* come here a lot. Did I know they were going to be here tonight, at the exact same time we were? No. But does it surprise me? Not really."

My eyes burned. I couldn't believe this was happening with Ben—Ben, who seemed so easy.

"What about *Breyer's Town*?" I asked. "You clearly warned them to stay away from that topic of conversation."

"Are you kidding me? You never mentioned it to me once, and now you're offended that no one brought it up? I don't know what you want."

What I wanted was to be the kind of person who could sit in a bar with her normal boyfriend and his normal friends and have a normal conversation. I wanted to be the kind of person who could answer a simple question like "What's your favorite food?" without feeling like if I said the wrong thing, the whole world might fall apart.

"I don't know what kind of relationships you've been in in the past," Ben said. "But this isn't how I do things. I'm not going to keep chasing you. I don't even know who you are right now. What happened to the girl I met at the bookstore?"

A taxi pulled up and I hesitated before opening the door. I didn't want to be like Caroline. I didn't want to spend my life trying to align myself with guys who could get me places or make me feel important. But the cab was there, waiting, and Ben had seen me for what I was, so I had no choice but to get in.

"The girl you met at the bookstore doesn't exist," I said.

He leaned on the open door. "This is really what you want?" He was beyond begging, beyond trying to convince me to come inside. I was beyond explanation. When I didn't answer, he said, "I hope you find what makes you happy, Michaela. Clearly, it's not me. But for your sake, I really hope you find it."

With that, Ben shut the door, and true to his word, he didn't follow me.

CHAPTER TWENTY-ONE

I've always thought the way you feel about a breakup says more about who you are as a person than it does about the relationship. When Deacon broke up with me, I was inconsolable, and I felt like that meant I was weak. When Burke dumped me and I didn't care, I thought that made me shallow. With Ben English, I didn't know what to make of how I felt, but something told me I was a severely screwed-up individual.

Maybe Caroline was right about leaving up my wall. Maybe life was easier that way. If I'd actually opened myself up to Ben, things would have ended anyway. That was how it worked. Then he would have ended up engaged to someone else, and I'd find myself hoarding his most precious belongings and avoiding my bed because the sheets smelled like his skin.

I wanted to let myself feel worse about Ben. I wanted to be the kind of person who cried into her pillow and ate ice cream and called her girlfriends to vent. That's what Daisy would have done, but all I could think about was how suffocated I felt when his friends were talking to me, how panicked I became at every simple question he posed. His last words about hoping I found what made me happy stuck in my head like an old Boyz of the Nation song, and no matter what I did, I couldn't shake them.

My every urge told me to go downstairs, plop down on Josh's couch, and tell him what I was feeling. Somehow, he always had a way of making my abnormal and nonsensical thoughts seem normal and full of sense. Knowing he was two floors below me and that I couldn't even speak to him made me nauseated.

I looked out my window, half expecting to find Ben standing outside in some big romantic *Say Anything* moment. All I saw was a cluster of girls heading up the street in search of a cab. It was clear they were in pursuit of a hot new club—a place where they could party away the worries of the week. It was early November, but they were all dressed in low-cut tanks and strapless dresses. Their flesh was turning purple, but what did it matter? They looked good. Rewind two months and that had been me. I didn't know why I thought there was more to me than drinking and dancing until dawn. Maybe that was all I had to offer the world. Maybe I was just the girl who used to play Daisy Breyer.

I'd been fooling myself with Ben, pretending to be a normal girl in a normal relationship who went to movies and talked about her interests. That wasn't me. Breaking up with Ben the English teacher wasn't any different than breaking up with Burke the ballplayer or Jordan the chef or Lewis the photographer. I'd move past him the same way.

Before I had a chance to second-guess what I was doing, I changed out of my jeans and slipped into a Missoni minidress. I was already starting to feel more like myself. I was about to throw on a pair of never-worn Jimmy Choos when I spotted the heels Caroline had pushed on me earlier that night, right where she'd left them. I'd thought my refusing them had been some grand statement, but now I saw they were just shoes.

They pinched my toes a little when I stepped into them, but by the end of the night I'd feel numb, so I ignored the pain and headed downstairs.

I didn't care what club I went to—two months out of the circuit might as well have been two years. I scrolled through the contacts in my phone while I waited for a cab, looking for someone to go with, someone who could give me the inside track to what was happening where. I couldn't remember the last time I'd spoken to half these people, but with this crowd, that wasn't really an issue. Someone could be your mortal enemy one day and your best friend the next. Even though I despised Portia Ambrose, an heiress-slash-model I used to party with, I sent her a text and asked what was going on. I knew I'd been out of the loop for a long time when she replied two seconds later with Jungle and I had no idea what or where she meant.

As it turned out, Portia's club of choice was exactly where Magic once stood, only it now had a new name, new ownership, and no more rules about Day-Glo necklaces. The line of people waiting to get in wrapped around the block, and the sidewalk was vibrating from the thumping music inside. If I wanted to stop myself from thinking, this place looked like the perfect remedy. I headed past the masses and went straight for the door, but without CeCe or any of the frenemies who preceded her by my side, I felt kind of pathetic, especially when I realized I had about five years on everyone there. I almost worried I wouldn't be let in, that I'd be told to go to the back of the line and wait like everyone else—until I saw Bobby the Bouncer.

Bobby had been a staple in the club scene since I started making the rounds at nineteen. The names of the bars had changed, his hairline had gradually receded, but year after year, you could always count on seeing him behind some velvet rope or other. As soon as he saw me, he unlatched the chain and gave me a kiss on the cheek, leaving an oily residue of aftershave on my skin.

"Michaela Turner," he said. "Rumor had it you left us all behind."

I flashed him the smile I reserved for acquaintances of the party world. I was a little scared by how easily I slipped back into it. "There have been a lot of rumors about me. I hope you don't believe them all."

"Only the things I've seen with my own eyes."

I tried not to remember the many instances he could have been referring to. He'd been there for the Deacon years. He could have written a book with the things he'd witnessed.

The club may have changed since the last time I'd been there—as its name implied, it was now suited up with leopard-print walls and tiger-skin rugs—but the crowd was exactly the same: trust fund guys practically having sex on the couches with girls who wouldn't have given them a second glance if the guys weren't rich and the girls weren't drunk; socialites trying to inconspicuously wipe their noses after trips to the ladies' room; celebutantes dancing on the bar, sans panties. Maybe Ben's friends weren't so bad, after all.

I didn't see anyone I knew, and I started to worry that the text had been a big joke, or maybe everyone had already decided this place was over and had moved on to the next activity. I didn't feel like drinking, but I needed something to busy my hands. I ordered a Stoli Raz and Sprite and was looking for a spot to position myself when I finally saw Portia Ambrose supporting herself on a nearby couch.

She gave me a glazed-over look when I sat next to her, whatever chemicals she'd ingested preventing her sight, mind, and speech from connecting. "Michaela!" She sounded surprised to see me. She clearly didn't remember the text. "Who are you here with?"

I shrugged and repeated her own question back to her. It

hadn't worked with Ben, but it would certainly work with Portia.

"Just Frankie and Sam and Natalie and Hunter and everyone." She assumed I knew who everyone included. The sad thing was, I did.

"So what are you doing here?" she asked, rubbing her eye and smudging her eyeliner in the process. She already had a charcoal line running from her other eye, so at least now they matched. "I thought you were over this or whatever."

I raised my drink and took a sip. "I'm here, aren't I?"

She leaned closer to me, though it was probably more for support than for any other reason. I couldn't help but notice that her excessive tanning had taken a toll on her skin, and her heavy makeup wasn't doing much to remedy the situation. She looked thirty-eight, though she was only twenty-eight, and her résumé claimed she was twenty-four. I always thought she and I were so different, but maybe we were heading down the same path.

I'd never been to a real high school, but I'd always imagined this scene to be a lot like one, and Portia Ambrose was its gossip guru. Within four minutes, I was completely caught up on everything I'd missed in the past two months. Apparently, a lot had happened while I was dating an English teacher. Dyana Wynters showed up at some club opening and everyone thought she was pregnant but as it turned out she was just in need of a colonic. CeCe had been thrown from a mechanical bull and everyone was pretty sure she'd fractured her tibia but she went to the hospital and luckily, there was just some minor bruising. As I listened to the full list of botched lip injections and bungled auditions, I found it hard to believe there was a time when I actually knew all these things, and a time before that when I actually cared. I'd forgotten that by walking into this club, I was opening myself up for just as much discussion and speculation. If I said yes to *Crescent Grove*, I'd be inviting it even more.

"Sucks about Deacon, huh?" she asked. "I hear he and Shaunn are getting married next summer."

It was like she'd stuck her manicured hand into my chest and squeezed my heart with all the power her Pilates could muster. I could say a lot about Portia, but if she said Deacon had set a date, he had set a date.

"Next summer," I repeated.

She traced a line down the side of her glass and licked the moisture off her finger. "Hamptons."

I tried to push the image from my mind of Deacon, Shaunn, and all their guests decked out in white, under white tents on the white sands of a private beach. I tried not to imagine the look he'd have in his eyes when he said those two words, the two words that would officially start his life with someone who wasn't me. It took every cell in my body to maintain enough composure to smile, swallow, and say, "I don't see what that has to do with me."

She shrugged with a little self-satisfied smirk. "I'm just saying." Then, as if the entire conversation never happened, she grabbed my hand like we were best friends. "Oh my God, you know who's here? Travis." Before I had a chance to react, she waved an arm in the air and said, "Look, there he is!" I tried to make a getaway, but it was too late. Travis Howard was heading our way. I thought I wanted to be my old self again, and Travis was definitely part of that life, but the closer he got, the more I wanted to duck behind the couch and crawl out of the club unnoticed.

Before he reached us, Portia jumped up and said, "I've totally gotta piss." She was gone within seconds, and I was left on the couch, alone—completely sober—with my annual one-night stand approaching.

"What's up, Michaela Rose?" He sunk down next to me, a beer in one hand and what appeared to be a Jack and Coke in the other.

"Hey, Travis." I searched for something interesting to say, something to make this less uncomfortable. This was a man I'd slept with—many times. I had to be able to hold a conversation with him. "What have you been up to?"

He shrugged, taking a swig from his glass and chasing it with his beer. "Touring."

I waited for him to elaborate or ask what I'd been up to. I shouldn't have been surprised that he didn't. Travis and I never talked unless we were so drunk we could barely stand. Scratch that. Once we got to that point, we were doing everything but talking. The last time I'd seen him was the day Burke broke up with me, when he was peeing into a toilet full of my vomit. That wasn't a memory I wanted to reminisce over, so I asked, "How long have you been in New York?"

"Few days. I was gonna call you."

He wasn't. Travis and I never hooked up twice in a twelve-month period.

We shared another moment of silence, me trying to think of something to say, Travis tapping the bottom of his beer bottle on the knee of his leather pants. I wondered if he'd been wearing the same pair all these years—if these were the ones I always stumbled over on my bedroom floor, or if he had a closet full of them. Afraid that Travis would misconstrue my looking at his pants as my wanting to get into them, I looked him in the eye and asked, "So are you working on a new album or promoting older stuff or what?"

"New stuff," he said. "And older stuff."

I suddenly knew how Ben must have felt all night, except that Ben actually cared about my answers, or nonanswers, as it turned out. I tried to remind myself that this was what I wanted—no talking, no feelings, no emotion. I should have been happy that Travis was his usual monosyllabic self.

He drained his drink and put the glass behind him, leaving his right hand free to trace the letter *M* into my palm with his thumb. This was always step one. Step two was me bringing my hand to his chest, and step three was him sticking his tongue down my throat. For someone with so many tattoos and piercings, Travis was a stickler for a good routine. It seemed to throw him that instead of doing my part, I decided to persist in the riveting conversation we had going.

"So are you still living in LA?"

He nodded. Then—shock of the century—he asked, "You still at . . . ?"

"Yeah," I said. "Still in the West Village."

Apparently, this was enough talking for one night, because he said, "Some things never change," then immediately asked, "Wanna go upstairs?"

The few sips of vodka I'd had turned in my stomach. Maybe I'd grown too accustomed to Ben and his hand-holding and we-can-take-things-slow speeches, but I'd never remembered Travis to be so seedy. I had to remind myself of the reasons I ran from Ben in the first place, and that Travis offered no questions, no strings.

"What's upstairs?" I knew very well that the answer wouldn't be *a beautiful view of the city.*

Travis nodded toward the shag-carpeted staircase, leading to a darkened upper level. "A bigger couch."

I swirled the ice around my glass, trying to think of one good reason I should say no. Travis Howard had always been exactly what I'd needed in the past.

"As soon as I finish this drink," I said.

Travis never smiled, but a mischievous light flickered in his eyes as he took the glass from my hand and sucked down its contents. "Now are you ready?"

I thought about Ben, about the look on his face when I left him on the sidewalk, the look of disappointment when he realized that no matter how hard he pushed, he wasn't going to crack into some hidden depth I'd been holding out on. I needed to stop thinking about him. Caroline had always taught me to leave the past in the past, and though it had only been a few hours, I had to put Ben into that compartment of things gone by, along with that normal girl I'd pretended to be.

"Let me run to the bathroom," I said. "I'll meet you upstairs."

I slipped away to the ladies' room, where the conduct was anything but ladylike. One girl was throwing up, one was having the longest pee in history, and another was passed out on the floor. This was my scene, all right.

I sat down on the chaise longue and practiced my breathing exercises, telling myself I was making too much out of this. This was who I was. I wasn't the girl who dated high school teachers. I was the girl who hung on to engaged ex-boyfriends because they made her feel needed and had drunken one-night stands because she was bored and alone. Ben had freaked me out with his questions and prying and getting-to-know-you talk, and I needed to be happy that Travis didn't want to talk at all. Ben expected me to be something I wasn't; Travis never expected anything more than a good time.

When I got upstairs, I didn't see Travis, and I felt a flash of relief. I looked over the banister at the club below, trying to see if he was still down there, or if he'd recast the role of "Easy Girl in Bar #1" and had already left with my replacement. I could see Portia on yet another couch, sandwiched between two guys I didn't recognize, and who the next morning she wouldn't recognize, either. I spotted a few other familiar faces, doing body shots and flashing body parts, just as they had when we were all nineteen or twenty. There was a reason I'd loved this world so much back then. It was a place where I could escape, where I didn't have to be the girl who used to be on TV, where I could just be a girl who looked good and had too much to drink and who guys wanted in their bed. It didn't matter that I didn't know who Michaela Turner was apart from Daisy Breyer, because no one cared. I didn't know why it suddenly felt so demoralizing.

"Michaela Rose."

I turned and saw Travis, lounging on a leopard-print couch in the corner. The minute I approached him, he pulled me down, slid his hands up my dress, and started smothering me with alcohol-induced kisses—first my earlobe, then my neck, then my chest. It seemed to occur to him that maybe it was bad form to reacquaint himself with my breasts before properly kissing me on the lips, so his beer-and-Jack-soaked mouth found its way to mine as he started to unzip his leather pants.

"How do you know no one else is going to come up here?" I asked, my lower lip getting snagged on the new hoop that was jutting through his.

He pulled back, his hazel eyes so bloodshot they almost looked amber. "You serious?"

Of course I was serious, and also kind of offended that the idea of showing some decorum was so preposterous. Then I remembered that the first time I hooked up with Travis was in the coatroom of a club just like this, so I could kind of see where he'd get that idea. At the time, Deacon had just smashed my heart to pieces by sleeping with a girl who "meant nothing" to him, and I wanted to get back at him by doing the same. I made it out to be more than it was to Deacon, telling him Travis had written a song for me, too. I never told him that "Michaela Rose" was only a substitute for "Lyla Jane" because Travis had just broken up with his girlfriend and didn't want to use her name in his song. Of course, Deacon knew me enough to see through my facade. "You're nothing more to him than a warm body," he'd said. "And all he is to you is an excuse to avoid dealing with what's really going on." I had been so furious that that was his only reaction, but now I could see he was completely right. For six years, whenever I needed him, Travis Howard had been my escape route.

I was using this whole scene as a shield, just as I had when I was nineteen, because it was easier, safer. But between coke-nosed Portia and the vomit party in the bathroom and Travis and his what's-the-big-deal-about-having-sex-in-public eyes, I had to admit that maybe this wasn't who I was anymore. I didn't know if this was ever who I was. I didn't want to end up like Bobby the Bouncer, or Portia Ambrose, or Travis Howard. I was twenty-seven years old, and if I couldn't stick around to answer one simple question for the guy I was dating, I would end up like everyone else here, or worse.

"I can't do this."

Travis squinted. The alcohol he'd consumed seemed to cause a delay in his understanding. "We can go to your place if this bothers you."

I shook my head. "It's not that. I just—I have to get out of here."

"Is it Deacon?"

"No," I said, feeling satisfied that not everything in my world lived and died by Deacon King.

"And you don't want to go to your place?"

"No." I was definitely done with taking Travis back to my place.

He shrugged, leaning back into the couch, completely unaffected. "All right."

A part of me actually felt bad leaving him there. I wanted to tell him there was more out there than Magic or Jungle or whatever this place would be called in another two hours, but I knew Travis wouldn't get it, or just wouldn't care, so all I said was, "I'm sorry about this."

"It's cool," he said. "I'm gonna go back down to the bar."

I started down the stairs, hearing Travis call behind me,

"See you around, Michaela Rose." I almost turned back and told him that he wouldn't.

I DIDN'T CALL TO TELL HIM I WAS COMING. I ONLY PRAYED that he was home, that he was alone, and that he'd let me in. Holden started barking when I knocked on the door, and after a minute or two, I could hear Ben's voice hushing him. The sound of Ben's footsteps neared the door, and I swore I heard him sigh before unbolting the locks.

He looked tired, worn out, done. I hadn't expected him to welcome me with open arms, but I thought he would have cooled off a little bit. Before he could tell me to go away, I blurted out, "I don't want to be this way."

He pressed his hands to his eyes, either debating if he should send me away or regretting that he'd opened the door in the first place. "What are you doing here?"

"Can I come in? Just let me come in for a minute."

He didn't step aside. I was afraid he'd send me away, but then he looked behind me like I might start disturbing his neighbors, sighed, and let me in.

All of his lights were out and the TV was off. He flicked on a lamp and stood there, waiting for me to go on. When I didn't, he said, "So, what? What are you here for?"

I didn't know how to respond. On the ride over, I thought of all the things I wanted to say to him, all the things I wanted to say to myself. Now that I was there, now that I had to apologize to the only person who'd been truly kind to me in as long as I could remember, I couldn't find my words.

"What were you doing?" I asked.

"Sleeping," he said. "I was sleeping, Michaela. It's three thirty in the morning."

I looked at his cable box and saw he was right. I'd forgotten what a time warp those bars can put you in.

"I'm sorry." I turned toward the door. "I'm so sorry. I didn't realize what time it was. I'll go."

"I'm up now," he said. "You've obviously come here to say something, so say it."

I looked from Ben to the dog, feeling like I was on the biggest audition of my life. In the cab, I imagined that I'd present him with this eloquent monologue, convincing him of all the reasons we'd be great together. Now all I could say was, "I just—I decided—I want to be with you."

He didn't smile, take me in his arms, or kiss me like someone on TV might. He covered his face with his hands, sank into an armchair, and let out a long laugh-like moan. "You've got to be kidding me."

"That didn't come out right," I said. "I just meant—I'm sorry I screwed up tonight. But I want to get past this."

He shook his head, weary, exhausted. "It's not that easy. It wasn't just tonight."

"I know," I said, the words I'd been practicing on the way over resurfacing in my mind. I knelt down on the floor next to his chair in the same way Daisy used to when she pleaded for a puppy or begged to stay up past her bedtime. "I know I've been all over the place, basically since the day we met. I know you asked me simple questions and it seemed like I just didn't want to answer them, but I will. It's hard for me, but I will. I don't want to be this way. I want to change. I want to be with you."

I waited for him to say something. I waited for him to at least look me in the eye, but he just rubbed his hand over his face again and said, "Please get up."

I hesitated, but figured if I wanted him to hear me out, I should probably cooperate. I moved to the ottoman and sat facing him. "Please don't make me leave. I want to talk."

He finally looked up at me. "Oh, now you want to talk? After all these weeks, this is the moment you decide you want to talk?"

My gut instinct was to look away, but I forced myself to keep staring him in the eye. "It's hard for me to trust people."

"So you've mentioned. But I'm sorry, at some point, you're going to have to get over that."

"I'm trying," I said. "It's just—my whole life I've had to worry that everything I do and say is going to end up in a tabloid and that people are going to judge me for not growing up exactly like Daisy Breyer should have."

"And that's how you want to go through life? Avoiding anything that makes you uncomfortable?"

That wasn't what I wanted, but I didn't know how to make him see that. I wanted to be the kind of person who could let someone like Ben in. I wanted to stop reminding myself that the only person I'd let see me as I was—flaws, scars, and all—crushed my heart time and time again.

"That's what I'm saying," I said. "I don't want to be this way. Ask me something. Ask me a question about myself and I'll tell you."

He sat there, quiet for a moment. "Look, you seem a little drunk right now, so—"

"I'm not." I opened my eyes wide so he could see that, despite reeking of Travis's Jack and Coke, I was completely sober. "I promise."

At that word, he let out a slight "Ha."

"I'll tell you things," I said. "What do you want to know? My favorite foods. I have two. Grilled cheese with tomato and turkey clubs. There was this diner called Bennett's that my best friend, Josh, and I used to go to when we were kids and we would always split grilled cheese and turkey clubs because I had to have a taste of both. And I knew that he would've rather had a burger because he loves burgers, but he'd get the turkey club anyway because he knew it was the only good meal I'd eat all day."

"Michaela—"

"What else do you want to know? Ask me anything. I'll tell you anything you want to know. Anything I can answer. Just ask me something about myself and I'll tell you."

"No." His raised voice caused the dog to stop chewing his toy and lift his head. "I'm a person, Michaela. A human being, who had feelings for you. I'm not some easy fix for whatever you're going through. I'm a person."

For a minute, neither of us said anything. Ben seemed to be composing himself; I just didn't know what to say. He broke the silence with a long exhale, and when he started speaking again, he seemed a bit calmer.

"Can you look at me and tell me honestly—honestly—why you came here tonight?" The way he said that word, *honestly*, made me think I hadn't been fooling him as much as I'd thought the last few weeks.

"I don't know what you mean."

"I mean, did you come here for me? Because you wanted to see me, and wanted to make us work? Or did you come here for yourself?"

My throat contracted into an involuntary swallow. "I came here for you."

"Really? What is it about me that you like?"

My flesh burned. "I don't know what you mean," I said again.

"That day at the bookstore. Why did you talk to me? Why did you agree to go out with me? Why did you continue to go out with me?"

My face started to flame. "You were the one who gave me your number."

"That's not what I'm asking. Why did you go out with me?"

I thought back to the corner table in the café, when he had no idea that the girl hovering around us on the phone was talking about me. I thought about how good it felt when I flashed him those famous green Daisy eyes and he only saw them as my own. After weeks of half-truths and ignored calls, I finally gave Ben English the honest answer he was looking for.

"You wanted to get to know me," I said. "You weren't interested in anything else. I could just be a normal girl with you."

Ben nodded, like this was the answer he'd expected. "So it wouldn't have made any difference if I were any other guy. It was all about how I made you feel, what you needed. It had nothing to do with me."

"No, that's not what I mean," I said. He'd completely misunderstood. I tried to think of one thing that made me want to date him—one thing that made Ben *Ben*. One thing that could prove I was dating him because of who he was, and not because of who I was when I was with him. The entire time I dated Ben English, I thought it was unlike any relationship I'd ever been in. But the truth was that just like with Burke Sanders and Travis Howard and even Deacon King, I kept going back to Ben because there was something I needed from him. It may not have been status that I was looking for, or wild sex, or love, but it was a selfish reason just the same. I wanted to fit into the idea of normalcy that Ben had carved out for me. I needed him around because I needed to believe that whatever he saw in me was actually there.

"You see something in me that no one else sees," I said, trying to cover the bubble growing in the back of my throat. "I want to be who you think I am."

Ben didn't come any closer. He didn't reach for my hand or tell me it was all going to be okay. He stayed where he was, hands in his pockets. "I only wanted you to be yourself. And I'm sorry, but that's not something I can help you with."

I nodded, searching for the strength to stand up, searching for the courage to tell him that the reason I couldn't be myself was because, without someone else to define it for me, I had no idea who that was. "I'm sorry I came here," I finally said, not quite able to look him in the eye. "I'm sorry for waking you up and—I'm sorry."

I forced myself off the ottoman, managing to keep my back to him through my brief journey to the door. I could feel him following me, but pretended I didn't know he was there. And because Ben English was a good person, the type of guy a girl should want to date, he put aside any hard feelings and made his last words to me kind and polite.

"I really wish you the best, Michaela."

BY THE TIME I GOT BACK TO MY BUILDING, THE SUN WAS coming up. The sidewalks were populated with joggers getting a 5 a.m. run in before the workday. I was exhausted; my feet, mind, and heart ached, and all I wanted to do was climb into bed, though I doubted I'd be able to sleep. I didn't even care about the disapproving look Phil gave me as I passed through the door. My dress was rumpled from Travis's hands, my makeup was running worse than Portia's had been, and I reeked of alcohol. I deserved his judgment.

I needed a shower. I needed to eat something. I needed to be alone, and I definitely needed to get out of Caroline's shoes. The absolute last thing I needed was to see Josh coming down the stairs as I waited for the elevator.

He was obviously heading out for his morning run, and he was obviously expecting to see me as much as I was him. When he spotted me, looking the way I did, he stopped mid-step, probably debating which would be more awkward—if he brushed by me as if he didn't know me, or if he ran back up the stairs, pretending not to see me at all. I figured I'd save him the discomfort and looked away, pushing the elevator button a few more times. I'd been on the verge of tears all night, but it wasn't until I saw him that I could feel them brimming to the surface. I wanted to grab him, fall to my knees, and apologize.

I wanted to tell him about the week I'd had, starting with how I'd lost my best friend. I wanted to tell him I missed him and beg his forgiveness—but I'd experienced enough embarrassment that night to last the rest of the year, so when the elevator finally came, I stepped in and pushed the button.

The doors were halfway shut when the toe of his sneaker forced them back open. Josh stood before me, looking a little angry, a little agitated, and a little disgusted. I wasn't ready for another fight. One cruel word and I knew I wouldn't recover.

"I really don't want to ask you this," he said, "but are you okay?"

My nose and throat tingled, the final warning sign that the tears were about to fall. He was looking at me as if he were a concerned neighbor, a stranger seeing someone in distress and, though he knew it was none of his business, thought it only right to ask. The appropriate response in a case like this would be, "Yes, I'm fine, thank you," letting us both off the hook. But since it was Josh, I told him the truth.

"No. I'm not."

Before either of us felt the need to say any more, I pushed the button again, shutting him out so he wouldn't be able to hear me when I finally started choking back sobs.

CHAPTER TWENTY-TWO

I called my cleaning company the next day and told them services wouldn't be needed until further notice. I had no place to go, no one to talk to, and no idea what I was supposed to do next, so I figured that until I knew how to clean up the mess that was my life, the least I could do was clean up my apartment. The harder I scrubbed my shower tiles and kitchen counters, the more my mind wandered, dwelling on every bad choice I'd made over the past nine years. All morning, I found myself wishing I had the kind of mother who'd understand, the kind who'd listen and tell me everything would be okay. A part of me actually thought about calling her, hoping that maybe Caroline would choose this moment to dig up some maternal bone that had been buried deep inside her body. Then I got a text from Portia Ambrose.

> Last night was crazed. Jungle so over. Y didn't u tell me about CG?

It took me a minute to figure out what *CG* was, and even after I considered *Crescent Grove*, I told myself she had to be talking about something else. Until I Googled my name and saw it everywhere.

> Daisy Does Daytime.
> Turner Turns to Soaps.
> Breyer Babe Goes Villainous Vixen: Inks Deal for Sudsy Serial.

I felt sick to my stomach. When all I wanted to do was hide from the world and get my mind straight, my face was plastered all over the internet.

I knew if I called Caroline from home, she'd make some excuse about not being able to see me, so I waited until I got to her hotel and called her from the bar downstairs.

The bar was an old-fashioned place with mahogany fixtures and leather booths and stools. I'd spent years of my childhood in bars just like this. Caroline wasn't a drinker, but she knew where the money was, and somehow always had a way of knowing which executives drank at which bars on which nights. It was a place like this where I scored my first agent. Caroline stood out in the lobby, pinched my cheeks to give them a bit of color, and told me to go up to the table in the corner and ask if anyone had seen my mommy. I was scared, but she reminded me of that Shirley Temple movie we'd watched the night before. Didn't I love it? Didn't I want to sing and dance and make the whole world smile? Didn't I want to show everyone how remarkable I was? I did it, because I wanted to make my mother happy, and within months, thanks to a string of cereal and fruit juice commercials, we went from living in a run-down studio to staying at a beautiful suite at the Four Seasons. When she gave me those instructions, she knew exactly how everything would play out. In the back of her mind, she must have seen the Macy's parades, the promotional trips to Disney, the eight *TV Guide* covers. With that one decision, she had written a script for the next twenty-four years of my life. And now, with *Crescent Grove*, she was trying to do the same thing all over again.

Caroline may have sounded collected on the phone, but when she entered the bar, I could tell she'd been more ruffled by my impromptu visit than she wanted to let on. Her hair was flawless as usual, but her ever-perfect makeup was minimally applied, and judging by the divorce settlements spilling from the top of her wrap dress, she'd gotten dressed in a hurry. She still didn't look all of her forty-nine years, but she looked as close to it as I'd ever seen.

"Hello, Gorgeous." She slid into the leather booth across from me. "This is a pleasant surprise."

"Here are your shoes back." I put the shopping bag I'd brought them in on the table. The handle, frayed from my hand, betrayed that I'd been more nervous than I wanted to admit.

"Oh." She looked in the bag, then pushed it aside. "I'm sure your new boyfriend adored you in them."

"Actually," I said, "we broke up."

She looked surprised by my flat-out honesty. It wasn't something either one of us was used to, but I wasn't going to fabricate any more scenarios about boyfriends or stomach bugs or people painting my apartment. Not to her, not to anybody.

"I'm sorry to hear that." She didn't sound sorry at all. "I'm sure you'll find someone else soon enough. You always do."

Something about the way she said that word—*always*—made me so angry that for a moment it outweighed my feelings about *Crescent Grove*. She hadn't been part of my life for over a decade. She had no right to speculate on what I always did or didn't do. What made me even more furious was that she was right—after ten years of absence, she could see something in me that I hadn't realized myself until the night before.

"That's not the point," I said. "I don't want to find someone. I have no business being in a relationship right now."

I waited for her to ask me why, or what led me to this epiphany, but she just nodded and directed her gaze toward the bar. "Good for you. Take time to focus on you. Just remember what I always taught you. Keep your options open."

I followed her line of vision and was frustrated to see that while I was trying to talk to her, she was making eyes at a thirty-year-old bartender. "You're engaged," I reminded her. "And you're old enough to be his mother."

She shrugged. "Only because I started so young."

I'd heard that line hundreds of times growing up. "I'm sorry to have been such an inconvenience," I said. I waited for her to protest, to throw out some line about how I made her life what it was, but she didn't even seem to hear me.

"I'm trying to tell you something," I said.

"And I'm listening, Gorgeous," she said, turning her attention back to me.

"Why did you put out a statement that I was doing the show?"

Before she could answer, the bartender made his way over to our table. His timing was so impeccable I had to wonder if my mother had sent him some sort of signal.

"Caroline," he said in what sounded like a French accent. "And friend. Can I get you anything?"

Caroline cocked her head and looked at me. "Gorgeous? Something to eat? Drink?"

"No," I said. "Thanks."

"Just the usual for me, then," she said, then nodded toward me and said, "Why don't you make it two?"

The bartender tapped his hand on hers and left it there for a second longer than necessary before walking away.

"I said I didn't want anything," I reiterated once he was gone.

"It's just a little tea with lemon, honey, and ginger root. It does wonders for the skin."

"But I said I didn't want anything," I repeated. "Why did you say I was doing the show?"

I almost expected her to play dumb, to say she had no idea what I was talking about and curse whoever leaked it for ruining my big return. She twisted her necklace back and forth and said, "It wasn't me. It was Peter."

She was such a good liar that I didn't know whether to believe her or not. But there was a sort of vulnerability in her tone that made me think there was more going on than I knew.

"Why would Peter have done that?"

She looked down, running her hand back and forth across the side of the table. For the first time since she'd announced her upcoming nuptials, it occurred to me that she never wore an engagement ring.

"He needs a decision," she said. "Sooner rather than later. He just thought maybe you needed a little push."

With those three words, I knew the whole thing had been Caroline's idea. It would take me all day to count the little pushes she'd given over the years. Walking off set to give the studio a little push. Fabricating French lessons and ballet skills and horseback-riding abilities to give my résumé a little push. Everything dating back to that day I walked up to the table of executives was the direct result of a little push.

"So you told him to do it," I said.

"He needs an answer," she said. "There's a lot riding on this, and we can't wait forever."

"You shouldn't have blasted it out to the whole world hoping to force me into a decision. If you wanted an answer, you should have come to me."

"I've tried that," she said. "And you've been avoiding it."

I couldn't deny that she was right, but I didn't know how to justify saying no when I had nothing else, and didn't know how to justify saying yes when it wasn't what I wanted. I was terrified of severing ties with my mother again if I decided against it, but even more terrified of having her around if I agreed.

"I needed time," I said.

The bartender came back over with our honey-lemon-ginger-root teas and set them down on the table. The minute he approached, the intensity that had been forming on Caroline's face slid back into a relaxed smile. "Thank you, Gorgeous."

The bartender nodded, looked over at me, then back at Caroline before heading off.

"Why is it so important to you that I do this show?"

"It's not important to me. I want it for you," she said. "Every decision I've made since the day you were born has been for you, to give you a better life."

"That's bullshit." I was surprised at how loud it came out. "Every decision you've made has been about you. What anyone can do for you. It's all about what you need. It has nothing to do with me."

A chill passed through my body when I realized I'd heard those words less than twenty-four hours before. I had harbored so much anger over the years, thinking of how my mother had nearly destroyed me by pushing me in front of the cameras, by never letting me become my own person, by leaving when I needed her the most. I never stopped to think that her pattern with men, her rootless life, and the way she refrained from anything resembling real emotion could have carried an influence just as strong.

"I'm sorry you feel that way, Gorgeous," she said, her tone softening slightly. "You can think what you like, but I'm doing this to help you."

"No, you're not." I looked back at her hand, thought of her engagement, and asked again, "Why is it so important to you that I do this show?"

She tucked a strand of hair behind her ear and took another sip of tea. "I just told you. Whether or not you choose to believe me is up to you."

I could never believe her. When I was younger, I sometimes wished she'd be less honest with me, when she'd hold nothing back about dates she went on, or how she really felt about the network, or what she thought of poor Katrina's lack of talent. It wasn't until I was a teenager that I realized occasional transparency wasn't the same as honesty.

"Why aren't you wearing an engagement ring?" I asked.

She put down her glass and rubbed her ring finger, consciously or not, I wasn't sure. "I'm forty-nine years old. It's my fourth marriage and Peter's third. I hardly think we need a ring."

"Okay, why don't you live together?" I asked. "I'm sure he has a place here in the city. Why are you staying in a hotel?"

Her lips spread into an overly wide smile. "It's only temporary. This arrangement works better for us right now."

I nodded. "Do you have a date set?"

She almost flinched, but played it off as a curious squint. "You're awfully inquisitive today, Gorgeous."

"Do you have a date set?" I repeated.

She leaned back in the booth and crossed her arms. "No."

"Have you made any arrangements?"

"Peter has a place in the Hamptons," she said. "We'll probably do something out there."

The mention of the Hamptons gave my heart a painful flick, but I ignored it and went on. "Are you actually engaged? Or is this whole thing some kind of set up?"

"Of course we're engaged. What kind of question is that?" She looked wounded that I would even ask. In my gut, I believed her, but I couldn't forget that she'd taught me everything I knew about bending the truth.

"We're getting married," she said, as if she could read my

doubts. "I told you before. We have a few wrinkles to iron out first."

"Meaning me."

She forced a straight grin. "You could say that."

"How am I a factor? What does my doing the show have to do with you and Peter?"

She let out a sigh, as if this conversation had gone on long enough. "Let's just say if you don't do it, it would put an unnecessary strain on an already flawed relationship."

I thought back to when I was little, and how every time I wanted to give up acting, she would pull something like this. Sure I could quit *Breyer's Town*, but did I want to go back to living in that tiny apartment with no hot water? No, I wouldn't have to go for that commercial if I didn't want to, but it would make paying the electric bill a little difficult. I had been trying to back out of this business for longer than I could remember, because it was never something I wanted. It was always Caroline. Every time I came close, I caved and went back because that was what she needed, and I couldn't disappoint my mother. But I wasn't a kid anymore, and she'd made enough decisions. This wasn't her life. It was mine.

"And what would you do if I said no?" Because she was my mother, I held out hope she'd say that she would still support me, that she would love me, and that she was glad I was finally making a choice that was right for me and me alone.

"I'm hoping that's not something we have to deal with," she said.

In the script that Caroline started penning for me at three years old, she probably saw a scene just like this in our future. She certainly hadn't wished for my hiatus from acting, but she probably factored it in just the same and saw this moment, this conversation, as the turning point that brought me back. And I could tell by the look on her face that in this scene she wasn't expecting me to go off book. She wasn't expecting that when she said the line, *I'm hoping that's not something we have to deal with*, my answer would be, "It is."

She took a moment, not yet accepting it. "Is this about Joshua? Because he failed? Because we've talked about this and I told you that wouldn't happen with you. That boy is not talented in the way that you are. He never was. You have been gifted since the day you were born and if you walk away from that, you'll never stop regretting it."

"This has nothing to do with Josh."

"That sounds familiar."

"It doesn't," I said. "This has to do with me."

She was silent for a minute. Then, because she was Caroline, and because she never gave up without a fight, she sat forward, plastered on that huge smile she'd always used with the network when negotiating my salary, and said, "Gorgeous, think about what you're doing. You're emotional right now. The announcement about the show threw you off. I get that. But don't walk away from what you excel at. This is your God-given talent. This is what you were born to do."

For the first time in my life, I felt completely certain when I said, "No, it's not."

Ten years before, when I had the conversation with Caroline about ending my career to go to college, she didn't speak to me for four days. Then she booked me an audition, thinking I'd change my mind, and when I didn't go, the silent treatment stopped. She was perfectly civil to me for two weeks. Not maternal, because she'd never been maternal, but civil just the same. Then she announced, quite formally, that she was leaving the country. She didn't tell me in the way a mother would tell a daughter, didn't think about how it might affect me, didn't act like it was personal at all. She said it as if we were business partners who'd realized that, while it was disappointing, this arrangement just wasn't working out. It was the exact same tone she used now, when she took one last sip of her tea, folded her hands, and said, "Well, then, I guess we're done here."

The tiniest voice in the back of my mind asked if I knew what I was doing. I had no plans for the future, and by walking away from that table, I was walking away from the only chance to reconnect with my mother.

"It's so easy for you," I said.

"Nothing about this is easy," she said. "You think I want to see you throw away your life?"

I wasn't throwing away my life. I was throwing away the idea she had for it.

"I'm talking about you throwing away your child."

She'd never seen me as a child, so I never saw myself as one, either—not when I went to work for hours every day, not when the world thought they knew me because I was in their living room every week, and certainly not when I was sixteen and my own mother decided I was no longer needed. The day she left, she proved I was nothing more than a tool that had stopped serving its purpose, and maybe that was why I let Burke and CeCe and so many others treat me the same way. If I was being honest, that was probably why it was so easy for me to use Ben, too. But people weren't tools. I wasn't a tool. I was a child.

I slid out of the booth, took my coat off the rack, and said, "I guess you're right, Caroline. We are done here."

Before walking away, I reached into my purse, pulled out the check she'd given me weeks before, and placed it on the table. "I'm not going to cash it."

I knew I didn't owe her anything. I knew it was my money and that she never should have taken it in the first place. But now that I'd said no to *Crescent Grove*, even though I didn't know the full story about Peter, I had a feeling she was going to need it.

I'D ALWAYS THOUGHT NOTHING COULD HURT WORSE THAN being rejected by my mother. When she left me the first time, I could barely function, and if it wasn't for Josh, I probably would have ended up hospitalized for starvation or sleep deprivation. When she wrote the tell-all about the disappointments I'd caused her, I pored over that article for weeks, scrutinizing every word, and believing everything she said about me. Now, after leaving her at that hotel, I felt sad because she was my mother and I wanted her to be supportive of me, and I felt pity because there were no signs of her ever changing. But mostly, I felt like I could breathe. I'd finally listened to myself and not her manipulation. And there was only one person I wanted to share that with.

I threw my stuff upstairs when I got home, then immediately ran down to Josh's apartment and knocked on the door. Eventually I'd tell him about Caroline, but first, I needed to tell him I missed him and that I was sorry.

I could hear rustling within, and I worried for a minute that he'd see me and not open up. Panicked, I knocked again, a little harder, a little louder. Then I heard his voice, the familiar voice that had been a comfort to me since I was a kid. "Yeah, I hear you, wait a second."

He opened the door, his messy blond hair curling out from under a backward blue baseball hat, dressed in black mesh shorts and the gray hooded sweatshirt he'd owned for a hundred years. He didn't look overly thrilled to see me, but he didn't look like he was about to slam the door in my face, either. He just looked like Josh.

He leaned on the doorframe, pulled his hat a little off his forehead, and said, "Hey."

"Hi." I didn't have to say anything else. Just standing there with him brought me a sense of comfort I'd been missing for weeks.

"You busy?" I asked.

He shrugged. "Not really."

"Can I come in?"

He stood back, allowing me through. His apartment was a little messier than usual, but it wasn't a disaster. The TV was on, the blender on the counter held one of his protein shakes, and there were three or four mismatched sneakers scattered across the floor. Everything looked normal. Except for the pile of cardboard boxes stacked up in the corner.

"What's going on here?"

He poured some of his shake into a glass and sat down on a kitchen stool. "Just packing some stuff up."

I peeked in the top box. It was filled with movies and a few books. "What do you mean you're packing some stuff up?"

He didn't answer. He just sat there, drinking his shake. I walked over to him, pried the glass away from his lips mid-sip, and stared him in the eye.

"Christ, Turner, you're gonna make me choke."

"What do you mean you're packing some stuff up?"

He took off his hat and put it on the counter behind him, running his hands through the mess on his head. "I'm getting rid of the apartment."

I figured I hadn't heard him right. Maybe he was still mad and this was his way of messing with me. There was no way he'd leave.

"Are you moving in with Morgan?"

He let out a half sigh, half snort. "No."

He stood up and started to walk away, so I grabbed his wrist. "Can you please tell me what you're talking about?"

"Can you please let go of my wrist?" he asked. "I'm just going to the fridge."

I hesitated for a second before letting go. He pulled out a beer for himself and opened a raspberry hard lemonade for me. Apparently, he thought this conversation needed more than a protein shake, but I wasn't having it. I put the bottle down.

"Josh."

He leaned his elbows on the counter. "I need to get out of New York."

"So take a vacation."

He almost seemed humored by this suggestion. "I definitely need more than a vacation."

My heart started throbbing. I had to sit down, because I couldn't breathe. "I don't know what you mean. Where are you going?"

"Home to Florida, for now."

"Florida is not your home," I said. "You haven't lived there since you were a kid. That's not your home. This is your home."

He laughed bitterly. "This is definitely not my home. It's a fishbowl. I'm tired of it."

"If this is about your show—"

He rubbed the tiny scar above his eye. "Please don't talk about the show."

"I'm just saying, if that's what this is about, you don't have to leave New York because of it. I'm sure you were amazing." Meaning it more at that moment than I even realized, I said, "I'm sorry I wasn't there. I should have been there for you. I wanted to be there but—I screwed up. I'm an awful friend and I screwed up." My pulse throbbed in my ears. I didn't want to be selfish, and I didn't want to make it about myself, but I couldn't help saying, "You can't leave me."

He looked at me for a long moment and for a while neither of us said anything. I knew Josh and he knew me and he had to have known how sorry I was—more than my words could even convey. We stared at each other silently, the only sounds in the apartment coming from the action movie on TV and Josh's fingernail scraping the label on his beer bottle.

"I was a shit show," he said.

"I'm sure that's not true."

"It is," he said. "It was embarrassing. The minute I got on that stage, I knew all anyone cared about was seeing Joshie Mac. I'm not that person anymore. I don't think I ever was."

I wanted to lean over the counter and hug him, to tell him how badly I understood, but his body was closed off.

"You weren't there, Turner. The show ended and Morgan came backstage cheering for me like I'd just climbed Mount Everest and you weren't even there."

"I know." It was all I could say. I thought back to that half-empty club, and how I'd been able to feel Josh's anxiety in my bones. "You trying this wasn't a mistake, though. You love music."

"I do," he said. "But I'd be happy if I never set foot on another stage."

"So what are you going to do?" I thought he might tell me some brilliant plan—some secret wish he'd always harbored or some incredible dream he'd just realized.

"Honestly?" he said. "I have no idea."

I sat there for a minute and breathed, still hoping I'd somehow misunderstood. He'd never make an impulsive decision like this. He'd never leave the city.

"You've lived in New York for over ten years," I said. "You have one bad experience and you're leaving?"

"You know it's something I've been thinking about for a while," he said. I didn't know it. Yes, he said it all the time, but I'd thought it was just him being in a bad mood. "I have to move on, and as long as I stay here, that's never going to happen."

I tried to process his words, tried to understand what he was saying. "What about Morgan? Is she going with you?"

He took a long drink of his beer. "Morgan and I aren't together anymore."

This is what happens when you stop speaking to your best

friend. One day, you know everything about him; the next, he's breaking up with his girlfriend and selling his apartment.

"Why?"

"She was a fan. You called it."

A wave of guilt washed over me. "I had no right to say that."

"Well, it was true. It wouldn't have worked out. We were on two different planes. Hers is actually going somewhere."

I thought about the look on his face when Caroline compared his teenage music video to Morgan's actual career in medicine, and how quickly Morgan jumped in to say she was the lucky one. "She really liked you."

He shrugged. "Maybe she did. But she also had my poster on her wall when she was in high school."

"Everyone had your poster on their wall when they were in high school," I told him. "You can't blame her."

"Just like you can't blame all the people who call you Daisy?" When I didn't respond, he said, "Did it ever occur to you that maybe you're not the only one entirely screwed up by this whole fame thing?"

I hated to admit that it hadn't. For years, I'd put all my issues on display for Josh, while he sat there and listened and tried to make me feel better. I knew I was a terrible friend, but if he hadn't sat there eating his bagels and reading his paper, saying things like "the fact that I was in some pop group doesn't define me," maybe I could have helped him.

"You always acted like you were totally fine," I said. "You always let me go on talking and talking and you never hinted that you felt the same way. You let me go on thinking you were the perfectly well-adjusted one and I was the one with issues."

He scratched his scruff with the tip of his beer bottle. "Well, of the two of us, I'm definitely the well-adjusted one."

"I'm serious," I said. "You used to talk to me."

He stared at me. "You used to talk to me, too."

I looked around the apartment again. Between the sugary cereal collection, the piles of video games, the weight machine, and the acoustic guitars, you'd never know whether this was a kid's bedroom, a college dorm, or a bachelor pad. "We really are two screwed-up individuals," I said. I wanted to say more. I wanted to tell him about Katrina's wedding and ask if he'd still be my date, because I didn't know how I could go without him. I wanted to tell him about Caroline and the week I'd had with Ben and *Crescent Grove*, but at that moment, none of it seemed to matter.

"Does it bother you that you have no idea what you want to do?" I asked.

He twisted his beer back and forth, probably wondering if by answering, he was forgiving me too quickly. "I don't know."

I knew he was thinking of more than that, so I didn't budge. "Does it bother you?" I asked again.

"Of course it bothers me, but what chance did we have? I mean, when you're a kid, you're supposed to have fun and figure out who you are, and then when you're older, you go off to work and start your career."

"Right."

"We never did that," he said. "When everyone else our age was messing around, we were working our asses off. We never got to think about what we wanted. Maybe that's why it's so hard for us to do it now."

I couldn't decide if I wanted to smile or cry. This was why Josh had been my best friend—my only friend—all these years. He had a way of saying exactly what I felt before I even knew I felt it.

I didn't want to start crying, and I didn't want him to think I expected his forgiveness, so I just nodded and sipped the drink he'd given me. Then I almost spit it out.

"God, McKenzie, how old is this?" I looked at the date stamped on the bottom and saw it had expired five years before.

He cracked a smile. "I don't know. You bought it."

This was not the hard lemonade I bought. It couldn't have been. When I bought this, Josh was still a Boy of the Nation. It was New Year's Eve, and he didn't want to go out because, well, he was one of the biggest superstars in the world. So we got beer and tried to make these fancy appetizers we'd seen on a cooking show, and when they all ended up burnt, raw, or falling apart, we tried to make pancakes, and when those didn't work out, we ate an entire box of Cap'n Crunch and fell asleep before the ball dropped. When I thought about that, and about him not living downstairs anymore, I felt like throwing up.

"When are you leaving?"

I prayed he wouldn't say anytime soon. Maybe he was just consolidating, trying to clean some things out. I didn't expect him to say, "Three weeks, but I'm flying down there tonight to look at some places."

I wanted to talk him out of it, beg him to stay, but maybe he had a valid point about leaving New York. Maybe he wouldn't be able to figure things out if he stayed here any longer, where everyone had a preconceived idea about him, where every step he made was speculated on and scrutinized. There was so much more I wanted to say to him, so much more I wanted to talk about, but another knock at his door prevented it.

He looked at me, probably wondering the same thing I was—if I was already there, who else could it be? Maybe it was the wrong door, or maybe he had more friends in the building than I thought. Maybe it was Morgan begging him for a second chance. He walked over to the door, looked through the peephole, then back at me. The tiny bit of warmth I'd worked so hard to build back up had vanished completely.

He opened the door, and I didn't need to see the person on the other side to know who it was. I only had to hear, "Hey. Is Mickie here?"

CHAPTER TWENTY-THREE

Josh stood, silent for a moment, beer in one hand, doorknob in the other. If this had been a movie, Josh would have told Deacon to get the hell out and slammed the door in his face, or maybe, just maybe, spat his drink at him. He might even have asked Deacon to step outside so they could finally settle this bad blood, once and for all. But this wasn't a movie, this was real life, and in my life, the best friend stared at the ex-boyfriend and said, "Yeah. She's here."

He didn't make room for Deacon to come in, didn't move at all. He remained where he was, leaning on the doorframe, drinking his Budweiser like he had all the time in the world. Judging by Deacon's tone when he said, "Christ, McKenzie, I need to talk to her," his business was a bit more urgent. Of course, with Deacon King, when it pertained to Deacon King, it was always urgent.

Josh didn't respond. I started to think maybe he'd throw Deacon out, after all. But then he flung the door wide open and retreated back to his corner, not even looking at me as he said, "It's for you." He started putting together more boxes, which Deacon took as an invitation to come on in.

He looked as though he hadn't shaved in days, his hair was sticking up in unruly tufts, and his eyes had that wild bloodshot glaze that only lack of sleep and a strict diet of cigarettes and alcohol can create. In his ripped jeans and thin Doors T-shirt, he looked exactly as he had when I first met him—a little older maybe, but there were no signs of that clean-living, blazer-wearing fake vegan I'd faced at Intuition. For months I'd thought that if he could only be the old Deacon again, I'd be happy; now, seeing him this way, despite the involuntary thrill that passed through my senses trying to give me emotional amnesia, all I could see was the man I gave my whole heart to, the man who returned it to me shattered, time and time again.

"What are you doing here?" I asked, but he didn't seem to hear me. He took my hands in his and pulled me up off the stool, swaying back and forth to some imagined beat in his mind. I knew that look in his eye—it was the look that said, *Oh, Mickie, do I have something to tell you.* I wasn't quite sure if it was hope I was feeling or fear of what that something might be.

"You need to come with me," he said. "Jay's waiting in the car downstairs."

I drew my hands back and curled my fingers inward, trying to fight that tingling sensation that took my body prisoner every time he touched me. I glanced over at Josh, who took a momentary pause from his packing to turn up the TV.

Deacon's energy could be infectious, and I knew it would take everything in my power not to get sucked in. I had to remind myself of Shaunn, of the red walls and white carpets and silk sheets that made up their life together. I had to remind myself of the wedding date in the Hamptons, and tell myself that as much as I wanted to believe we could be the same people we were eight years before, or even three years before, maybe too much had changed. If I thought about who those people really were, maybe that wasn't such a bad thing.

I grabbed my drink and clasped it with both hands so I wouldn't be in danger of his taking hold of them again. "I'm in the middle of something."

He shot me a humored, confused stare. "Mickie, you don't understand. You need to come with me. McKenzie won't mind." He looked over his shoulder as if considering Josh for the first time. "You care if I steal my Queen, McKenzie?"

Josh responded by slapping a loud strip of tape on one of his boxes. "I don't think that's her name."

I wasn't sure if Deacon chose to ignore him or if his hearing had gotten so bad that he actually missed Josh's answer. He ran one hand over his beard and scratched his stomach with the other, rolling back and forth on the balls of his feet like a child who had to pee.

"Come on, Mick. Let's go. You need a coat? I don't think you do. Mine's in the car but it's not even bad out."

He took a pack of cigarettes out of his back pocket and pulled one out. Josh didn't turn around, but just as Deacon was about to flare up his lighter, he said, "Can't smoke in here."

Deacon turned back to him, the unlit Camel hanging from his lip. "Seriously?"

Josh finally looked up. "Yeah. Seriously."

Deacon scoffed, the concept of being told *no* completely foreign to him. He stuck the cigarette behind his ear. "Okay, now we really have to go."

There was a time when I was enamored by these high-speed allegro moments of his. I used to think they were a sign of his brilliance and passion for life. Now I just wanted him to get to the point.

"Deacon," I said. "What's going on?"

He stopped fidgeting and grinned, beamed actually, his eyes even brighter than when they'd been airbrushed on the cover of *Rolling Stone*. He glanced around at some imaginary audience in the room, then lowered his voice and said, "It's done."

Everything froze—my heartbeat, my brain, even Josh's packing. He couldn't possibly have been saying what it certainly seemed like he was saying. I'd longed for the old Deacon, but I never thought about what I'd do if I got him back.

"What do you mean?" I asked.

"I mean I finally did it." He placed a hand on each of my hips, drew me close, and kissed my forehead, my mouth, my neck.

Despite what I knew was right or smart, my pulse throbbed. I tried to gain as much control of my breath as I could so I didn't sound like melting putty when I said, "I don't think this is the place to be talking about this."

"Which is why I have the car downstairs." He pushed my hair back, touched his lips to my ear, and whispered, "I think it's my best yet."

A cold sting shot through my veins. "You wrote a song."

He nodded, that gleam in his eye igniting even more hearing the words from someone else. I should have known there was only one thing that could make him smile like that. I felt stupid for thinking he could have meant anything else.

"You have to come hear it. I'm going to the studio right now to lay it down and I need you there." He grabbed the bottle from my hands, took a swig, and put it back on the counter. "This is disgusting. How are you drinking this?"

I looked to Josh, thinking he'd say, "I told you so," but he just made another louder-than-necessary point of tossing some books in a box and throwing it on top of his pile.

Deacon's smile faltered a little when he realized I wasn't moving. "I thought you'd be more excited."

"I am," I said, and a part of me meant it. I was excited for him, thinking back to those balled-up papers of scribbled notes and that untouched custom-made piano. For his sake, I prayed the song was as brilliant as he thought it was, but I wasn't feeling personal gratification about it, not in the way I used to.

"Well, come on, then." He tugged my hand again.

"I told you. I'm in the middle of something."

"Just go, Turner," Josh said. "Really."

I released my hand from Deacon's grip and walked toward Josh. "No. I want to help you. I want to talk. I want—" I looked around at the history he was packing away, the thought of him leaving making me sick inside all over again. "Please just let me help you."

"Don't need your help. I'm perfectly capable of doing this on my own." He shot Deacon a look. "I'm not that codependent."

Deacon turned. "Do you have a problem with me, McKenzie?"

Josh snorted. "Just get out of here, please. Both of you. Before I say something I shouldn't."

"Josh." I wished I could be more composed, wished I knew the exact thing to say. "You can't keep being mad at me."

"I'm not mad," he said, completely devoid of emotion. "I'm busy."

Deacon stood in the doorway, one foot already in the hall. "Come on, Mickie. I don't think we're wanted here."

I looked Josh in the eye, afraid that he'd forgotten my apology, worried that if I walked out that door, the gap I'd tried so hard to narrow would split right back open. He stared back and didn't seem to be daring me, didn't seem to be testing me, just seemed to be laying out the facts when he said, "This is what you wanted."

I didn't know how to respond. I only knew how I felt, and at that moment, I only wanted to stay.

"Turner," he said when I didn't move. "I'm telling you to go."

You'd think this would be nothing considering what happened with my mother hours earlier, but Josh's telling me to leave was a hard punch to the stomach versus Caroline's mere sting. Yes, I wanted to have the kind of mother Katrina had, the kind you could talk to and rely on, but I didn't. This was the hand I'd been dealt. But the thought of losing the comfort and peace of Josh—that was unbearable.

"I'm going to deal with this and then I'll come back and help you."

He turned away. "Not necessary."

"I'm coming back," I said. "I'm coming right back."

Josh pinched the bridge of his nose, like if he stood there silently enough, long enough, I would give up and leave. "I told you I'm going away for a while. My flight's at eight."

I looked at the clock. It was almost two. "I'll be back by then. I'll be back and we're going to talk. What time are you leaving?"

He shook his head, probably knowing as well as I did how impractical it sounded. "I don't know. Five, five thirty."

I didn't know how I was going to make it, but it was Josh. Not making it wasn't an option.

I was afraid to push it any further. As I forced myself out of the apartment, the ache inside me grew stronger with every step I took away from him. I couldn't imagine what that pain would feel like with a thousand miles between us.

Once I was out in the hallway, Deacon tried to wrap his arm around me. I swept past him and pushed the elevator button, but he still didn't get the hint.

"What was his problem?" he asked.

"He's going through a lot right now. And he's mad at me. Rightfully so."

"He'll get over it."

I turned to face him. "I don't think he will. I told you we had a fight. I told you I don't know if we'll ever be friends again. Why did you assume I'd be at his apartment?"

"I was right, wasn't I?" He pushed the button a few more

times, like that was somehow going to get us downstairs faster. "Come on, Mickie, it's you and McKenzie. It'll be fine. It always is."

"It won't be," I said. "He's moving."

He blinked. "Where?"

"Florida." Saying it made my heart hurt.

Deacon got into the empty elevator. "I wouldn't worry about it."

I didn't follow him in. "What do you mean by that?"

He sighed and held his hand in front of the elevator door, waiting for me to join him. "McKenzie won't move to Florida. There are people who do things and people who talk about doing things. He's a talker. Now come on, Jay's waiting."

I got in the elevator, mostly because I wanted to hear the rest of this. "He's moving to Florida," I said. "He's tired of New York. And to be honest, I don't blame him."

He looked baffled that I could say that. Deacon was one of those people who thought the entire world lived and died by his city. Although he'd toured the globe, though he himself was born in Tallahassee, he still had a hard time remembering there was civilization outside of Manhattan.

"Then good for him." His tone clearly indicated he'd believe it when he saw it. I wanted to keep at it, wanted to tell him he was wrong, but I knew there was no use in trying to talk to him about anything when he was preoccupied by his own creative genius.

"You could have called me, you know. If you went upstairs and I wasn't home, you could have called me."

"You seemed pissed at me the other night. I didn't know if you'd answer, and I need you to hear this song." He smiled like someone had just whispered all the secrets of life to him. "It's good, Mickie. It's really good."

I wanted to tell him that the last thing I cared about was hearing his song, but somehow it didn't seem fair. If we hadn't talked that night on the fire escape, he would have gone on with his meat-is-murder, sunglasses-at-night persona, and wouldn't have given a second thought to selling out. I'd needed him to be that man I so desperately loved, and now, aside from the fiancée, that man seemed to be back. I should have been happy; like Josh said, this was what I'd wanted.

When he realized I wasn't saying anything, he turned and looked at me, his eyes taking on that bruised little boy luster he'd perfected over the years. It was the same look he'd given me when I caught him cheating or when he blew off our anniversary for a three-day bender—one part manipulation, but one part genuine fragility. It was a look I'd asked for, a look from the man I thought I needed. So when he asked, "You do want to hear it, don't you, Mickie?" I felt like I had no choice but to say, "Yes."

I HADN'T BEEN TO THE STUDIO WITH DEACON SINCE HE RE-corded *The Queen*. Back then, we had to travel to this tiny place upstate, which was a big deal for a band who'd recorded their first demo in their drummer's parents' basement. The guys were so excited you'd have thought they were at Abbey Road. Now Deacon had his own state-of-the-art space in the city, which he explained in the car made more sense to have at his disposal for times like these. "And," he added, "if I let anyone else use it, I pick up a producing credit."

"Do you know anything about producing?"

His eyes crinkled into a laugh. "I know my bank account likes it."

The last time I'd been in the car with Deacon, he'd spent the entire drive on the phone. This time, he couldn't stop talking. He was going to lay down a raw cut, he said, one take—just him and the piano, something he could show his label before he recorded it for real. He knew the minute the executives heard it, they were going to want to rerelease his album and feature this song as a bonus track single. I had to wonder how much of his bravado was real, and how much he was using to psych himself up. He knew as well as I did that if this song wasn't as good as he thought it was, the old Deacon King—the brilliant songwriter, the man rife with talent and imagination—would be nothing but a thing of the past, if he'd ever really existed at all.

"What does Shaunn think of the song?" I asked. I had to. After that night at his apartment, I couldn't ignore her anymore.

He kissed my palm. "You're the first one I'm playing it for."

I nodded toward our driver. "Really?"

He grinned and kissed me again. "Jay doesn't count."

I didn't know what to make of him playing the song for me first. I wanted to believe I was the only one he wanted to share it with, wanted to think he could let his guard down with me in a way he couldn't with Shaunn, but at the end of the day, she was the one he went home to. She was the one he said those words to. I could try to convince myself all I wanted that I was the one he was opening his heart to, but when all was said and done, she was the one he was opening his life to.

Once we got to the studio, it became clear why it'd been so difficult for Deacon to find that starving piano-tuner-by-day/songwriter-by-night harbored inside him. The size of the place wasn't overwhelming, but the fact that it belonged to Deacon alone made me realize that, thanks to his dance hits and cartoon songs, he'd become a bigger success than I'd realized. From the moment we walked in the door, everyone from the receptionist to the engineer addressed him as "Mr. King," catering to his every need and whim. There was no doubt in my mind that every one of them had signed one of his famous NDAs, because not a single person so much as blinked over him bringing a girl who wasn't his fiancée into the studio. It was no wonder why he thought he could get away with anything; apparently, he could.

Deacon kicked his shoes off before heading in to record. He always said he had to have a clear mind in order to write, record, or perform, and he couldn't get there if he had the dirt and grime from the city trailing on his shoes. He gave me a quick kiss and finished off his prerecording ritual by asking, "You'll tell me what you think?" It was the same thing he did in the old days, before he cut his hair and stopped eating meat and bought a ring for someone else. I waited for that thrill I always used to feel, that nervous anticipation that the song I was about to hear was as much mine as it was his, but now, the only nerves I felt were for him. The flash of insecurity in his eyes told me that, despite the gold records and state-of-the-art studio, a part of him missed that twenty-three-year-old kid who could churn out masterpieces just as much as I did.

Jay and I stayed with the engineer in his booth, and I watched as Deacon sat down at the piano, skimming his fingers over the keys. He'd always said playing was like trying to seduce a beautiful woman—you couldn't just go for it, you had to warm her up a little, caress her, love her. When we were younger, I'd started many fights by accusing him of loving his piano more than he loved me. Seeing him now, I knew that I was right, especially when he said into the microphone, "She's not 'Cilla, but she gets the job done."

I turned to Jay. "Is it really any good?"

Jay almost smiled. "Just listen."

Deacon's back rose into a deep breath and he started in on the piano. The music seemed to pass through his body, forcing his shoulder blades to dance, his ribs to move up and down under his threadbare T-shirt. I couldn't help but think of the night I first saw him play at that piano bar, when I was nineteen and in complete awe of him. I remember thinking I had never been as consumed by anything in my life as he had been by the Otis Redding song he was playing. Pretty soon, the way he felt about music became the way I felt about him, and for a while, that had been enough. I was the girl he wrote songs for, the girl he put on his album covers, the girl who made him better. He needed me when no one else wanted me, and he saw me for who I was and he loved me for it. For those reasons, I madly loved him, and for those reasons, I still loved him, and for those reasons, I probably always would, but now, watching him play again, I didn't feel the way I thought I would.

Before he sang a single word, I knew he'd been right about the song. It wasn't exactly like the early sound he'd been trying to re-create—it was more complex, more mature, deeper. The melody alone told me that whatever he'd been searching for, whatever had been holding him back, was now yesterday's worry. The lyrics were beautiful and raw, and told the story of a green-eyed girl and a blue-eyed boy who wanted more than anything to find the people they used to be. Artistically, it was his best song yet; it was the natural evolution from the boy genius I'd so passionately loved to the man he'd grown into.

He remained still after he played the last chord, hovering over the piano in silence before he turned around to look at me. He looked satisfied, proud, but still a little anxious for my reaction. When I nodded my affirmation, he broke into a grin, bounding off the piano bench and practically running in to meet us.

"Did you like it?" he asked, but before I could answer said, "Gavin, can you play it back?"

The engineer cued it up. Deacon stood staring at the floor, gnawing on his thumbnail, a little out of breath as he listened. His right leg was bouncing like crazy, and his T-shirt was moist with sweat. I laid a hand on his back to try to calm him down, but he didn't seem to notice—nor did he seem to notice the engineer saying, "It's great, Mr. King," or Jay clapping a meaty hand on his shoulder and adding a "Good work, D."

As far as Deacon was concerned, he could have been alone in that room with just his song.

There was a knock at the door and the girl from the front desk popped her head in. "I have the stuff you wanted?"

Deacon didn't appear to hear her. "Can you play it back again?"

"D," Jay said. "You want the stuff you ordered?"

Deacon looked up. "Oh, yeah, no, I do, yeah. Bring it in."

She opened the door and wheeled in a cart with chilled champagne and a tray of sushi. She started to leave but Deacon called back to her.

"No, hey, Holly, stay a minute. Tell me what you think of the song. Actually, go get everyone. I want everyone to hear this."

Within minutes, the room went from four of us to twelve, and while everyone listened to the second playthrough, Jay handed out champagne. I couldn't help but notice he gave me less than everyone else. I guessed our momentary alliance was over.

"Sounds great, Mr. King," front desk Holly said—purred, really. Deacon clinked his glass with hers. In the old days, I would have been insane with jealousy, wondering if he had something going on with her. Now I could see he was far too consumed by the song to even know who was toasting him.

While everyone congratulated him and showered him with praise, I sat silently, sipping my eyedropper of champagne and keeping my eye on the clock. I didn't belong there. I belonged back at the apartment, helping the one person who had never turned his back on helping me.

I stood up and touched Deacon's hand. "I think I'm going to get going."

He looked at me, suddenly alert, like he'd just realized I still hadn't said a word. All he had to do was scratch the side of his neck and say, "Hey, Jay?" and just as quickly as the room had filled, we were left alone. In a matter of seconds, he went from a boastful rock star to a nervous kid seeking approval. "Did you really like it, Mickie?"

"It's perfect, Deacon."

He lit up, his beard scratching my face as he leaned in to kiss me. He turned and took the champagne out of the bucket, refilling our glasses. "Come on. You can stay for a few more minutes." He stuffed a sushi roll in his mouth and offered me the tray.

"I didn't think you liked sushi," I said.

"I like sushi," he said through a mouthful of food.

"You used to celebrate recording with Jack Daniel's and bacon sandwiches."

He laughed and took a sip of his champagne. "I did, didn't I?" He lifted his shirt a little and scratched his stomach, rearranging the sushi on the tray with his other hand.

"What happens to the people?" I asked. "In your song. What happens to them?"

Deacon raised an eyebrow and shrugged. "I guess you have to draw your own conclusions." He wiped his mouth on his T-shirt and turned to play the recording again. I didn't know how he could do it—how he could write a song so poignant, so personal, then completely remove himself from what it was actually about. He didn't care that he hadn't given the green-eyed girl and blue-eyed boy any kind of resolution; he'd gotten what he needed for the sake of the song—what happened to them after didn't matter. Maybe he liked it better that way. Maybe if they always stayed just as they were—screwed-up, confused, going around in circles—he'd always have something to write about.

"Why did you put me on the list for your show that night?" I asked.

He looked surprised, almost defensive. "What do you mean?"

"I'm not looking for a fight," I said. "I'm really not. I just want to know. You have so many people around you. You have a fiancée. You have a whole life I'm not a part of. Why after two years did you seek me out?"

I could feel my final hopes in Deacon King resting in that question. A small part of me thought if he really had grown and changed, like his music seemed to indicate, he could finally say something I needed to hear.

He leaned back on the soundboard, considering me for a long moment. "Why are you asking me this?"

"Please," I said. "Just answer me."

He raised his eyes to the ceiling. "I don't know. I told you before. You're the only person who won't bullshit me."

"It has to be more than that," I said. "Why me?"

"Come on, Mick. You know why."

"Tell me."

He focused all his attention into swirling the champagne around in his glass. "No one else knows me like you do."

"And?"

"And what?"

"And is that it?"

He finally looked up at me. "I've told you this a thousand times."

"Tell me again."

He reached out one hand and pulled me toward him, turning on those bruised baby blues one more time. "I'm my best when I'm with you, Mickie Mine. I need you to remind me of who I was, before all this." He lifted my hand, brought it to his lips, and said, "I need my Queen."

He was right about one thing. He had told me this a thousand times. I'd never let myself admit what he meant.

I looked up at his album covers that lined the walls, just as they did in his apartment. There was my bare back, in a gold frame above a gold record, the word *Queen* scrolled across my shoulders. For so many years I'd loved that picture, loved that the man I loved loved me enough to put me on display for the whole world to see. Now I could see it wasn't me at all; it was Deacon King's faceless muse.

"And that's all this was about," I said, giving him one last chance to show me something, to prove I wasn't just a tool to him like I was to Caroline.

His smile faltered. "Isn't that enough?"

It was a question I should have asked myself a long time ago, but back then, I wouldn't have given myself an honest answer. Back then, I'd only have heard that he needed me, and that would have been the end of the conversation. This incredible talent, this strong, complicated, once-in-a-lifetime man needed me. He needed a girl to write songs for, to think of when he sat down at that piano. He needed a girl who'd tell him what she thought, whose back he could put on album covers and whose troubles he could put to beautiful melodies for the whole world to hear. It wasn't one-sided. I needed someone to understand me and love me for the person I was, and at one time, I have to believe he did, but things had changed. He'd moved on with his life—he was eight-time Grammy winner Deacon King, who had a studio and a staff and a fiancée to cater to his every desire—but he still needed me to be the mixed-up muse I was at nineteen. He needed me to play a role just as much as the people at *Breyer's Town* had, and I needed more than that.

Something inside me wanted to give him one last kiss, but I didn't trust myself. I wanted to be composed, and strong, and graceful, but I could still feel my heart knocking through my chest when I released my hand from his. "I really do love you, Deacon King. And you should be so proud of your song, because it truly is beautiful. And I hope you keep this up, because you're better than what your label wants you to be."

He squinted. "What are you doing?"

I swallowed hard. "I need my key back. And I can't have you calling or coming by anymore."

He stood up straight, looking as though I'd just slapped him. "Why are you doing this?"

"We're not the same people anymore," I said. "You're getting married next summer. You're moving forward. Let me."

Without so much as a hesitation, he said, "Well, what if I don't?"

"If you don't what?"

"Get married," he said. "What if I don't?"

I looked around for accomplices, hidden cameras, some indication that this was a cruel joke. "That's not a fair question."

"Sure it is." He put down his glass and moved his hands to his hips, determined. "What if I call it off?"

In that moment, I felt sorry for myself, because I wanted to believe he meant it; sorry for Shaunn, because she thought she was marrying someone who loved her; but mostly, sorry for Deacon, because this change of heart had nothing to do with his feelings for me or his lack of feelings for his fiancée. It was about his music, his muse, and when it came right down to it, his piano. He loved that piano more than he ever loved any woman, loved it more than he loved himself. At the end of the day, the only thing that mattered to him was his career, and he thought he owed it all to his 'Cilla.

"What if I told you that you can have the piano?"

He remained still. This wasn't how things worked between us. In the past when we ended things, I would hoard his belongings or throw them in the street. "I didn't say anything about the piano."

"You didn't have to," I said. "It's yours. I should have given it to you a long time ago. I'll hire someone to come get it." I held out my hand, waiting for my key.

"Was it the song?" he asked. "Did you not like it?"

"The song was brilliant, Deacon. I told you that."

"Then have I done something wrong?"

I thought back to when he broke up with me the second time, those five words that haunted me, that caused me sleepless nights and tear-filled days. I'd replayed those words over and over in my mind, wondering what I could have done differently, wondering what he could have meant. Now I understood.

"This is never gonna work."

I'm not sure if he was remembering that day in my bed, too, or if he was already mentally composing our final breakup song. He pulled his key ring out of his pocket and slid my key off, but held it in his hand for a minute. He didn't even sound like he cared about convincing me when he said, "It's not about the piano, Mickie."

The whole situation would have been comical if it wasn't so pathetic. If I was watching this happen to somebody else, I'd want to shake the girl for loving a guy like this in the first place, for missing him already even though she knew what was best for her. I definitely would have thought she was crazy for still wanting to help him even as she said goodbye.

"I really think you should try to fix things with Petie," I said. "You need someone around who knows you and who will look out for you. You need your best friend."

I thought he might say I was right or throw out one more plea to get me to stay. All he did was hand over my key and say, "If this is what you want."

I still wasn't sure what I wanted, but I needed a different story. I buried the key deep in my pocket and gathered everything within me to remain strong when I said, "Goodbye, Deacon."

I tried my best not to look at him as I made my way to the door, knowing that if I glanced back, that Band-Aid I'd strategically placed over my heart might soften and fall off. Just as my hand touched the doorknob, he said, "Wait."

He came toward me, and I kept my eyes on the ground, believing like some wild animal that if I stayed still enough, he'd just keep walking. As I felt his lips press against my forehead, all I could think about was that first night I'd met him, when he kissed me outside the bar and said he had a serious feeling I was the kind of girl he'd never get over. A small part of me wondered if he still felt that way, or if he ever really had—if it was just one of his famous lines. I told myself that whatever he had to say now, I wouldn't let it haunt me for the next two years. For once in his life, he actually did say something I needed to hear, something that showed me I'd just done the best thing I could have done for myself.

"Don't hire someone for the piano. I'll get one of my own guys."

THE GOOD THING ABOUT MY FRANTIC CAB RIDE HOME WAS that I was so consumed with making sure I got back before Josh left that I didn't dwell over what I'd just done. Sure, my legs still had a wobbly I-can't-believe-I-went-through-with-that shake, and my pounding heart still hadn't fully found its rhythm, but my main concern was the clock ticking away in front of me.

Of course, I'd hurt myself in the time department, because when I left the studio, full of adrenaline and racing emotions, I thought I was running earlier than I was. I thought I had enough time to pop into a diner and pick up two sandwiches—a grilled cheese and tomato and a turkey club—as a peace offering. It wasn't Bennett's, but that didn't matter. I needed him to know he could move to Florida, he could move to Timbuktu, but he would never not be my best friend. I just didn't plan for the long line or the guy behind the counter getting satisfaction out of making the sandwiches as slowly as possible.

Phil gave me a strange look as I burst past him—maybe because I was running, maybe because my take-out bag smelled a little rank, or maybe because I had a few lines of mascara smudging down my face. (Okay, so I might have cried a little after I left Deacon. I'm not perfect.) I got in the elevator, pushed ten, and nearly collapsed against the wall as I rode up to his floor. I was definitely going to need to start hitting the gym more often.

I took a few deep breaths when I got to his door, planning what I should say. I wondered if I should tell him about Deacon, if he'd even care to hear about Deacon. I wondered if I should say I was sorry again, or if he was tired of hearing my apologies. I wondered if I had the right to ask him to stay and not leave me when I knew that leaving New York was probably the best thing he could do.

I knocked on the door and waited to hear his familiar shuffling within. After a few seconds, I tried again, harder, louder, squishing the sandwiches in the process. Still no response. It was only four forty-three, and he'd said he wasn't leaving until five or five thirty, but then I thought about how much Josh hated airports, and how he probably got nervous about check-in, changed his mind, and left earlier, thinking there was no way I'd actually come back. I tried his doorknob, not that it would do any good, because even when he was home, it was always locked. In a last-ditch effort, I gave the door one more knock and called his name so loud that I'm sure I disturbed more than one of our neighbors, but it was no use. I could see under the door that his lights were out. He was gone.

CHAPTER TWENTY-FOUR

Josh had given me a key long before I moved into the building. He'd been on tour a lot, and he wanted to make sure I always had someplace to stay if I needed a break from Caroline, or later, when I needed an escape from the dorms. I hated that I'd never told him how much it meant to me.

When I opened his door the next morning, I half expected him to be lounging on the couch, watching *Scarface*, drinking a protein shake. Even though he was a thousand miles away, even though he'd taken down his pictures and had started boxing up his belongings, it felt like he was there. It smelled like him and looked like him, and the slightly messy paint job on the walls had been rolled on by him. I had burst into this apartment on so many occasions with the urgent need to share some story, or when I needed a good laugh or, more often, a good cry. Josh was always on the other side of that door, ready to share whatever it was with me. I didn't know how I'd survive Katrina's wedding without him the following week, let alone the city without him forever.

One benefit of being Caroline's daughter was that I'd become an expert packer by the age of seven. Left to his own devices,

Josh would never remember where he packed anything, and any fragile items would be shattered by the time he got to Florida. It was probably a little creepy for me to be slinking around his apartment uninvited, especially when he had issues with his privacy. (You may remember the story from a few years back about the woman who was caught stealing his garbage scraps from outside the building and, for reasons that have yet to be determined, was feeding them to her calico, Squashie Mac.) Still, this was Josh. We'd been in each other's business since we were kids, and if he could buy me tampons, the least I could do was pack up his underwear.

Every time we moved, Caroline told me not to dwell. Thinking led to regrets, and regrets led to delays. To actually become attached to anything would be inconvenient. Moving, possessions, even where we lived, were best kept unemotional. When I started packing Josh's things, I tried not to think at all, tried to let my hands do the work and let my mind take a rest, but every item I packed was drenched with memory. The sweatshirt he always wore at night. The beer steins he'd collected from around the world. I couldn't pretend that somebody else lived there, that these were somebody else's dishes and sneakers and guitar picks and movies. It was impossible to work on autopilot when everything he owned was completely, utterly, and totally Josh.

I spent the entire day on his living room and kitchen, went back to my apartment only for sleep and a shower, and got back to work on his bedroom first thing the next morning. I knew he'd be back for at least a few days before he left for good, so I kept the bed made up and set aside some clean clothes and a few other necessities in an unsealed box labeled **Things You'll Need Before You Go.**

The last space I had left to sort out was the spare closet. If Josh was anything like me, that would be the catchall for his junk, and the biggest pain to put in order. I opened the door and, sure enough, it was bulging with souvenirs, hand weights, golf clubs, and skis. A stack of old magazines sat in a cardboard box on the floor, and I smiled when I saw they were all a decade old, and all featured Boyz of the Nation on the front. It was like the Daisy doll I had stuffed in the back of my closet—embarrassing, haunting, but somehow wrong to throw away. Looking at those covers, I couldn't believe how young he was. I'd never imagined that either of us had aged over the years, but now I could see that the boy I'd relied on so much—he was just a boy. He shouldn't have had to deal with press conferences and six-pack abs and twenty-three-hour workdays and red-eye flights across the globe. He should have been allowed to be a kid. As much as I couldn't bear the thought of him leaving, he deserved to do what made him happy. He deserved to figure out what that was.

There was a bag in the corner behind the golf clubs, and I expected it to be filled with more Mardi Gras beads and poker chips. I hoped it wasn't porn. I looked inside and instead of kitschy collectibles, I found a stack of CDs. I was about to kick myself for already sealing up the Music/Movies/Other Media box when I realized they weren't just any CDs. There was a Simple Minds CD. And the soundtrack to *Pretty in Pink*. And the Smiths. These were my CDs. CDs I'd loved, that I hadn't listened to in years. I couldn't fathom why they'd be in Josh's closet.

I flipped over *The Queen Is Dead* and read through the track listing. Those CDs immediately reminded me of a small window in my life I'd forgotten about. A time post-Daisy and pre-Deacon when I was actually trying to figure out who I was—before Caroline took off and before I failed at college and before I met the man who muddled my mind with his passion, when I was just a girl with a really great friend and the possibility of a future where I could be myself and not who everyone wanted me to be. I was just a girl who loved ’80s music and who couldn’t wait to figure out what else she loved. Then Caroline left, and everything changed, and I’d been afraid that what drove her away was me trying to be me. I was petrified of losing anyone else, and that, I remembered, was why Josh had the CDs. When I first met Deacon, he’d made one of his blanket statements that there was no such thing as good music after 1980 (a complete lie, because we all know his feelings on Lionel Richie) and I was so desperate for him to love me that I told Josh he could have them. He’d said that he’d hold on to them, that he knew I’d want them back someday. I should have known he’d keep his word.

I thought I’d be physically exhausted by the time I finished packing, but once I stacked up the last box, it was only my heart that felt the strain. It killed me that Josh was leaving this way. It wasn’t just because of the rift I’d dug between us, though that was a huge part of it, and it wasn’t just that he’d no longer be footsteps away. It was that look of defeat when he said he was moving back to Florida. He’d always been ambivalent about where he came from. I wished he was going somewhere or doing something he could be passionate about.

I knew I’d ruined things between us. I knew if he wanted to forgive me, he would have returned my calls. I just needed him to know how I felt, and that if he was ever ready to speak to me again, I’d be there, waiting. I grabbed one of my markers, flipped over a sheet of labels, and laid it on top of the first box he’d see when he came in. On it I wrote:

I’m so, so sorry. I can’t say it enough. Love you always and always.

M

PS—I took my CDs

MY PLAN WHEN I GOT BACK UPSTAIRS WAS TO TAKE A HOT shower, listen to my newfound CDs, and scratch up some dinner that didn't come from a take-out box. I had to stop dwelling on Josh's leaving because, as much as it pained me, it was something I was going to have to get used to. When I entered the apartment, I realized I'd also have to get used to the gaping hole in the center of my living room.

It shouldn't have thrown me, because the piano had been gone for days and I had wanted it gone. I guess I thought with 'Cilla out of the apartment, the place would finally feel like it was mine again, but it didn't. After spending the last few days at Josh's, my apartment felt sterile. Foreign. Cold. I didn't feel like I'd reclaimed my own home; it just felt like Deacon had partially moved out.

I started by getting rid of his ashtrays. Four ashtrays, and I didn't even smoke. I hated smoke. When we first started dating, I begged him to quit, and once, for sixteen hours, he did. After that, I gave up and let him do whatever he wanted, because part of what he wanted was me. From there, I let him pick out the atrocious leather couch that reminded him of Graceland and the gaudy glass coffee table that went along with it. Making this place my own again was going to take serious work.

I scanned the apartment and took a quick inventory of everything I'd need to get rid of to free myself from Deacon. As far as furniture went, the only things that hadn't been his direct choices were a chaise longue, two dressers, and the bed—and the bed, well, that had enough memories of its own. He could hold no claim on the kitchen, but what hadn't come standard with the apartment had been purchased at the suggestion of Jordan the chef, that one month we'd dated. Even Burke had left his mark—he'd bought me the TV because he said I needed to watch his games on a bigger screen. I thought about Josh's apartment, how I'd gone with him when he bought his furniture and how I'd helped him paint every room with colors he had chosen. My paint had been picked out by an interior designer who thought my aura exuded lavender and selected shades meant to be bold yet serene. Packing up Josh's apartment broke my heart because it said so much about him. I'd lived in mine for almost a decade and I felt no attachment to it.

I went to my spare closet and looked inside, hoping to find some clue, something that could bring me forgotten happiness in the way the long-lost CDs had. I tore that closet apart, looking for some piece of myself, but all I found was Caroline's tabloid. And Burke's jersey. And the stupid tiara CeCe had made me wear on my birthday. And a Day-Glo necklace hanging off my Emmy. I didn't know who this life belonged to, but it certainly wasn't me.

I had let down that sixteen-year-old girl with her affinity for '80s music and not-quite-developed plans for the future. I had let her get so wrapped up in the fear of failing and getting hurt that I never let her try anything at all. I had let her end up in an apartment she never really cared about, with a string of guys she never particularly liked, with one undeserving guy she loved too much. I had let her settle for being a girlfriend or a muse or a one-night stand instead of letting her figure out who it was she wanted to be. True, Caroline had hurt me, and so had Deacon, and maybe Daisy had, too, but I was the only one to blame for the fact that while everyone else in my life was moving forward, I was left behind with a color scheme chosen by an interior decorator, with Elvis-inspired furniture chosen by my ex-boyfriend, in a city chosen by my mother.

I wasn't hungry anymore. I wasn't tired, and I didn't feel like that shower. I slipped in the soundtrack to *Pretty in Pink*, sank into the chaise, and waited for the welcome sounds of "If You Leave." God, I loved that song. I had forgotten how much I loved it.

There was something stuck to the back of the CD case, and I flipped it over to find a yellowed napkin, ripped from age and ink. In Josh's messy handwriting, it read,

To do by 25: Get a dog. Surf more. Master Rodeo Flip. Order double fries.

A half laugh, half cry escaped me. I vividly remembered him writing this over lunch at Bennett's when we were teenagers. He was sick of worrying that whatever he ate was going to result in a pimple or a disappearing ab, and said that one day, he would do whatever the hell he wanted. When I asked like what, he jotted it all down. When I told him those were some pretty impressive goals, he slid the napkin over and said, "Let's see if you can do better."

Slowly, I peeled the napkin away from the plastic, and there, in faded writing, my sixteen-year-old self reminded me of everything I never followed through on.

1. *Graduate from college*
2. *Learn to drive*
3. *Move to San Francisco*

San Francisco. I could have cried when I thought about it. I had desperately and passionately wanted to live in San Francisco.

I looked around the apartment at the art prints on my walls—London, Paris, Venice—cities I'd never been to, cities I had no connection to, cities that wouldn't hurt if people asked me questions about them. The only color picture was the one of San Francisco that Deacon had bought me. At the time, I thought it was a romantic gesture, that I could have the best of both worlds. Now, I saw it for what it was: a consolation prize.

I'd only been there once, when I was fourteen, but I fell in love with everything about it. The ocean, and the weather, and the way the buildings and houses and streets looked like nothing I'd ever seen in New York. There was so much to see, but I never felt suffocated. I was only there for four days, and for three of those days I was shooting. On my one day off, I begged Caroline to please let me to go the beach instead of running lines, and I'm not sure if she felt bad because I'd recently been rejected for a handful of roles or if she thought I'd be more marketable with a little sun on my skin, but she said yes, and to this day, when I think about it, it was the happiest memory of my childhood. I loved the sound of the ocean after hearing nothing but cabs and construction my whole life. I loved that it was chilly and I had to wear a sweatshirt on the beach. I loved that I could see the Golden Gate Bridge and the feel of the sand beneath my toes. I loved it.

When I first met Josh, he'd laugh when I talked about San Francisco like it was some magical place, but at the same time, he agreed. We'd talk about how one day, when we were old enough, when he was tired of touring and I was finished with college, we would live there, side by side on the beach, and we would drink all the coffee we wanted because no one would tell us it would stain our teeth or stunt our growth, and we could eat grilled cheese with tomato and turkey clubs every day just because we wanted to.

It wasn't one big thing that made us not go. It was just life. Caroline said if I insisted on going to college, it would have to be in New York, to leave the window open for auditions. Then she left anyway. Josh stopped touring but kept the same apartment because that was where he lived. I dropped out of college and moved upstairs because I didn't know where else to go. We never had a solid plan about going to California. But remembering how passionately I felt about the idea made my eyes sting with emotion—I'd forgotten that underneath Daisy

Breyer and Deacon's Queen and Burke's Babe and Caroline's Gorgeous Girl, there was still someone there who felt. Who wanted things. Who actually had a mind and a heart and a voice of her own, waiting for someone to listen.

I looked around the apartment, thinking of all the work I'd have to do if I wanted to make it my own. I wasn't sure I wanted to. I wasn't sure I wanted to live in this building anymore, or even this city. I wasn't sure what I was going to do or what I wanted to do, but for the first time in a long time, that blank slate didn't feel so blank. It didn't feel like a curse. It felt like the possibility of promise.

CHAPTER TWENTY-FIVE

The universe gifted Katrina with an unseasonably warm wedding day. She looked beautiful, but more than that, she looked happy. I'd always thought her childhood was so charmed but maybe she had a difficult time adjusting after the show ended, too. Maybe she'd just figured things out a little bit sooner than I had.

I sat next to Uncle John and his wife, Jasmine, at the ceremony. Uncle John was happy to see me and the truth was, I was glad to see him, too. When he asked how I'd been, I said I was okay, and when he asked what I was up to, I told him—I was putting my apartment on the market, and I was applying to colleges in San Francisco.

His reaction was classic Uncle John—a slap on the knee and a "Get out of town!"

I smiled, and because I knew he loved a corny joke, I said, "I told you. That's what I'm doing."

He let out a good laugh, one that was probably too loud for church. "I'm proud of you, kiddo. You've always been the smartest person in any room I've been in. Any college would be lucky to have you."

I'd been so fortunate to have him while I was growing up. I once read somewhere that something like 80 percent of TV viewers wished that Dr. Breyer was their real father. I always wished Uncle John was mine. After the show ended, I felt like I'd lost a family, and I'd always thought that when he checked on me through the years, insisting on birthday lunches and inviting me to holidays, he was doing it out of obligation. I never stopped and let myself consider that he actually cared. For that and more, I said, "Thank you."

He put his arm around me and kissed the top of my head, like he would when I was a kid, when I'd flub a line, or when I was too tired to do another take, or when I'd ask why I couldn't just go home. I sat for a moment, enjoying that comfort.

"So," he said, giving my shoulder a little tap. "Where's my friend Josh?"

It pained me to say, "He's not coming."

"He's not? That's a shame. I always love seeing him."

"Me, too." It wasn't that I couldn't handle this crowd without him. I just missed him. I missed his company and his unwelcome opinions on my wardrobe choices and his witticisms about the crowd around us—especially when I saw Mrs. Wilder's silver-sequined Mother of the Bride dress. I knew I had to get used to life without him. I only wished it didn't hurt so much.

At the reception, Katrina must have told me a dozen times how happy she was to have me there. Although my prior record was against me, I truly meant it when I told her I wouldn't have missed it. She took my hand and introduced me to her guests, if not like my big sister, then at least like a childhood friend. I should have done a better job of staying in touch with her over the years. It would have been nice to have someone around who had battled the same war.

It was a little awkward when dinner came, because I didn't know anyone at my table except for Uncle John, and he was off mingling. I was glad in a way, because at least no one I knew would be there to witness me eating two meals. The chicken looked delicious when the waiter placed it in front of me, and since Katrina had borrowed me through the salad course, I was kind of thankful I'd ordered another for my phantom guest. Then the waiter placed a second plate before the empty seat next to me, and it was definitely not the same dish.

"Excuse me?" I said before he walked away. "I think that was supposed to be another chicken."

The waiter looked at me, then pointed to the place card. "Blue ribbon means beef."

"I'm sorry," I said, "but there must be a mix-up because when I RSVP'd, I ordered two chickens."

The waiter picked up the place card and handed it to me, as if that would help. "Red ribbon means chicken, blue ribbon means beef. You have one red, one blue."

How kind of him to explain my primary colors. I didn't want to make a fuss when I had no guest to speak of. I considered telling him to take it back, but I figured Katrina had already paid for it. Uncle John was always one for seconds anyway, so I said, "That's fine."

The waiter walked away and I started in on my meal. It was good, but definitely not worth arguing over. The beef actually didn't look so bad, so I reached over and started cutting a piece off, and then I heard his voice.

"I can't believe you ordered me the chicken."

I turned around in my seat. I never thought I'd be at a loss for words with Josh, but this was the closest I'd come. "Hi."

He indicated my fork, still stuck in the center of his prime rib. "Hungry?"

"What are you doing here?"

He shrugged. "Apparently, I RSVP'd." He sat down next to me. "I take it you'd like some beef?"

"What are you doing here?" I asked again.

"Did you not want me to come?"

"Joshua."

"Katrina called me," he said. "Wanted to make sure I knew the chicken had a cranberry walnut sauce. She remembered I was allergic to walnuts, which you clearly forgot. Unless this was your way of killing me off?"

"I didn't know it had walnuts."

"So, are you going to keep your fork on my plate all night or do you want some prime rib?"

"A taste, please."

He cut the meat while I held it down with my fork. "I thought you were in Florida," I said.

"I got back last night. Here, give me your plate."

I handed it over and held my breath before asking, "When do you leave for good?" I waited for him to say that something fell through, that he'd changed his mind, anything.

"Two weeks."

A sting pricked my heart. Especially when he said, "Did you catch Elaine Wilder's Mother of the Bride dress? I didn't realize that when disco died, they turned the mirror balls into formal wear."

I put my fork down and lunged into the tightest hug I'd ever given him. "Thank you for coming."

"Sorry I missed the ceremony," he said. "It took me a while to get dressed. Someone packed up all my shirts and ties."

I smiled and dabbed a tear. When he noticed, he said, "Christ, Turner, don't cry. You knew I wasn't going to stay mad at you."

"You weren't?"

"Don't get me wrong. I was pissed—really pissed—and thank you for packing up my stuff because, well, now I don't have to. But come on. You know you didn't have to do that."

I untangled myself from his hug, needing to hear it again. "I thought you were going to hate me forever."

He tugged my hair. "I've been telling you since we were kids. I'm stuck with you for life."

A mass of relief melted through my body. He was still Josh. As mad as he'd been at me, as much as I thought I'd ruined things, he was still Josh.

"Can we please dance?" I asked.

He made a face. "A minute ago you were so hungry you were going to eat two meals."

"We can go get sandwiches somewhere after."

"And you know what dancing does to my knees."

"Please?"

He stood up and held out his hand. "You're gonna be the death of me, Turner."

We headed out to the dance floor, and once I was in his arms, I felt more relaxed and comforted than I'd felt in years. It wasn't romantic. It wasn't sexual. It was family.

I could have stayed in the silence of his company forever, but Josh had to break it by saying, "Phil tells me you got rid of the piano."

"He really needs to stop discussing me with people."

"Is it true?"

I nodded. "I ended it. For good this time."

He was quiet for a second before saying, "I hope so."

He'd heard it all before—my saying it was over, my swearing up and down that I'd hate Deacon King until I died. There wasn't anything I could say that would convince him this time was different. All I knew was how I felt, and for now, that was the best I could promise.

"So I have to tell you something," I said.

"Where you packed my underwear?"

I whacked him. "Didn't you see the box I left at the foot of your bed?"

"Must have missed it."

I held on to him tighter. I wanted to soak him in for as long as I could. "I know you probably don't even care, because you're leaving anyway and I'm sure you'll make a million friends and forget all about me, but I thought you should know. I've decided to move to San Francisco."

He stood still. "What do you mean?"

"I mean I'm moving to San Francisco," I said. "You know I always wanted to go."

He let go of me and rubbed his hand along his scruff, like he always did when he was utterly baffled. "I know. I know you always wanted to go—"

"We both wanted to," I reminded him.

"I know," he said again. "But—shit, we were kids."

"I don't think I've matured very much. Have you?"

"Can you be serious for a minute?"

"I am being serious," I said. "This is what I want to do."

He stared at me as if deciphering whether I was telling the whole truth or leaving something out. "You didn't consider telling me this?"

"You never returned my calls."

"Well, I was pissed at you."

"Well, I'm telling you now."

"Well—" He paused and looked around the hall. "We're not going to talk about this here. We're going to get some cake, go outside, and you're going to tell me everything."

And I did. We stood out on the balcony for at least an hour, having the kind of talk we should have had years before. I told him it wasn't a decision I'd come to lightly, but I also didn't want to overthink it, because I was tired of overanalyzing everything, tired of worrying what everyone else would think. I told him I'd be going the following week to look for a place, and that once I found one, I was going to put my apartment on the market and go. I told him I was scared because I had no idea if it was the right thing or the wrong thing or if I'd hate it there and immediately regret what I'd done, but I had to try, because if I was being honest, I'd never really tried at anything. I told him I didn't want to live that way anymore.

He listened, as he always had. "And you promise this has nothing to do with Caroline or Deacon or any other guy you might have met while I was away?"

I shook my head. "It's all me."

He was silent for a minute, listlessly tapping his cake plate on the banister, looking up into the New York City sky. "Does it scare you that you won't know anyone out there?"

"Yes. But I won't really know anyone here anymore, either. At least no one I care to know." I looked over at him. I wished I'd realized sooner that he'd been going through the same things I had.

"Can I ask you something?" I said.

"Sure."

"Do you want to go to Florida? Do you think you'll be happy there?"

He hesitated, tapping his plate a few more times. "Why would you ask me that?"

"Because," I said, "you're the only person I have in the world, and I need to know you'll be okay. I will miss you more than I have ever missed anyone, and it will kill me to have you on the complete opposite end of the country, but if you think moving there will really make things better, that's all I need to know. So do you want to go to Florida? Do you think you'll be happy there?"

An audible sigh breezed through his lips. "I don't know. I'll be able to golf year-round. And surf. And I'll be near my family, which I guess is a good thing. Maybe. I don't know. I mean, I hope so. I guess I won't know until I get there."

"Think you'll master a rodeo flip?" When he didn't respond, I said, "I found our napkin. Order double fries. Get a dog. Surf more. Master rodeo flip."

He looked confused, but then he said, "Where in the Christ did you find that?"

"Your closet." I dragged my fork through a dab of frosting on my plate, making a little design while I worked up the courage to continue. "They have nice beaches in California, you know. Golf courses, too. And it's not as hot."

Josh had never been impulsive a day in his life. I knew he wouldn't change his plans without thinking about it. I also knew by his silence that he was thinking about it.

"You and me side by side on the beach," I said. "Eating turkey clubs and grilled cheese. That was the dream."

"That was the dream." He was quiet for a minute, then he asked, "What was on your napkin list?"

I told him. He laughed. "It's going to take someone with a lot of patience to teach you how to drive."

I shrugged. "Well. If you know anyone."

Gazing at the lit-up skyline, looking down into the busy streets, it was almost possible to hear the dreams being made—the prayers of the musicians, artists, and hopefuls waiting for the city to bring them everything they'd ever wished for. I thought about how every day, people came to New York looking for their every happiness. I wondered what it said about the two of us that we had to leave to find ours.

A gust of late-autumn air passed over, a whispered goodbye from the place where we tried to grow up. Josh wrapped his jacket around me, and I rested my head on his shoulder. The music and laughter from the reception floated through the open door, but what I could hear most of all was the familiar comfort of his breath.

"You want to go back inside?" he asked, warming my arm with his hand.

I shook my head. "I'm okay right now." And for the moment, I was.

For the moment, that was enough.

★★★★★

ACKNOWLEDGMENTS

This book never would have made its way into the world if I didn't have my own A-list around me.

I couldn't ask for a better champion than my literary manager, Liza Fleissig, who met this novel with such enthusiasm from day one. From our very first phone call, I knew I had the exact right person in my corner. There aren't enough thank-yous in the world.

My editor, Leah Mol, understood the heart of these characters right away and made the book all the better for it. I couldn't have wished for more talented and thoughtful hands to usher Michaela into the world. I owe endless gratitude to the MIRA and HTP teams who brought every bit of this book to life in ways I couldn't dream of. A special thank-you to Amy Wetton and Kimberly Glyder for creating a cover I'll never stop pinching myself over.

I will forever be grateful for my time in the Emerson College MFA program. Without the incredible Kim McLarin and Jessica Treadway believing in me as a writer and teaching me so very much, this book would not be here. I can't say it enough.

Endless thanks to Ann Garvin, Laura Bird, and every one of my Tall Poppy Writer sisters. This world would be a better place if everyone were as supportive and generous as this group of women, and I am so, so lucky to be in their fold. Thank you to Maddie Dawson, Kristy Woodson Harvey, and Aimie K. Runyan for giving this novel an early look and cheering it on so kindly.

This book has been a part of my life for so long, which means that it's been part of my family's and friends' lives, too. I'm grateful every day for the beautiful branches of Burnses, Snows, and Raymonds making up my family tree. A special thank-you to Arlanna Snow and Allison Segalini, my cousins by birth and sisters by choice, for filling every chapter of my life with fun, and for being the first people I go to when I want to talk about nostalgia.

At its core, this is a story of friendship, and I'm so thankful for my best friends of over twenty years, Lee Burgess and Kate Wills, who have let Michaela crash more outings and conversations than I can count. Of course, infinite thanks to my furry sidekick, Ollie Twist, the heartbeat at my feet, who was by my side through every rewrite and always let me know when it was time to get some fresh ocean air.

I'm so grateful for my brother and sister-in-law, Mike and Erin Burns, who open their doors to me every time I'm too consumed with the plots and characters spinning through my mind. They're funny and smart, and best of all, they gave me my favorite person. The day I became an auntie, I gained a bestie for life. One day, my strong, hilarious, brilliant niece will read this book I wrote in between our very important dates with Barbie, games, and American Girl. I aspire to be half as cool as she is.

Most importantly, I owe everything to my parents, Michael and Cheryl Burns. I became a reader in their laps, and I grew up in a house full of books. Even better, I grew up in a house full of love. From the day I was born, they told me I could be whoever and whatever I wanted, and they always encouraged me to follow my own dreams. I know not everyone is so lucky. I am so glad to be their daughter.

One final note of appreciation to the young entertainers who have entered our lives through the screen and on the radio, gifting us with years of joy. I wish them the privacy and peace they deserve.